Foreword

One of Emma's favourite sayings is 'yo
up'. Some of life's craziest situations ha.. a..ually happened and
many novels and thrillers are based on real life. Even the most
creative of imaginations would be challenged to come up with a
storyline to equal many things which occur. As a nineteen year' old
student studying abroad, Emma was surprised when a fortune teller
told her that one day she would write a book. Whatever about, she
mused to myself at the time. Many years later the book became a
reality.

The journey began twenty years ago. It led to many unexpected and
startling discoveries and it took several years to piece together the
parts of a bigger and complex puzzle to finally get the clear picture.
The findings could profoundly affect not only our own lives but
those of our children and grandchildren. Knowledge is power and
allows us to act and still make a difference.

The story is one where determination and courage triumph and the
good side of human nature prevails, restoring one's faith that
justice can still be secured. Even if it often means fighting long and
hard to come out on top, fuelled by the belief that this is simply the
right and only thing to do. Emma thanks her family and friends from
the bottom of her heart for their unyielding support without which
the outcome might have been very different and dedicates this
book to her two dear children.

This novel is based on a true story. However, all characters
appearing in this work are fictitious and any resemblance to places,
events and real persons, living or dead, is purely coincidental.

Images in the book cover courtesy of Pixabay.com. Free of
copyrights under Creative Commons CC0, available for commercial
use.

Chapter 1

At 12.25 pm the train pulled slowly away from Charing Cross Station. It was a warm sunny summer's day. The train crawled onto the old iron bridge over the river Thames. Emma looked out of the window and admired the London skyline. She was on her way to Tunbridge Wells to visit her good friend Carla. Soon the train had gathered speed and was crossing green meadows. Emma admired the scenery and sweeping hills of the Kent countryside for a while before looking at her watch. She was expecting an important phone call at 1.00 pm from her lawyer on the continent. She felt happy and relaxed believing the call was just a formality.

At 1.03 pm Emma's mobile phone started humming in her handbag. She reached down and flipped the reply button.

'Hello Hubert. How did things go?'

'I am afraid there are complications, the custody of your children has been transferred temporarily to your ex-husband.' he replied in a curt, business like and impersonal manner.

'What but how can that be?' Emma enquired in a shocked voice, suddenly overcome with concern and fear.

'There will be an in-depth enquiry into the situation by the competent authorities.' he replied.

'Then I must come over and see the children.' Emma urged.

'I am afraid not, the court has refused all visiting rights. I will fax you a copy of the judgment and then we can talk next week.' And with that the line went dead.

Emma sat speechless in the train. The beautiful lush nature outside the train window no longer seemed at all alluring. She tried to call her ex-husband Paul but there was no answer. She felt tears start to well up in her eyes. 'Pull yourself together.' she muttered to herself. 'There must be some huge mistake. This cannot be happening.'

Ten minutes later the train arrived at Tunbridge Wells station and Emma met Carla at the station entrance.

'Hello my dear it's lovely to see you again.' Carla said chirpily taking Emma in her arms and giving her a big hug.

'Carla something terrible has just happened.' Emma blurted out immensely relieved to have a trusted friend to share the devastating news with. 'I have just lost custody of the children.'

'What no, that cannot be.' Carla replied looking on in astonishment.

'Well that is what my lawyer just told me over the phone twenty minutes ago. He says he will fax me a copy of the court judgment he received this morning. Can I give him your fax number? He does not have a fax number so he cannot send me the judgment unless I tell him where to send it.'

It was the late 1990s and although it might seem incredible to many today, at that time fax was still the fastest way of sharing documents.

'But of course you can as soon as we get back to the house. There must be a mistake. It is outrageous.' Carla continued. 'Everyone knows you love your children to bits and are a great mother.'

Carla squeezed Emma's arm in reassurance and opened the car. They drove the five minutes to the house in relative silence both trying to digest the news.

Both women waited anxiously in front of the fax as it peeped and started to transmit a copy of the judgment.

Emma read it through and with each page she was gripped by a little more fear and trepidation. She explained to Carla what was written in the short three-page document. Hubert had been right.

'Let's go in the garden and have a drink and a bite to eat.' Carla suggested a concerned expression now engulfing her attractive features. 'The judgment does say temporary custody' Carla continued trying her best to sound optimistic and positive 'so all is not lost and you must go back to the continent as soon as possible and sort this out.'

'I know.' Emma replied. 'That is exactly what I intend to do first thing tomorrow morning.'

At 2 am Emma eventually fell into a restless troubled sleep. Up at the crack of dawn and on autopilot after less than three hours' sleep, she was through the Channel Tunnel and already knocking on Hubert's door before lunchtime. She wanted answers and a clear path forward. Above all she wanted to hold her young daughter Olivia and her young son Sebastian in her arms again. They were due to return to her in three days' time following a three and a half weeks' holiday with their father. Obviously everything was now on hold.

Chapter 2

During the car journey back to the continent, Emma's head was spinning. She was trying to understand how she could possibly find herself in such a dreadful predicament. Separated from her lovely son and daughter and without any visiting right. After all this was Western Europe. 'Start from the beginning.' she told herself, retracing her youth, how she met Paul and what had gone wrong with the marriage and subsequent divorce. She tried to make sense of what had happened so unexpectedly. She knew that only then would she be in a position to find the solution.

Emma had always loved travel and languages so it was no surprise to her family and friends when she announced following her studies that she would go and live and work abroad for a couple of years. She met Paul two years later at a party arranged by a mutual friend and there was an instant attraction. Paul was tall, good looking and charming and Emma was soon smitten. Three months later Paul asked Emma to marry him. Emma called her parents in the evening to announce the news. They were surprised but less enamoured by what they had just heard.

'It is too early.' Emma's dad insisted. 'You don't know each well or long enough and you are married for an awful long time. Think carefully before rushing into something you might regret later.'

Paul's parents also thought they should wait. Paul was an only child doted upon by his mother. She had lost her first son during childbirth when the gynaecologist, apparently celebrating his son's 21st birthday when she went into labour, arrived much too late and under the influence of alcohol. The baby received a blow to the temple with a pair of forceps and died three hours later. Paul's parents were grief stricken and when Paul arrived eleven months later he was understandably the apple of his mother's eye and could do no wrong.

Young and headstrong Paul and Emma married a year after their first encounter. They enjoyed a big white wedding in England followed by a smaller civil ceremony at the local registry office on the continent to make things official on both sides of the channel. Emma found a job and the couple moved into a nice neat bungalow in the countryside forty minutes from the capital and started life as a happily married couple.

Things were idyllic at first but after several months Emma started to notice how Paul became possessive and controlling with bouts of jealousy if she went out without him, albeit to exercise class with some girlfriends. A fit of jealousy provoked a car accident when Emma accelerated through an orange light on her way home from work in a bid to avoid arriving five minutes too late and incurring yet another line of questioning. In the process she wrote off Paul's new car. She was so shaken she did not drive for several years and pushed for the couple to move to the capital so that she could get around with public transport.

Paul's mother insisted on retaining a very active role in Paul's life, continuing to do his washing and ironing and visiting the couple's house when they were at work and moving the furniture around. Emma stood her ground and refused to give up seeing her girlfriends. She was a warm, friendly outgoing person who had grown up surrounded by a wide circle of friends and attached a great deal of importance to good friendship. She loved Paul and could not understand why he tried to control her. It would not have occurred to her to cheat on her new husband. She constantly tried to reassure him of this fact.

After one year Emma found a demanding job in an international company with increased responsibility and a much higher salary and the couple enjoyed a full and active life, marred only intermittently by Paul's jealousy and his mother's meddling. They travelled widely including to the Far East and all over Europe. Six years into the marriage Olivia was born and just under a year later Sebastian arrived to complete the family. The couple bought a large flat just before the property boom of the late 1980s and were able to sell at an ideal moment and purchase a beautiful old farm house close to the forest and five minutes from the capital. Paul and Emma had everything to be happy.

A year later Emma's father died suddenly of a heart attack and Paul's father fell ill and was diagnosed with lung cancer. It was a big double blow to the family who lost both fathers in the space of nine months. Olivia and Sebastian never really got to know their granddads which pained both Emma and Paul.

In the early 1990s Paul had the opportunity to secure a very good job as commercial director. The conditions were excellent. He seemed really enthusiastic and Emma persuaded him to take the job promising to support him one hundred percent. The job was challenging but also very interesting and Paul spent many evenings working away. Emma assumed the smooth running of the household, arranging her job so that she always left the office to pick up the children late afternoon and could spend quality time with them. In busy periods, she would turn on her computer when Olivia and Sebastian were in bed and continue working.

Eighteen months later, Emma pointed out to Paul that he seemed to be spending more and more time engrossed in his new job and perhaps it would be better to try to find a better work life balance. To Emma's shock and surprise, Paul exploded and punched Emma in the face, grabbed her hair and pulled her to the kitchen floor and started kicking her hard in the legs and ribs. After four blows Emma jumped up overcome with indignation. She grabbed a solid oak chair from the adjoining living room, lifted it above her head as though it weighed nothing and centring her gaze firmly on Paul said very calmly and with a great deal of commitment that if he ever laid another finger on her, she would personally send the chair crashing down on his head and that would be the end of him.

Paul looked shocked and retreated to the bathroom. That evening something broke inside Emma.

Next day Paul arranged for the company photographer to come around to the house. The photographer had already offered several times to pop by and take pictures of the family which Paul and Emma could also share with family and friends abroad. On Saturday morning Emma got up and went to the hairdresser. That afternoon, she sat smiling for the photos with her legs and ribs still throbbing. In the evening Paul and Emma attended the annual dinner arranged by Paul's company. Over the years she had learned to cover up her real feelings and put on a brave face where necessary. It worked. Nobody was any the wiser and the evening passed by really well. Paul continued as if the incident had never happened.

Three months later Emma was invited to accompany Paul and five of his colleagues and their spouses on a long weekend to Paris. One colleague in particular, Lea, made a special effort to befriend her. Emma had an uneasy feeling about the sincerity of this particular lady but being in a business environment, was too polite to say anything. She reassured herself that she would not see much of Lea afterwards anyway.

Paul started to be absent several evenings a week then started to spend each Wednesday night away. His lack of interest in family life increased. He was often rude and critical of Emma when he was at home. Mutual friends started to confide in Emma that they had noticed a change in Paul's behaviour and did not appreciate the way he talked to her in public. Emma tried to play it down confirming that Paul was under a lot of stress at work and things would get better.

Then Emma noticed that their joint account started to drift into the red. She did not understand why and started to worry. She knew that their mortgage was high but their two salaries were more than enough to cover all outgoing expenses. When she tried to discuss it with Paul he became angry so she left it, afraid he might fly into another rage. He also flatly refused to share his credit card statements with her so she had no way of determining how to correct the situation. When her cash point card failed to work at the supermarket one Friday evening as she stood with the week's shopping, Olivia and Sebastian and a long queue of people behind watching her curiously, she decided enough was enough.

She went back to the car and cried with frustration and worry. The next week she opened her own bank account and arranged for her next salary to be paid into it. Paul insisted all bills be split equally even though he now earned twenty percent more than Emma. She did not argue. Having at least some control over her own finances was more important to her.

The following spring Paul mentioned to Emma casually over dinner one evening that his colleague Lea had left her husband. Emma just nodded failing to make any particular connection. She now had enough preoccupations of her own. Paul's mother, who had now been widowed for several years, was still meddling in the household. However, Emma did not make a fuss as she was sympathetic that the old lady was still getting over the loss of her husband and knew that she absolutely adored her grandchildren, Olivia and Sebastian. She would often say that they were the only valid reason she wanted to carry on.

After Paul had been especially rude yet again, Emma could not take it anymore. She was beginning to lose her confidence and self-esteem. It was finally clear to her that she could no longer continue like this and she successfully convinced herself that she deserved better.

'I want a divorce.' she told Paul flatly.

'OK.' he replied coldly. 'I will do the necessary to draw up the papers for a mutual consent divorce as its quicker, cheaper and easier.'

It sounded rehearsed and Emma was sure he had pushed her to react this way. Emma decided to hop on the plane for the weekend and go over and see her sister Laura in England to clear her head and get some sound advice. Laura was very sympathetic. As they went for a long walk across the fields, Laura reassured Emma not to worry, that in two years she would say that it was the best thing which could have happened to her.

'You really do deserve better.' she reassured her sister. 'You are still young and you have your whole life ahead of you.'

When Emma arrived back on the Sunday evening, a mutual friend Janine called to say she had heard that Paul and Emma were separating. Janine was a stay at home mum married to one of the country's top bankers.

'Don't sign anything.' she insisted. 'I know a retired judge from the golf club. He still handles divorces and other litigation for people to keep his hand in. You should get really good professional advice before you go any further.'

'OK thanks let me have his name and telephone number and I will see what he has to say.' Emma replied.

Emma called Jules Mercier and arranged to meet him the following Saturday morning. It was a step which was to radically change the next few years of her life.

Chapter 3

What had surprised Emma upon her return from her sister's that Sunday evening was that the terms of the mutual consent divorce were already written up and waiting for her. Emma played with Olivia and Sebastian before putting them to bed and told Paul that she would have a look at the proposed terms next day in the office. She felt she was being rushed and wanted to study this important document in detail and in her own time.

It turned out to be quite generous. Paul had left Emma all the furniture and offered to pay child maintenance of 400 € per month following the sale of the house. Most importantly he had left Emma exclusive parental rights for the children whom she had been practically bringing up alone over the previous two years. Paul requested a visiting right every second weekend and half the school holidays. He would take his personal belongings such as his stereo and the speed boat he had purchased four months earlier with his bonus and a sum of money his mother had apparently given to him following a small win on the lottery.

Emma was in agreement with the terms but wanted to see what additional professional advice the retired judge would offer her prior to the signature of any legal document. The mutual consent route certainly seemed the best one to take in the interest of the children.

Emma got up early on the Saturday and set off to meet Jules Mercier. Paul asked her if she felt it was really necessary to seek legal advice. His ever interfering mother had taken Emma to one side the day before and declared that if Emma did not claim more than 400 € a month in alimony then she would not claim back from Emma half the sum she had given Paul and Emma to clear their overdraft the year before, the origin of which still remained a mystery to Emma. Emma replied that the 400 € per month Paul was proposing was fine. She had already calculated that with her salary and the proposed maintenance payment she could still offer the children a comfortable and stable future. She told herself that there was no need to take either party to the cleaners as this would only lead to more problems later. Gosh Emma thought to herself, I am so glad dad pushed me and my sister Laura to work hard at school and be financially independent. If not, I would be in a right old pickle now.

Emma rung the bell of the villa where Jules Mercier was living a mere five-minute drive from home. The door opened and an elderly, very distinguished looking gentleman with grey hair and glasses stood in front of her. He looked like a retired judge with a lifetime of experience and Emma felt she must be in good hands. Jules firmly shook Emma's hand, smiled reassuringly and invited her into the living room. The sun was shining through the large bay windows and she looked out over the large, well-kept garden.

'Have a seat.' he said beckoning her to sit down on the comfortable brown leather sofa. Jules sat down on the adjacent sofa and observed her calmly.

'Well.' he said at last. 'What can I do for you? I understand you want to divorce by mutual consent. Why don't you start from the beginning and tell me what happened?'

Emma was still confused and hurt. Just where did she start if she wanted to sound objective? 'My husband is completely absorbed by his job and has been for two years and he shows very little interest in his marriage and his family. In addition, when he is at home he is unpleasant. I don't think I can keep on living like this as all efforts to discuss the situation have proved futile so I agreed to go through with the mutual consent divorce.' she trailed off.

'Oh I see.' Jules Mercier added. 'It sounds as though he has somebody else.'

'Not that I am aware of.' Emma replied.

'Well maybe you should try to find out.' Jules Mercier suggested.

Emma handed him the proposed terms of the divorce which he studied carefully before commenting on the alimony sum.

'Why don't you try and press him for fifty percent more?' he retorted. 'After all life is expensive and will become even more so as the children grow older.'

'No I think I will cope just fine and what is being proposed is acceptable.' Emma confirmed.

She did not want to get into an eternal fight, fully aware that money and luxury were important, if not key elements, in Paul's life as well as his interfering mother's. Jules Mercier proposed to study the terms in detail and make a note with his eventual comments for the following week. Emma left feeling reassured that the case was in such capable hands. Jules Mercier had been proud to share details of his former career, that he had been a judge for several years as well as a member of the ministry of justice and had even drafted some new legislation which became law. Well if anyone must be familiar with the law it must be this gentleman Emma told herself confidently.

When she arrived back home, Paul was eager to discover how she had got on.

'Fine.' Emma replied adding 'But he suggested I should perhaps ask for more money for the children.'

Before even asking if she intended to do so, Paul went berserk and started screaming abuse at Emma. To eventually stop the tirade, Emma shouted back.

'Listen, rest assured I don't intend to ask for more but your behaviour is completely unacceptable. If I agree to a divorce by mutual consent it is for the good of the children but I question your motive, otherwise you would not be ranting and raving like a madman. Now be quiet the children can hear us.'

Emma and Paul spent the weekend far out of each other's way playing separately with Olivia and Sebastian. Both longed for the week to start so they would be even further apart. The shadow of Paul's mother hovered insidiously in the background and Emma could not help thinking that once she no longer had Paul in her life she was also freeing herself from this mother in law who continued to dog her existence. How she longed for freedom and peace.

Jules Mercier's comments arrived a few days later. They started off officially and in an old fashioned manner with the title 'Personal and confidential note for the attention of Emma Archer.'

Apparently the mutual consent divorce procedure had only been introduced a couple of years earlier so there were still very few legal books or notes written on the subject. The procedure lasted about five months and involved two appearances in court to sign the terms initially drawn up by the notary in the consent order, followed, a few weeks later, by the pronouncement of the decree absolute.

Jules Mercier went on to point out that on page two there was a phrase which stated that Emma Archer could not go and live abroad without the written approval of Paul Archer. He went on to elaborate that in Western Europe women enjoyed equal rights and they were far from being in a soap opera. In other words, he wrote and underlined, that if need be, she was free to do what she wanted but must advise the court administering the divorce in the interests of the children.

Regarding the clause concerning future modifications to the divorce agreement, i.e. in case of any major events the terms were susceptible to be reviewed, Jules Mercier highlighted that this became slippery ground. That in essence, the terms were made to last to avoid problems but that times and situations do change. He would be cautious because if things did not work out, the court would need to be consulted and if any problems arose from the divorce, he would recommend going to court to sort them out.

A few days later he faxed an addition to the consent order stipulating that Emma could not go abroad without Paul's permission with the children adding 'except for exceptional circumstances due to her profession'. Emma agreed to leave in that in such a case, she would pay travel expenses for the children to see their father. Paul accepted the updated terms without further ado much to Emma's surprise.

Jules Mercier was not in favour of Paul only starting to pay child maintenance after the house was sold but Emma was confident that she could sell the house relatively quickly and wanted to be as conciliatory as possible to avoid any further problems. Jules even reiterated the couple could put the house up for rent. Emma turned down the proposal. She had no confidence in Paul's financial management and the sooner she was free of this large financial responsibility and final legal tie, the better it would be.

The following weekend was Paul's mother's birthday. Ironically it also happened to be Emma and Paul's thirteenth wedding anniversary. Needless to say, one week away from signing the first papers for the divorce, neither was in a mood to celebrate or even spend time together. Paul wanted to go to the countryside for the weekend with the children and to take his mother out for her birthday.

Emma had always arranged her professional life around the children and made a point of never travelling at weekends. However, that weekend there was a European sales meeting in Frankfurt and she jumped at the chance to participate. It helped take her mind off the emotional upheaval for forty-eight hours at least. Back with the children on Sunday evening, they started to talk about the weekend and asked Emma if she knew that Lea had come along to the restaurant to meet grannie.

'No I didn't.' Emma replied trying to sound upbeat and changing the subject. Suddenly Emma had a very uneasy feeling. When the children were in bed, she called Paul and asked for an explanation.

'We are just friends' he replied 'and in any case it is none of your business because we are getting divorced next week.' and with that he hung up.

Jules Mercier's words came flooding back. 'Are you sure he does not have anyone else?'

Emma called Paul's mother and asked her what had happened during the weekend.

'Nothing.' she replied sadly adding that she had spent the most horrible birthday of her life.

Emma cast her mind back to all those Wednesday nights that Paul had spent away over the last eighteen months apparently abroad with colleagues on a business trip. Emma felt confused and betrayed. Anyway in the end what does it matter she told herself. The marriage is over. She thought about what her boss had told her at work the previous week. How brave she was to take such a major decision to divorce at a relatively young age and then with two young children. It did not seem brave, just painful.

Chapter 4

Friday morning Paul and Emma went to the notary to sign the consent agreement. The same evening Paul had planned to go on holiday with the children to the south of France. He now had his speed boat which he was eager to try out and was taking his mother along to look after the children and do the cooking. The notary hurried through the details, Emma and Paul signed and then parted company. It was over in less than five minutes. Emma wished Paul a good holiday and asked him to take good care of the children. Since they had agreed to divorce, Emma had lost nearly thirty pounds in weight. It was the most effective diet she had ever seen but not one she would recommend. She did not even notice until a friend commented and she stepped on the scales.

Emma spoke to Olivia and Sebastian on the phone several times during the following two weeks and could not wait for them to come home. They were due to arrive at Paul's mother's country house on the Saturday evening so she called on Sunday morning eager to hear their little voices and to know that they were back safely. She called several times but there was no answer. By early afternoon Emma started to get worried and rang two neighbours in the village. The next door neighbour informed her that yes they had arrived back safely but that Paul's mother had fallen down the stairs at midnight, fractured her arm and badly bruised herself. She had only been able to call for help in the early hours of Sunday morning and was transported to hospital where they expected to operate. Paul had not been there when it happened as he had driven the speed boat back to the barn where it was being stored. Paul was not answering the phone as he had gone for a walk with the children in the forest.

The children arrived home that evening and Emma gave them a huge hug. She had prepared their favourite dinner of roast chicken, baked potatoes and homemade apple sauce. She smiled as they both tucked in hungrily licking their lips and commenting how good it tasted.

'Did you have a good holiday?' Emma finally asked them.

'It was OK.' they replied in unison.

Then Olivia sat up in her chair and announced 'Lea came and shared daddy's room and they went away most of the time together on the boat and we stayed with grannie.'

They both looked at Emma and waited for her reaction. In two seconds everything fell into place. Paul's lack of interest in his family, his constant absences and provocative comments and condescending attitude. Emma tried very hard not to look shocked or hurt in front of the children. He could at least have had the courage to tell her face to face and end things honourably she thought to herself. But I suppose this is too much to ask. She felt tired and weary but at least the cat was finally out of the bag and she had to accept it and move on.

When the children were in bed, Emma called one of Paul's colleagues Alice with whom she got on well and told her what she had discovered. Alice was sympathetic and confirmed quietly that she had known about the affair for quite a while but did not feel that she could interfere and update Emma about it. Emma could not blame her. How many people would have actively got involved and then in a sensitive work environment too?

Paul came around to the house the following evening to fetch some clothes. He was flying the next day to the USA for a worldwide sales meeting. Emma was in the kitchen preparing dinner for herself and the children. It was shortly after a large passenger plane had crashed and he asked Emma if she would tell Olivia and Sebastian what a good father he was if he did not make it back. Emma stared at him in disbelief.

'Please get your clothes and leave. I don't have anything more to add.' she replied peeling the potatoes and hoping he would just go.

'No this is my house and I will not leave.' he taunted.

Emma had had enough. She said calmly 'If you don't leave, I will throw this glass of grapefruit juice over your head, suit and all'.

The time that Paul had doused her with coffee just before she left for the airport on her first business trip twelve years before, in an unprovoked jealous moment, came flooding back. It was not in Emma's nature to act impulsively or emotionally. In fact, Paul had often accused her of being too phlegmatic, which he referred to as a typically English trait. Paul stood his ground and refused to move.

'OK.' Emma announced 'Here you are.' She threw the grapefruit juice at him and waited for his reaction. At first he looked startled. Then he grabbed a tea towel, dried his face then carefully dabbed the drops off his shirt, jacket and tie. Emma carried on pealing the potatoes, hoping he would just leave.

'When I leave' he added 'please don't cut the arms and legs off my remaining suits.' Emma felt like laughing. It had never even crossed her mind. What sort of person would do something like that she asked herself?

The children were playing in the garden and unaware of the fracas. Emma took her coat, went outside, collected Olivia and Sebastian and took them to McDonalds for dinner. When she got back Paul was gone. She felt guilty about having thrown the juice and she promised herself that this was the last time she would do something so rash, emotional and out of character. When Emma told her sister Laura about Paul's request not to cut up his suits, she laughed and suggested Emma think about it seriously and use mum's whopping great pinking scissors in the process. The two sisters saw the funny side and had a much needed laugh over the phone.

'Never lose your sense of humour.' Emma muttered to herself. 'Otherwise you are dead.'

Over the next few days, Emma called Paul's mother regularly in the hospital to let the children speak to her. She had needed an operation and had a pin in her arm. She begged Emma to visit her at the weekend with Olivia and Sebastian before heading off to England on her planned summer holiday with the children. Emma was shocked by what had happened and felt sorry for Paul's mum. Even more so when she saw the alarming shade of black and yellow the bruising to her face and neck had caused. The old lady looked frail and weak. But her face lit up when she saw Olivia and Sebastian.

She explained to Emma that during the holiday she had gone down with a bout of food poisoning which she blamed for provoking the fall upon her return. She confided that she had told Paul she did not agree 'for that woman' to stay with them in the apartment. Paul had simply replied that he was paying the rent and his mother had nothing to say. Emma shook her head and changed the subject. After an hour she wished Paul's mum a speedy recovery and left with Olivia and Sebastian.

Events of the past few days had all proved a little too much and Emma decided to bring forward her holiday to see the family in England by three days. It was a relief to load up the car and leave the problems behind for two and a half weeks. Emma had arranged to go with her mum, Aunty Hilda and the children to the coast for a well-earned break. Emma's mum had booked them into a cosy hotel on the cliffs with a panoramic view of the sea. The fresh sea air was wonderful. They built sand castles on the beach with Olivia and Sebastian. The children loved paddling in the sea and the highlight of the day was a donkey ride at the end of the afternoon. For the first time in weeks, Emma slept well.

During this time Paul planned to come to the house and collect all his things. Friends and family were sympathetic about the impending divorce. It was the first in the family.

'Somebody has got to be the first.' Emma joked.

'It can happen.' they reassured Emma. 'You are still young and have a good job and your whole life ahead of you. Most importantly of all you have the children.'

Chapter 5

When Emma got back home, she decided to change the locks and put the house up for sale. Paul had collected his things as promised. There were some gaps where his stereo and other things had been so Emma moved the furniture around to fill them. She took some rubbish down to the garage and stumbled upon three dustbin bags which Paul had filled during the move. Out of curiosity stemming from her recent discoveries, Emma opened the bags and rummaged inside. She was surprised to see the statements and credit card details from her joint account with Paul. He had been very secretive about revealing details and Emma had been unable to grasp why their account had slipped so much into the red. She took them back upstairs determined to sift through them when she had a bit of time and see if she would glean anything new.

For years Emma had worked hard to have a dream home and the best environment for the couple's children. It seemed such a shame to put the lovely farmhouse on the market. However, so much had happened over the last few months that she was actually, to her own surprise, able to reason that the house was just bricks and that the sooner it was sold and she moved on, the better it would be. Focused on getting the best price possible and not appearing rushed to sell in a divorce case, Emma stayed clear of estate agents and chose to attempt, at least initially, to sell the house directly. She placed an ad in the local paper and had two calls on the first day. She arranged visits.

The house had lots of character, an open fireplace from the seventeenth century, a high wooden ceiling and beautiful nineteenth century doors taken from a manor house. It was situated two minutes from the forest and had a superbly equipped kitchen and luxury bathroom. The first couple fell in love with the property the minute they walked through the door. They returned three days later and informed Emma of their intention to buy. Emma was so pleased and immensely relieved. She had also managed to get ten percent above the market price and there was no agency commission to pay.

Emma had the deeds of sale checked by Jules Mercier who gave her the green light. He had been extremely surprised by the speed of the sale. He kept telling Emma that in his experience it could take over a year to sell such a property. Emma did not need obstacles she needed solutions and she called Paul and arranged for him to be there for the signing of the sale. He was also surprised but pleased, especially about the sales price.

At the beginning of September Paul and Emma made their first appearance in the family court to sign the first stage of the divorce proceedings. Emma had not even been in a police station in her life let alone in a courtroom in front of a judge and she found the whole thing completely daunting. The couple sat down in front of the judge, a stern looking lady approaching her fifties. She looked at the terms of the consent document and remarked what a shame it was to end a thirteen-year marriage with two small children and asked if Emma and Paul did not want to reconsider and try for a reconciliation. Emma muttered that Paul had been cheating on her for close to two years so there was little point in trying to save the marriage. Paul who had limited hearing in his right ear turned to the judge and asked what Emma had said.

'Nothing.' the judge snapped. 'I can see you have already done enough.'

The papers were laid out for signature. By now Emma was shaking. She took out her identity card from her wallet and was surprised to see at that moment how much her hands were trembling. She signed, made a quick exit to the car and headed back to the office. She was so mentally drained that she started to nod off in a meeting that afternoon. Her colleagues gently nudged her until she woke up with a start and re-joined the meeting. At 5.30 pm she headed off to pick up the children from school, relieved to be in their company and happy that this significant milestone was now behind her.

Following the holidays, Paul came every second weekend to pick up the children. Officially he was registered as living at his mother's address in the country but Emma knew following the children's first visit that he was living with Lea in a small flat in a large city 100 km away. He had rented the apartment next door to store all his boxes. Emma had no idea where the address was and Paul would not tell her.

Olivia and Sebastian complained how they were locked up alone overnight in the neighbouring apartment with just a baby phone for contact with their father which did not appear to function. In the morning they told Emma how they started to cry as they were all alone and no one came to fetch them. Emma was angry but felt helpless. What happens if there is a fire or something else happens she lamented. She contacted Jules Mercier and informed him about it. He replied that it was not normal but via his contacts he would have Paul followed and inform Emma of his address and telephone number. There would be a cost of course, money in hand, but by now Emma was worried and money seemed comparatively unimportant. Within a few days Emma had an address and phone number.

At a dinner party a few weeks later, a friend asked casually if Emma had heard that Lea had been fired by her company. Surprised Emma said no and asked what had happened. Apparently word had spread around the company about the affair. Questions had been asked about the many business trips Paul and Lea had made together. The General Manager had apparently arrived for the weekly meeting and had announced quite abruptly that Mr Archer had left his wife and children and was living with Lea and that Lea was no longer an employee in the company.

A couple of weeks later Paul called Emma. 'I have been fired' he began 'and it's all your fault.' Emma was flabbergasted.

'How can you say it is my fault?' she replied. 'If you were fired you only have yourself to blame.'

The following day Paul's mother wrote Emma a registered letter, copying Paul and claiming 5000 € or half the money she had given Paul upon his request to clear their overdraft with the bank. Emma was stunned. First of all, she had not spent any of this money, did not even know where it had gone and Paul's mother had told her a few months earlier that if she did not claim more than 400 € per month in maintenance for the children in the divorce settlement then she would not come back on the matter.

Emma was worried though as Paul's mother hinted she would take legal action if Emma did not comply. Emma's family urged her not to pay. Paul's mother wrote that as they had decided to sell the house and not take the future of their children into account in this decision and as the house had been sold for a good price, she felt it right to ask for return of the money.

Emma dug out Paul's bank statements which she had recovered from the rubbish, opened an excel spreadsheet and started to plug in the amounts, the dates and the places. She sorted by date and by location and looked in amazement at the picture which unfolded in front of her eyes. There were over forty business trips and accompanying receipts, often for a double hotel room, restaurants, perfume shops, flowers, all for over 4000 €. There were even some receipts from the same period for a single room accompanied by another receipt for the difference between a single and double as Emma found out when she called the hotel. Emma could only conclude that these were expenses Paul had run up and not claimed back from the company or at least not back into their joint bank account.

Emma felt betrayed, even more so that Paul's mother was now pushing her to pay for Paul's luxury living with his mistress and that Paul had on top, not paid Emma a penny since their separation for the clothing, schooling or upkeep of the children.

Emma wrote to Lea's former husband Alan who called her the day he received her letter. It was time for them to compare notes. If she was being attacked she might as well have as much information as possible to defend herself. The two had met on a couple of occasions. Alan went on to explain to Emma that he had discovered the relationship nearly eighteen months earlier and had almost picked up the phone to tell Emma what he knew. Following a trip to Vienna about six months into the affair, he had noticed a distinct change in his wife's behaviour. He called Paul and begged him to leave his wife alone so he could save the marriage but to no avail. He also discovered some hotel bills for a double room even though Lea maintained she had stayed the night with her son.

Emma now had enough information to be able to reply to Paul's mother. She wrote that the breakdown of her marriage had deeply hurt her, confirmed when the affair between Paul and Lea had started and attached copies of the hotel bills, restaurants, perfume etc. highlighting the large sums deducted from their joint account. The children were the most important thing in her life and if she got a good price for the sale of the house it was because she was fighting to be able to offer them a good future. She knew Paul's mother loved her grandchildren very much and that she could call them whenever she wanted. Paul's mother's accident was unfortunate and she hoped she would get better soon.

For years she had earned more than Paul but it had all gone into the same pot and she had never complained. It was now ironic that as soon as he earned more and they opened separate accounts, she still had to pay fifty percent of the bills. She had shared all her bonuses with him over the years but as soon as he received a big one, he bought himself a boat. Paul had even taken back the solid gold necklace his parents had offered Emma for their first Christmas as a married couple.

Emma tried to be objective and she had the letter checked by Jules Mercier before sending it. He commented about how much he appreciated the honest and charming style. A few days later Emma received a short reply from Paul's mother. She said the contents of the letter saddened her but her mind was made up. Both were to blame for the breakdown of the marriage. She thanked Emma for her acknowledgement that she loved her grandchildren and told her to forget about paying back the money, she would manage. Finally, she wished Emma and the children the best of luck in life. Emma now hoped that things would calm down but somehow she had an uneasy feeling that more was to come.

Chapter 6

Emma quickly found a new house to rent close to the children's school and five minutes from work. She could save thirty minutes' travel time each day which meant more quality time with Olivia and Sebastian. The children liked the new place. They had their own playroom and a nice big garden to play outside in the summer.

Jules Mercier was surprised that Emma had found such a nice place so quickly and for a reasonable price. He was dabbling in real estate himself and would have preferred to be the one proposing the property. She had him check the rental agreement which he confirmed was good to go. She moved in with the children over a long weekend and the following week handed over the keys to the buyers of the farmhouse they had sold. Slowly things were falling into place. In six weeks Emma would appear in court for the second time to sign the divorce and early the following year the divorce would be officially pronounced.

In the run up to Christmas a series of phone calls put Emma on her guard again. Two of Paul's former colleagues called her to tell her that Paul was telling everyone who wanted to listen that he had left Emma because she was a bad mother, an alcoholic and had neglected the children. Emma was shocked calmly confirming that this was absolutely untrue.

'We know it is unfounded.' they replied. 'This is why we are calling you. Take care. He may want to take the children away from you.'

Lea's husband, Alan, had also mentioned this to Emma. On his side, Lea had told people that Alan, in reality a respected doctor, was a manic depressive and needed hospital treatment which is why she had left him. Emma and Alan had actually laughed the accusations off together as being so absurd and a somewhat feeble and unconvincing attempt from the cheating pair to justify why their two marriages had broken down.

Then Cathy a good friend who occasionally looked after Olivia and Sebastian after school called to tell Emma that Paul's mother had contacted her to ask if she did not think that Emma drank too much and that the children were badly dressed and poorly fed. Cathy immediately denied this and warned Emma to be on her guard. The same thing happened to Valerie, another long standing family friend, who quite direct by nature, had immediately let Paul's mother know that she would gain absolutely no support from her in this respect.

Paul's mother was planning to leave for three months to America so Emma hoped her attempts to fabricate evidence would subside while she was gone and eventually disappear. Paul's cousin Claude had emigrated to America in the early sixties and made his fortune. He lived in one of those affluent places dotted with palm trees where the sun shines the whole year. It was a great way for Paul's mother to escape the cold winter months and get spoilt in the process. Emma had been the one to persuade Paul's mother to undertake the long plane journey and make this a regular event. Often the ticket would arrive, first class, and no expense was spared to pamper the old lady, something she admitted she really enjoyed.

Claude had lost his own mother several years earlier and saw in Paul's mum a replacement and he went out of his way to make her feel at home and spoil her. Claude was extremely well connected to some of Europe's top politicians, business men and famous people from the world of entertainment. The family would sometimes see his picture in magazines and hear stories of top events he had attended. Paul's mother had even met some famous stars at his house. In fact, Paul's mother had last been out to stay just after Paul and Emma started discussing the possibility of a divorce.

Worried, Emma consulted Jules Mercier about how to deal with the false accusations.

'Go to the doctor and get a blood test to prove you are not a heavy drinker.' Jules replied.

Emma did just that. She wanted to stay one step ahead and had a growing feeling of unease that Paul and Lea and Paul's mother would stop at nothing to gather whatever 'evidence' they could to use against her in the future.

Chapter 7

Like most of the country Emma had been closely following developments in the case of a series of child abductions, the discovery of the bodies of several children and the miraculous release of others alive who had been imprisoned in the cellar of a house. She shuddered at the pictures on TV and in the papers, watched the funerals with deep sadness and hoped that all involved would be promptly caught and brought to justice.

At Taekwondo class one Friday evening her friend Brigitte asked Emma if she would like to participate in a large demonstration planned in the capital in support of the parents of the children who had disappeared. The aim was to put pressure on the government for more clarity and an improvement in the policing and judicial system. Emma had grown close to Brigitte since her separation from Paul. She found her positive outlook contagious and it cheered her up. Brigitte was the same age as Emma and had a daughter the same age as Olivia.

A couple of months after becoming a mother, she was involved in a bad car accident when a young drunk driver crashed into her. She spent several months in hospital and had had to undergo a series of painful operations to rebuild her feet which were badly crushed. However, Brigitte loved sport and pushed herself to be as active as possible even though she admitted it was often painful. She had a very bright smile, wavy blond hair and big green eyes which sparkled and came to life when she laughed.

'Yes sure I will come with you.' Emma replied. 'Children are precious. We owe it the families of these poor children to show our support.' she continued.

On the Sunday morning Emma headed to the village where Brigitte and her husband Matthew lived. Olivia and Sebastian were with their father otherwise she would have taken them along. Susan,

Brigitte's young daughter, accompanied them as did quite a few other children from the village. They had their picture taken on the village square for a local newspaper then set off by coach for the capital. Emma had mentioned to her mum the day before on the phone that she was taking part in a peaceful demonstration. It was the first time in her life.

'Be careful.' Emma's mum remarked. 'Especially if the police are on horseback.'

It was the strangest and most moving demonstration Emma could have imagined. Most people were dressed in light colours. Many carried balloons. There were old and young and a rainbow of different races walking together in solidarity. There was a dignified silence and despite several hundred thousand people on the relatively narrow streets for as far as the eye could see, a remarkable discipline and respect. Emma found the whole thing very moving. There were pictures posted everywhere of the poor children, some murdered, some rescued but no doubt scarred for life and others still missing. The expressive stare on their faces was haunting. Emma asked her friends lots of questions.

'This is extraordinary.' she commented. 'Something just has to change after this.'

To Emma's surprise, they did not share her optimism.

'So many things are wrong with our system.' they replied. 'It will take an awful lot to improve it and then there are certain factions who do not want the truth to come out and they will do everything in their power to stop it.'

Emma did not understand. It would take many events and be several years before she grasped the full meaning of these words.

Chapter 8

Emma continued to be in regular contact with Jules Mercier. In light of the recent attacks from Paul and his mother, Jules said he would conduct an additional study to see if they could review Paul's visiting rights if they turned the mutual consent divorce into one for a determined cause such as adultery or unreasonable behaviour. A few days later, he concluded however, in an official note that even if they went down this long and arduous route, this would not change anything to the visiting rights already established and the youth court was the only competent authority to be able to do so going forward.

Jules Mercier had sent his summary of the situation to a longstanding associate with whom, he confirmed, he worked with more than regularly. He outlined the fact that the young children were locked up on several occasions overnight on their own when they went to stay with their father which perturbed them, as well as Paul's unreasonable behaviour and constant criticism of Emma. His name was Hubert Belette and Jules confirmed that in the event of eventual recourse to the court, Hubert Belette would represent them. Concluding his note, Jules Mercier wrote that he believed Emma had appreciated his work in which he had invested a maximum of time and effort and he had particularly appreciated their collaboration. Jules thanked Emma for the payment of his fees, some 1700 € handed over in cash during the four month' period.

Emma still felt confident with this retired distinguished former judge and grandfather who had worked at the Ministry of Justice and had written some of the country's laws. The situation was difficult but if Jules Mercier had everything under control and, as he said, an excellent lawyer friend to represent her interests if things did not improve, what did she have to worry about Emma reassured herself.

Emma remained cautiously optimistic that things could only get better. Time is a great healer she kept repeating to herself. The children were settling in well into their new school and making lots of friends. Most of Emma and Paul's mutual friends during their marriage had sided with Emma following the break-up which, to Emma's dismay, also served to wind Paul up.

Paul called the children three times per week as did his mother, usually on the day on which Paul did not call. When Paul came to pick up the children for the weekend, Emma stayed in the house. She was hurt by Paul's stories of her failings as a good mother and Paul's mother's attempts to gather 'evidence' she feared could only be used against her. Outwardly Emma remained positive and cheerful in front of the children but inside she began to worry and wondered where things were heading and when the onslaught would eventually stop.

Chapter 9

Within a week of the divorce being officially pronounced, two letters dropped through the post. The first one from Paul's mother claiming additional time with Olivia and Sebastian in the holidays. She blamed Emma for the situation and divorce as she did not see her grandchildren as often as before. The second one, a registered letter, from Paul.

Emma had to go to the post office to pick it up. Why send the letter by registered mail if there was not some ulterior and more sinister motive behind it she lamented to herself? Emma signed for the letter and returned to the car and tore open the envelope. As she read through the content, her hands started to shake. The letter was so mean, so full of untruths. She sat in the car for ten minutes in shock and dismay before setting off to the office.

Paul wrote that if Emma did not respect his wishes for the children's summer camp then he would react in due course. He blamed Emma for turning the children against him and for the loss of Lea's and his own job. He said enough was enough and they had decided to get the judicial authorities involved and nothing could now stop them. He added that if he had decided to leave home, despite the pain to leave his children behind, temporarily at least, it was because he could no longer be unhappy at Emma's side. She had made his life unbearable by her abominable character, he was forced to bring up the children on his own, that her chronic arrogance had displeased so many people who now supported him.

The tirade continued and just got worse and worse. He accused Emma of having totally failed as a wife and a mother, devoid of tenderness, love, comprehension, pleasantness which she reserved exclusively for her colleagues. She dressed and fed the children badly including giving them the green of the cauliflower to eat, which in his country was strictly reserved for farm animals. Under a p.s. at the bottom he wrote that he was going to ask the competent authorities to reduce the maintenance he paid for the children because it was Emma's fault that he had lost his job. With her substantial salary, without counting recent promotion and bonus, this should not pose too much of a problem for her.

Emma had never felt so shocked, hurt and unfairly treated in her life. She knew she should just ignore it but it was just so cruel, deliberately so she reasoned to inflict maximum hurt, weaken and subsequently destabilise her. She was frightened and for the first time suddenly felt very alone in a foreign country.

That weekend she sat down at her computer, took a deep breath, and decided to reply to Paul's mother's letter, copying Paul and Lea to put the record straight. Emma outlined how disappointed the letter had left her and that it was a pity Paul's mother could not follow the advice of her brother to remain neutral for the sake of her grandchildren. Everyone had the right to have an opinion, but it was best to be in possession of all the facts before airing it. Emma attached copies of the credit card statements proving Paul's infidelity and luxury living with his mistress, adding so much so that she had not had enough money to buy the groceries with her small children at the supermarket one Friday evening.

Emma reminded Paul's mother that her son had sometimes made her cry in front of Emma and the children if he did not get his own way and that he told so many lies about Emma that he was probably starting to believe them himself.

Emma wrote that Paul had recently called her in the office furious because she had spoken directly to Lea's ex-husband which she found normal as their lives had been turned upside down by the same phenomena and that they had just compared notes then wished one another the best of luck for the future. Emma added that she found Paul and Lea's arrogance amazing. That they believed they could do anything they wanted without the slightest comment from anyone.

She wrote that Paul's life had always been too easy and if he did not get his own way he became angry, even violent, and that this had been the origin of nearly every argument they had had during their marriage.

Emma added she was now very glad to be out of it and that she believed she deserved better. That there was something decidedly rotten about the whole episode and she was following the advice of her family and close friends and severing all contact with Paul and his mother as they were just out to hurt her and were not acting in the best interests of the children. Emma concluded that she would give a good education and future to her children with a solid preparation to face life successfully.

Emma asked Paul's mum to stop contacting her friends in a bid to secure a confirmation that the children were not properly looked after as people could not take her seriously. Finally, if she wanted to go to the seaside at Easter with Olivia and Sebastian she should do so during the week the children were with Paul since Emma had arranged to go to England for a week to see her own family.

Wrapping up the letter on a more conciliatory note, Emma wrote that she acknowledged the fact that Paul's mum genuinely adored her grandchildren and that she could call them whenever she wanted, that Emma was not difficult and had always been fair.

Emma knew that Paul would not take the reply lying down but naively hoped the proof and objectivity would show that she was not a push over and it might be preferable to look for a more peaceful solution. She expected retaliation but was not sure in which form.

The Personal Assistant to the Managing Director of Emma's company, Julie, was a friend. Instinctively Emma mentioned that if she should receive any suspicious looking post from Paul addressed to top management, then she should give her a call. Two weeks later the phone rang.

'Emma I have something which may be of interest.' Julie announced in an amused tone.

Two minutes later she arrived in Emma's office with a brown envelope addressed to the MD with a letter from Paul stating that he believed the company was a high-tech org. and not a bureau of private detectives or a sensational newspaper publisher. Perhaps certain of the company's employees had so far failed to grasp this fact and were using the company's resources to settle their little scores, indicating that Emma was posting her private post free of charge at the company's expense. The company actually had an internal system allowing employees to use the company's postal facilities for private mail to avoid losing time at the post office. Each employee paid for the service used and this is exactly what Emma had done. Emma thanked Julie

'Absolutely no problem.' Julie replied. 'Your ex does seem to be a bit of a basket case – you must be glad it's over.' she added wistfully as she left.

The following day Emma received an envelope from Lea returning the letter with a photo of herself, the children and Paul. Emma's face had been disfigured with a Hitler moustache. Emma was with a colleague when she opened the envelope and the photo fell out onto her desk. She looked at it for a moment in absolute amazement, showed it to her colleague and together they started to laugh at the sheer absurdity and pettiness.

Chapter 10

Jules Mercier had been monitoring the situation closely. Emma and Jules had already known one another for over nine months, had spoken at least twice a week and were beginning to form a friendly trusting relationship. In this time of turmoil, Emma was becoming emotionally dependent on Jules Mercier to support and reassure her that everything would work out fine. Something he did extremely well.

He was distinguished, experienced, well versed and fashionable. One of the highlights of his career had been a transfer to London representing his government where he often mentioned the wonderful time he had enjoyed. He had lived in a big house in Hampstead, was a member of one of the most prestigious golf clubs in the area and used to buy all his suits on Saville Row. He could not hide his love of all good things British which gave Emma an added comfort factor as the bombs continued to fall around her.

Jules Mercier prepared a letter to his longstanding colleague Hubert Belette recapping the details of Emma's file. He underlined that Emma felt deceived by the way the divorce had been handled and that she was particularly concerned by the way the children were perturbed during the visit to their father since he never looked after them alone, locked them up in a separate apartment overnight and constantly criticized Emma and her family in front of them. He therefore recommended to limit Paul's visiting rights to one day every two weeks and two weeks in the summer.

Emma had yet to meet Hubert Belette. She could only feel confident about his experience and expertise from the glowing reference, both written and verbal, provided to her by Jules Mercier. She desperately needed some good moral and legal support and felt increasingly vulnerable in light of the ongoing barrage of attacks for which most people, even in their native country, would be totally unprepared.

With almost clockwork precision, the first lawyer's letter from Paul's side dropped into Emma's post-box a few days later. It was what she had been subconsciously dreading but still dared to hope would not happen. The official letterhead jumped out at Emma as she unfolded the paper with what was to become an all too familiar sight. Victor Falconer and Partners stood out in bold, dark letters. Emma drew a deep breath and started to read. She was quite familiar with legal letters from work in a commercial context but was a complete novice when it came to the official exchange of correspondence in family matters.

The letter started that Victor Falconer had the honour to inform Emma that he was the counsel for Paul Archer and Lea Forest and that having divorced under a mutual consent agreement it was time to turn the page without acrimony. After only twenty seconds Emma felt the manipulation and irony of the letter. She read on. Emma's recent reply to Paul's mother with copy to Paul and Lea was considered completely ill placed, and seriously defamatory. Emma was expected to cease immediately with such inadmissible, intolerable, incomprehensible and aggressive practices which were no longer current. He concluded that he dared hope that Emma would understand not only her own interest but that of the children and put a definitive end to her vain accusations against his clients and stop, without the slightest foundation, to destroy their excellent reputation.

Emma sat down heavily on the sofa in disbelief and read through the letter again, carefully digesting every word and ensuring that her understanding was in fact correct. She felt uneasy and anxious and picked up the phone to call Jules Mercier.

'Don't worry.' he reassured her in a matter of fact manner. 'You have done nothing wrong. I will make an appointment for you to meet Hubert Belette who will send a reply on your behalf. He has a lot of insight, is above all shrewd and will represent you well.'

Next day Emma found herself sitting opposite Hubert Belette with Jules Mercier safely at her side. His office was large and crowded with hundreds of files. Stacks of paper were piled high at the edge of each desk. Some were dustier than others. In front of the small window, the metal structure of a fire escape could be seen. Jules Mercier handed over the letter from Victor Falconer and Hubert read it through briskly, peering intently through his small glasses perched precariously on the end of his pointed nose, his small balding head moving slightly from side to side as he scoured the content line by line.

Finally, he looked up at Emma and said 'Well we can't leave this letter unanswered. Your ex-husband is not acting in a very pleasant or responsible manner.'

Hubert's voice was sharp and business like. Emma remembered Jules Mercier's words. He is one of the best and has a very smart mind.

'I will fax you a draft of the reply.' Hubert added handing Emma a piece of blank paper. 'Please write down your details and I will open a file. By the way I will need payment of 500 € to be made by end of the week, administrative expenses you will understand.' he said smiling for the first time.

Of course Emma understood. By agreeing to a mutual consent divorce in the best interest of the children, under the pretext that it was fast, more cost effective and caused less confrontation between the parents, Emma was now being drawn, against her will, into a costly legal wrangle. She felt uncomfortable but what choice did she have?

The next day a copy of Hubert's reply to Victor Falconer came through by fax. He introduced himself as Emma's counsel and went on to point out that Paul and Lea had provided an erroneous view of events and suggested Victor Falconer ask his clients to stop bothering Emma by telephone or letter including to her employer, reiterating that they had elements in their possession which would stand up in a court of law. From their side, they would not tolerate the continuation of the situation. He concluded asking Paul to pay the deductions he had made on three previous occasions from the agreed maintenance payment otherwise they would have to take matters further.

Scarcely one week later, a reply arrived from Victor Falconer and the plot began to thicken. Emma and Hubert's threats did not worry Paul who had strictly nothing to reproach himself. The deductions from the maintenance payments were for half of the household bills which Paul thought Emma should pay, incurred prior to the sale of the house.

A new element was introduced to stigmatise Emma's inflexible, provocative and confrontational approach. Victor Falconer claimed that Paul had written twice to Emma explaining that he wanted to spend the second half of July in the south of France with the children on holiday. Emma had not received any such letters from Paul. She had arranged for the children to go to the beavers' summer camp with their friends during this period. Victor Falconer continued that Olivia and Sebastian no longer liked to go to the brownies and beavers and they had complained on various occasions to their father that Emma forced them to participate against their will in different activities which they did not enjoy.

The letter finished with a short but significant sentence that it was not confidential. Only two years later was Emma to discover that a non-confidential or official exchange of correspondence between lawyers could be used perfectly legitimately, if both agreed, as evidence against one or the other party. Unwittingly Emma was being drawn into a meticulous and pre-meditated plan to blacken her name and distort the facts which could then be used against her in a future court hearing. However, her instincts were at this early stage dulled by the almost blind trust and belief in Jules Mercier as an honourable retired judge and former member of the Ministry of Justice. Brought up to respect justice and authority, it was inconceivable for Emma that a judge's intentions could be less than one hundred percent upright.

Emma advised Hubert Belette to reply that in order to avoid prolonged quarrels and to the disappointment of the children, she would cancel their participation in the beavers and brownie's summer camp and that Olivia and Sebastian could go with their father to the Cote d'Azur during the last two weeks of July. She requested that Paul take care that they were not exposed to too much sun and wore a life jacket while at sea on Paul's speed boat. Hubert added that it was time for Paul to behave like a responsible parent abandoning his vindication which was all the more amazing since the current situation was judicially attributable to him. The letter was non-confidential and was even underlined as such.

Emma now hoped that all outstanding issues had been resolved and that things would progress peacefully. However, she knew deep down that this was probably not going to be the case. Her fears were confirmed a day later when Brigitte and her husband, one of Paul's former best friends, informed Emma that they had just received a letter from Paul informing them that during the divorce he had left his children behind, temporarily at least, and that he would forgive them for siding with Emma initially urging them to reconsider their allegiance. Emma shuddered.

This was yet one more clear indication that Paul had every intention of trying to gain custody of the children which left Emma very wary and worried. She knew she was a good mother who dearly loved her children but she was abroad and one would be naive to assume that prejudices do not exist, especially in the provincial courts, even if she had lived and worked abroad for many years and spoke the language fluently.

The next official letter from Victor Falconer arrived a week later and Emma was dismayed, shocked and frightened by both the style and the content. She found it difficult to imagine that any serious lawyer could write such things. Surely there must be some ethics among the legal profession she tried to reassure herself. She felt she was being morally harassed with the aim of destabilising her. Stay calm she told herself reaching into her inner resources to find the strength and resolve to do so.

Victor Falconer claimed that Paul could not accredit to Emma the image of a role mother. Had she forgotten that while in her care and as a result of her negligence, Olivia had sustained second degree burns on her arm from the sun and Sebastian had lost the end of his index finger in an accident in the home. More recently during the first week of the Easter holidays spent in England with their mother, Paul had welcomed back his children in a state of exhaustion to such a degree that he had had to call a doctor during the night who was, in addition, willing to provide a witness statement and the necessary medical certificate.

What was Emma to do? Not only was it completely untrue but the first two allegations were exact problems which Paul had encountered while looking after the children alone in the past and now he was trying to pin them on Emma. She had not made any issue in the past putting them down to a simple accident or the normal ups and downs encountered with children growing up.

The doctor's certificate really made Emma sit up. It smacked of the mother cum son conspiracy which had manifested itself on numerous occasions since her separation from Paul. Following the Easter break Emma had arrived back home from England at 4 pm. During the holiday Olivia and Sebastian had been in bed at 8.30 pm each evening and had led an active but well balanced life. Paul was away on business so his mum and Lea came to pick up the children. Olivia and Sebastian were not keen to go and Olivia clung to Emma and kissed her three times before opening the door and heading

44

slowly towards the waiting car. The children explained to Emma that they did not like it when Lea referred to their mum as a witch and they were forced to change their clothes upon arrival and were often shouted at. Emma encouraged them to go. She certainly did not want any trouble for breaking any part of the mutual consent divorce settlement, all the more so now, with Victor Falconer hot on her heals.

Paul's mum was delighted at the prospect of being the one in charge of the children that Friday evening, and had prepared a voluptuous meal which she urged her grandchildren to eat. Olivia was sick and when she eventually fell asleep was awoken in the early hours by a doctor Paul's mum had called who subsequently examined her. Emma wondered under the circumstances if any doctor would issue a certificate which could be used against her as indicated in Victor Falconer's letter. She tried to reassure herself that this was highly unlikely. Also, that Paul would have to prove his allegations which he would be unable to as they were clear invention on his part.

Emma called Jules Mercier and they met for lunch. She had faxed him a copy of the latest letter and turned to him for moral support.

'Archer is mad.' he retorted. 'Take no notice of him.'

'But what about his lawyer Falconer?' Emma argued. 'How can he write such things without checking their authenticity first?'

Jules Mercier answered Emma's questions confidently and with authority. He managed to dispel her mounting concerns. They started to talk about other things, England, travel, politics, their respective families and friends. They laughed a lot together and got along well. Their conversation came easily. Emma had introduced Jules Mercier to some of the better restaurants in the suburb where she worked. Excellent food, reasonably priced and friendly service. Their lunches started to become a regular occurrence. At the end of the meal, Jules Mercier would look to Emma to settle the bill. This was the unspoken rule as he was providing valuable advice and moral support. Emma did not mind. Having such an experienced member of the judiciary on her side made her feel more secure, especially in light of the constant unprovoked attacks on her capacity as a loving and responsible mother.

Chapter 11

A few days later Emma received notification that another registered letter was waiting for her in the local post office. She signed for the green envelope looking inquisitively at the round stamp embedded with the letters Youth Court. Whatever is this now she sighed as she opened the letter struggling at the same time to open the door to escape from the cramped confines of the tiny post office.

She stood on the cobbled courtyard outside surrounded by trees and listened to the leaves rustling in the wind. She took a deep breath and started to read. It was of course a letter, as the envelope so clearly signified, issued by the provincial youth court and attaching a request from Paul's mother to obtain an official visiting right as a grandparent.

Emma's heart sank. They were actually serious about pulling her to court. Ironically the request was in Paul's handwriting and Paul's mum had just added her signature. They were requesting an official visiting right of one weekend per month from Friday to Sunday outside of the time allocated to Paul plus all the holidays where Emma could not personally look after the children and had to have them looked after by third parties who were not declared to the authorities as official child minders. An asterisk indicated the large salary Emma was earning plus the maintenance Paul was paying. A date was given for the introduction of the case at which time a date for the exchange of papers and the appearance in front of the judge would be agreed.

Emma called Hubert Belette. In his usual business-like manner, he made an appointment for her to come and see him to discuss how they were going to handle the case. First and foremost, he requested, with a big smile, a second advance payment of 500 € for opening another file. Emma started to get the distinct impression that money was very close to Hubert's heart.

He informed Emma that he would go to the provincial court for the introductory procedure and it was not necessary for her to accompany him, only when the case came in front of the judge.

Hubert called Emma a few days later. 'It is extraordinary.' he claimed. 'Your ex-husband and mother in law were there and they tried to influence me. They talked to me for over an hour and tried to persuade me that they had a strong case and to pull me on their side. Of course I must notify their counsel by a confidential letter that this is not standard procedure.'

Emma was surprised but not surprised. A few days later Emma received a copy of an official letter from Hubert Belette to Victor Falconer confirming that he had learnt from Paul and his mother that he would be representing them in this case and looked forward to meeting him, and fixing dates for exchange of documents prior to the hearing by the judge. Emma was nervous but curious to meet Victor Falconer, to see what he was like in real life. His letters were so manipulative, aggressive, and sly. In one way he frightened Emma as it was becoming clear he had no scruples whatsoever but on the other hand she was indignant and determined to continue to defend her position and her reputation as a good mother.

Hubert Belette had not really indicated to Emma very much at all about what she needed for her defence. A good and worldly colleague gave Emma some valuable advice. Basically one should not rely on lawyers to do everything. A proactive role was needed and then one had to stay behind things to ensure they were actually done on time. Emma earnestly set about gathering evidence for her defence which she would present shortly to Hubert Belette.

Her first port of call was Cathy. Cathy had been recommended to Paul by a mutual friend just after the children were born and he decided that as his mother was not getting any younger and had decided to move to the country, Cathy should help with the ironing, particularly of his shirts, which his mother had always ironed and folded like a true professional. The first time Emma met Cathy was when she arrived at her house one evening with a basket of ironing. Cathy opened the door and the two women smiled at each other. They were about the same age and Cathy's daughter the same age as Olivia. Cathy was tall, chic, slim and energetic and took a distinct pride in her home and family. She had a very expressive manner and talked quickly, her voice almost singing melodically. Later Emma was to affectionately label her the 'white tornado' for her superbly efficient cleaning ability.

Emma explained briefly to Cathy what Paul and his mother were up to and showed her the court papers. Cathy shook her head in disbelief. She felt personally targeted by the reference to third party child minders not officially approved by the authorities. After all Paul had personally asked Cathy to look after Olivia and Sebastian after school and Cathy had done so much to help Paul's mother. She considered Olivia and Sebastian like part of her own family.

'Can you help me?' Emma asked. 'All I need is a simple confirmation for the court about the real situation.' she continued.

'Don't worry.' Cathy replied reassuringly. 'We all know how much you love your children and what a good mother you are. I will write a letter for the judge putting the record straight from my side.'

A couple of days later Cathy handed over the hand written letter to Emma. Emma thanked her, gave her a grateful hug and took it home to read. In a nutshell, Cathy confirmed her longstanding relationship with Paul, his mother, Emma and the children. She confirmed that Paul's mother had confided in her that her son did not respect her. Paul's mother loved her grandchildren to the point that she wanted to bring them up herself. For Paul's mother as well as Cathy, Emma's marriage was disintegrating. Paul was often away, especially on the Wednesday night and when he was home before

Emma, he did not even take the time to come and collect the children. It was always Emma who did so after work.

Paul was always criticizing Emma, that she did not do the housework, was a bad cook, could not take care of her family, that her family in England were dirty etc. Cathy contradicted these allegations highlighting that as Emma worked full time Cathy did the housework and ironing and everything was ship shape and Emma cooked a warm meal with fresh produce every evening for her children.

Cathy confirmed that Paul's mother had done everything to have her believe that Emma was not a good mother for her children and, together with her son, tried to use these so called pieces of evidence for her visitation rights, including trying to obtain confirmations that the children were badly clothed, fed and that Emma drunk too much. Cathy had confirmed this to Emma in the interest of the children and since Emma's letter to Paul's mother she had had no further contact with the Archers. In Cathy's opinion, the children loved coming to her place, and she would always look after them from time to time on the rare occasions that Emma had to travel for work. Cathy concluded that Paul's mother had no valid reason to present herself to the youth court.

Emma sighed with relief. At least someone has the courage to be honest she reassured herself.

Emma's next visit was to Valerie. Valerie had helped Olivia and Sebastian with their homework after school at 4 pm each day. Paul himself had approved Valerie's appointment interviewing her for over one hour. Valerie confirmed that she received a lot of affection from Olivia and Sebastian and considered them almost like her own children and Emma a good friend. She confirmed that Paul had only been twice to fetch the children over a three-year period and this during one of Emma's rare business trips, Paul had asked Valerie to look after the children one extra night but not to say anything to

Emma. As Emma had telephoned home that very evening to speak to the children, the truth had come out.

Valerie continued to look after the children with pleasure and help Emma from time to time in the holidays. She too confirmed that Paul's mother had done everything she could to darken Emma's image trying to extract from her a confirmation that Emma was a bad mother, the children were badly dressed, poorly fed and Emma drunk too much. However, Valerie denied the accusations and had soon made it clear that nothing would be gained from her in this respect. Valerie had even received anonymous phone calls when she looked after Olivia and Sebastian, in her opinion, to check who was with the children.

Again Emma was grateful for the honesty and support of yet another person who had become a good friend and an integral part of hers and the children's lives over the previous five years.

Emma's third and final stop was with Brigitte. Brigitte studied Paul's hand written request in his mother's name and tutted in disappointment. She immediately recognized the manipulation. After all she had witnessed first-hand the situation the previous July with the summer camp. She went immediately to the local town hall and requested a confirmation from the mayor himself and the mayor's office that Olivia and Sebastian had participated along with 220 other children in a summer camp organised by the local authority and not the social services as Paul and his mother were claiming in their court papers.

A programme with all the interesting activities was attached and Brigitte wrote a short letter in which she pointed out that as a friend of the Archer family for twelve years, she had proposed to both parents the summer camp since the activities were varied and sportive and very beneficial for younger children. As one of the supervisors, she was constantly available and the children went home with her and her own daughter every afternoon to be collected shortly afterwards by Emma. Brigitte added that they had seemed to very much enjoy their two week' participation and that Paul himself had seemed very satisfied when he collected the children on their last day.

Emma thanked Brigitte for her sincerity, grateful that friends had the courage and willpower to speak out and confirm the truth.

Emma handed over the three confirmations to Hubert Belette who drew up his written defence for the court hearing. He wrote that Emma had agreed to a divorce by mutual consent despite the affair her husband was having. As soon as the divorce was pronounced, her ex-husband and mother in law had not stopped to discredit her and the present request had been written by Paul in his mother's name. Paul's mother had never hidden her wish to bring up the children in place of their mother. It was a personal attack out of context.

Their demand did not take into account the rights of the maternal grandmother. The third parties referred to were people chosen by Paul himself to look after the children in the past and the summer camp issue was unfounded as the children had attended the two week' holiday activities with the agreement of both parents. The camp was organised by mutual friends and the local town hall and had nothing to do with the social services whatsoever. Paul's claims about Emma's high salary were also incorrect.

A few days later Victor Falconer replied with seven pages of additional dribble, inconsistencies and lies. It was just a foretaste of things to come. He claimed among other things that Emma had an aggressive attitude which was to the detriment of the children, that Paul's mother had brought up the children full time in the last three years of the couple's marriage. During and after their separation she had always made a big effort to remain neutral. Very often for professional reasons Emma was forced to leave the children in the hands of third parties. The children were always very happy and settled every time they saw their grandmother and a social enquiry could confirm such a finding. Attached was a certificate from the doctor confirming that after Easter and a week's holiday with their mother, Olivia was examined at night and found to be in a state of exhaustion which could be attributed to a lack of sleep.

So some unscrupulous member of the medical profession had gone along with the game after all Emma sighed to herself. Just where would these people stop she asked herself. Emma immediately visited her own family doctor and got a counter statement that the children were in excellent health and had not had any major health problems over the last four years. She also went to see the headmistress of the children's school who confirmed that Olivia and Sebastian had not been absent for illness for one single day over the previous eighteen months. Emma's employer also confirmed that she had travelled only eleven days in the last year, five of which were when the children were with their father in the half term holiday.

Emma forwarded everything onto Hubert Belette. She was beginning to feel like a private detective. It did not come naturally but she was learning fast.

A further letter by Paul's mother to the court was so petty and dishonest. It was the final slap in the face for the support and generosity Emma had shown her ex mother in law over the past years. She felt angry but also pity for the woman at the same time.

Paul's mother reiterated that her grandchildren loved to visit her in the country and absolutely detested to have to go to the summer camp run by the social services where their mother forced them to go. They had confided in their grandmother that their mother forced them to participate in a strange sport called taekwondo which she used to defend herself and she forced them, also against their will, to go to the brownies and beavers which they did not appreciate at all. She implored the court to give these two small children a little happiness and personal pleasure in their lives as they were already so perturbed by the hard and very unfeminine reactions they were subjected to.

Victor Falconer's final court papers appeared literally the day before the hearing. Paul's mother had managed to extract from a former neighbour a confirmation that she came frequently to the family home during the parents' professional absences to look after her beloved grandchildren who were always more than pleased to see her. The neighbour herself had four children and had given up work to dedicate herself to raising them and running the family home. Emma had shared the school run equally in the mornings and the two, in turn, had dropped each other's children off at and collected them from the brownies and beavers. Emma did not travel a lot and if Paul's mother came it was often on her own insistence as she was lonely and longed to see her grandchildren.

One day later, Emma received a handwritten note from the neighbour ironically asking Emma to forgive her for writing a confirmation for the court in Paul's mother's favour. She justified her action by pointing out that one had to be kind to older people.

The day of the court hearing arrived. Emma had arranged to travel to the provincial court with Hubert Belette. Hubert drove and Emma read the court papers as they whizzed past fields and open countryside.

'What do you think?' he asked Emma as she finished intently reading the final page of the case papers Hubert planned to present in her defence to the court and which she was also seeing for the first time. 'I included a request that Paul's mother pay you compensation of 500 €' he added proudly 'in damages for her wicked, reckless and vexatious action against you.'

'I bet she was pleased when she read that.' Emma replied. 'Do you really think the court will take that into account?' Emma asked.

'Well nothing ventured nothing gained.' Hubert retorted confidently with a touch of arrogance.

Emma still could not believe that Paul and his mother had gone to a court of law with what were basically a long list of lies and inventions and she was curious to see how the judge would react. They drove up to the large historic looking square on which the court building occupied a prominent position. Just what was Victor Falconer like Emma asked herself as they searched for a parking spot opposite the court. Well she was soon going to find out.

Emma felt her stomach churn as she stepped out of Hubert's old Audi and turned to walk towards this imposing building with its almost church like windows and huge heavy double black doors.

'If I remember correctly' Hubert continued guiding Emma along the pavement 'the youth court is not in the main building but we need to go through an arch at the side and it is just behind, look there in front of us.'

It was a relatively small and modern looking building. When they entered Paul was already there with his mother and Victor Falconer sitting in the small grey sparsely furnished waiting room. The two lawyers greeted one another smiling, shaking hands and introducing themselves, then their clients. Victor Falconer held out his chubby hand to shake Emma's which she reluctantly put forward imitating the gestures of the other parties. She mumbled hello to Paul and his mother.

Victor Falconer was small and stocky and Emma was a head taller than he was. His face however had pointed features, and what Emma found the most worryingly were his piercing eyes which fixed Emma briefly in a penetrating stare. He had a confident and unflappable air about him. His physic matched the sharpness, sarcasm and aggressiveness of the correspondence Emma had witnessed so far and on the receiving end of which she unwittingly found herself. Her instincts to be wary of this individual were confirmed. He looked and felt ruthless not to mention unscrupulous. She felt intimidated and anxious.

The two lawyers put on their black gowns in preparation for their entrance into the court room. The judge, prosecutor and court clerk arrived punctually together and the small group filed in behind them. The youth court was designed to be smaller and more familiar than the normal court and the room had two small desks for the court officials in front of which were a row of chairs. Emma and the group found themselves less than two metres away from the judge who opened the file, glanced up at the assembled group and promptly started the proceedings.

The judge, a man in his mid-forties with short dark hair and a round face, remarked that he had read the papers forwarded by the two parties. He then turned to Emma and with his features visibly softening, congratulated her on her excellent command of the local language. Emma sat in surprise before quietly muttering 'thank you your honour.'

He then turned to Paul's mother and, with a somewhat hardening expression, enquired why she was there today. She looked at Victor Falconer who nodded for her to reply. Paul's mother set off about how she loved her grandchildren and how well she and Emma had got on before the breakup of the marriage. She continued that because of the problems, she was no longer allowed to have any extensive contact with Olivia and Sebastian.

The judge then asked the lawyers from both parties to put forward their case. The court clerk busily took notes. The public prosecutor's office was represented by a young lady who sat motionless but attentive throughout. This was Emma's first experience of any sort of hearing or proceeding. Emma thought to herself at that moment that a mutual consent divorce was easier as the terms were already agreed upon upfront and the outcome predictable but now the outcome was unknown and depended on the opinion of the judge, the skill of the lawyers representing their case, the opinion of the prosecutor's office and who knows whatever else. From what Emma could gather, the judge and court clerk got to see the written evidence and submissions in advance. The public prosecutor's deputy listened to each counsel's speech then just before the wrapping up of the hearing by the judge, gave an opinion on the resulting decision in accordance with the provisions of the law which the magistrate or judge took into account in the final judgment.

The public prosecutor's deputy began to speak. The young lady raised her head and spoke loudly with a great deal of authority. She was a few years younger than Emma and could not have been out of law school for very long. Emma listened as she cited details of the recently introduced law about an official visiting right for grandparents and the fact that she fully agreed with the case put forward by Paul's mother in all aspects. Emma was taken aback by how one sided it seemed. The forcefulness and conviction with which this young woman had put forward her case bothered Emma. There seemed to be something she could not quite put her finger on.

The judge closed the hearing announcing the judgment would be pronounced in approximately three weeks' time. The small group filed out of the court room in silence. As Emma climbed back into Hubert's car she asked him how he thought it had gone. Hubert seemed agitated by the comments from the prosecutor's deputy.

'Let's wait for the judgment.' he replied starting the engine and roaring off direction home.

A month later Hubert Belette faxed Emma a copy of the judgment. Paul's mother was granted a visiting right of one weekend every school term or three times a year and four days in the summer holidays. The judgment stated that this was limited since Paul's mother also saw her grandchildren when they were with her son and that Emma also had to have some leisure time at weekends and in the holidays with the children. Furthermore, it was not in the interest of the children for the rhythm of their daily life to be constantly upset. Finally, one also had to into account that time should be available for the children to spend with their mother and other members of the maternal family. Emma had to drive the children to the country and Paul's mother had to bring them back after every visit.

Hubert Belette's fax was defiant of the judgment which he described as contrary to the normal jurisprudence of the court which had failed to take into account any of the arguments put forward in his case. He suggested Emma introduce a similar request for a visiting right for her own mother and appeal against the judgment.

Emma's instinct told her to let this one be and not to prolong the matter any further. The judgment was not catastrophic. Emma's mum saw her grandchildren in the holidays when they went to England and she came over in the summer to see them too. Emma reasoned that it was in Hubert's interests to multiply court proceedings as he was getting paid for each one.

Perhaps Paul and his mother would now let the children and Emma lead their lives in peace. This was Emma's hope at least. She called Hubert and told him she accepted the judgment and expressed her desire to simply turn the page.

'OK' he replied simply. 'Just another little matter' he added quickly. 'I had quite a lot of work on your file and will require another payment of 600 €. If you don't mind you can give this sum to my wife in cash.'

Not wanting to be difficult as Emma knew she needed good legal support more than ever, she obliged against a written receipt. What

Hubert does with the tax man is his responsibility she told herself. She had other things to worry about.

Chapter 12

Things did not improve of course. Paul and his mother continued to vent their frustration via Olivia and Sebastian constantly criticizing Emma, her family and friends and anything they considered an obstacle to their full control of the children. Upon their return from visits, the children confided in Emma. To Emma's relief, they added that they did not believe any of it.

Emma's mum had always maintained that the children were at least four years more mature as a result of everything they had recently witnessed. Nevertheless, Emma felt helpless. She tried to reassure the children that the comments were not important and they should take no notice. She gave them lots of love and attention but deep down she was angry and frightened. How can they do this to the children she kept asking herself. They were often uncomfortable before a weekend visit to see their father and sometimes Olivia would wet her bed after she returned on the Sunday evening.

Emma was at a loss what to do. She made a list of the particularly cutting comments and sent it to Jules Mercier and Hubert Belette with a request for guidance and help. Paul continued to regularly tell the children that Emma was wicked and did not love them, was a bad mother and gave them trash to eat. When Emma's mum and Aunty Hilda came to stay in the summer holidays he called the children and told them that these two old women were dirty and fed them garbage. He told the children that Cathy who came to help with the cleaning and ironing was Mrs Excrement.

Paul's mother added that Cathy did not iron their clothes well and she could tell her for all she cared. No one was spared. Valerie was referred to by her surname and as that fat woman. Emma's sister Laura and her brother in law as people Paul did not appreciate and their eighteen month' old son as a horrible wicked little boy. Lea of course joined in the affray referring to Emma in front of the children as a witch, a cow and a wicked woman.

Meanwhile Paul had found a new job as a commercial manager in an international company. A former colleague called Emma to tell her that she had heard that Paul was telling his new company that he had custody of his children since his marriage had broken down because Emma was a bad mother and an alcoholic. Be careful the former colleague warned Emma. Emma really began to wonder if she was not confronted with three psychopaths. If it had been on an even playing field she would not have minded but to put innocent and vulnerable children through this was just inexcusable. Emma feared Paul knew all too well that the children were her weak flank and he was using them to get right back at her. Emma's hands were tied.

On the advice of Hubert Belette and Jules Mercier she made an appointment with a well-known child psychologist. Emma explained the situation and asked her to interview the children to see that they were not being damaged by the constant barrage of criticism they were being subjected to and to speak to Paul and Lea and ask them to behave more responsibly. Jules Mercier was very categorical. In his opinion Paul was simply 'crazy'. 'You have to go to the youth court and ask for a social enquiry and limit his visiting rights if this continues.' he kept repeating to Emma.

Jules Mercier continued to call Emma regularly and they met two to three times a month for lunch in their favourite Italian restaurant. They usually spent the first half an hour talking about the latest developments in Emma's case then the conversation wandered to other topics. Jules Mercier continued to reassure Emma that all the problems would be sorted out soon. The youth court would investigate the situation and Paul would be asked or forced to toe the line in the interest of the children. Of course, Hubert Belette was a very good lawyer, on the ball, vigilant and he would continue to represent Emma's best interests in the court.

Sporadically Jules Mercier would mention his time at the ministry of justice. He proudly repeated that he wrote some of the country's laws. He had married young into a wealthy family but had left his first wife when his children were very young. His son had never forgiven him for it even today. He then met a beautiful actress and they married. It was during the busiest part of his career and she soon became bored with his constant absences and took a lover. One day the justice minister came into his office and asked why he looked depressed. Jules explained that his wife was having an affair.

'Oh' the minister had replied with a wry smile 'shall we catch her red handed for adultery?'

'Yes.' Jules replied in immediate agreement and the justice minister promptly picked up the phone and called the police chief muttering some details which Jules had written down shortly before on a piece of paper. What followed next really merited being part of a film.

As Jules Mercier carried on with the story Emma stared at him in disbelief but also amusement. They laughed together at the prospect. Jules because he had actually lived through it and Emma because for her, such things were practically unheard of and had an almost absurd side to them.

The amorous couple were in a villa with a large garden surrounded by trees. Several officers took up strategic positions hidden in the undergrowth and behind the trees. One of the officers ventured up to the door and rang the bell. He announced that the lover was about to be busted for adultery and the place was literally surrounded. Startled, the lover ran out of the house in his underpants with a gun in his hand and started shooting wildly in the air. He was soon brought under control by the various armed officers who emerged from their hidden vantage points. The official report on the adultery was established and used in the divorce proceedings much to the initial fury of Jules' second wife.

'Well' Emma remarked to Jules following the story. 'it certainly helps to have friends in high places.'

'Yes' he smiled knowingly. 'It certainly does.'

As had become customary, Emma settled the bill and they agreed to call one another the following week.

Chapter 13

The date for the meeting with the child psychologist arrived. Emma had tried to play it down in front of the children. She told them they were going to see a lady who liked children, who would have a chat with them and who was there to make them feel better about mummy and daddy splitting up. Emma gave the psychologist a first name, Colette, to make the whole thing sound less official.

Emma could not help questioning herself and the whole nonsensical situation she now found herself in. Things had deteriorated to such a degree that they now had to seek professional help. Just what had gone so horribly wrong she kept asking herself. How could I have done things better?

Emma parked the car on the busy main road and tried to find the entrance to the practice. She quickly pressed the doorbell then held the hands of Olivia and Sebastian, a jest aimed at reassuring them. There was no answer. Emma tried the door and it opened.

'Is there anybody there?' she enquired.

Eventually a voice called back 'Yes please take a seat in the waiting room and I will call you when I am ready.'

The voice was rich, relatively deep and surprisingly soothing. An attractive middle aged lady emerged a few minutes later. She spent half an hour with Olivia and half an hour with Sebastian and then conferred for ten minutes with Emma. The child psychologist agreed to contact Paul and ask him to come and see her.

She tried a couple of times unsuccessfully by phone then sent a letter to Paul four weeks later, explaining that in the interest of the children it was important that she meet Paul and Lea on the request of Olivia and Sebastian to alleviate certain difficulties experienced during time spent together. She wrote that the children did not dare to broach the subject on their own and she hoped to serve as an intermediary since the relationship with Emma was too strained. She added that she did not have the impression that Emma was trying to manipulate the children against their father.

Paul refused to go, later stating that the child psychologist could not be considered impartial. This was difficult to believe but as Emma was already beginning to suspect, Paul had another agenda and finding a peaceful solution while the children were still in her custody was just not part of that agenda.

Chapter 14

The summer holidays arrived and Olivia and Sebastian left again with their father and Lea to the south of France. This time's Paul's mother did not join them. The only thing Emma asked before they left was that Paul take special care to put a life jacket on the children when out at sea with the boat as they were still not very strong swimmers.

Olivia and Sebastian arrived back and proceeded to tell Emma how they had been forced to stay without a life jacket in the open sea for over one hour at the insistence of their father together with Lea's youngest son, as their father wanted to take an afternoon nap. Olivia, cold and tired, had clung to the ladder of the boat and started to cry. A passer-by on another boat had stopped to ask her if she needed help. Meanwhile the other two children were on the point of crying too. Paul apparently slept on, unconcerned by the situation. Emma was speechless. She went out into the garden and walked around deep in thought.

'What a nightmare. The children could have drowned. How utterly irresponsible.' she whispered to herself. She felt like crying but had to put on a brave and normal face in front of the children who had now come out to join her. What was Emma to do? If she tried to talk to Paul or make the slightest comment, he just insulted her. She was just immensely relieved Olivia and Sebastian were home safe and sound.

The following week Emma met Jules Mercier and Hubert Belette in their favourite Italian restaurant to discuss the next steps. Emma was so glad that Jules Mercier was on her side. His experience and knowledge would be invaluable against Paul and Victor Falconer who were now clearly out gunning for her. The lawyers' letters came thick and fast. Up to year end over twenty, many of them marked 'official' mentioning how inflexible and unreceptive to dialogue Emma was, especially regarding planning of holidays, how she made unilateral decisions on visiting rights although whenever she sent Paul anything, she always used the word 'proposed'. How she forced the children to do things they did not want to like attending the brownies and the beavers. Emma had sighed. Here we go again. Attending the brownies and beavers was something they had done for three years, originally with the mutual agreement of both parents, and with a great deal of pleasure.

Emma, Jules and Hubert ordered their favourite pasta dish, a carafe of house red and started to discuss what their options were. Emma's concern lay with the continuing conflict and the longer term effect on the children. Jules Mercier was very matter of fact.

'I said it right from the beginning' he stated with authority. 'Paul is mad and you should file against him in the youth court and ask for a social enquiry or child psychologist report. Ask for his visiting rights to be reviewed, say every second Saturday and two weeks in the summer.'

Emma thought back. True Jules Mercier had suggested exactly this to Emma and Hubert Belette in writing one year ago.

'I agree with you my dear Jules.' Hubert added taking a large sip of red wine and swilling it around in his mouth in appreciation before swallowing noisily. 'I can do the necessary in the next two weeks.' he continued, trying to dust off a small drop of red wine which had dripped onto his lapel.

Emma looked at these two experienced men sitting opposite her and thought that they could not both be wrong. The most likely outcome she assumed would be that the court would see clear and caution Paul and things would then improve.

'OK go ahead.' Emma concluded. She paid the bill and headed back to the office blissfully unaware that the first nail had just been hammered into her coffin.

A fortnight later she received a copy of a letter which Hubert Belette had addressed to Victor Falconer. In a nutshell, it stated that Hubert was forced to note that Paul did not miss any opportunity to show his aggressiveness and lack of psychology with regard to the children as well as to their mother. Not content to attack his ex-wife, he also wickedly ran down his ex-wife's family and any other person who did not agree with his theories. As all attempts to find an amicable solution seemed to be condemned to failure, his client regretfully had to address the youth court. Enclosed was the request submitted to the court. The rest of the file would follow shortly.

The request was succinct. The visiting rights foreseen in the mutual consent divorce were turning out to be unfavourable for the children. In spite of all amiable attempts to find a solution for the problems caused by the irresponsible exercise of the visiting right, the children were often left on their own, especially at night, the relations with the concubine of Mr Archer imposed on the children led equally to perturbations and created sleeping problems which Paul Archer attempted to attribute to Emma.

Mr Archer had refused the amiable intervention of a child psychologist who would have been able to find a solution after having heard the children, in the sole interest of the children. Therefore, the visiting rights should be amended to one day every fortnight from 8.30 am to 5.30 pm and that this visiting right be exercised by Mr Archer and not a third party, as too often the case, currently to the disappointment of the children. He concluded that the court should order a social enquiry or child psychologist's report if it required additional information.

Victor Falconer immediately sprang into action and writing directly to the President of the Youth Court formally contested all allegations requesting the affair should go in front of the judge before any exchange of paperwork or counsel's speech. A week later, Hubert Belette confirmed that the court had advised it wanted to hear the parties up front due to limited resources to decide at that time whether to request a social enquiry, child psychologist intervention or family mediation. The date for the special hearing was fixed for just before Christmas.

It was a very cold but clear day as Emma stepped into Hubert Belette's old Audi for yet another visit to the provincial court. Once again they whizzed through the countryside past open fields but this time they were covered with a white glistening frost. The sun shone weakly through the scattered clouds casting a hazy but golden light for as far as the eye could see.

The children had just finished school the previous day and were all set to head off to England with Emma for a traditional family Christmas. The car was already packed and as soon as Emma arrived back, they planned to set off. Emma's thoughts were already with the family in the quaint little village where Laura her sister and family lived, the candle lit children's Christmas service in the thousand year' old church, drinks in front of the open fire, turkey and trimmings and lots of presents for the excited children. The scene seemed very reassuring and welcoming following the traumatic year which had just passed.

Hubert drove onto the large square and the provincial court building stood imposingly in front of them. The sparse waiting room in the youth court had not changed. It felt even colder in the winter as Emma huddled into her warm coat. Paul and Victor Falconer were already there and the ceremonial greetings and shaking of hands took place.

The court officials arrived and the assembled group followed them in silence up the narrow stairway into the court room. The judge was stern, dark haired and very serious. He wasted no time in starting the proceedings and abruptly asked on what basis Hubert requested a social enquiry. Hubert started to explain.

'Where is the letter from the child psychologist?' the judge demanded.

'I am afraid I can't show you that' Hubert replied 'as my adversary has not yet seen it and we were told this hearing is only preliminary, to agree how to proceed and fix an eventual date for the exchange of correspondence.'

The prosecutor's deputy nodded in agreement. Then the judge turned to Emma and fixed her with a cold stare.

'So what is the problem?' he requested dryly.

'I am worried about the children.' Emma began trying to sound constructive. 'They have been locked up alone overnight and this frightens them.'

The judge turned to Paul who nodded in agreement. 'There was a baby phone connecting the apartments.' Paul explained.

'But it did not work.' Emma added.

'What else?' snapped the judge fixing Emma with an even colder stare.

'The children who are aged just 7 and 8 are sent out alone into the centre of town when they visit their father.' Emma courageously continued. 'I don't think this is appropriate especially in view of the recent child abductions and murders. These poor children were the same age as my own children.'

'Is that all?' the judge replied mockingly.

Emma looked at the judge for an instant in absolute disbelief and mistrust. She quickly gathered her courage and added.

'Please rest assured your honour, I would not waste your time or my own if I did not have some serious concerns to raise about the welfare of my son and daughter.'

The prosecutor's deputy proposed that a new date be fixed for deposition of all documents and that the resulting judgment notify all parties of the new date. Hubert Belette and Victor Falconer who had said surprisingly very little during the hearing both agreed. As everyone stood up to leave the court, Paul went over to the judge and shook his hand and thanked him. How strange Emma thought to herself. Never seen that done before. With hindsight though, it could have been a very different handshake.

Chapter 15

Emma and the children arrived safely in England. Emma's mum and Aunty Hilda had already arrived at Laura's for the large family Christmas.

'Well how did it go in the court?' they asked Emma as they made a pot of tea in the kitchen, Olivia and Sebastian having run off to play with their little cousin.

'Strange set up.' Emma replied. 'I don't think things are done the same way over there.'

'What do you mean?' they both enquired.

'I don't know exactly.' Emma said thoughtfully 'Paul actually admitted that he locked the children up overnight alone and instead of pursuing this further or being concerned, the judge seemed to put me on trial and play the whole thing down.'

'Well I think you will just have to wait for the judgment' Emma's mum concluded. 'You have had a hell of a year dear so forget about it for a few days and enjoy yourself with us and the children.' she said reassuringly squeezing Emma's arm and smiling.

Emma smiled back. 'I guess you are right mum. By the way you look tired. Are you OK?' Emma asked a little concerned.

'Yes I am just fine.' Emma's mum replied chirpily.

'Make me a promise.' Emma continued. 'When you get back home in the New Year, do go for a check-up at the doctors. You have not been for close to twenty years. It is just a routine visit but you don't look your normal good self.'

'Fine I will think about it.' Emma's mum promised.

Christmas was wonderful but it passed by very quickly. Before Emma knew it, she was driving back to drop the children off to spend New Year and the second half of the school holidays with Paul and his mother.

The judgment was pronounced middle of January. Instead of giving a date to present the case with evidence as indicated in the wrap up of the recent hearing, it simply closed the file under the pretext that although there was a difference of opinion on certain points, these were not susceptible to justify such a radical change to the visiting rights of the father and that Emma and her counsel had not brought any tangible element justifying a change to the terms. The child psychologist's letter of course could not be used at this hearing to justify the need for further intervention by an expert body.

Furthermore, the judge went onto emphasise that each party was free following a divorce to found a new family and that the former partner had no right to put any obstacles in the way. In obvious support of Victor Falconer's only argument that Emma was being difficult because Paul had recently announced his remarriage to Lea. The relationship between parents and children was the responsibility of both parents who should ensure that the children had the most frequent, intense and fruitful relationship with the other parent and never took the child hostage or used him or her as a messenger.

Hubert Belette was furious. He insisted to go immediately to the appeal court. Jules Mercier confirmed the decision reiterating that such a judgment was highly unusual. Emma saw no alternative but to pursue the current line and for the truth to eventually come out. Otherwise how else was the situation to be improved? Hubert Belette filed his appeal in the capital.

Chapter 16

'So what did the doctor say?' Emma asked her mum over the phone middle of January.

'I don't know yet.' she replied. 'I am waiting for the results of tests next week.'

'How are you feeling mum?' Emma continued.

'OK but a bit tired.' Emma's mum answered.

'Listen you call me the minute you get the results, promise me.' Emma encouraged.

'OK will do. Speak to you soon.' She concluded. 'Love to the children.' and she hung up.

A few days later Emma's mum called back. 'They are admitting me to hospital for further tests and apparently I have jaundice.'

'Jaundice what is causing it?' Emma enquired suddenly overcome by concern.

'I don't know yet and that is what they want to find out.' Emma's mum replied.

The children were with their father the following weekend so Emma booked a flight, and called Aunty Hilda and her mum to tell them that she would be arriving on Friday evening. She went straight from the airport to the hospital with the taxi. She stopped in her tracks as she entered the hospital room. Emma's mum looked so ill. She was yellow, frail and frightening fragile. Tears welled up in Emma's eyes and she suddenly felt very worried. Emma's mum had always been so strong all her life. She had been such a moral support to Emma during her divorce from Paul and the subsequent harassment. Now here she was in such a vulnerable condition.

Emma's mum was pleased to see her daughter and they talked for a long while.

'When will you know what the problem is?' Emma enquired.

'In a couple of days normally.' her Mum replied. 'But they are not giving anything away for the moment.'

Emma's uncle arrived and Emma saw from his expression that he too was very concerned.

'Don't worry.' Emma said as she hugged her mum on the Sunday afternoon before heading for the airport. 'They have made so much progress today in modern medicine, they can cure just about anything.' Emma concluded trying to convince herself more than anything that things would be fine.

The following week Emma received a call from her sister Laura who had been up to hospital and spoken to the doctors.

'It is bad news I am afraid.' Laura announced. 'It is pancreatic cancer.' The big C word knocked Emma flat. It was everyone's worse nightmare.

'Is there a cure?' was Emma's first question.

'We are looking at the moment but this specific cancer is particularly voracious and they say mum is too weak to operate.' Laura explained sadly.

'What are we talking about time wise?' Emma asked dreading the answer.

'The doctors say maximum six months.' came the reply.

Emma sat at her desk and felt the hot tears streaming down her cheeks. A colleague came into her cubicle and seeing Emma left in a hurry. Shortly afterwards Emma's boss arrived.

'Whatever is the matter Emma?' she asked in a concerned voice. Emma started to cry again and Hallie her boss put her arms around her.

'You know' she confided in Emma. 'I had cancer when I was twenty-one and beat it against all the odds. Let's look on the internet together to see what the latest medical advances are.'

Emma went into a daze. Suddenly time seemed so short. She planned the next half term holiday in February with the children to go to England to see the family. Originally she had wanted to go skiing but now everything was put on ice. Olivia and Sebastian had barely known their grandfather when he died. Now they were going to lose their grandmother. Emma was temporarily inconsolable.

In February Emma and the children returned to England to see Emma's mum for the week. She was very ill but had returned home and Aunty Hilda had moved into the family home to look after her. Aunty Hilda was Emma's mum's sister. She had never married and was like a second mum to Emma and Laura. She had, for as long as Emma could remember, accompanied the family on their summer holidays and was always there for Easter, Christmas and many other family gatherings including many Sunday lunches.

The doctors were very worried and now did not even expect Emma's mum to make it past their original prognosis of August. Despite her frailness, she was so happy to have Olivia and Sebastian around her. They were too young to grasp the gravity of the situation and Emma did not want to burden them either. The week flew by and Emma and the children returned home to the continent.

The following Monday evening after a weekend with Paul, Emma was giving the children a bath when they innocently dropped a bomb shell.

'You know what daddy said?' they confided in Emma. 'He says he is glad that grandma is ill and hopes she will not get better. She deserves it and that is what happens to wicked people.'

Emma was dumbfounded. She told Olivia and Sebastian that they should not take any notice of bad things which daddy said about mummy or her family and friends. Emma had to leave the bathroom. She was upset yet so angry at the same time. As soon as the children were in bed she called Paul on his mobile.

'Whatever have you said to the children this time?' she almost screamed. 'How dare you? When are you eventually going to stop with your inadmissible behaviour? she demanded.

'I do not have to listen to any comment from you.' Paul retorted indignantly and he promptly hung up diverting his phone to his voice mail.

In desperation, Emma called her best friend Rachel who was a social worker and a haven of good advice.

'It is disgusting.' she said. 'Take no notice. Don't let it get to you. That's what they want. He won't change so you will just have to let it go in one ear and out of the other. Rise above it.' she advised. They had a long chat and Emma went to bed feeling slightly better.

Spring arrived. Emma's mum seemed to be getting stronger. She had always been a good little fighter all her life and both Emma and her sister knew she was going to battle on right up to the end. There was no known cure so, as difficult as it was, they were slowly reconciling themselves to the fact that they had to make the most of the precious time which was left.

For Easter, Emma's mum had booked them all into a four-star hotel on the seafront complete with indoor swimming pool for the children, sauna and Jacuzzi for Emma and Aunty Hilda. They had a wonderful week and each day was special and they lived it to the full.

Paul and his entourage continued their unfair tirade. Olivia and Sebastian returned from a weekend to claim that Paul's friends had told them at a party that their mummy was really not a very nice person. In Emma's next letter to Paul to arrange the proposed split of the coming weekends and summer holiday, she asked him again, in the sole interest of the children, to request his circle to stop telling their children that their mum was not a nice person. Emma wrote that personally she did not care what his so called friends thought about her. Most of hers thought that he was behaving in an absolutely appalling manner but at least they were intelligent and considerate enough not to say this to or in front of the children.

Still deeply shocked and hurt by Paul's recent comments about her dear mum, Emma decided to heed Rachel's wise words to not fall into the trap of letting it continue to get to her.

A few days later Emma discovered two pre-addressed and pre-stamped envelopes in Olivia's room tucked under the sofa bed, one from Paul and the other one from his mother.

'What is this?' Emma asked in surprise.

Olivia seemed a bit startled that Emma had found the envelopes but then went on to spontaneously explain that her dad and grandmother had asked the children to write to them, especially if they were unhappy. Sebastian entered the room and not wanting to be left out confirmed what Olivia had said adding that he also had two envelopes in his room.

'Well that is all right' Emma said reassuringly. 'There is nothing wrong with that. You can write and let them both know what you have been doing this weekend.' Emma added.

Olivia and Sebastian had been to brownies and beavers with their friends and they had had a barbecue in the forest and sang around the campfire until early evening. They had come back full of stories about how enjoyable it had been. The children agreed and sat down to write the letters. Emma posted them next day hoping the message was clear but nevertheless concerned about just how far these people were continuing to go to try to manipulate the children.

Chapter 17

Things at work had been going well. Since the separation Emma had worked very hard in the knowledge that the future wellbeing of her children depended on it. She dropped Olivia and Sebastian off at school in the mornings and picked them up every afternoon, often continuing to work through the lunch hour with a sandwich at her desk. In busier times, she would carry on working in the evenings from home on her portable computer once the children were in bed.

On the rare occasions she had to travel for work, Cathy or Valerie were always there to help out. The children had known both friends for over five years and felt completely at ease in their company. Emma did it for the children. There was now only one salary to offer them the best in life and a good future.

In May, Emma received an interesting offer of promotion from the president of one of the US subsidiaries proposing her a worldwide directorship based in New England. It was a wonderful opportunity and a definite move up the career ladder. Emma liked New England, and had quite a few American friends there. The standard of living was very good. There was the coast, the mountains, the sporting activities and also some very good schools.

It was tempting. However, Emma knew and could understand that Paul would never agree for her and the children to move to the USA. Also, it was unfair as he would not have had regular contact outside the school holidays as agreed in the mutual consent divorce. Also with mum so ill, Emma knew she wanted to stay in Europe and make the most of their remaining precious time together. Emma thanked the president for the offer which she said she regrettably had to turn down for personal reasons.

A short and rare trip to London for one and half days in May confirmed to Emma that things were not about to improve. Emma had arranged to leave Olivia and Sebastian with Cathy and her family and take the last flight out on the Tuesday evening. She was due back early Thursday afternoon, had a barbecue planned with the children that evening and had taken the Friday off to be with them as Olivia and Sebastian had a day off school.

Paul's mum called Emma on her mobile on her way to the airport to speak to the children. Emma told her to call them at Cathy's which she did without major incident. Five minutes later Paul called and started shouting at the children then threatening Cathy and her family that he was going to arrive at her house with the police and a bailiff to take the children away by force. Olivia admitted being frightened every time she heard a car pass fearing the police were about to arrive.

Cathy and her daughter frantically left ten messages on Emma's mobile which was switched off during the flight asking for guidance. Emma was upset. She could not even go away for one and a half days for work without her friends being harassed and her children frightened. She called Hubert Belette who confirmed Paul had no authority to put his threats into practice and to forget about it.

Paul later claimed that Victor Falconer had sent Hubert Belette a letter asking to have the children on the Thursday which was a national holiday but Emma had no knowledge of any such letter being received. Later this incident was predictably to be used by Victor Falconer to justify Emma's lack of flexibility regarding Paul's visiting rights.

A few weeks later Emma received another offer of a job promotion, this time from the UK office. The net salary was double what she was currently earning. The job was close to London and half an hour from her sister Laura's home. Emma would have a home office and if she found a house near the airport she could fly the children back to see their father at her expense every second weekend and half of the school holidays and still honour the terms of the mutual consent divorce. They could also continue to see Emma's mum in her final days. Suddenly it seemed possible and worth evaluating.

Emma rang Jules Mercier to check out the legal aspects.

'You are covered of course.' Jules replied confidently. 'It says in the terms of your divorce which you drew up together that for exceptional reasons due to your profession you can go abroad with the children. You just need to pay the travel expenses for them to see their father and to respect the visiting rights of your ex-husband.' Jules added emphatically.

This was a former judge and member of the ministry of justice speaking and Emma felt confident that the advice was flawless. Jules suggested Emma call Hubert Belette to get a second opinion and confirmation which she did.

'Are you one hundred percent sure?' Emma asked. 'Should we not first ask the court for an official approval anyway?' Emma continued.

'No' Hubert replied almost too abruptly. 'Over here we do not need to do that sort of thing. The terms of the divorce are clear and signed by both parties and ratified by the youth court.'

'Well how do we proceed then?' Emma asked.

'I will write a registered and official letter to Victor Falconer advising him that you have been posted to the UK and, in accordance with the terms of the mutual consent divorce settlement, you will honour your ex-husband's visiting rights.' he explained.

'OK.' Emma agreed. Given the latest deterioration in the relationship with Paul, she considered it undesirable to discuss the issue further with him.

So much for good and sound advice. Emma excitedly prepared for the move, a new chapter, a new beginning and hopefully some much sought after peace. Still unbeknown to her, and her family and friends who had been following developments closely, Emma was being led into an enormous trap for which she would pay a very high price for several years to come.

Chapter 18

It was a warm summer day and Jules Mercier and Emma had just discovered a new watering hole in a quaint little restaurant opposite the forest run by a friendly family where the food was quite extraordinary.

'So how are your plans coming along to move back to the UK?' Jules enquired sipping the house red which had just arrived at the table.

'Fine' Emma replied. 'As you can imagine I am very busy. I signed my UK contract. The movers are due to come in mid-July.'

'Oh that's fast' he added. 'Where are you going to live?'

'Well I have been quite lucky.' Emma went on. 'It just happens that an English colleague is moving and has rented me his house, three bedrooms, opposite playing fields, nice area, not far from the airport so the children can hop over to see their father every fortnight.'

'What about the lease on your current house?' Jules enquired always interested in any property as he was himself working as an estate agent to boost his income.

'Well you know the owner is quite reasonable and my company agreed to pay the three month indemnity for terminating the contract early so he has agreed to find new tenants for me which is quite a relief as I have so many other things to take care of.' Emma added.

'You work for a good company.' Jules Mercier replied thoughtfully.

'Yes I know.' Emma said. 'I am very fortunate.'

'What about the children's schooling?' Jules continued.

'Well that was my biggest concern.' Emma admitted. 'However, I have been lucky there too because I found two places in one of the best schools in the area. I visited the head mistress, a charming lady, saw the class where Olivia and Sebastian will be starting and met the children. They all looked so sweet in their neat little uniforms and were all so polite, friendly and well behaved. It reminded me of when I was at school.' Emma remarked nostalgically.

'Well it sounds as though you have everything under control.' Jules smiled.

'Well I do hope so.' Emma replied.

'Cheers.' Jules suddenly piped up. 'Raise your glass to England.'

'Chin Chin.' Emma replied. 'You know Jules' she confided. 'going through a divorce is very tough as well as getting back on track afterwards. I worked hard for fifteen years to build up something, had a lovely house then lost it overnight. With this new job, I have doubled my salary and can now afford to buy a new property on my own which will also be an important investment for the future and for the security of the children.'

'Hmm' Jules agreed. 'I know what you mean about losing everything.'

'Oh?' Emma asked in surprise looking over to Jules to discover more.

'Yes' he continued reflectively, his thoughts appearing to run off into the past. 'I once had a beautiful castle but I had to sell it.'

'That's a pity.' Emma replied wondering if he would elaborate.

Nothing came so Emma changed the subject. 'I just hope Paul does not react too adversely to my move.' she went on 'The children have been through so much.'

'I don't think so.' Jules reassured Emma. 'In any case it is covered under the divorce agreement ratified by the youth court and you are adhering to the terms you agreed by returning the children every second weekend at your expense to see their father.'

'Yes I know.' Emma stated. 'But you know how he is.'

'Don't worry.' Jules replied. 'Hubert will take care of notifying your ex-husband and Victor Falconer and they will just have to go along with it. So what about holidays?' Jules enquired.

'We are going to the USA.' Emma explained. 'We are staying with friends in New England who also have a holiday home on the Cape. We are there for the fourth of July which is always great fun and I want the children to see the wonderful firework display.'

'Yes I like the States too.' Jules added. 'My daughter lives there.'

'Oh great.' Emma added. 'Do you see her often?'

'Not really.' Jules replied.

Emma continued to explain her plans for the summer. 'Then afterwards the children are with their father in the south of France, then with their paternal grandmother at her house in the country and for the final two weeks of August with my mum, Aunty Hilda and myself in England. It will be mum's last summer holiday with them. Time is so short.' Emma said sadly.

'Yes it tough.' Jules Mercier replied. 'I also lost my mother to pancreatic cancer.'

Emma paid the bill and they parted, promising to call one another the following week.

Emma hurried around trying to finalise everything before the holidays in America. She visited the children's current school and explained that the children were moving to England in the next school term. At the same time Hubert Belette informed Victor Falconer by registered letter of the planned move emphasizing the fact that Emma intended to respect the visiting rights stipulated in the divorce settlement.

One evening after dinner Emma explained to Olivia and Sebastian that they would be moving to live in England after the summer holidays. At first they both looked a little worried.

'But we don't read and write yet in English.' Olivia pointed out.

'But you speak English fluently and the school is really going to help you get up to speed.' Emma reassured them. 'You will see within one year you will be flying' she added. '

'We love visiting England.' Sebastian joined in. 'I just hope that it will not be too difficult at school.'

'Me too.' Olivia added.

The holidays in America were thoroughly enjoyable. Olivia and Sebastian were excited about their first long haul flight. The stewardesses kept them entertained with a string of toys and books throughout the flight. They took it in turns to sit by the window. Their American friends welcomed them like members of the family. During the holidays between activities, Emma read to the children in English and encouraged them to start reading.

Upon their return, Emma drove Olivia and Sebastian to Paul's mother's home in the country, sad to leave them for three and a half weeks. She had so many things to do in this period. Move countries, houses, start a new job, prepare everything for the children's arrival and smooth integration into their new life. However, as every summer, she was going to miss them an awful lot. Emma comforted herself with the fact that middle of August she was going to spend a memorable holiday with her mum, aunty Hilda and the children which gave her something to look forward to.

Although frail, Emma's mum was determined to get away with her grandchildren to the seaside for a final summer holiday. She remained brave and dignified in spite of her constantly deteriorating health.

Emma gave Olivia and Sebastian a big long hug before they got out of the car. Paul's mother came running out of the house towards them and swept them along with her through the front door. They looked back and Emma gave them a final wave and blew them a kiss before driving off.

A couple of days before the move, Emma called the children. Paul's mother answered.

'So you are moving back to the UK?' she asked dryly.

'Yes I have received an important promotion.' Emma replied.

'I will pass you the children.' she replied and was gone.

Chapter 19

Two days after the move, just as things were almost straight in the new house, Emma received a call from the European headquarters.

'Emma we have just received a fax from your lawyer. It looks important. We will fax it over to you.'

Emma waited on the other end of the fax wondering what on earth was happening now. The fax was short and snappy, just like Hubert Belette's recent manner. For the first time, Emma felt slightly irritated. She read the contents and took a deep breath. So this is why Paul had remained so quiet after receiving notification of her move.

Victor Falconer had just filed two actions in front of the provincial youth court. The first requesting transfer of custody of the children to their father and the second an emergency action to be judged in a public hearing in the coming three weeks just before Emma was due to be reunited with the children. He asked for temporary transfer of custody to the father pending an in-depth enquiry given the fact that Emma had already left the country.

Hubert Belette suggested that Emma meet him as a matter of urgency. He concluded the letter by asking for another payment, this time of 1000 € for these two new procedures. Initially the seriousness of the situation did not quite sink in. Emma poured a glass of wine and sank down into the sofa and started to read Victor Falconer's court papers. She sat up in indignation. This man was a compulsive liar but a very good one and from what she had seen so far from the courts, they could not or did not want to see through this charade. A wave of anxiety swept over her.

The emergency action stated that for more than a year, Emma had intensified her provocations towards Paul, making false accusations and criticisms about him in front of the children in contradiction to the very clear recommendations which had been made to her last

January in a judgment by the provincial youth court. As a result, the two children had expressed a clear desire to reside principally with their father.

Emma had prepared her move to the UK in secret and undoubtedly her decision had been stigmatised by her discontentment with the judgment made by the youth court in January.

Hubert Belette's letter advising of Emma's move was dated 25th June but had not arrived until 2nd July, after Emma's departure to the USA with the children on holiday. This was, Victor Falconer, claimed in deliberate and complete violation of the agreed terms of the divorce settlement.

Paul feared Emma's moves were a deliberate attempt to cut him off from his children who had for many months anyway already clearly expressed their clear wish to live principally with their father and his new family.

The above request covered just the temporary emergency measure. Emma read on to see the additional arguments developed for definitive transfer of custody. She shook her head in utter disbelief. It was a complete turning of the tables.

- As soon as the divorce was pronounced it was clear that she had accepted it badly and held a firm grudge against her ex-husband and used the children to get back at him.

- She kept his visiting rights to a minimum, incessantly modified amicable agreements made and refused all dialogue, with many official reminders going unanswered.

- She made a fantasy request to reduce Paul's visiting right, simply classified by the youth court as such. In particular, her motivation should be noted (remarriage of Paul) and the corresponding advice in the judgment which she had superbly ignored.

- She had categorically refused to grant Paul's mother a visiting right which the mother had then been forced to obtain by addressing her request to the youth court.

- She constantly criticized Paul and Lea in front of the children.

- She systematically interrogated the children after each visit to their father.

As a result, the children had noticed a difference of atmosphere with the home of the mother. Their father who had since remarried was attentive and always there for his children and they enjoyed themselves immensely with him.

The children complained that their mother often left them for several days with different people when she went abroad for professional reasons even refusing that the children visit their father during the school holidays.

It was clear that Emma's departure for England was not connected to exceptional circumstances due to her profession but that she was putting into practice the threats she had made to Paul's mother a year previously that she was going to go abroad and prevent Paul from seeing his children again.

Paul could not agree to his children going to live abroad. It really was against their better interests. He travelled rarely and Lea was a house wife available full time for the children with whom they enjoyed an excellent relationship. Emma travelled regularly and left the children with different child minders.

It was dangerous to interrupt their schooling again now that they had excellent results. The children barely spoke English.

Emma was utterly flabbergasted. She had never seen such a collection of lies before. She turned to the inventory and supporting documentation to see which evidence they were presenting to justify the points they were making. A list of thirty-three letters popped out at her. A few between Paul and herself but for the most part, between Victor Falconer and Hubert Belette full of invention from Victor Falconer's side, some defended by but most not even answered by Hubert Belette.

Emma was distraught but could still not sincerely believe any serious court of law could take such evidence on face value. What worried her however, was that enough seeds of doubt had been sown for the court to give Paul the benefit of the doubt and the fact that she was now established on the other side of the channel did not help her case. She fell into an uneasy sleep.

Next day Emma called Jules Mercier. 'Have you heard the latest?' she asked.

'Yes Hubert called me to update me.' he replied.

'Well what do you say?' Emma demanded

'Just a hick-up.' he replied reassuringly. 'I will come with you to the hearing in August.' Emma felt relieved. At least she was going to have some experienced back up.

'Listen Jules. I need your help. A lot of Paul's case is based on the fact that I am a career woman unavailable for my children and Lea a housewife. You know this is nonsense. I go every morning and evening myself to the children's school. Lea has a shop in the centre of the city where they live and works every day, including Saturdays, until 6.30 pm. In the holidays the children even have to sit in the backroom of the shop until she is ready to go home and some Saturdays she even sends them out into the centre on their own to look at the shops when they are bored. During this time Paul is working and travelling of course. However, we need proof. I need a private detective to take photos of her working and opening and closing the shop. We simply can't just accept all these lies.' Emma stated.

Emma's boss had been an officer in the army during her late teens in the intelligence section and she had strongly advised Emma to start to gather evidence in a few crucial areas.

Jules Mercier hesitated looking at Emma in surprise. Emma felt guilty that she was having to go to such extreme measures to prove such a simple but important point.

'Well if you can't help me Jules, please say so.' Emma continued. 'Then I will find someone who can.'

'No, no it is fine.' Jules finally replied. 'I know someone, someone very good. It will cost you of course but I think it is worth it.'

A couple of days later Emma heard about Ivan, a gentleman with whom Jules Mercier regularly cooperated. 'We will go together and do the necessary next week.' he promised Emma.

'Good' she replied relieved that at least something was being done to dispel some of the lies now directed against her. She added 'Listen I am coming over tomorrow. On Saturday I have to go for four days to the USA so let's stay in touch. I am then going to stay in the country for as long as it takes to see Hubert and finalise our case. Want to come along?'

'Fine' he replied. 'Look forward to it'.

The day after her return from the US, Emma picked up Jules Mercier and they set off to see Hubert to put together the reply and approach for the imminent court hearing. Hubert had moved offices recently. His new office was surprisingly much bigger, lighter, more spacious. It did not seem quite so cluttered and the numerous files seemed to have received a much needed dusting prior to the move. Even his jacket seemed to breathe new life.

Hubert was definitely not the best dressed man in the world in stark contrast to the immaculate dress sense of Jules Mercier. Hubert did however enjoy good food, wine and travel. Jules Mercier confided in Emma that he even thought that Hubert might be keeping a mistress. Hubert hurried around and made everyone a cup of tea before sitting down to discuss what their optimal course of action should be. Hubert perched himself on the end of his chair and looked at Emma and Jules with an air of authority.

'Well, Victor Falconer's case is definitely full of untruths.' he started. 'We will of course vehemently deny them and set the record straight. You are adhering to the terms of the divorce agreement. We have enough proof that this a premeditated step by your ex-husband.' reiterated Hubert looking straight at Emma.

'I agree.' Jules Mercier chimed in.

'I do hope so.' Emma added. 'Here are the financials of Lea's shop.' she continued holding out an eight-page report. 'As you will see she transferred her business officially via the trade register into Paul's name a few days after our divorce so she could say she is a house wife which we know she definitely is not.'

'Yes precisely.' added Jules Mercier. 'I am going with Ivan end of next week to take some photos of her working in the shop.' he explained to Hubert.

'Very good.' replied Hubert. 'This will be important to attach to the file I will submit to the court. I already have the confirmation from four of your friends and acquaintances about your attributes as a good mother.' continued Hubert turning again to Emma. 'I have also received the doctor's confirmation of your mother's medical condition and the fact that this will be her last summer with her grandchildren. Now what about the children's new school?' Hubert enquired.

'Well I have the prospectus plus a letter of congratulations from the Archbishop of Westminster about the high academic standards.' Emma explained.

'Good, send me a copy right away and I will attach the letter from the child psychologist which the youth court refused to take into account last time around.'

Hubert seemed satisfied and so did Jules Mercier which put Emma a little more at ease.

'Please send me a copy of our written defence for the court as soon as you can.' Emma urged Hubert. 'I want to read it through in advance and see if there is anything else we should add to strengthen our case.'

'No problem.' Hubert replied.

They shook hands and agreed to meet at the entrance of the youth court the following week for the all-important custody hearing.

Chapter 20

Emma flew over the night before the hearing. She drove the next morning with Jules Mercier to the provincial court. They met Hubert in the large reception hall of the main court building. It was humming with activity. Lawyers were everywhere in their black gowns, conferring with their clients, checking final details. Unfortunately for Emma it was becoming an all too familiar sight. Emma sat down at a table with Jules Mercier and Hubert handed over his written defence.

'The photos are attached.' he said.

'Yes you can't imagine the fun Ivan and I had taking those.' Jules Mercier added excitedly. 'We hid behind the clothes racks apparently undetected. In fact, Lea seemed to have confined herself to a back room of the shop probably doing some paperwork or the like so Ivan called his wife from his mobile and she then called the shop asking to speak to Lea who then came out, under the pretext of applying for a job.'

Emma smiled at the prospect. The photos were really quite good. Clear with the date and time marked on the back. Emma felt a tinge of guilt for having gone to such lengths but how else was she ever going to begin to disprove all the lies written about her and defend her case and her right to bring up her own children?

'When did you file our defence? I did not receive a copy in advance to check and I did ask you specifically to send me one' Emma asked Hubert.

'Oh it is not yet done.' he replied. 'I finished it yesterday evening and will give it to the judge this morning.'

Emma was irritated. 'Is this not a bit too late?' she protested loudly.

'Oh no it is quite usual especially in these emergency hearings when time is short.' he defended himself.

Emma turned to Jules Mercier and he nodded in agreement. Emma read the defence through quickly. It seemed concise and covered all the main points which had been discussed. In short, it confirmed that she was adhering to the terms of the mutual consent divorce which Paul now had no intention of respecting. That Emma had always scrupulously respected his visiting rights.

That Paul was fully aware that Emma's mother was terminally ill and this emergency measure should in no way prevent Emma's mother from spending the last two weeks of August with her grandchildren as planned.

That all issues should be raised and debated in a full custody hearing in the early autumn. If Paul had such first-rate aptitudes for the perfect education of his son and daughter, then previous tensions should have been avoided but as an only and very spoilt child, egocentric with a fiery temper and occasionally violent, this did not appear to be the case.

Furthermore, it did not give Paul the right to take the children away from their loving and capable mother at any price, notably in order not have to pay maintenance he had previously agreed to, exclusively for the children.

He concluded that it was curious to note the apparent availability of Lea compared to Emma since it was a proven that far from being a housewife as stated by Victor Falconer, she had a full- time job running a shop and Emma had no intention of ceding her role to a substitute mother, in addition to someone who the children did not appreciate.

Suddenly Emma saw Paul and Victor Falconer hovering in the aisle looking in their direction. Hubert went over to them and shook their hand. He then returned to Emma and Jules.

'They want to know who Jules is.' he said with a smile.

'Did you hear that?' Jules asked Emma. 'They are really wondering who I am.' Jules seemed really amused. Emma could not understand why until much later of course.

Everyone stood up and filed into the court room. It was a public hearing and there seemed to be over one hundred people packed in there.

'I am going to stand at the back.' Jules Mercier explained to Emma. 'You go next to Hubert. Don't stand next to me.' he added.

Emma looked at him for a moment in surprise and edged her way over to where Hubert Belette was standing. Most issues were sorted in a matter of five minutes. Their case took over half an hour. Victor Falconer opened the proceedings from his side speaking for twenty minutes. The room was packed and everyone looked and listened. Hubert followed with his defence for a further ten minutes.

Then the public prosecutor's deputy turned to Emma and snapped 'I checked with the police and you already officially left the country beginning of July.'

'That is not correct.' Emma protested as politely as she could.

'You also appealed against a previous youth court judgment.' she continued.

Emma looked towards Hubert for help. The court clerk looked at Emma sympathetically.

'The judgment will be pronounced in one week's time.' the judge wrapped up. 'Next please.'

Emma was shaken. Who was this young woman from the prosecutor's office? She seemed vaguely familiar. Emma thought back. It was the piercing voice more than anything and the haughty manner, how she raised her head and spoke with such absolute authority crushing anything around her. She reminded Emma of the trainee who had presided in the hearing over a year ago when Paul's mother had applied for her own visiting right. I will see when the judgment is issued Emma told herself.

Emma joined Hubert and Jules Mercier again outside the courtroom.

'I do not feel very comfortable.' she confided in them.

Hubert was angry with the prosecutor's deputy. 'You were on holiday beginning of July with the children.' he said. 'You had definitely not officially moved out of the country. She should check her facts more carefully before making such strong and sweeping statements.' he concluded.

Emma nodded in agreement.

'Don't worry.' Jules Mercier concluded. 'Courts do not take away small children from their loving mother without a very good reason. It is practically unheard of.'

Chapter 21

Emma was still in a state of shock and functioning on auto pilot following the news the previous day that she had temporarily lost custody of her two young children. When she pulled up outside Hubert Belette's home at 11.30 am on the Saturday morning she wanted answers to her questions and above all solutions. Hubert did not seem surprised to see Emma but could not hide his displeasure either at being disturbed during the weekend.

'Morning Hubert.' she began and losing no time immediately got down to business 'So just what happened? How come not only do I lose temporary custody of my children but I don't even have an official visiting right? Do you realise the situation in which I find myself today? It is absolutely outrageous.'

Hubert looked uncomfortable, irritated, almost annoyed.

Emma felt herself getting annoyed too and fought not to show it. She needed this annoying little man on her side to try to reverse the damage which had just been done.

Eventually Hubert replied. 'It was a bad judgment. It just needs careful handling. It is just a matter of time.'

'Matter of time?' Emma repeated. 'I don't have the right to see my own son and daughter and you say it is just a matter of time? How much time? You know Paul is going to make it very difficult for me to have contact with them.' Emma continued her voice getting louder by the second.

'Keep calm. Getting wound up won't help.' Hubert replied almost patronisingly which just served to wind Emma up even more.

'And what about my dying mum?' Emma went on. 'The children should now be spending their last summer holiday with her. She was so looking forward to it. How can this happen? Didn't you see it coming and why didn't you point out the potential risk and I would not have moved without the written green light from the court? You were so sure I was covered by the mutual consent agreement.'

Hubert took a deep breath and tried to get on top of things.

'Look it is the weekend so there is not a lot I can do today or tomorrow but I promise first thing Monday I will contact Victor Falconer and sort out a visiting right. I fully agree with you that it is completely unacceptable that you are not officially allowed to see your children.'

'You bet.' Emma replied. 'I am postponing my return to the UK early next week until I get some answers and a clear path forward. This is simply and utterly outrageous, outrageous.' she repeated.

Still seething, she left Hubert to enjoy the rest of his weekend. She got back into the car and for an hour drove around aimlessly. She was not officially resident in the country anymore and felt completely helpless. After a while Emma stopped for a cup of coffee and then headed to Valerie's where she was staying. Valerie was her rock and she was sure she could pour out her heart and get good solid support and advice which would not help the situation this weekend but would help Emma put things in perspective and plan her next step.

On the Saturday evening, Jules Mercier had insisted that Emma come over for dinner. He wanted to discuss the judgment with her and find out how she was going to react. At 7 pm she rang the doorbell. She was still in a state of shock and dismay and in no real mood to be chatty. She felt badly let down by the system and desperately missed Olivia and Sebastian whom she had not seen for over four weeks. Now she did not even have an official visiting right. It was inconceivable.

Contact over the phone was also proving to be very difficult and she feared it would only get worse. Emma's mum had been bitterly disappointed about not being able to spend her final summer holiday with her grandchildren and this only added to Emma's frustration. She just wanted to sleep. This was the only way she could temporarily forget about the situation.

'Come on in.' Jules beckoned warmly giving Emma a kiss on each cheek. 'How are you?'

'Terrible.' Emma replied.

Dominique, Jules' bubbly third wife arrived. She also kissed Emma on each cheek and told her how surprised she had been about the judgment.

'You have got to fight to get them back.' she encouraged Emma.

'I know that is exactly what I intend to do.' Emma replied. She wondered where she was going to get the energy from as she felt so flat and empty.

'You must go to appeal.' Jules added. 'When are you seeing Hubert again?'

'Next Monday.' Emma replied. 'I am going to come back and live and work here.' Emma suddenly confided in Jules who handed her a welcome glass of red wine.

'What and leave the promotion and everything behind? You have only just moved over.' he quirked.

'I know and I don't care.' Emma replied. 'They are my children and for me they are the most precious thing in the whole world. Promotion or no promotion.' Emma continued

'Well how are you going to do it?' Jules enquired suddenly looking serious.

'Tomorrow morning Sunday I have a meeting with the European management and together we will call the president and sort something out. I worked hard before and they indicated on the phone that they will do everything they can to help me.' Emma explained.

'That is very good of them.' Jules Mercier replied looking at Emma inquisitively over the rim of his smart glasses before asking half-jokingly if she was having an affair with the President.

Emma was in no mood for such flippant comments and replied 'Don't be ridiculous Jules.' She could not help thinking what a strange comment that was to make.

'Well as I said earlier' Jules continued reassuringly and changing the subject 'it is practically unheard of for children to be taken away from a loving and capable mother and it is just a matter of weeks before you will get them back through the appeal court. After all the temporary judgment is only valid until 1st December and that is only three and a half months away at most.'

Emma left feeling slightly more confident.

On Sunday morning Emma found herself back in her old office. The two directors explained that they had already spoken to the president and the company would take her back immediately in her old job. They explained that they would go with Emma on the Monday morning to the HR department and sort the whole thing out.

'Don't worry.' they urged Emma. 'Things will work out.'

Emma hugged them both and felt tears coming into her eyes. 'I don't know how I can ever thank you both.' she said gratefully.

'Don't. Just concentrate on getting Olivia and Sebastian back. Now are you sure that your lawyer is up to it?' they both asked, almost in unison.

Together the three of them called Hubert Belette and told him the news. What do you need from our HR department for the appeal was the question they asked? Emma put Hubert on the loudspeaker and the two directors listened. Hubert seemed surprised and hesitant. Emma's two colleagues looked at one another with raised eyebrows. Subconsciously the first seeds of doubt were planted in Emma's mind.

'You know he has to be good.' Emma said trying to convince the two directors. 'After all his has been highly recommended by a former judge and member of the ministry of justice.'

'OK you must know but keep a close eye on him.' they advised.

'I will.' Emma replied.

On Monday in the office Emma's colleagues were shocked by the judgment and they rallied around giving Emma much needed comfort and encouragement. They told her it would be great to have her back. Emma had told her mum, Laura and Rachel about the decision over the phone. It is the best move you can make under the circumstances they all confirmed. You have to go back and fight them on home territory. There is very little you can do from England.

The HR department issued a confirmation that Emma was going to come back and work in the country and also offered to pay her relocation fees in full. Emma had insisted that they did not need to do that, admitting that she should have been more vigilant. Consider it done had been the reply as this situation is so unfair.

Emma was so grateful and relieved. She felt the situation was totally unfair but to have this confirmed by friends and colleagues from so many different nationalities gave her confidence that justice would eventually be done and the children would soon be coming home.

Chapter 22

On the Monday afternoon Emma met Hubert. He had sent a fax informing her that since their appeal against the file which had simply been closed some six months previously by the provincial court was still pending, the request from Victor Falconer and Paul to transfer custody of the children was on hold in the provincial court and could not be processed until the appeal court had taken the whole case into account which it had the right to do. He added that naturally Paul and Victor Falconer were not pleased with this development.

Emma felt slightly relieved that the case was going to be judged next time by three experienced judges who were bound, she thought, to be more neutral and impartial and would actually take the time to get to the bottom of things.

Hubert then requested payment of another 700 € for opening yet another file. Emma was not pleased but with her children now being held hostage, she felt it was not the right time to start haggling over legal fees. Emma reluctantly called her mum and asked her if she did not mind advancing the funds. She would pay her back in the coming two months. By now Emma's mum was frail and thin. At the beginning of the year the doctors had given her until August but here she was now still battling gallantly on. Emma's mum took her bag and got on the bus and went down to her building society in the centre of town. She arranged for immediate transfer of the funds to Hubert Belette's account.

Emma walked into Hubert's office. He shuffled towards her and shook her hand in a business-like fashion. He made a cup of tea for them both fishing out the teabags which he proceeded to throw in the bin under his desk leaving a couple of stains on the light carpet.

'Before you ask,' Emma announced. 'the funds will arrive this week on your account from my mum. She is not well but she went into town especially.' Emma continued wanting him to know.

'Excellent.' Hubert replied. 'Now let's look at this appeal.'

'I want to see my children. It is my right' Emma interrupted. 'What have you done to make sure this happens and when will that be?'

'Yes yes.' Hubert replied almost impatiently. 'I will make the necessary arrangements with Victor Falconer this week.'

'When will that be?' Emma insisted. 'My things are still in England and I will be arranging my move soon but meanwhile I have to plan.' she continued.

'Yes yes' Hubert replied. 'As soon as I have everything by the end of the week, I will let you know.'

'Only then?' Emma asked.

'Yes.' Hubert replied categorically.

Emma took a deep breath. For the first time, she felt like shaking then throttling Hubert but knew it was out of the question. She had to stay calm, clear headed, composed if she was going to get her children back. It took an enormous amount of self-control. They agreed on the general content of the appeal which Hubert promised to finalise by end of the week as well as the arrangements for Emma to see the children.

Emma felt completely punch drunk from the events of the previous days. Meanwhile she had Olivia and Sebastian briefly on the phone but they seemed frightened, confused and distant. All Emma could tell them to try to reassure them was how much she loved them.

Emma decided to stay in the country for two more days to gather additional pieces of evidence for the appeal. She ran around, the picture of Olivia and Sebastian never far away which suddenly gave her a new surge of energy.

Several friends confirmed that she was a good mother, clean, well-organised, and focused on the wellbeing of her children. She never drunk more than two glasses of wine with dinner, when she drunk at all. The headmaster of the children's former school was very sympathetic and issued a letter that he would take the children back immediately with open arms, even in the middle of the school year. The head of the parents' association of the school, the mother of a friend of Olivia, confirmed what a good mother Emma was in all respects.

Her employer confirmed she travelled infrequently. Emma's direct boss that she planned all her professional life around the children dropping them off and collecting them personally within school hours.

Two of Paul's former colleagues confirmed that he had told everyone who wanted to listen that he had custody of the children, even before it happened, because Emma was a bad, neglectful mother and an alcoholic. Both colleagues said that there was no evidence that this was true and they believed the whole case had been premeditated by Paul.

She sent everything to Hubert Belette and headed back to the UK. She had the move back to start planning. She was also going to spend the weekend with her mum, something she had done every time she was in England, savouring each moment and trying not to think that their days together were numbered. Emma normally took her mum and Aunty Hilda out for lunch to a nice country pub.

On Friday, Hubert sent Emma a copy of an official fax from Victor Falconer. It urged Emma if she was true to herself to drop the appeal and return for a full custody hearing to the provincial court in the real interest of the children. It confirmed that Paul would stop paying maintenance payments and he was not opposed to discussion and had in fact been searching for this with Emma over the last two years without obtaining it from her side. Finally, in the short term, Paul was not hostile to Emma having contact with the children up until 1st December.

Hubert had replied a day later that he had lodged an appeal and would ask the court of appeal to take all the previous procedures into account, to put an end to a situation created by Paul who had never intended to respect the mutual consent divorce he had signed and who interpreted it according to his personal needs. It was also inadmissible that Emma, the mother and the dying grandmother were deprived of all contact with the children up to 1st December. Emma felt relieved that the appeal was lodged and just hoped now that things would move fast.

Emma tried all week to reach Olivia and Sebastian but without success. She left five messages on Paul's mobile phone but to no avail. She called Valerie on the Friday evening and asked her to find out the telephone number of Paul's home. She called on Saturday morning at 9 am knowing the children would be up but Paul still sleeping. It was now nine weeks since Emma had last seen her children and she missed them so much.

Lea answered the phone and passed Emma the children as she had requested. Emma had spoken to Olivia for about two minutes telling her how much she loved her, how hard she had been trying to get hold of her and her brother and that they would soon be together again and that mummy was doing everything to sort things out as soon as possible. Suddenly, Paul awoken by Lea in the meantime, grabbed the phone and started to shout at Emma.

'You certainly know how to annoy people. I am going to change the phone number of the house and my mobile too.' he threatened.

Emma replied calmly that she had tried for five days to reach the children and she would call as often as necessary until she succeeded. Paul stated that the children were profoundly perturbed after speaking to her last time. Emma shot back that under the circumstances it was hardly surprising. She then asked Paul to pass her over to Sebastian which surprisingly he did.

Afterwards Emma jumped in the bath happy to have spoken to her children for a mere five minutes. Funny how one becomes grateful for small mercies she told herself. As she jumped in the car for the three-hour drive to visit her mum, Emma noticed that she had five missed calls and two voice messages. It was Paul with yet another one of his monologues.

'Yes I will continue because I have not finished.' he began. 'Nobody has heard the children yet. Olivia is OK but Sebastian is perturbed. It is unfortunate but the child does to dare tell you what he really wants. I have told them that if they want to be with you then I will drive them back but they do not. It is not easy for an 8 and a 9-year-old to tell their mother because they don't want to displease her. They are frightened of hurting you because after all they love you but they also love their father and they prefer to stay here with us. You won't accept that so too bad for you. We will no doubt have to fight this one out right up until the end. It is the children, I repeat the children, who will decide. I take into account what the children want and I would like you to do the same. But if you don't want to, carry on with the procedures; there is no problem and you will see what the outcome will be. OK goodbye. The children have your number and will call you but please do not call on a Saturday morning when everyone is asleep. But then thinking about other people's interests has never been one of your strong points now has it!' and he was gone.

Two minutes later the second message began 'Yes, it is me. I simply want to say the following. I have given Olivia and Sebastian your mobile number so they can call you when they want. We have told them they can use the phone and shown them how to use it. Now you must understand that if I am in the office or travelling, I cannot always jump when you decide that I should jump. When I called the children at your place the line was not always clear but I had to put up with it. I find that quite scandalous but I can't walk around with my mobile all the time, and be completely at your disposition to do what you want when you want OK? Now one more little detail. It is your fault that you have not seen the children for weeks. If you had called me after the judgment to say you wanted to see the children, I would not have put up any opposition but no you say nothing and yet again you have gone to appeal but then you only think of your own interests and could not care less about what the children think. Well good. Continue, continue there is no problem, no problem. We can carry on to the finish perhaps like this for another ten years. I don't give a damn because if you think you are tough I am even tougher so you had better believe me OK, Me, I …. End of message.'

Emma shook her head. The tone was the usual one when Paul wanted his own way. Aggressive, domineering, mocking, insulting. She shuddered. She knew the children were under a lot of pressure and must feel frightened. It was obvious Paul's tactic was to keep the children with him for as long as possible with limited contact to Emma then convince the court they were settled and bully them into saying they wanted to stay.

Emma felt helpless. She knew it was going to be a long and arduous fight. Family and friends told her she owed it to the children to continue to try to get them back home adding they will grow older, they are intelligent and their fear will subside. Just give them lots of love and support in the meantime. They need you now more than ever before. Emma sighed. It was difficult. She made a recording of Paul's monologue and sent it to Hubert Belette for information.

Chapter 23

The hearing in the appeal court was fixed for early September. Another public hearing this time in an even bigger and even more imposing court room. Emma had flown over the night before. In a recent letter to Victor Falconer, Hubert Belette had expressed his desire to plead their case at this particular hearing and finish everything. Jules Mercier insisted on coming along for moral support.

They waited for three hours before they were called forward. In the meantime, Hubert had darted over to Victor Falconer to greet him, shake hands and they laughed and joked together. When he came back he saw Emma's expression.

'Don't think we know each other well.' Hubert commented to Emma. 'It is perfectly normal for two lawyers to chat in court.'

'Oh.' Emma replied ironically. 'Is that so?'

Jules sat by Emma's side. They were deep in conversation observing the goings on in the court room and trying to calculate when it would be their turn. Jules suddenly looked over to the round like figure of Victor Falconer and asked Emma if she found him attractive. Emma laughed in utter surprise about the absurdity of the question adding how could she possibly like anyone who had written so many nasty lies about her. Hubert joined in the conversation.

'Mr Falconer was just asking me if Jules here was your fan club.' he added.

Jules laughed. 'Tell him yes of course.' he replied.

Emma did not find the conversation very amusing. Then again she was probably completely missing the concealed irony of it.

Their names were called and they negotiated their way past the dozens of black cloaked lawyers in front of them and up to the bench.

'We have come from the provincial youth court you will understand.' Hubert explained with a smile as if this was some known phenomena.

'Yes I understand.' replied the judge returning the smile.

They spoke briefly among themselves in legal terms which were unfamiliar to Emma. The judge and court clerk both wrote something down, the two lawyers thanked them and returned to their places.

'Well what was that all about? Emma asked Hubert anxiously. 'It was too short. When do I get my children back? When do I even get to see them again?' she demanded trying to sound calm and constructive.

'The other party are not yet ready with their written defence so we had to agree upon a final date for exchange of papers so that a final date can be fixed for the hearing.' Hubert explained in his matter of fact way. Jules Mercier nodded in agreement.

Emma's heart sank. She had so much hoped for progress that day. She had come all the way from London, sat for three hours waiting for the case to be heard and then for a mere five minutes only to learn that they were no further forward and she had still not seen her children. She could have wept.

'Come to my office.' Hubert requested. 'I need you to sign a paper for you to see your children this coming weekend.'

Emma had no choice. She obediently followed Hubert out of the courtroom. They did not exchange a word until they arrived some five minutes later in front of his desk. Emma signed the letter which basically said that she agreed to respect the terms of the latest provincial youth court judgment transferring temporary custody to Paul and that she could see the children against the surrender of theirs and her British passport which would be returned when the children were handed back over to their father. She felt humiliated but had no choice.

A few days later Emma received a copy of a letter stating that Paul and Lea had arranged a weekend at the seaside with the children and as Emma's request had arrived too late, they could not cancel. However, in agreement with the children, Paul was going to cut short this weekend and Emma could see the children for three hours on the Sunday afternoon. Victor Falconer concluded by officially requesting Emma's party in future to contact them with more advanced notice.

How could this possibly be Emma asked herself. She had been pushing Hubert since day one for access to see her children. She was livid but helpless and did not know anymore who to blame. She felt completely and utterly manipulated.

Valerie and her mother had opened-up their home for Emma to stay whenever she was in the country pending her relocation back. Valerie and Emma had become close friends. Valerie was a tower of strength for Emma during this difficult period and was a haven of good, sound advice. Valerie had been through a difficult period a few years before. Her husband had had an affair with a young woman interested in the family fortune. Her ex-husband had then left Valerie. Her soon to be ex mother in law had told her, and anyone else who cared to listen, that Valerie was lazy and incompetent although she had practically run the office and done the accounting of the family firm for seventeen years as well as bringing up two children.

Valerie knew what Emma was going through and often said that unless one had been there, one could not begin to imagine the pain and moral prejudice.

Emma waited anxiously for Paul's car to pull up outside Valerie's house at 4 pm on the Sunday afternoon as arranged. At last the children were there and they stepped down nervously from the car. Paul came to the back of the house and the children ran into the house to Valerie and her mother while Paul and Emma sorted out the paperwork.

'Passport.' Paul demanded.

'OK.' Emma replied and handed him over the older now invalid one which she had declared lost and had recently found at home wedged between the bed frame and the mattress. You clever so-and-so she thought to herself as he took it almost triumphantly from her. He did not ask her for the children's British passports. She took just a little comfort from the thought that she could have left the country with Olivia and Sebastian there and then but obviously she was not going to as she had to be whiter than white to have any chance of officially recuperating the children.

'Mum is not well.' Emma continued. 'She has not got much longer to live. I want to visit her soon with the children.'

'Well OK' Paul replied. 'but only if you do not regain custody of the children at the end of the temporary judgment period on 1st December and if you agree to wait for the hearing in the appeal court which is not yet fixed.'

'No.' Emma replied resolutely. 'That is blackmail and I am not going to go along with it.'

'Well that is your choice. I will be back in three hours.' Paul replied and he left.

Emma was shocked. 'Did you hear that?' she whispered to Valerie.

'I know.' Valerie replied. She had always had excellent hearing. 'It is inhuman.' she added. 'Now don't waste any time. You have only three hours with the children so make the most of it.'

Emma, Olivia, Sebastian, Valerie and her mother talked together for thirty minutes. Olivia and Sebastian gradually started to thaw as the conversation revolved around the things they enjoyed doing and activities they had all done together in the past. Then Emma drove with Olivia and Sebastian to a large park where the three of them used to go together on many an occasion. They walked in the woods and ate ice cream.

Emma observed the children as they played and ran between the trees. They seemed to have grown over the last ten weeks. They also looked sad. She kept hugging and kissing them. By the end of the afternoon they were much more relaxed and responding to affection. When their father arrived to collect them, Emma hugged them goodbye and promised to call them the following week.

'Don't worry' she reassured them. 'We will see each other regularly from now on.'

Emma turned to Valerie. 'It is going to be a very long road back.' she said.

'I know.' Valerie replied wisely. 'You are going to need lots of courage and lots of patience but you will get there in the end I know it.'

Emma thanked her friend, jumped in the car and set off for the long drive back to London painfully aware that with every passing minute she was getting further and further away from Olivia and Sebastian.

Emma had to explain to her mum and family why she still had no official visiting right nor any date for her mum to eventually see her grandchildren for probably the last time.

'You must not go back to that provincial kangaroo court.' Emma's mum stressed, obviously pained by the whole experience. 'Even if I never see Olivia and Sebastian again they know I loved them. Never give in to blackmail do you hear me?' Emma's mum continued.

'Yes mum.' Emma replied and headed into the kitchen to make a pot of tea her eyes filling with tears.

Aunty Hilda followed her. She was indignant.

'This Hubert Belette, is he trustworthy?' she asked. 'Remember you are in this situation because he gave you some very poor advice prior to your departure to England.' She reminded Emma.

'I am told he is very good by a former judge and member of the ministry of justice and the contents of the defence so far seemed to have had all the main points in them.' Emma explained.

'Yes but you had to do a lot of the running to get the evidence together and guide him in the right direction.' Aunty Hilda added.

'Yes you are right, but I thought this would help accelerate things. You know lawyers are always so busy.' Emma continued.

'Hmmm' aunty Hilda concluded, not convinced, reaching into the fridge for the milk.

Chapter 24

Emma's official move back to the continent was planned for early October. Aunty Hilda came over to help with the packing. Emma's mum who was now too weak to do anything physical stayed with Laura, Emma's sister. Emma and her aunt worked solidly from morning to dusk packing box after box after box. Wrapping things which had been unwrapped just a few weeks previously.

Emma was pushing Hubert to arrange her next weekend with the children and this time the whole weekend and not just a few hours. She was at an exhibition when a fax came through from Hubert to her hotel. It had been a long day and she sat down wearily on the bed and starting to read wondering what was in store for her this time.

It was a three-page letter in the now familiar style of Victor Falconer accusing Emma again of a host of things, in particular, not filing any papers in the court for either of the two appeals and trying to drag things out until 1st December at which time the temporary judgment transferring custody to Paul would expire.

Paul agreed for Emma to see the children the following two weekends at Valerie's provided she surrender her passport and that of the children. Paul did not agree for the time being to a trip for the children to visit Emma's mother stressing that the children were far from enthusiastic about the long trip and if Emma's mother could make it down to London by car she could easily make it over to the continent. Tears rolled down Emma's cheeks at the sheer audacity and unfairness of the situation.

She picked up the phone to call Hubert at home. He was not particularly happy to be disturbed in the evening but Emma did not care. She was completely confused and needed answers.

'What is this about us not presenting our paperwork to the court?' she demanded. 'You confirmed to me weeks ago in two separate faxes that the necessary was being done. Why all of a sudden this problem?' she challenged him sniffing loudly.

'Don't believe Victor Falconer.' Hubert replied. 'He has to present his papers first then only then can I reply.'

'Well do something to make him.' Emma suggested. 'We cannot carry on like this. Things have to move. Time will start to play against us soon.'

'I am doing all I can.' Hubert retorted but Emma was not convinced.

'It is inadmissible that my mum cannot see her grandchildren.' Emma continued between sobs. 'The doctors gave her until August and now we are two months past the date and she is getting weaker by the day. We went away last weekend to Oxfordshire with my sister and family' Emma lamented 'and mum had looked forward all weekend to having her grandchildren on the phone and Lea refused to pass them over to us. This is a completely unacceptable situation. You have to do something.' Emma pleaded.

Hubert's voice became irritated. He was not accustomed to dealing with emotional women.

'As I told you, I am doing everything I possibly can, now try to get some sleep. As you can see, you will be seeing your son and daughter two more weekends this month.' he replied and hung up.

Emma took a bath and fell into an uneasy sleep.

On Friday afternoon Emma drove over to the continent so happy to be seeing her children again that weekend. She had arranged to have dinner with Jules Mercier on the Friday evening upon her return. They met up in their favourite Italian restaurant.

'Jules I really need your help. This is turning into a nightmare.' Emma pleaded.

'Don't worry you will get the children back latest beginning of December. Courts just don't take children away from their mothers. It is almost unheard of.' he reassured Emma.

The small carafe of house red had arrived and Jules poured them both a glass.

'There seems to be a problem with transfer of paperwork between lawyers.' Emma continued.

'That will be sorted. Hubert is on the ball. We have a very strong case.' he said soothingly.

'Paul is blackmailing me.' Emma blurted out. 'He says he will not let Olivia and Sebastian see their dying grand mum unless I agree not to regain custody of the children on 1st December. There must be a law against such things.' Emma implored.

'Not really, but you should tape the conversation.' Jules advised. 'Now when are you moving back?'

'Ten days from now.' Emma replied.

'So soon?' Jules seemed surprised. 'Have you found anywhere to live yet? As you know I am working for an estate agent and we have some nice flats currently on our books.' Jules enquired.

'Thanks but it is all taken care of. I found a really nice little villa, very good price too. It is only fifteen minutes from work, five minutes from the children's former school and close to Valerie and other good friends of mine. There is a small, well-kept garden too for Olivia and Sebastian to play in.' Emma announced proudly.

Valerie had helped her find the place and had called the owners the day the ad appeared in the paper. They were an elderly couple and the most important criteria was that they rented their property to a quiet, trustworthy person. The meeting had gone really well and Emma had signed within forty-eight hours.

'Where did you meet your wife Dominique?' Emma asked changing the subject.

'Oh she walked into my office one day and things sort of went from there.' he replied. 'You know.' he added proudly 'I was earning 30.000 € per month and used to give Dominique a monthly allowance of 2.000 €.'

'Lucky lady.' Emma added. 'I wish someone would do that to me. I like Dominique. She is good fun. You two seem to get along really well together.'

'Yes we do.' Jules added pensively. 'But times are much harder today than they were a few years ago.'

Emma paid the bill and they went their separate ways agreeing to meet up again once she had moved back to the country.

The children arrived the following morning. Emma was so pleased to see them.

'Passport please.' Paul demanded. Emma handed him the one declared lost and cancelled and smiled as he proudly took it from her.

She hugged Olivia and Sebastian and told them all about the nice things planned for the weekend. She had arranged with the parents of their friends from their former school to go to a pleasure park for the day. They were twelve in total. The autumn weather was beautiful and everyone had a wonderful time. The parents of their friends were shocked by the judgment and showed Emma their solidarity. The children got along really well and Emma revelled in the pleasure and relaxation on their faces as they raced from one ride to the next.

Emma broke the news to the children that she was moving back and felt their relief. She asked them if they would like to go back to their old school. 'Oh yes mummy' they replied. 'And also back home to you.'

The following weekend Paul could not drop off the children as he was working so a letter arrived from Victor Falconer advising that Paul's mother would meet Emma at the railway station with the children. Emma had not seen or spoken to Paul's mother since the judgment. The train arrived and Paul's mother tottered towards her with the children.

'Emma I am so sorry; children should be with their mother.' she declared attempting to put her arm comfortingly on Emma's.

'Please don't touch me.' Emma retorted, cringing as two passers-by stared at her. She gave Olivia and Sebastian a few coins to buy an ice cream at a stall 15 metres away and keeping an eye on them, turned to Paul's mother.

'Listen to me.' Emma began calmly. 'You have plotted right from the beginning to blacken my name and help your son snatch my children away from me. It is a little too late now for regrets.'

'This story has nothing to do with me.' she protested.

'Well frankly I am not convinced.' Emma shot back. 'If there is any sincerity in what you are saying then you will write to Hubert Belette and confirm that I never threatened you a year ago to go abroad and prevent Paul from ever seeing his children again. You probably know this lie was in Victor Falconer's case against me and it was one of the elements which spooked the court into taking custody from me, at least temporarily.'

Paul's mother looked uncomfortable. 'I need your passport.' she said.

'Here it is and I suppose you need the paperwork signing again so where is it?' Emma replied.

She signed the paperwork and walked away with her children to the car. She told Olivia and Sebastian about the nice things planned for the weekend. Time flew by and Sunday evening was there again before they knew it.

Emma had to drive over one hour in the opposing direction to drop off the children at their father's before heading back to England. It was 2.00 am when she eventually arrived back home. She almost fell asleep on the M25 fighting desperately to stay awake. At least when you move back, you won't have this nightmare return journey she reassured herself trying to look on the bright side.

The day of the move arrived. The same jolly team of international movers who had relocated Emma a few weeks' earlier turned up to bring her back.

'What you again?' a burly removal man asked her in surprise.

'Afraid so.' Emma shrugged. 'Just one of those things.'

Valerie was at the other end to help with the unpacking. Cathy had been the day before and given the house the white tornado treatment. Valerie had even wallpapered the kitchen for Emma before she moved in. How lucky she was to have such good friends Emma told herself. She immediately felt at home in the new place. It was cosy, comfortable, light and the furniture just seemed to fit perfectly.

Friends and family suggested Emma visit the British consulate, explain her predicament and ask them for guidance. She set off one sunny morning, a copy of the file and court papers in hand. She waited her turn in the long queue and eventually arrived at the counter.

'I have a small problem.' she started. 'I got divorced nearly two years ago and was granted custody of the children. Now they have been taken away from me by the authorities in a very questionable judgment and I don't even have a visiting right. They are also British citizens.'

'Well I am afraid this is a private matter.' the lady behind the glass replied. 'We cannot help and we cannot give you any advice either.'

'But surely there must be something you can do?' Emma pleaded.

'Afraid not.' the lady reiterated. 'Unless your husband is beating you up and putting yours and the children's lives at risk, then we can't possibly get involved. Sorry.' she continued. 'I would ask you to come into the office for a longer chat but as you can see we are really busy today and somewhat short staffed.'

'Here is the file anyway.' Emma gestured. 'Please take it and attach it to your records.'

The lady took the file and Emma left walking almost mechanically down the steps and through the revolving bullet proof door. Suddenly she felt really alone. It was clear she was going to have to get herself out of this fix using her own steam. And who said prejudices only happen in faraway places she asked herself morosely.

Emma called Ivan who had taken the photos of Lea working in the shop to tell him she was back in the country and to thank both him and his wife for their help and support to help gather this important piece of evidence proving that Lea was certainly no stay at home mother.

'No problem.' replied Ivan. 'You seem to have got yourself into quite a fix.'

'It is terrible.' Emma replied. 'Sometimes I don't know if I am coming or going.'

'Why don't you come over for dinner one evening?' Ivan suggested.

'Yes thanks that would be nice.' Emma replied.

They fixed a date and Emma set off. It was only five minutes away from the new house. Ivan was tall, athletic, muscular and good looking. He gave the impression that he was not the sort of man to mess with. Jules had described him as a friend in security who helped him out from time to time. Emma got the impression that he was much more than that.

Ivan's wife Nathalie was by contrast small, slim, bubbly with startling blue eyes and naturally blond curly hair. She had an infectious laugh. Their five year' old daughter was exceptionally sweet and Emma got along with her immediately. She pulled Emma up to her bedroom and proudly showed off her latest toys. It was really good to be close to children again. It was something Emma was missing.

Ivan and Emma talked about different things as Nathalie prepared the dinner. Then Ivan remarked that he would quickly solve Emma's problems if it were left to him.

'How?' she asked curiously.

'We would go together to find your ex-husband and tell him that he had better start behaving responsibly and toe the line otherwise he would get punched.'

Emma laughed at the prospect. 'Sounds great but he would use it against me. They already blacken my name when I do nothing wrong. Imagine what they would do if I actually did something?' Emma explained. 'Lea and her first husband allegedly slashed one another's car tires during their divorce. Can you imagine?' Emma continued. She had always been shocked when she heard this story.

'Well if you and I went to Paul's place in the middle of the night and let his tires down then daubed paint over his lovely new BMW would you feel better?' Ivan asked chuckling at the idea.

'Sure but I could never agree to that – unfortunately, really unfortunately.' Emma added with a laugh. 'Just imagine we would then tell Jules what we had done.'

Suddenly Ivan started to laugh. He laughed so loud he was almost crying. Emma thought it was amusing but not hilarious.

Eventually Ivan stopped laughing and looked at Emma seriously.

'You know what?' Ivan hinted to Emma at the end of their enjoyable evening. 'Your problems could be related to Jules and Hubert Belette.'

'What do you mean?' Emma exclaimed in surprise.

'Think about it and good luck.' Ivan concluded as Emma left. Emma was confused. These comments did not make a lot of sense until much later of course.

Chapter 25

Early October Emma received a letter from Hubert Belette advising her that the date for the appeal court hearing against the temporary emergency judgment had been postponed to late January of the following year. This was contrary to what he had told her two weeks previously. The official confirmation arrived the next day from the court. Emma was shocked and in panic.

Mum will probably not be here anymore she wailed to herself and how can I possibly go another three months without my children. In the same fax, Hubert confirmed that he was doing his utmost to have an even earlier date for the first appeal which would settle the whole custody issue and this time in front of the appeal court, youth court section. Jules Mercier seemed to think that they were on the right track, reassuring Emma with every phone call that things would work out well for her and the children and everything would be solved in the very near future.

The children were due to spend their first weekend with Emma in the new house. Emma was looking forward to it and had lovingly arranged their new bedroom with all their toys and pictures. It looked cosy and inviting. Paul dropped them off on the Saturday morning. They came through the front door curious and excited about what they were to discover.

'Passport.' Paul demanded.

'Listen.' Emma protested. 'I am back in the country now so why do you still need my passport?'

'My lawyer says it is necessary.' Paul insisted.

'OK so here it is.' Emma said handing over the invalid one.

Paul drove off. He arrived back five minutes later knocking on the door and asking Emma to sign the usual declaration.

'Getting forgetful now are we?' she remarked ironically as she handed over the signed copy.

Olivia and Sebastian really seemed to like the new house. The bathroom had a huge tub and given their size, was almost like a mini swimming pool. Emma had also arranged for them to see their old school friends. Friends had always been important for Emma and she encouraged her children to have an active social life participating in dance classes, sporting activities, language classes, brownies and beavers on top of the school curriculum which they had done with enthusiasm.

To Emma's dismay, they had confided in her that they had been very worried about their new life in England because daddy had told them their mummy intended to send them to a very strict boarding school and subsequently they would not see either of their parents very often at all. Emma had to neutralize this fear now as soon as she could. Luckily she had a good job and lots of friends supporting her as she battled to get her children back home to live with her. It could have been much worse she consoled herself.

Emma urged Paul both directly and via Hubert Belette to let her go back to England during the half term holidays with Olivia and Sebastian to visit her mum for the last time. The answer remained categorical. Emma could see the children early November for six days but had to stay in the country. She began to feel increasingly desperate and heart broken.

Late October Paul dropped off the children one Saturday morning to spend the weekend with Emma. Meanwhile, Emma had followed Jules Mercier's advice and had purchased a Dictaphone which she positioned strategically behind the front door on top of the electricity box. How dare he blackmail me and my family like this she muttered to herself. Paul knocked on the door. Emma switched on the recorder and opened the door with a smile. The children ran inside the house. Emma closed the door between the living room and the hall.

Paul handed her the declaration to sign and asked again for her passport. She objected but he insisted that it was a continued necessity since she insisted to pursue her appeal in the appeal court. Emma took a deep breath and reiterated calmly but firmly that she wanted her mum to see her grandchildren for the last time.

'Agreed.' Paul repeated. 'But then you must agree to leave the children in my custody on 1st December when the temporary judgment expires because the appeal court hearing is in January.'

Emma continued undeterred. 'But you can't prevent the children from seeing their grandmother who has so little time left to live.'

'OK but the children are settled in their new school, they are happy, everything is going well.' Paul argued.

The couple disagreed on this point of course. Paul became more and more agitated. He accused Emma of trying to abduct the children, of being unreceptive to dialogue. Emma accused Paul of premeditating the whole thing and neglecting the children by locking them up alone overnight. She added his motives were principally financial. She pointed out that Paul ironically blamed her for losing his job, when in reality, according to what she had heard from an ex colleague of his, it had probably been due to him fiddling his expenses. Nothing to do with Emma. Paul looked at Emma in surprise before getting even more wound up.

'Put it in writing and I will sue you.' he threatened his voice rising two octaves.

Emma continued calmly adding that she found Paul's behaviour deeply dishonest to say the least. Paul retorted by saying it was the children's choice where they wanted to live and that the judge should listen to them.

Emma turned the conversation back to her mother and the request to take the children to see their grandmother for the last time.

'Only if you consider the 1st December and end of the temporary custody period as null and void.' he said again.

'That is blackmail.' Emma retorted as resolutely as she could.

'Perhaps.' Paul admitted ironically.

'You cannot play with grandparents like that.' she went on refusing to give in. 'The provincial court is not the competent authority in this affair anymore. Everything is now in the appeal court.' Emma added.

'Perhaps but it is not sure, not sure yet.' Paul replied. 'Hubert Belette is not telling you everything. I will tell you as much because … well I don't want to say anything anymore.'

'Carry on.' Emma prompted him, suddenly very curious by this admission.

'No you have to sort things out with your lawyer.' he went on. 'This is what you hope but the provincial court is completely competent. In addition, you have made grave accusations about the provincial court and for that reason you are going to have problems, huge problems because you think you can do anything but you have put your hand in a large wheelwork, a massive cog, you are going to see, you are going to see, you are going to have huge problems.' Paul announced with conviction and slightly triumphantly.

Emma was shocked but quickly regained her composure. She continued undeterred. 'I find it absolutely disgraceful that you are using blackmail so that my dying mum cannot see her grandchildren anymore.'

'No your mother can see the children' he continued 'but I do not see why I should always make a step towards you and you lead me by the end of the nose. If I make a step you make a step too. It is as simple as that.'

'The children will go back to their former school on 2nd December.' Emma added with conviction.

'We will see about that.' Paul shot back. 'Now give me your passport.' he demanded.

Emma almost threw the passport at him. He grabbed it and drove off quickly without looking back.

Emma was perplexed by the conversation and tried to make sense of it. She dared not tell her mother that they were coming to see her at half term. Nothing was sure. She felt concerned by Paul's words. Why was Hubert not telling her everything? What did Paul know that she did not? What was this big wheelwork and cog he referred to? Her mind raced. She had no answers and drained she went into the living room to play with Olivia and Sebastian and make the most of their precious hours together.

When the children were tucked up in bed, Emma made a couple of extra recordings of the conversation and as soon as they were on their way back to their father's the following afternoon, she set off to see Hubert Belette for an explanation. She took a seat in Hubert's living room on his dark brown checked sofa. His wife busied herself clearing away the dinner plates. Their small poodle kept jumping up and licking Emma's face. She diplomatically tried to push it away. It had already laddered her tights and although, in general, she was fond of dogs, this little thing was becoming a bit of a pest. Emma's mind was focused on Hubert's reaction. She put the tape in the player and they sat back and listened. His face remained expressionless throughout.

'What does Paul mean that you are not telling me everything?' she probed.

'Oh nothing.' Hubert replied. 'I cannot possibly think what he could mean. Do you have copies of the recording?' he asked Emma.

'Yes there are three.' she replied holding them up. 'One for you, one for Jules and one for the court.'

He thanked her and she left.

The day before the half term holidays, Paul called Emma in the office.

'If you don't let me go next week to England with the children to see mum before she dies' Emma said calmly and with a great deal of conviction 'then I will see that you regret it deeply for the rest of your days.'

There was a brief silence.

'OK' Paul replied. 'You can go. If anything happens to your mum before she sees Olivia and Sebastian for the last time, then I will not forgive myself.'

Emma could not believe her ears. The conciliatory moment was short lived.

'I am going to prove to the court that the children were not well followed in their last school when they lived with you.' Paul continued.

'Don't even try.' Emma advised. 'You know full well that they both had between 86% and 92% on their last school report.'

Paul hung up. Emma felt immensely relieved that the trip with the children to England was approved. She called Hubert Belette to get it in writing before calling her mum and aunty Hilda. The last thing she wanted was to give her mum the good news then to disappoint her. End of the afternoon, the long-awaited fax authorisation arrived and Emma made the phone call.

A couple of days later Emma was driving onto the ferry with Olivia and Sebastian safely in the back of the car. They stayed five days in the house where Emma had grown up. Emma's mum was now extremely frail but so pleased to see her grandchildren. She bought them their favourite sweets, Cadbury chocolate and Lincoln cream biscuits, two new Disney videos and made her last ever outing into town to buy them new anoraks and boots for winter. They savoured every minute. In no time at all, they were back and Emma dropped the children off at their father's place with a heavy heart.

Chapter 26

The following week Emma received an official notification from the court that Paul and Victor Falconer had filed another emergency action against her, this time in the provincial court in the city where Paul and the children were officially registered as living. They requested a prolongation of the temporary custody order indefinitely or until the final decision in the appeal court, whenever that would be.

In dismay Emma read through the document. It was an elaboration of the one filed the previous summer, full of lies and unjustified attacks on her person. Victor Falconer was now on home ground as well and the city had a well-known reputation for scandal and manipulation where things had their very own specific way of being handled. Emma's anxiety rose. She had just enjoyed a wonderful week with family and here she was being thrust into the gladiator's den once again.

Victor Falconer's papers highlighted the perfect willingness of Paul to spontaneously organise contact between Emma and the children, a conciliatory attitude which sharply contrasted with Emma's marked refusal to dialogue. He reinforced the danger which existed that Emma would take her children hostage again. Nothing justified the children being transferred in the middle of the school year back to their mother with whom they had very regular contact anyway. Emma suddenly felt sick.

There were of course now some new pieces of 'evidence' added to the file. Four of the teachers from the children's new school had given statements in Paul's favour confirming how settled the children were and what a good family background Paul and Lea provided. Paul's cleaning lady provided a written confirmation that she was aware of all the problems which Emma was causing Paul and his family, adding that at their father's place the children were treated like a little prince and princess, well dressed and well fed, which was not the case with their mother as they often arrived in a lamentable state with dirty, shabby and worn clothes, including safety pins holding the zip of an anorak together for over one year. Of course, the medical certificate from the family doctor was attached alleging Olivia had returned from England and a stay with her mother the year before in a state of exhaustion. Another of Paul's acquaintances, who had probably seen the children only twice, confirmed that when Emma called the children on the phone they had tears in their eyes and did not appear to want to speak to her.

Emma jumped into what was becoming an all too familiar defence mode providing counter evidence for the hearing. Valerie gave her a confirmation that as a former seamstress she had replaced the zip in the anorak which had stuck and broken within five days of it happening. Emma produced proof that she had spent over 700 € on the children's clothes, shoes and activities in the previous four months since the beginning of the school year. When this was presented to Victor Falconer and Paul the day of the hearing they shuffled uncomfortably.

Why do I have to go to such lengths? Emma asked herself. Any pretext was good to bring her down, even try to break her spirit. She remained indignant and determined for the children, refusing to let it get to her too much.

It was dark when Emma picked up Hubert Belette from his home for the hour drive to the provincial court in Paul's home town. She went into the living room.

'There please put those papers in my briefcase for me will you?' Hubert asked Emma. 'You know I have a bad back and cannot carry anything so I am going to have to ask you to carry everything for me today.'

'OK no problem.' Emma replied. 'When did you present the papers to the court for this hearing?' she asked. 'I have not seen a copy yet and I did ask you twice to see them in advance.'

'Oh I will do that this morning.' Hubert announced in a matter of fact manner.

'What again so late?' Emma lamented not wanting to be confrontational but now really concerned about a further delay which could jeopardize their case.

'It is OK.' Hubert replied curtly. 'The judge will read them before the final decision.'

Emma glared at Hubert. She was not so sure anymore. She thought back to the meticulously detailed submissions or written defence given to the court already by Victor Falconer, absolutely jam packed full of inventions but so well presented and suddenly felt very vulnerable and frightened.

'Do you have all the statements and evidence I gave you recently?' she asked Hubert anxiously.

'Yes.' he replied. 'Most of it is in my briefcase but I have not had any time to make any copies so I will give the originals to the court. Now come on.' he urged.

Emma had already been waiting for ten minutes and was beginning to feel annoyed. She really started to wonder if she had got the right lawyer. She picked up the briefcase and followed Hubert out of the house to the car.

When they arrived in the city they could not find the youth court as it was quite a distance from the main court building. Eventually, after asking several people, Emma and Hubert arrived nearly one hour late and Paul and Victor Falconer were starting to look worried. Hubert handed over his written defence and Victor

Falconer studied it quickly to see what additional evidence they had produced to counteract his latest tirade of inventions.

He was not happy about the confirmation and receipts for 700 € which Emma had spent on new clothes and shoes for the children nor two former colleague's statements about Paul's premeditated plan to snatch the children away from their mother. It was yet another public hearing to make an emergency decision. Again, the room was full of strangers listening and watching. They would again be watching her fight for her children in a language which was not her own. Emma felt that this was an intrusion into her private life but what choice did she have?

This time the judge was a lady. Their case was called forward. Victor Falconer began again with a series of untruths followed by Hubert who attempted to put their side of the story. The judge looked at Emma as if she was waiting for an explanation from her side.

Emma explained to the judge that she loved her children and was a very good mother adding that she certainly had not abducted them and the proof was she had moved back immediately to the country as soon as it was evident that there was a problem. In her opinion, things should now return to the situation before she left for England in line with the terms of the mutual consent divorce. At that point, Victor Falconer interrupted Emma and started turning things around again. Emma turned to him and said as calmly and as confidently as she could.

'Now look here why don't you just be quiet for a minute? I was in the middle of explaining the situation to the judge. You tell nothing but lies. You are a disgrace for your profession.'

The court fell silent. Emma felt at least twenty pairs of eyes fixed on her. Hubert continued.

'Look.' he said holding up the cassette which Emma had given to him and which contained Paul's admission that Emma did not know everything and had put her hand in a large wheelwork and was going to face huge problems. 'The children want to go back and live with their mother. There is no reason for the temporary judgment to be prolonged. Emma Brown is now back in the country.' Hubert stated with conviction.

Emma had recently reverted back to her maiden name and she was now happy that she was no longer referred to as Mrs Archer but Mrs Brown. Suddenly, on seeing the cassette, Paul panicked. He turned to Victor Falconer and said in a loud whisper 'Oh god I knew she was capable of doing something like this. I warned you.'

Victor Falconer's sharp features remained unflappable. Unperturbed he continued on with his counsel. Suddenly Emma noticed a marked change in the expression of the prosecutor's deputy, a middle aged man with a pointed face. Until now he had been sitting quietly watching the procedures, looking slightly bored by it all. Now all of a sudden he was very attentive, watching Victor Falconer with a complicity which Emma found completely strange and inexplicable. His eyes smiled and he hung onto every one of Victor Falconer's words.

'Well.' the judge finally suggested. 'Maybe we should give Mrs Brown a visiting right to see her children.' speaking about Emma as if she was almost abstract and not even present.

The prosecutor's deputy suddenly spoke wrapping up the procedures. 'The children should stay with their father.' he announced emphatically. 'There is no reason to change anything until the final custody hearing.'

'You can't take children away from their mother like that.' Hubert almost shouted at him.

'The hearing is over.' the judge announced. 'You will receive the judgment within the next ten days.'

It was what Emma had dreaded but also expected. She walked past Paul on her way out and whispered 'You have won this battle but you will not win the war.'

During the journey back Hubert tried to reassure Emma. 'Don't be pessimistic, we have not got the judgment yet.'

'I know what the outcome will be.' Emma replied flatly. 'The only place where we will get a fair hearing is in the appeal court.' she added. 'These provincial courts are so biased, one sided. It is unbelievable.'

The day the judgment was due to be pronounced, Emma tried to get hold of Hubert. She called his office and his home but no one seemed to know where he was.

'How can he do this to me and just disappear?' Emma lamented. She picked up the phone to call Jules Mercier. Whenever things were tough or difficult she always called Jules. He made her feel better, gave her hope and was her sounding board.

'Well that is strange that you cannot get hold of him. I have no idea where he is either, but don't worry I will call some friends in the court and we will get a copy of the judgment sent through.'

That afternoon Emma received a copy of the judgment. It was as she had expected. The temporary judgment was prolonged indefinitely and to top it all, Emma still had absolutely no official visiting right to see her children. She remained indefinitely at the mercy of Paul and his camp. The judgment stated that it was not in the interest of the children to change family environment and school again until a final custody decision was made, an appeal having been lodged with a date of late January for the proceedings.

In addition, Emma had produced no confirmation from her employer indicating that she was going to stay in the country. Emma was particularly put out with this last point. She had called

Hubert with her two directors nearly three months previously to ask precisely what he needed for the court and she had given him a copy of her new employment contract which deliberately stipulated that the company could not ask her to move more than twenty-five kilometres from their current location. She had even given Hubert a copy of her first salary slip following her return to the country. How can this be she asked herself feeling annoyed, surprised but completely helpless and manipulated.

Chapter 27

A couple of days later Emma received the call she had been dreading from Aunty Hilda. Her dear mum's health had deteriorated sharply and her days were numbered. Emma booked a flight immediately and flew over to England that evening.

Emma's boss was very supportive. She sympathetically told Emma to take as much time off as she needed. Emma's mum had never liked hospitals and had expressed her wish to die at home with her family around her. Emma's sister Laura was also driving up with her two year' old son that afternoon.

They were very difficult days and they got through them in a sort of a daze. They had always been a close family and that helped in these moments of extreme sorrow. Emma's mum got weaker by the day and was soon confined to bed. She was frightened of course. No one wants to let go of life. Emma, Laura and Aunty Hilda took it in turns to sit by her bed both day and night.

'I am so glad you came over.' she said holding Emma's hand and turning to face her. 'You carry on fighting to get those children back do you hear me? And don't trust that rich cousin living in the USA. This situation did not happen on its own.'

'Yes mum.' Emma replied stroking her mum's hand.

'I am very proud of you Emma and also of Laura. You are a credit to your father and myself.'

Emma's eyes filled with tears. Her mum weighed scarcely more than 6 stone by now and it was heart-breaking for Emma to see her mum who had always been so strong and supportive waste away in front of her eyes. Two days before her mum passed away, Emma received a phone call early one morning from Cathy.

'Hello.' Emma replied sleepily.

'Emma' Cathy announced. 'You have been burgled. I came around to the house this morning and it was so cold in the living room. I went into the kitchen and the door to the garage was open and the garage window was smashed.'

'Oh' Emma replied. That was all she could muster. She felt so empty and dazed and even an earthquake could not have moved her.

'Don't worry.' Cathy continued taking things in hand. 'I will call the police and get someone round to repair the window. Take care now and let me know when you will be coming back.' and she hung up.

'What was that?' Laura asked rubbing her eyes and slowly waking up.

'Oh my new house has been burgled.' Emma replied flatly adding 'You know when it rains it pours.'

Laura shook her head. Two days later in the early hours Emma's mum passed away. It was early December. The undertaker came in the middle of the night and took her away. Emma thought her heart was going to break as they carried the coffin out of the house. Laura, Emma and Aunty Hilda hugged and comforted one another. They made a cup of tea and sat silently together lost in their own thoughts and grief.

Emma's mum had fought on valiantly for eleven months, five months longer than the doctors had originally given her. Emma was due to see Olivia and Sebastian for the weekend and Laura and Aunty Hilda encouraged her to go back the following day to prepare for the weekend. She also had the burglary to sort out. As the taxi drove across the hills to the airport, Emma looked up at the full moon shining brightly which seemed to follow them all the way. Her mum felt close. She was now at peace and would no longer be suffering Emma tried to comfort herself.

Emma phoned Valerie from the airport and Valerie promised to come over when she arrived home. Cathy was also there to greet her.

'We are so sorry about your mum.' they both said hugging Emma. 'Me too.' Emma replied, hot tears streaming down her face.

'You know.' Valerie began. 'We have been thinking. This burglary is very strange. Nothing is upset. Just a few cupboards open but nothing taken. Just your jewellery box is on the landing floor as if this is what they were after.'

'The police did not dust for finger prints.' Cathy added. 'They just opened a file confirming the break-in which you will need for your insurance company. Has anything been taken from the jewellery box?' she asked.

Emma looked before replying 'Yes just some minor items in gold, but this is strange because my engagement ring, wedding ring and the diamond and emerald ring which Paul bought me during a trip to Sri Lanka are still there. They were together with the other stuff so I don't understand why there were not taken too.' Emma concluded.

Cathy and Valerie looked at each other. 'Emma' Valerie continued. 'I had our locksmith come around to look at the damage because you are going to have to put new locks on the kitchen door. He took a look and asked me if you had problems with someone because it appears to be a very professional sort of job.'

The two locks on the kitchen door had been meticulously carved out to get into the house. Emma reached into her handbag and took out the cassette with the recording.

'They could have been looking for this.' she said suddenly feeling uneasy. 'I will have some more copies made and sent to friends in five different countries for safekeeping.' she added.

That evening Olivia and Sebastian arrived for the weekend. Emma broke the sad news about grandma whom they had seen less than one month before and they both cried. Emma joined in. They spent a quiet weekend together. It was a comfort for Emma to have the children there and to hug them.

She flew back to England the following week to make arrangments for the funeral with Laura and Aunty Hilda. It was a very emotional week. Family, friends and neighbours were wonderful. Emma's mum had been well liked and had helped so many people in her life. Everyone wanted to pay their respects.

The day after Emma arrived back, she flew with three colleagues on a four-day trip to the USA for a worldwide meeting. Her boss assured her she did not have to go.

'We understand if you prefer to stay in the office after all you have been through in the last couple of weeks.' Emma insisted on going on the trip as she wanted to keep herself busy and did not want time to reflect. It was still all too painful.

Opening hours in America were quite something, especially in December with the run up to Christmas. Emma managed to get some Christmas shopping done after the meetings in fact quite a lot of it and it was a great comfort to buy Olivia and Sebastian some nice clothes and a mini computer each for Christmas.

'It is great for the US economy when you European ladies get loose in the shops.' the American president of the company joked.

Waking up from the overnight flight back as the plane came into land, Emma reminded herself, as a reflex action, that she would have to call her mum to tell her she had arrived back safely. Suddenly she remembered that mum was now gone and tears came into her eyes. God how I am going to miss her Emma told herself.

Chapter 28

The day of her return from the USA, Emma met Jules Mercier and they went to their favourite Italian restaurant for lunch.

'We just have to get the children back in the appeal court end of January.' she declared desperately.

'Yes it will be OK.' he reassured her.

'But I have not seen any of Hubert's papers for the court yet.' she protested. 'He keeps telling me he is finishing them. Then every week there seems to be another delay. It is worrying me. We cannot afford to miss yet another deadline. I am sending him fax reminders every other day and also calling him at home. You know he has problems with the other lawyer his is sharing the new office with. He tells me she will not let him install a phone line and that he suspects she may be fiddling with his computer when he is not there and deleting some files. You know Jules this is really concerning me. It is not normal. However, I am trying my best to find a work around. I now drive all paperwork and supporting documents in the evening to his house ten minutes from the office and drop them in his letterbox. I have told him if he needs any photocopies I will make them in the office and drop them off the same day. You see Jules I really am doing everything I possibly can to help. All Hubert needs to do now is finish and file our defence. Everything is clear and we have so many elements and pieces of evidence I simply do not understand it.' Emma explained in frustration.

'We still have time.' Jules reassured her. 'The deadline to deposit the papers with the court should be two weeks before the hearing.' he added with authority.

'Yes perhaps but why leave everything to the last minute?' Emma continued undeterred. 'We have already lost so much time. It is much better to be early for once. Just what is the matter with him Jules? Has he got personal problems?' Emma suddenly asked.

'Well yes.' Jules admitted. 'Recently his daughter from his wife's first marriage committed suicide and his wife is taking it rather badly. When they married he insisted she put the daughter in a home. Then they had another daughter together, you know you met her once, and now she will not speak to her father anymore.'

'Oh.' Emma said in surprise thinking to herself what a horrible thing to happen and suspecting there was a lot more to this story than met the eye. 'We all have problems but we have to try to not let them interfere with our work.' Emma confessed in her defence and also from her own personal experience. 'Will you speak and write to him Jules please?' Emma pleaded. 'He will listen to you perhaps more than me.'

'Sure I will do it next week.' Jules replied.

Emma paid the bill and they parted.

Christmas came and Emma headed to her sister Laura's home. They had a quiet time very much aware of the empty place at the table. Mum was often in their thoughts but they put on a brave face for the children. That is what she would have wanted they told themselves. Laura's parents in law were also there. Her father in law had just retired. He had been a solicitor all his life, like his own father who had also been a prominent member of the law society. He asked Emma how things were going in the courts. She briefly explained the judgments so far. He looked concerned.

'Emma I do not have a good feeling about this whole affair. I do not trust their system. Something is amiss. It is not normal. Things are obviously done very differently over there.' he confessed.

An unease swept over Emma. She was still persuading and reassuring herself that she would regain custody of her children in the appeal court end of January. Now here was a professional opinion sowing the seeds of doubt. She tried to remain optimistic but she also began to worry even more.

As soon as she arrived back the first thing she did was to fax and phone Hubert asking for a copy of the court papers covering their impending appeal. It was already early January and the days were ticking by.

'Come to my office tomorrow.' he proposed as though he now had everything under control. 'We can finalise everything together.'

Emma arrived five minutes early anxious and eager to finish things. She told herself that she was not leaving until she could see that everything was done. Hubert was in a shabby brown jacket and dark trousers. He darted around notably to the kitchen to make some tea and his business like impersonal manner combined with his somewhat high pitched voice was beginning to seriously grate on Emma for the first time.

Hubert handed Emma a copy of their case defence with supporting documentation. It seemed to be in order and what they had discussed previously with Jules. Emma read the supporting pieces of evidence again. She fell on a handwritten letter from her mother back in August following the provincial court judgment granting Paul temporary custody addressed to the appeal court which Hubert had asked her to write. Aunty Hilda had immediately taken the bus into town to fax it through from the town stationers. Emma's eyes filled with tears as she read it through but she also felt frustrated and angry. The letter had never been presented, the summer holiday had never happened and it was now too late anyway.

Mr President it began. I am deeply shocked by the recent emergency judgment preventing my grandchildren from visiting me from the 15th to 30th August. I am suffering from pancreatic cancer and unable to travel long distances and I was so much looking forward to seeing Olivia and Sebastian again. Time passes by so quickly and as each day comes, I treat life as a bonus. An added bonus would be to see my grandchildren. Thank you.

'So' Emma asked sternly for the first time looking up from the letter in her mum's familiar handwriting. 'just where are we?'

'Well as you can see' Hubert explained 'everything is ready. We just need to file.'

'So what are you waiting for?' Emma challenged. 'We are in court in under three weeks and even Jules confirms it is now high time to make sure our papers are filed with the court.' Emma continued.

'I will do the necessary this week.' Hubert replied.

'How can I be sure?' Emma shot back.

Hubert stared at Emma in surprise.

'If I say it will be done it will be done.' he almost snapped back.

'I am going to Malta for four days' end of the week for an international sales meeting.' Emma explained quickly changing the subject. 'Before I leave I will fax you the phone and fax number of the hotel so if anything comes up you can reach me. OK?'

'Oh Malta.' Hubert exclaimed. 'Yes I like Malta, know it quite well.' he quirked.

'Really? Did you use to go there on holiday?' Emma asked.

'No.' Hubert replied proudly. 'Just to conclude contracts, arms contracts, used to be my specialty.'

Emma sat back in surprise. She felt uneasy. What in the world was a lawyer whose specialty was negotiating arms contracts doing defending her and her children in a complex family case? The two did not seem compatible. She thanked Hubert and left. As she waited for the lift to take her down to the ground floor, her mind shot back two years ago to the time she had dropped in at Jules Mercier's house to hand over a paper for the mutual consent divorce proceedings and Jules had said to her in amusement 'Hey look there on the TV news they have found a large consignment of arms stashed away in my old house which is now empty.'

Emma shuddered. It must be a complete coincidence she tried to reassure herself. This man was a former judge and member of the justice ministry and it was inconceivable that he could be involved in something so improper. She quickly dismissed it from her mind and hurried back to the car.

Chapter 29

Emma spent another enjoyable weekend with Olivia and Sebastian. She was now seeing the children every second weekend as so generously authorised by Paul. Emma had decided to take the children to a child psychologist to ensure that they felt OK and that no longer term damage was being done as a result of the ongoing conflicts with Paul and their changing circumstances. The children drew pictures and started to talk frankly.

Life in their father's home was quite severe. They did not have a lot of friends. They preferred their former school. They were shouted at if they did not conform. They remembered daddy often shouting at mummy. They did not like the girl who looked after them after school. They missed Emma. The child psychologist concluded to Emma that if Olivia and Sebastian were still reasonably balanced and not over duly perturbed by the whole affair, it was principally thanks to Emma and the love and support she was giving them in the less frequent moments they spent together. She advised Emma to keep this up and reassured her that she was on the right track. Emma felt relieved. Once the children come back we can carry on with our lives without any scars from the past she told herself.

As she walked to the car, her mind wandered back to a conversation she had had with Lea's former husband, the doctor, following the temporary custody judgment. He had confided in Emma that Olivia and Sebastian might not be happy in their new home. Lea could never accept anyone else's children. She had even given her own children a hard time. His own daughter from his first marriage had refused for four years to come to the house to see him because Lea had been so mean to her.

Lea had also recently told his daughter that she was glad she had left her father because Paul had lots of money and could keep her in the style in which she thought she should be accustomed. Emma had laughed at the irony of these words. Many of her friends including Rachel had since warned her that Paul would soon be after her for maintenance for the children. He loves money they said, you know him. The children are also a means to increase his monthly income.

Chapter 30

It was over one of their familiar lunches that Jules Mercier first shared with Emma his deep interest in freemasonry. Until this conversation, Emma had very little knowledge of what freemasonry comprised. She knew only that it was a secret association of men who formed a sort of brotherhood, helped one another in friendship and gave to charity.

She had an uncle who was a freemason but he had spoken very little about it. It just did not seem to be one of those things which people asked questions about or perhaps, put more succinctly, were encouraged to ask questions about.

Jules went on to explain what a significant part of his life freemasonry was, how good it was to belong, what a pleasure it was to be able to help out a fellow brother and then added proudly that his father had been one of the top freemasons in the country.

'Oh' Emma commented in surprise. 'So how long have you been a mason then?'

'Oh a very long time.' Jules replied nostalgically. 'Over forty years.'

'And what about Hubert then, is he also a mason?' Emma enquired.

'Oh yes he is also a mason of course.' Jules confirmed as if it was a given.

The conversation moved on to other things.

'Hubert has submitted his written defence to the appeal court this week.' Emma updated Jules. 'Only a few days now and we will be in court. I really do hope to get the children back. I miss them so much.' Emma added.

'It will work out.' Jules said comfortingly. 'You are a good mother and they will not deprive you of your children.'

Emma asked the waiter for the bill. She was intending to go to court with Hubert the following week.

'Keep me posted on developments.' Jules asked Emma kissing her on both cheeks and saying goodbye.

'Don't worry I will.' she replied. 'You will be the first to know.'

The appeal court hearing was getting near. With every approaching day Emma became more nervous. The future of her children, their happiness depended on it. The day before the hearing she received a phone call from Hubert Belette.

'I can't stay long.' he said. 'I just wanted to let you know that tomorrow's court hearing has been postponed. Very important matter came up you understand, to do with paedophiles. This has to take precedence over standard cases like ours. But don't worry I will soon receive a new date for the hearing, maximum a couple of weeks and then I will call you back.'

Before Emma had chance to utter a word he was gone. She sat in her office stunned and shocked. She had been preparing herself psychologically for so long for this big day which had been officially confirmed to them nearly four months ago and then suddenly it was just postponed like that. Something was amiss. Emma just could not buy it. She went home in a pretty sombre mood. Angry, disappointed but feeling equally helpless.

She decided to call Jules Mercier next day and play hell. After all he had sung Hubert's praises so loudly and recommended his services. Emma had trusted Jules as an honourable retired judge. Now he had to find them a way out of this latest unfortunate predicament.

'Please don't' get angry with me.' Jules pleaded to Emma next morning on the phone. 'I am on your side. I wrote to Hubert as promised and told him to submit his papers. If the court decides to change the date, then it is out of our control.'

'I don't trust this latest delay.' Emma went on. 'You cannot tell me it is normal. We wait four months for a hearing in the appeal court and then it is suddenly postponed the day before. Sorry Jules it just does not add up.' Emma objected almost shouting.

'Then call the court yourself. You can get the number from the director of enquiries. It is the fifth chamber.' Jules suddenly proposed.

'I will.' Emma replied sharply and hung up. She looked outside her office window at the well-kept lawns and felt almost ashamed of her outburst. She sighed, picked up the phone and got hold of the number she needed to call the court. After three rings the court clerk answered.

'Hello.' Emma said trying to sound as polite and as business like as she could. 'I really would be most grateful for your help. My name is Emma Brown and my case number 322 was due to be heard this morning. Apparently it has been postponed. Could you kindly give me the new date?'

'Yes just a moment.' the court clerk replied as she checked her papers. 'Oh' she exclaimed adding 'Well actually your ex-husband and your counsel Hubert Belette are currently in the court room fixing together a new date with the judge. It appears that not all the defence papers were submitted on time.'

'Thank you very much for the information.' Emma blurted before putting down the receiver. She clenched her fists. 'I don't bloody well believe it.' she muttered to herself. 'I am going to strangle someone.'

Initial anger was soon overcome by worry. Her children, when would she now get them back? It seemed endless. Whom could she trust? Literally the whole system, even her own counsel seemed to be working against her. It was an absolute nightmare. She would give Hubert Belette two hours to get home from the court for lunch then she would call and confront him. Boy was she mad. She told herself maybe it was better she calmed down before she called, lest she say something rash.

Emma got up from her desk and headed to the toilet. On her way back she bumped into her boss in the corridor.

'Are you OK Emma?' her boss enquired concerned. 'You don't look very happy.'

'I am not.' Emma shot back. 'I think my lawyer is double crossing me.'

'What?' her boss exclaimed in surprise. 'You have to be kidding me.'

'Afraid not.' Emma assured her. 'I just called the court.'

'Gosh, you have to dump him, get rid of him immediately. He is bad news. A huge liability. Listen our company attorney is visiting me this afternoon. When we have finished, I will ask him to come over and see you and you can ask for his advice.' she continued helpfully but obviously perplexed.

'Thanks a million.' Emma replied gratefully. 'What would I do without you?'

'Find another one.' she laughed.

At lunchtime Emma called Hubert's home. His wife Suzanne answered.

'I need to speak urgently to your husband.' Emma began.

'I am afraid he is not here. Can I take a message?'

'Yes.' Emma said loudly. She hesitated. It was not fair to shout at this poor woman. It was not her fault and from what Jules Mercier had told her recently, she already had enough problems with the recent suicide of her daughter.

'Look Mrs Belette.' Emma explained calmly. 'I have a big problem. Your husband told me that our court case was postponed unilaterally by the court and when I checked myself with the court, it appears that he was arranging a new date with my ex-husband and his counsel in front of the judge. You know yourself how long I have been waiting for this hearing and how important it is for me to regain custody of my children. Just whatever is going on?'

'Listen I am really sorry.' Suzanne replied sympathetically. 'I have absolutely no idea. You really must speak to my husband.'

'OK'. Emma said. 'I understand so why don't you please ask him to call me as soon as he gets home.'

'OK' she agreed. 'I will pass on the message.

That afternoon Emma's company attorney Edgar came into her office. She stood up and greeted him. They had worked together on a couple of occasions in the past and got on well.

'Nice of you to stop by.' Emma began gratefully.

'Yes I understand you are having a few problems with our legal system.' he continued.

'Just a few.' Emma replied ironically. 'Listen Edgar I could really do with a bit of sound advice.'

'No problem Emma.' Edgar continued helpfully. 'Now what is the issue?'

Emma briefly explained the situation.

'It sounds as though you urgently need a lawyer you can trust.' he announced emphatically.

'I will put together a file for you with copies of the judgments so far and submissions from both parties as well as the two outstanding appeals and if you could direct me from there I would be very grateful.' Emma offered immediately. 'By the way what do I owe you?' she asked.

'Nothing.' Edgar smiled. He looked pensive as he stood up and shook her hand before leaving.

They agreed that Emma would provide all the papers and Edgar would study them and come back to her within the week.

That afternoon Paul called Emma in the office. He seemed triumphant. He announced that the appeal had been postponed until the end of April and that he would confirm the dates on which she could see the children up until Easter. She listened partly in shock but partly because she wanted him to carry on talking.

He went on to tell her that he was of course a member of two national organisations which helped fathers to secure parental rights and support in cases where children were abducted by their mother. Emma almost sobbed at the irony. How clever he was. It was just amazing how the truth could be distorted she told herself.

He went on to rub in the fact that the judges were against her even that very morning in the appeal court because she had tried to reduce his visiting rights then abduct the children. He went on to say that if the children wanted to come back and live with Emma, then the first thing he would do would be to drive them back himself but not until a social enquiry or interview of the children by the judge had clearly revealed this. Emma felt so manipulated and trapped. She mustered some courage and replied. 'Victor Falconer played the system to prolong the proceedings in your favour.'

'Perhaps.' Paul replied with a certain degree of irony.

Paul wrapped up the call reminding Emma that he was not forced to give her a visiting right to see her children, he simply did it for the children. She had never felt so alone or abandoned by all reason in her whole life. She was further away than ever from being reunited with her children. The only thing she wanted to do was to go home and sleep and forget about everything for a few hours.

Hubert Belette came back to Emma a few days later with Jules Mercier. He was apologetic. It was a genuine case of the court postponing because Victor Falconer had not presented all his papers on time. A new date was set for end of April for the appeal against the emergency temporary custody decision but in the meantime the first appeal against the provincial court judge who had refused a social enquiry would be reactivated by Hubert and all papers lodged promptly with the appeal court, youth section. The details of the case were apparently the same and Hubert intimated that this case could even be heard before the appeal scheduled for late April and they could regain custody of the children then even earlier.

'You know.' he stressed quite emotionally to Emma's surprise. 'I told your ex-husband that it was inhuman to treat your dying mum like that. I laid into him now you understand. I don't agree at all with what he did.'

'Fine.' Emma replied 'Then please do the necessary with the next appeal.'

However, she did not trust Hubert anymore, not one inch, and she earnestly awaited Edgar's feedback. It came a few days later.

'Emma,' Edgar explained over the phone. 'the adverse party have succeeded in painting to the courts a completely black picture of you. When you tried to reduce your ex-husband's visiting rights they saw you as a trouble maker and gave him the benefit of the doubt.'

'But I had several genuine concerns about how he was looking after the children at the time.' Emma replied. 'Does this have no significance?'

'Well your counsel could have expressed them in a better way without asking for such a drastic measure.' Edgar continued.

'I see' Emma replied. 'and now I don't even have a visiting right to see my own children and have seen them for just thirty-eight days in the last nine months.' Emma went on.

'Emma you urgently need a very good lawyer you can trust and who is an expert in family law.' Edgar explained. 'We have to start to completely turn around this devastating image which has been painted of you.'

'OK.' Emma admitted as the light began to dawn on her how badly advised she had been. 'So where do we go from here?' she asked Edgar.

'Listen I am not an expert myself in family law but I know a good person, a lawyer himself who can definitely point us in the right direction.'

'Fine.' Emma replied very gratefully. 'Can you please set up an appointment as soon as possible for us to meet?'

'Consider it done.' Edgar declared his voice sounding friendly and reassuring. He was certainly trying his best to help.

Although Emma began to see things more clearly, she still had difficulty accepting that the judges involved so far had not scratched a little deeper below the surface and she could not help feeling uneasy that some additional forces might be at play against her. However, she had no idea yet just what those could be.

Chapter 31

As Emma had been expecting for a while, Hubert Belette called her to advise that Victor Falconer was insisting that Emma start to pay Paul a maintenance payment for Olivia and Sebastian. The sum of 400 € per month was mentioned. He stressed that this was in accordance with the jurisprudence of the courts and could be imposed retroactively.

Emma had had considerable expense breaking the lease on her house in England to move back and felt this was the final insult. The little money she had left over she preferred to use to spoil the children when she was lucky enough to have them in her company. In addition, they had explained to Emma that they had to wear second hand clothes and hand me downs from Lea's son. Treats were rare and they participated in no extra curriculum activities.

Emma ran a report on Lea's business. They had run up losses of 20.000 € over a nine-month period. Emma's colleague who had grown up in the town Paul and Lea were now living asked her parents to go and check out the shop. They reported back that it seemed to be closed for transformation but the shop keeper opposite had confirmed that it had gone bankrupt. A further informal enquiry with other neighbouring shop keepers revealed that Lea had a reputation for badly treating her staff. Emma called Hubert back.

'The answer is no.' she stated emphatically adding 'Over my dead body.'

'But you might be forced to contribute.' Hubert insisted.

'Let them try.' Emma responded emotionally. 'I will go to the end of the earth to reveal this incredible set up. Now enough is enough do you understand me?'

'Yes.' he replied.

A couple of weeks later the children inadvertently let slip that their dad had claimed that Hubert Belette had mentioned that Emma was crazy.

'Oh.' Emma exclaimed. 'I don't think so do you?'

'No mum.' they both replied.

Emma asked herself just how could Paul have possibly heard and then said that unless ……

Middle of February Emma called the appeal court clerk, youth section, to check if Hubert Belette's written defence had been received as he had already promised twice over the previous couple of weeks. Nothing had been deposited so far. Emma sighed, then sat down and wrote Hubert a letter.

As she had so far received no definitive date from his side, she had called the appeal court herself only to be stupefied to learn that no date for the hearing had been fixed despite his written promises. She demanded immediately an explanation from his side. She reminded him that it was the third time in three weeks that he had hidden the truth from her and she could not and would not continue to work in this manner.

She reminded him her children had been torn away from her seven months ago in a very bad judgment and she did not even have a visiting right. She reminded him she had spent close to 5000 € on his fees for this service. She and her children were suffering considerably from the situation and in short it was completely unacceptable. She demanded an immediate written response. She copied Jules Mercier. Jules called her first.

'That was quite a tough letter you wrote to Hubert.' he remarked.

'Yes I know.' Emma defended herself. 'But what do you want me to do? My back is against the wall. Anyway, I am already looking for a new lawyer.'

'What?' Jules exclaimed instantly. 'I can help.'

'No thanks.' Emma retorted. 'Hubert was your hot tip and look where it got us, nowhere apart from a whole lot of trouble.'

'Well I will write him a letter and give you a copy.' Jules offered appeasingly. 'Yes, it is unfortunate he was always so good in the past. I really do not understand what happened this time. I really do apologise Emma.'

A few days later Jules Mercier handed Emma a copy of a letter he had sent to Hubert asking him to explain why there had been so many delays and why it appeared that Victor Falconer was calling the shots at his leisure. He went on to write that he understood nothing anymore and invited Hubert to meet him at his initiative and explain. He hoped Hubert was not angered by his letter but he had to respect his clients. He asked if Hubert wanted to drop the file which he hoped to avoid. He signed it fraternally yours, a reference, Emma wondered, to their warm and longstanding masonic relationship.

Paul had decided that in March he was going skiing with the children then the following weekend to Euro Disney. As a result, Emma did not see Olivia and Sebastian for four weeks. These seemed some of the longest of her life but there was absolutely nothing she could do about it.

She used the time to try to sort out her new legal counsel. She had accompanied Edgar to meet his friend, a young academic type with glasses and a tank top. They had spent two hour discussing the file around the kitchen table in his flat. He got up a couple of times to make tea and the three of them continued with the discussions as they sipped the warm brew.

He basically confirmed what Edgar had said. Emma's name had been severely blackened and now they had to start to repair the damage. He knew one of the best lawyers specialised in family law who also lectured at the university.

Getting the children back home would be a very long and hard process and they might even have to stay with their father until they were eighteen years old. Emma stood on the pavement with Edgar afterwards in the dimly lit street. It was raining and the scene just seemed fitting as she felt the hot tears roll down her cheeks. Edgar looked at her sympathetically.

'We will do everything possible to help you regain custody of your children. Now think positive.' he told her.

Emma thanked him gratefully for all his help and they agreed to speak the following week.

Edgar called Emma a few days later.

'I spoke to my friend again.' he said. 'Although he was a little pessimistic at the beginning, he thinks that if you can show that you were set up, this puts a completely different light on things. When are you seeing the new lawyer?' he asked.

'Next Tuesday.' Emma replied.

'Good luck. Keep me posted and let me know if you need any more help.' Edgar offered encouragingly.

Emma nervously went into the new lawyer's office. She had read the file in advance. She was about Emma's age, attractive with noticeably penetrating eyes and she exuded authority and experience despite her relatively young age. Emma could easily imagine her lecturing at the university. She had a large picture of her two smiling children on her office wall.

'Lovely children you have.' Emma commented.

'Yes' she smiled. 'Now about your file.' she continued immediately getting down to business. 'You have been very foolish and badly advised. How could you try to reduce your ex-husband's visiting rights? This is like a red rag to a bull in court especially when the judge is a man who has just gone through a painful divorce himself.' she asked looking Emma straight in the eyes.

Emma looked back at her sheepishly. 'There were issues with the way the visiting right was taking place. Even the child psychologist was concerned.' Emma explained.

'Well for one I would never have advised you to take the route you did.'

'It is a pity I did not have you as my lawyer at the time.' Emma commented 'Can you please help me?' Emma asked almost pleadingly.

'Not personally.' came the reply. 'I am much too busy to take on such a complicated case but I think I know someone who can. This lady has a lifetime of experience and she actually trained me. You are very hurt and shaken and she will also help you to put things back into perspective.'

The lawyer stood up and handed over to Emma the name and address of Mrs Sinclair. They walked together to the lift.

'You know' she concluded wistfully. 'your ex-husband has acted in a very irresponsible and selfish way. The children will not forget and it risks to boomerang back at him in the future. Good luck.'

They shook hands, Emma thanked her again and she left.

That evening Emma had arranged to go with a former colleague and friend to London for the weekend to meet up with two of their good friends. She left her car in the little village outside his home and they set off together in his sports car. She told him about her meeting that afternoon.

'Emma you must never give up. You must carry on and you will succeed eventually.' he assured her.

'Yes I agree.' Emma replied starting to feel more confident that she was about to get back on a better footing. 'Thanks for the words of encouragement.' she smiled.

They had a great weekend and it allowed Emma to enjoy herself and take her mind off things for a couple of days at least. Olivia and Sebastian were skiing with their father although it should have been one of the weekends assigned to Emma. She made a conscious effort that she was not going to let it get to her.

Chapter 32

The following week Emma went to meet her new counsel, Mrs Sinclair, for the first time. Edgar had been kind enough to make the introductory call on her behalf. He had confided in Emma that Jules Mercier had called him directly to see how things were going and asked if he could help. Edgar had replied politely no thank you.

Emma was nervous. Just where was she going to begin? It had become such a complicated story. Mrs Sinclair opened the door and beckoned her to come into her office. She smiled welcomingly. Emma immediately felt at ease. Her office was tidy, light, there were a lot of files and activity but things looked so much better organised than what she had witnessed so far with Hubert Belette. This was a first good sign. Mrs Sinclair herself was distinguished, chic, well dressed. She looked decidedly younger than her age.

'Well young lady.' she smiled looking straight at Emma. 'Why don't you explain what I can do for you?'

They conversed for about an hour. Emma did most of the talking trying to explain as clearly as she could everything which had happened since the beginning. Mrs Sinclair listened intently only interrupting from time to time when something was not one hundred percent clear. Emma saw Mrs Sinclair forming a picture of her case in her mind, working out what the strategy should be. When Emma had finished, Mrs Sinclair sprang into action.

'Well the first thing we must do is get the file from Hubert Belette. I will write to him immediately.' she announced. 'We only have six weeks until the court hearing and we have to move very fast. I am staying at home over the Easter weekend. How about you?'

'I should have the children the week before so yes I am also free that weekend.' Emma replied adding 'You know my file takes precedence. I am free to help you at whatever time suits you best.'

Emma had wanted to go to Tenerife with Olivia and Sebastian the first week of the Easter holidays and take Aunty Hilda with them. She had done so much to help Emma's mum during her illness nursing her for nearly one year and Emma had always considered her like a second mum. With the change of lawyers, the authorisation from Paul had not been forthcoming so Emma had not dared book anything. Suddenly all flights were booked.

The authorisation arrived two days before the holiday. Determined to still have a break in the sun, Emma booked them all on a scheduled flight to Nice for a week finding a comfortable hotel via the web with an indoor pool for the children. She made the reservation. It was all done within half an hour much to her relief. She was determined that Paul and company were not going to scupper her plans. Aunty Hilda was thrilled. She admitted she loved the South of France and actually preferred it to Tenerife. Olivia and Sebastian were excited. They were taking another plane and going to the seaside and they loved swimming, so the pool was a big plus too.

Emma's file finally arrived from Hubert Belette the morning before their departure. It had taken one month and three letters from Mrs Sinclair, numerous phone calls and the intervention of the president of the bar following two letters from Mrs Sinclair and one from Emma herself. The file was in an utter and total state of disarray.

Aunty Hilda and Emma worked non-stop for ten hours to classify and file all the correspondence in chronological order so that Mrs Sinclair could already begin to work on it. Luckily Emma had kept detailed copies of most of the correspondence and court rulings which she had handed over to Mrs Sinclair as soon as she had agreed to take on the case so they could make a start.

'They are not going to make it easy.' Aunty Hilda commented. 'I never liked that Belette fellow, smelt a rat from the beginning.'

'Aunty Hilda,' Emma confessed as they were having dinner together that evening. 'I have something to share with you. You know how much I miss mum. Well I did something which you might not entirely approve of but with the most honourable of intentions. Last week I went to see an internationally renowned medium with Valerie. Valerie told me that this special lady could transmit messages from loved ones, always with a positive intention. The medium works with the police to help locate missing children. She has a good reputation, has been on TV and radio, and has foreseen many a natural disaster. She also fights for the rights of underprivileged children and animals. She recently lost her husband and told us she sits in his armchair in the evening chatting to him.' Emma smiled.

The prospect of the medium chatting to her late husband from his armchair seemed so ironic, almost funny.

'Oh!' replied Aunty Hilda her interest surprisingly aroused. 'Tell me more.'

Emma continued. 'She works with photos of loved ones, deceased of course. Remember the lovely black and white portraits of mum and dad in their early twenties? Well I took them along.'

Suddenly Aunty Hilda seemed intrigued. She did not scold Emma for having dabbled in what some might consider the occult or unknown.

'I laid the photos along with everyone else on the table and waited.' Emma elaborated. 'Suddenly the medium picked up mum's photo, held it up and asked in front of the eighty or so assembled audience who it belonged to. I hesitantly put up my hand.' Emma admitted. 'The medium went onto describe with precision mum, her character, her life, what she died of and even explained the pain she had in her ankles during the final months of her illness.'

'Dropsy?' Aunty Hilda interrupted.

'Exactly.' Emma replied. 'Well she confirmed that mum is now happy and was standing at the side of a gentleman with a very large moustache. I admitted, when she asked me, that I did not know who that could be. Have you any idea Aunty Hilda?'

Aunty Hilda looked at Emma in astonishment then added almost in a matter of fact manner 'oh that's our grandfather.'

It was now Emma's turn to look back in astonishment.

'What else did mum say?' Aunty Hilda prompted.

'Well the medium apparently told me that mum was really insisting on passing on a very clear message which happens quite rarely.'

'What message?' Aunty Hilda asked taking a sip of sweet white wine. She suddenly looked quite moved. The sisters had been close for over sixty years. Emma felt tears coming to her eyes.

'She insisted that I should stop worrying, that everything would work out OK and that I would get what I wanted at the end of the summer.'

'She meant get the children back.' Aunty Hilda added.

'Naturally, it could not have been anything else.' Emma confided. 'It meant so much to me. It gave me such a boost at a time when I was really at rock bottom. Mum is still there for me after all and now I feel I have the necessary strength to carry on for as long as it takes.'

'Good for you.' Aunty Hilda replied resolutely. 'You know mum was a fighter all her life. Always for a good cause. You will get Olivia and Sebastian back.' she said reassuringly. 'We are all one hundred and fifty percent behind you.'

For the first time in months Emma felt optimistic again. Her resolve strengthened and her natural energy seemed to return.

'I got a message from dad too,' Emma added with a smile.

'Oh what?' asked Aunty Hilda.

'Well he was up a ladder stocktaking of course.' she added fondly. 'Typical dad always working.'

'Did he say anything?' Aunty Hilda asked.

'Oh just that things were fine and he found it amusing that I had come with such a young photo of him in his prime. He wished he were still that handsome.'

They both laughed standing up to carry the plates to the dishwasher. They had an early start next day and wanted to get an early night.

The holiday was really enjoyable. Aunty Hilda and the children left following their Easter break together and the house was suddenly quiet and empty again. To take her mind off the emptiness, Emma concentrated fully on finalising with Mrs Sinclair their written defence for the impending appeal court hearing end of April.

Of course Victor Falconer had not remained idle and had updated his previous defamatory case against her, all thirty pages, with a couple more statements from the children's current school about the wellbeing of Olivia and Sebastian in the paternal home. Lea, after the photos of her activity in the shop, remained a house wife but surprisingly now working just a few hours a week. Paul was the unsung hero, spontaneously and instantly offering Emma regular contact with her children, the proof being that her counsel Hubert Belette had not even felt it necessary to officially ask for a visiting right.

What a coincidence Emma remarked ironically with hindsight. She asked herself yet again how far these people would go to distort the truth. What never failed to amaze her was that they did it with such impunity.

During the Easter weekend Emma and Mrs Sinclair set to work. They worked three days' non- stop even downing tools one day at midnight. They formed a good team. Emma provided the background and the justifying evidence and Mrs Sinclair put it all into a very structured and clear case in their defence.

'Judges don't have a lot of time or even patience to read very long and complicated documents.' she confided in Emma. 'It is important we get our point across in an easy and convincing manner.' she continued.

They both knew that it had become a complicated case which therefore presented them with a challenge. Victor Falconer knew this and was obviously turning it to his advantage. As Emma drove home in the early hours feeling rather drained, her thoughts turned to Olivia and Sebastian who were tucked up in bed over one hundred kilometres away. Telephone contact was being made as difficult as possible. Four days a month was all she had with her children but she made sure it was sheer quality time.

For the first time in months Emma felt they were making progress. Now someone in authority would listen and take their case seriously she told herself. For the first time officially, Mrs Sinclair seemed to shed some light on the origin of the problem. Emma had been the victim of wrong advice and serious negligence for which she could not be blamed both at the base of the problems as well as in the management of the procedures.

The animosity which had grown between the parties and was evident by the exchange of correspondence which Paul had tried to pin exclusively on her, was obviously attributable to both of them. It was proven that Paul had premeditated events, having no intention of adhering to the terms of the mutual consent divorce agreed a few months earlier. Mrs Sinclair sent her written defence to the court the day before the deadline and they waited.

Jules Mercier called Emma the day before the deadline anxious to know how things were going.

'How are you sweetheart?' he asked in his familiar fatherly tone. 'What is happening with the papers for the court?'

'I am fine' Emma replied. 'but I still think we have some lost ground to make up.'

'You know Emma I am not happy about you going to this Mrs Sinclair.' Jules continued almost possessively. 'I know some of the best lawyers in the country, expensive of course but the best. Are you sure that you don't want to reconsider?'

'I am absolutely sure.' Emma replied resolutely. 'Mrs Sinclair is also among the best in the country in her field and comes highly recommended from several reliable sources.'

'Well I think I should go and see her.' Jules suggested. 'I don't know her but I think her associate used to drive a black jaguar.'

Emma was surprised. 'No thanks Jules.' she hit back. 'I don't think that will be necessary. I think that everything is under control. Of course if we need any advice we will ask you.'

There was a short silence on the end of the phone. 'On the other hand I am thinking of suing Hubert Belette for negligence.' Emma continued.

'Oh!' Jules retorted in surprise. 'You know over here that is not considered standard practice.'

'Neither is what Hubert did to me apparently. Now what would you do in my position?' Emma challenged him.

'Write and complain to the president of the bar.' Jules suggested confidently before adding 'But if I were you, I would do it before the summer, because the president, who is a good friend, is retiring in June. You know also that the 5000 € which Hubert took from you in fees, well I did not get a cent of it I assure you.'

Again Emma was surprised by the comment. She asked herself if she was not overreacting by sensing a complicity, even a protection at play. She told herself that she needed to fully focus on the next court hearing and distractions would have to wait including nailing this infuriating double crossing little Hubert Belette who had caused her children and herself so much grief along the way.

She had become emotionally dependent on Jules Mercier but was now acutely aware of how poor his recommendation had been. She was also wary as a result but it was still inconceivable for her that this honourable retired judge and meanwhile friend could be anything but well intentioned.

Subconsciously however, she knew for the time being that she needed to keep Jules in view and remain on good terms as there was a lot more to this story than met the eye. She remembered the words of Edgar's lawyer friend. If you can prove you were set up, then you improve your chances of securing a positive outcome.

Chapter 33

Just as things seemed to be moving in the right direction, the next bombshell arrived. It was a sunny afternoon and Emma was driving along one of the tree lined avenues of the capital on her way to meet Mrs Sinclair when her mobile phone rang. She diverted to hands free. It was her sister Laura.

'Bad news I am afraid. Brace yourself Emma.' Laura announced in a sad voice. 'Aunty Hilda is dead.'

'What oh no.' Emma groaned as she threw back her head in disbelief. 'Oh god no.' she screamed and started to sob. She slowed down as she could hardly see the road in front of her as the tears flowed freely. 'Whatever happened?' she wailed.

'It was an accident in Spain. She drowned in a shallow lagoon. They think she had a heart attack and lost consciousness. They tried desperately to revive her but it was too late. She would not have known a thing. Of course the friends she was holidaying with are completely shocked.' Laura explained calmly, herself deeply shaken by this tragic and unexpected turn.

'I don't believe it.' Emma sobbed. 'She was only with us three weeks ago and we had a great week with the children in Nice. On the Sunday before she flew home, we went to visit the tulip fields together with Valerie. You know how much Aunty Hilda loves flowers, well she really relished that day.' continued Emma trying to convince herself that this just could not be true.

She was heartbroken. Life was just so unfair and this was a double blow so shortly after the loss of her own dear mother. In a matter of months, Emma and Laura were back in their hometown where they had grown up and had many happy childhood memories arranging yet another funeral. They were again united in sorrow. Sorting out the contents of Aunty Hilda's bungalow they stumbled

174

upon the old family photographs. The grandfather with the large moustache stared out at them proudly in several of them.

'Aunty Hilda we love you take care and say hello to the rest of the family for us' Emma whispered. Somehow she was comforted by the fact that she knew they were not far away. She could almost feel their presence at certain moments.

Chapter 34

A couple of days before the appeal court hearing, Mrs Sinclair and Victor Falconer agreed to make a request to the court to assign a child psychologist who would interview the children and enlighten the court about the best custody arrangement in the sole interest of the children. They would make a report, under oath, to be submitted latest by end of July in time to settle everything for the beginning of the next school year. In the interim, Emma was to receive as a temporary measure an official visiting right of every second weekend and five of the eight weeks in the summer. This seemed the only logical way forward.

Olivia and Sebastian seemed anxious to come back and live with Emma. Life with their father and Lea seemed tough. They confided in Emma that they were often criticized unjustly and shouted out. Olivia, sad to return one Sunday evening, had been dragged up the stairs by Paul in front of the whole family, hit and thrown on the bed and left without anything to eat until the next morning under the pretext that she was sulking and therefore behaving like her mother which was considered completely unacceptable.

Emma was deeply saddened but dare say nothing. She feared anything she said would be completely turned around and used against her in the final hearing. Mrs Sinclair's strategy was to rebuild her image so aptly decimated over a two year' period. It was extremely difficult for Emma to swallow but she knew it was an important long term investment.

Emma was confident that the child psychologist would quickly uncover the truth. A call from a wise and worldly friend put her on her guard again. She told her that this was a good step in the right direction but warned her to make sure the psychologist was not unnecessarily biased in Paul's favour. These experts are nominated and that also often means for their allegiance to those whom nominate them she pointed out.

As soon as Mrs Sinclair received the appeal court judgment assigning an expert to interview the children, she called Emma in the office. She was obviously very pleased about the outcome, commenting positively that at least things would move forward now. She confirmed that she would write immediately to the expert to fix the first meeting. She added that they needed to have the report by the end of July as specified by the appeal court judgment to be able to plead their case in front of the court before the start of the next school year. She emphasised that there was no time to lose.

Emma felt relieved that her new counsel was actually being so proactive. After having had to chase Hubert Belette during months to do even the simplest of things, this was like a breath of fresh air. Emma's feeling of well-being was to be short lived. Mrs Sinclair called her three weeks later to confirm that the expert assigned by the appeal court was too busy and would not be able to complete the task. Emma was speechless.

'What?' she exclaimed.'

'I know.' Mrs Sinclair replied. 'As if they could not check this beforehand.' she added.

For the first time Emma detected an irritation in Mrs Sinclair's voice.

'You are absolutely right.' Emma chipped in. Her mind went back to the appeal court hearing. Sat up high on the bench with such an air of authority had been five court officials. Three appeal court judges, a court clerk and a general counsel for the prosecution. She had felt small and almost intimidated during the short hearing.

'This is unbelievable. What happens next?' she asked Mrs Sinclair all too aware that time was ticking by.

'Well the association where the psychologist works has proposed two young ladies instead, one a child psychiatrist and the other a psychologist. However, your ex-husband has refused so I have no choice but to file an emergency action for the appeal court to assign another expert.' she explained.

'How long will this take?' Emma enquired.

'I will finish the papers by tomorrow evening and file the morning afterwards so within two to maximum three weeks we should be back on track.' she replied. 'I will advise Victor Falconer this afternoon what I intend to do.'

Emma thanked Mrs Sinclair in advance for keeping her posted and told her how much she appreciated her efforts and support.

Paul obviously knew now that the children were going to be interviewed and as Emma expected, he did everything he could to keep the contact she had with them on the phone outside the four days she was entitled to see them every month to a minimum. She found this frustrating and unnecessary but could do little about it apart from remaining calm. She knew they were pushing her hoping she would do something rash which they could then pin on her and use against her and she was determined not to play ball.

She agreed to call Olivia and Sebastian three times a week for just fifteen minutes each time. She became accustomed to the standard replies. No, children are in the bath. No, the children are eating. Call back later. She would call back later and the phone would ring and ring and no one would answer.

One day she finally managed to reach Olivia and they had only been on the phone fifteen seconds when Lea ripped the receiver from Olivia's hand and shouted at Emma that she needed to use the phone and Emma should stop bothering them before abruptly hanging up. Emma was shocked but furious.

Each time it was Lea who played these games with Emma. Paul never answered the phone. He was working or was away. Emma left a couple of messages on Paul's mobile phone outlining the difficulty she was having to speak to their children and reminding him that she had never played such games with him and asking him to put his house in order. To no avail.

Undeterred she went out and bought the children a mobile phone. Bright yellow with fun keys and a card which she could recharge remotely. During the next visit she handed it over to them. They programmed in her phone numbers and those of their friends and the children recorded a joint greeting. They were excited. 'Our own mobile phone.' they exclaimed proudly.

'Yes now we can chat without problems three times a week.' Emma explained

'Good mummy. You know it is not much fun knowing that you are trying to reach us and Lea is doing everything she can to make it difficult.' Olivia explained with a wisdom which surpassed her years.

Paul of course was not pleased and two days later, true to form, another nauseating and official letter dropped on Emma's desk from Victor Falconer, forwarded by Mrs Sinclair. Victor Falconer claimed Olivia and Sebastian had explained to their father that Emma had given them each a mobile phone and made them promise not to say anything and to call their mother in secret every single day. This type of step was considered vexatious since the children were able to spontaneously call their mother three times a week without the slightest obstacle being put in their way.

In addition, Emma was putting the children under pressure telling them that if they did not tell the expert that they wanted to come back and live with her, she would disappear abroad and they would never hear from her again. Furthermore, Emma had brought the children back after the weekend having neither taken their bath nor having eaten. Finally, she constantly criticised Paul and Lea in front of the children. Victor Falconer asked Mrs Sinclair just what Emma was looking for and asked her to talk Emma around to a more accurate analysis of the situation.

Emma had grown to detest Victor Falconer. He had absolutely no scruples whatsoever. She was beginning to consider him as a real public danger.

'Don't worry.' Mrs Sinclair reassured Emma. 'Let's sort out this new date first before replying and clearly putting the record straight.'

The day Mrs Sinclair was due to file the emergency action for the appeal court to assign a new expert, Mrs Sinclair received a call from the head of the association confirming that Paul now accepted the amiable modification and proposed the first meeting mid-June between the parents and their respective legal counsel but without the children. The sum of 500 € was requested from each parent to cover the fees.

Again Emma had to dig into her savings. Emma was so glad her job was so busy and challenging, and last but not least, well paid. It kept her sane and allowed her to focus on something positive and not only the problems she continued to face with Paul. She was quite surprised that Paul had suddenly changed his mind.

Mrs Sinclair now set about replying officially to Victor Falconer's latest tirade of untruths. She formally contested the facts as presented by Paul. Emma had not given two mobile phones to the children only one so they could communicate without passing by the landline. On several occasions Emma's phone conversations with her children had been interrupted and terminated by Lea. Emma firmly denied returning the children without having eaten and had never said that if they did not say they wanted to return, they would never see her again. She regretted that after each weekend the children spent with her they were subjected to a real interrogation upon their return and hoped that the forthcoming expert's report to objectify the situation would put an end to the war of accusations pursued by Paul Archer.

A day later Victor Falconer came back with yet another official letter. Mrs Sinclair put the record straight immediately nipping it in the bud. His letter could not be accepted as official (to be used as evidence later) as it did not meet the requirements. If he insisted, he could always get a second opinion from the president of the bar. Mrs Sinclair confirmed that she intended to be very attentive as to the contents of official letters sent to her by Victor Falconer because it was obvious in the past, and without any reaction from her predecessor, that the content had been rather a counsel's speech for Paul (or in any case a reproduction of what Paul had said) rather than an official communication.

This confirmed what Emma had known for a few months already. The only real 'evidence' they had against her was a long string of official letters from Victor Falconer full of one untruth after the other. She was stunned to see the courts had so far failed to pick up on this and expressed her concern to her sister Laura in one of their weekly phone calls.

'But nobody has really examined your case in any detail.' Laura reminded her.

She was a scientist with a very responsible job and had such a clear analytical mind, something Emma had always admired.

'It is a temporary measure which is becoming a permanent one.' Laura added. 'As they say possession is nine tenths of the law. Hang in there girl. Keep plodding on. Remember softly softly catch the monkey. You owe it to the children to remain strong.'

'But they are my children and they are growing up so fast and it is all precious time I am missing with them.' Emma lamented.

'I know.' Laura replied. 'I sympathise. We all do. I know you are on an emotional roller coaster but try to think clearly. Detach yourself. Try to foresee what their next step will be. Play them at their own game. I am convinced you will win in the end. Paul has never been as clever as he likes to think. Life's circumstances always catch up with dishonest people in the end. Meanwhile, be yourself and enjoy every minute with the children. They are very smart kids and they are growing up fast which means they are also going to see things as they really are sooner than you realise. Now let's just hope these experts assigned by the appeal court are up to it.'

'Oh I really do hope so.' Emma replied as they said goodbye and promised to call each other the following week. She was so lucky to be surrounded by such a supportive group of kind, level headed people be it family, friends, or colleagues.

Chapter 35

One good thing about the appeal court judgment was that Emma had temporarily gained a small but official visiting right to see the children every second weekend and five of the eight weeks in the summer holidays valid up until the end of August. The judgment said that she could collect the children from their new school at 4 pm on Friday and had to return them to their father's for 8.00 pm on the Sunday.

This meant at least three hours driving each weekend but Emma was grateful for small mercies and it meant quality time with the children even during the car journeys there and back. Emma had a comfortable company car, her petrol was paid and her driving skills over longer distances, on the motorways and in all sorts of weather had definitely improved since her divorce from Paul.

Following the judgment transferring temporary custody to Paul, Emma had telephoned the headmistress of the children's new school to introduce herself and request a copy of their school report so she could follow their progress. The headmistress had asked Emma to fax her details and to remind her if she forgot. Emma sent the fax and waited and waited. When she was sure the reports were issued, she sent a fax reminder with the word reminder typed at the top in large letters.

She felt completely excluded from her children's schooling. At Olivia and Sebastian's previous school the teachers had been very neutral to both parents as is only right in any divorce case. Here where Paul lived, in this sombre looking school in the city centre, she felt like a black sheep. The foreign mother who had tried to abduct the children and goodness knows what other stories Paul had told about her.

The confirmations from the school about the children's well-being in the paternal home kept flooding in with every court appearance.

Emma decided not to lower herself to try to clear her name and limited her contact to picking up the children at the school gates.

In spite of this, she was the victim of another vicious and official letter from Victor Falconer accusing her of taking unilateral and aggressive initiatives and profiting from a visit to the school and making declarations which once again could only turn against her. She actually laughed at the absurdity. This particular letter sent to Hubert Belette the previous year appeared as evidence in Paul's favour in his appeal court case at which time Emma saw it for the first time.

Olivia and Sebastian had kept in regular contact with their friends from their former school. They all lived within a ten-minute drive from Emma's new house and it was not uncommon at weekends and in the school holidays when the children were with Emma for their friends to come around to play or for Emma to take them all on an excursion for the day to a fun park or the seaside. The other children's parents were wonderful. They understood her difficulties and were very supportive.

In May they received an invitation from the children's former school to attend the annual school fete. Olivia and Sebastian were excited to go along and say hello to their former teachers. It was an exceptionally sunny and warm day for the time of year. The children ran around from stall to stall with their friends while Emma chatted happily to the other parents in the school yard.

Emma's mind jumped back to their first day at the school and how she had held their little hands accompanied by her own mum who was over for the week and all this before her mum's fatal illness. Those happy carefree days now seemed so far away. There was only eleven months' difference between Olivia and Sebastian. After their nursery schooling, they had expressed a clear wish to be in the same class at school which the headmaster had agreed to.

'How is the new school?' the headmaster asked Olivia and Sebastian.

'Oh not so good.' they replied. 'We prefer this one.'

He looked at Emma with a smile. 'I hope this will come out in the experts' report.' he said as the children ran away to play in the sandpit.

'So do I, so do I.' Emma replied.

Chapter 36

Of course Jules Mercier was never far away. He called Emma at least once a week and they continued to go for their regular lunches.

'So what is new?' Jules asked Emma as he lifted his glass of house red in their favourite Italian restaurant looking at her through his smart glasses. 'To a successful expertise.' he proclaimed.

'To success.' Emma replied as their glasses clinked together. 'Well next week is the first meeting with the two experts.' she explained. 'It is without the children so I suppose they want to talk to us about the background and meet the parents in general before interviewing the children.'

'Are the lawyers going to be there?' Jules enquired.

'Apparently yes.' Emma replied. 'No doubt Victor Falconer will try to distort the picture as usual.' she added with a certain irony gained from bitter experience.

'Don't worry.' Jules reassured her. 'It is obvious children are better off with their mother at that age. Besides they have nothing to reproach you for. Just be yourself.'

Then to Emma's surprise Jules Mercier added 'Don't you think we get on well? I told Dominique the other day that you are my mistress.'

'You what?' Emma exclaimed. 'I don't think so. You are old enough to be my father and besides I know and like Dominique so there is no way I could be your mistress.'

Jules looked back at Emma in surprise.

'Well I meant my intellectual mistress.' he corrected himself smiling as if it was a joke.

'OK if it makes you feel better.' Emma replied somewhat caught off guard by such a strange statement.

'How are you and Dominique getting on for the moment?' Emma asked after a short period of reflection.

Now it was Jules' turn to look a little taken back by the question.

'Not too bad.' he answered also after a moment of reflection. 'Money is a bit short though. As you know Dominique works in the shop I told you about and the owner is a strange fellow and she has not been paid for over 6 weeks.'

'Surely that is illegal.' Emma pointed out. 'Doesn't she have an employment contract? Of course Jules you are best positioned with your experience to advise her about her rights and options.'

'It is the daughter too.' he continued. 'She comes around every weekend and it annoys me.'

'But Jules it is normal.' Emma replied. 'Dominique is her mother and weekends are in part to see family members. You can't imagine how happy I would be if I saw my children every weekend like most normal parents.'

'But she is not very intelligent and has a coloured boyfriend.' he almost protested.

'Well that is her choice. There is nothing wrong with that.' Emma retorted. 'As long as she is happy and he is a nice guy you should not worry. She is over eighteen and it is her life.'

They changed the subject. Jules asked Emma to let him know how they got on with the first meeting with the experts. She assured him she would. She requested Jules to ask for the bill. He looked at her in surprise.

'I will pay.' she added reassuringly. 'As the man I just want you to ask for it, that's all.'

He raised his hand to beckon the waiter over to the table. Emma paid and they parted.

Chapter 37

Emma had discussed with Mrs Sinclair the form the first interview with the experts would take. Her concern was what background information they needed to do a good job. Their case had become so horrendously complicated. How could they introduce it in a simple and clear way?

Mrs Sinclair made a two-page summary setting the scene. It began that at this stage of the expertise it was important to be strictly objective without going back to the long thesis and events developed so far in the judicial debate. She briefly pointed out that as soon as the mutual consent divorce was announced there had been a serious attempt to put into question Emma's capabilities as a good mother and she had had the sentiment that this was a manoeuvre to take her children away from her which was the start of a painful conflict. It was even more distasteful in Emma's opinion since less than a year previously Paul Archer had recognized what a good mother she was by agreeing to the mutual consent divorce and transferring to Emma exclusive custody of the children.

Emma was unfamiliar with local laws and had been badly advised about her move to the UK by her former counsel, a second event which had added oil to the fire. However, realizing this was an error, she had immediately come back to the country but had no visiting rights and depended on the good will of her ex-husband to see her children. Initially being deprived of contact with the children, she now saw them every second weekend.

Before any judicial conflict, she had seen a renowned child psychologist and asked her to intervene to alleviate the conflictual situation in the sole interest of the children but Paul had refused to cooperate. So if the expertise was now urgent it was because it alone would allow the court to fix, in a serene manner, the parental rights which should happen before the start of the new school year as the decision would influence the choice of school as the parties did not reside in the same town.

Mrs Sinclair gave Emma a copy of the brief up front. She read it through. It seemed a very clear and fair assessment of the situation and she hoped it would set the scene for an unbiased debate and thorough expertise. The night before Emma took a relaxing bath and went to bed early anxious to be rested and alert. This was a very important meeting and it had to go well for Olivia and Sebastian's sake.

Emma arrived five minutes early at the address marked on the letter head. It was an old town house converted into offices. The ceilings were high with carved designs. The floor was tiled in a stylish manner. The walls were painted in a light and cheerful colour and pictures hung on the walls. The doors were paned with small glass windows and likewise exuded good taste. Plants were dotted around to finish the pleasant decor which no doubt helped put the many visitors, parents and children alike, at ease.

Emma entered the waiting room. Paul and Victor Falconer were already there. She nodded a polite good morning and went to the seat furthest away from them and sat down. A minute later Mrs Sinclair's colleague arrived. Mrs Sinclair had an important medical appointment so her colleague was standing in for her. Mrs Sinclair had assured Emma that she had briefed her colleague well. She was young, very pretty, smartly dressed with startling green eyes. They greeted one another and she took a seat next to Emma.

'Did you receive a copy of the brief from Mrs Sinclair?' she asked Emma.

'Yes thank you very much.' Emma replied.

There was a total silence which engrossed the waiting room as both Paul and Victor Falconer stared straight ahead at the wall in front of them.

'I also have a copy for Mr Falconer.' she said standing up to hand it over. Victor Falconer read it through quickly and then handed it over to Paul who proceeded to read it through more slowly and carefully.

Mrs Sinclair's colleague turned to Emma with a smile and said 'Well this is an amazing case you have. What a negligent counsel you had before. I have never seen anything quite like it in my career.'

'I bet.' Emma replied very deliberately. 'It does of course all depend on whether it was deliberate and planned negligence.' she continued watching the expression of Victor Falconer. He did not flinch. His sharp features remained expressionless as he continued to stare ahead at the wall.

At that moment Mrs Barry, the psychologist bustled into the waiting room, introduced herself and beckoned the group to follow her up to the first floor for the start of the interview. They filed behind her up the wooden staircase and into a light room with low sofas and a wooden coffee table in the middle. Emma sank onto the sofa. It did seem incredibly low, too low. Mrs Barry sat on a normal chair in front of them with her colleague Dr Robert.

'Well I received Mrs Sinclair's brief as she is unable to attend herself in person.' Mrs Barry began.

'Yes.' explained her colleague. 'Unfortunately she is in hospital and has to have surgery.'

Mrs Barry went on to explain the procedure and opened her diary to fix first a date to see each parent for one hour then two dates to see the children, once with herself and the other with Dr Robert. Both children would be interviewed for one hour by both experts then a preliminary report issued. Both parties would then have the chance to give their input before the final report was published.

Mrs Sinclair's colleague insisted on the shortest possible date for completion of the task as time was of the essence. It was agreed 15th August which was tight but still just before the start of the new school year but six weeks later than the original deadline in the appeal court judgment. Mrs Barry touched on the different proceedings and judgments so far. This association of experts obviously also worked for the provincial court as well as the appeal court.

'What was the name of the judge who classified the case to review the father's visiting rights two and a half years ago?' Mrs Barry suddenly asked.

Emma was surprised by the question. What difference should it make she asked herself. These experts were assigned to make an impartial report about the best interests of the children.

Mrs Barry turned to Victor Falconer for an answer.

'I don't know.' he replied. 'I would have to check my file.'

Mrs Sinclair's assistant, completely new to the file, could also not provide the answer.

'It is Judge Granger.' Emma replied. She had had ample time to study the judgments which had played such a key role in her current predicament and almost knew them by heart.

Emma was pleased that on the next occasion she would actually drive the children for their interview with the experts as they were with her at that time for the summer holidays. She had taken two weeks' holiday in July to be with Olivia and Sebastian but had not booked any holiday abroad, only too aware of being available for the interviews. They would stay at home and go on lots of interesting day trips, see friends and just enjoy being together. Besides all the legal bills were taking their toll. It was time to economise.

They finished the interview and filed down the stairs into the hallway. Emma agreed to go for a coffee with Mrs Sinclair's colleague before heading back to the office. As they left, she noticed Victor Falconer deep in conversation with Mrs Barry. She felt uneasy. This was not a good sign. Victor Falconer was an expert at distorting the truth. I really hope that these experts are smart she thought to herself as she stepped out into the sunshine and walked towards the nearby cafe.

Chapter 38

Emma arrived for her hour interview with Dr Robert. She was young, attractive, well dressed with a very pleasant and receptive manner as one might expect from someone in her profession. Emma calmly explained basically what Mrs Sinclair had put in her brief and pointed out that the breakdown of her marriage had been precipitated by Paul's fiery temper and unreasonable behaviour which she could no longer accept. She loved her children and was a very good mother and was suffering enormously by being separated from them. The situation was not being helped by Paul's rigid attitude and apparent attempts to limit their contact to a bare minimum. At the end Dr Robert smiled and simply said that now she understood and everything seemed much clearer.

A few weeks later Emma drove Olivia and Sebastian along for their interviews with the experts. Emma did not want to ask questions nor guide the children about what they should say. This is what she knew she should not do. She just encouraged them to be honest and tell the truth as they had done six months earlier with the child psychologist Emma had consulted upon her return from England.

Afterwards Olivia confided that she had told the experts about Lea painting a Hitler moustache on a photo of mummy and that she wanted to change school and return to her former school which actually meant she wanted to come back and live with Emma and see her friends again. OK Emma reassured her. If you said that then you have a good chance that this will happen. Sebastian joined in the conversation. He said that he had told them that life living with their dad was difficult as they were treated severely and often shouted at.

'OK let's wait for the report. Meanwhile let's have a great summer together.' Emma said enthusiastically.

'Yeah' they both shouted in unison.

Emma returned, this time to speak for an hour to Mrs Barry. Her questions were very focused and she was much more forthright than Dr Robert. She drilled Emma for the third time about why she had tried to leave the country without telling her ex-husband personally.

'Because as I told you,' Emma replied 'our relationship was extremely strained. After Paul's inadmissible comments to the children about my dying mum and his subsequent insults when I tried to ask him not to say things like that to the children, I decided it was futile to even attempt to discuss anything further with him. Please bear in mind that this was after two years of constant harassment.' Emma concluded.

'In addition, the divorce settlement clearly stated that I could leave the country with the children for professional reasons and I double checked in advance with my lawyer to be one hundred percent sure that I was not doing anything improper. Also with a retired judge who helped draw up the terms of the mutual consent divorce. With hindsight, I was obviously very very badly advised.'

Mrs Barry stared at Emma. Emma continued.

'You do realise that this is a set up?' Emma said as calmly and as convincingly as she could. 'If I do not regain custody of my children, I will go to the European Court of Human Rights. This situation is absolutely unacceptable.'

Mrs Barry tutted loudly and suddenly looked annoyed.

'Even if it takes me years, I will divulge the truth.' Emma continued.

The interview was coming to an end. 'You know what is really sad?' Emma concluded. 'One of Paul's prime motivators for separating me from my children is that he wants money. He wants me to subsidise his lifestyle as I did for many years during our marriage.'

Mrs Barry suddenly nodded and admitted to Emma's surprise, that ninety-five percent of cases passing through her offices were motivated by money interests and the parents used the children as pawns. They shook hands and Emma left.

Chapter 39

Emma waited for the preliminary report from the experts. Mrs Sinclair had left the hospital and asked her how it had gone. Emma confirmed that it had seemed to go OK but it was difficult to tell beforehand and of course they would need to see the report to really know. They waited and waited and the preliminary report still did not arrive. Emma became anxious as she saw the end of August approaching. The final report should have been filed with the appeal court by middle of August. Emma called Mrs Sinclair ever second day and she, in turn, wrote to the experts.

Ten days later the preliminary report finally arrived. Mrs Sinclair called Emma to come over to collect a copy. Emma walked in to her office. Emma started by enquiring about Mrs Sinclair's health and if she was recovering well from the recent operation. The two ladies got on well and Emma really liked Mrs Sinclair as a person and both admired her and was grateful for her legal experience and above all support.

'Take a careful look and let me have your comments as soon as possible.' Mrs Sinclair requested handing over to Emma a copy of the preliminary report.

'What does it say?' Emma asked earnestly.

'Poor, poor Emma.' Mrs Sinclair replied. 'I am most perplexed. I really do not know what to say.'

Emma's heart sank. As she headed for the lift to take her to the ground floor, she continued reading the first page of the report. She was suddenly worried about what set of hurdles she was going to be faced with next. She arrived home, took paper and pen and went systematically line by line. She was very disappointed. At best the report was discriminatory.

There were many anomalies but the main ones which Emma documented for Mrs Sinclair was that Paul had literally looked after the children on his own during the first three years of their childhood. This was completely untrue. He arrived home one hour before she did thanks to his flexible hours in sales then as soon as Emma arrived, they shared quality time together with the children, both feeding bathing and putting them to bed. In addition, of course there was no mention of years four to six when Emma brought up the children almost single handed as Paul was always away working. To top everything, this particular remark had been placed under the section Emma Brown as though she had even admitted it.

The next irregularity was that Emma's problems had only started once temporary custody was transferred to Paul. This was blatant. Emma had spent nearly half of the time with Dr Robert explaining the difficulties she had had just after the mutual consent divorce was pronounced, the negative effect on the children and Paul's premeditated actions. She had made this clear to Mrs Barry too providing many examples. Just how could they justify this? Even Victor Falconer wrote that this was untrue in his feedback.

The report went on that Olivia claimed she was unhappy in her current school as the children made fun of her accent and she wanted to change class and be with her brother. Olivia had clearly told Emma that she had said she was unhappy in her current school and wanted to go back to her former school.

Emma took out a letter Olivia had written herself to her best friend one month earlier following the school fete. Her friend's parents had forwarded Emma a copy just in case. Olivia clearly wrote that she was unhappy in her new school and by far preferred her former school. She had drawn a big sun above a picture of her former school and admitted she missed her friends who were much nicer there too. She gave her mobile phone number so they could call her. Emma asked Mrs Sinclair to send the letter to the experts as well as to point out that the school results were much better in the former school. Olivia had seventy-five percent on her last school report compared to ninety percent when she was in her former school and living with her mother.

Emma casually asked Olivia if she was sure that she had said she wanted to go back to her former school because this was not in the report. Olivia replied categorically yes adding that she did not like Mrs Barry. She had practically asked no questions and had spent half of the interview playing with a little power ball.

Finally, the preliminary report confirmed that Emma saw her children regularly and there was no problem in this area either which was quite unbelievable given the minimal contact she had had with her children since the provincial court judgment. The fact that the mobile phone she had had to purchase to overcome the numerous problems was now even confiscated from the children or as Paul admitted, placed in his office in the basement where incidentally the children could not hear it ring when their mother called them. Emma had also mentioned this and had given further examples of how difficult it was to enjoy a normal contact with her son and daughter.

There were a few small things in Emma's favour. The children admitted Lea called their mummy a witch and had disfigured a photo of her with a Hitler moustache.

Mrs Sinclair with all her wisdom, experience and skill replied objectively in a three-page letter to the two experts. This was followed by an aggressive tirade of untruths from Victor Falconer extending to seven pages accusing Mrs Sinclair of giving a personal account of the history, which was even more amazing and inaccurate since she had only taken over the file a few months earlier. A diarrhoea of words on a constipation of ideas. It was difficult for Emma to read let alone digest but by now she should have been accustomed to it.

Mrs Sinclair replied succinctly and skilfully wrapping up the debate and pushing for the final report finding the means to give to each parent the place which he wishes to have and which the children expect of him. Despite the well-known urgency, the final report was only filed in October, nearly three months after the date specified by the appeal court judgment and well into the new school year.

To top everything, Mrs Sinclair and Emma had discovered that the delay was for the most part attributable to a break in at the premises of the experts where their computers and notes had been stolen. Emma froze when she heard the news. She immediately thought about her own suspicious burglary eleven months ago. Her family and friends were as disappointed and as concerned as she was.

She rang Jules Mercier.

'There is a fiddle going on here. The delay in the filing of the experts' report is due to a burglary at their premises. Remember I was also burgled. It is more than coincidence.' she complained. 'I feel like going to the police and informing them about my concerns and telling them the whole story so that they can pursue this line of enquiry.' she continued.

'Don't do anything without me.' he urged Emma. 'I will check a few things out then let's have lunch to go through this in a calm and structured manner. I know a little restaurant we have not been to together. Here is the address. How about 12.30 pm tomorrow?'

'OK' Emma replied. 'I'll see you there.'

'Bring a copy of the final report with you too'. Jules asked.

Emma met Jules in the restaurant. He kissed her on both cheeks then sat down and asked to see the experts' final report. Not much of the content had changed despite their feedback. However, the experts had added their findings which clearly stated that the children were perfectly happy in the maternal home too. They had nothing to prove the contrary.

It mentioned that Emma felt very wronged and that she even thought she could go to the European Court of Human Rights as she felt her whole being and right as a mother had been denied. The children were victims of the conflict between adults which should be settled so they could see and love both parents without fear of criticism. However, Emma's suffering from being separated from her children was sincere and significant and she found the situation intolerable. Any judicial decision would not be enough to sort out the deeprooted conflict and whichever parent did not have the children in the week should have them one weekend then the Saturday of the following weekend.

'Well based on this report' Jules said looking at Emma intently 'the children will stay with their father and you will have a very generous visiting right.' He pulled out a piece of paper and pen and started to draw the number of days per year Emma would have the children which was all weekends and a larger part of the holidays and tried to convince her that it was a good deal as it was all quality time.

Emma bit her lip.

'You are sweet when you bite your lip.' he smiled at her.

'It is a set up.' she repeated her voice trembling. She felt angry, hurt and betrayed.

Finally, she continued 'I did nothing wrong. It is my fundamental right to bring up my own children, bring them to school every day, follow their progress, put them to bed. Have daily contact with them. I cannot accept to see them just at weekends with all the difficulty I have to maintain even normal telephone contact when they are with their father. I will not pay Archer to dress them in second hand clothes and for his new family to insult me on every occasion. These experts are not honest. My friends warned me. I will not accept this report. It is rigged.' she concluded her voice become stronger and more and more determined.

Suddenly, Jules Mercier looked worried.

'And this burglary.' she fired at him. 'What did you discover then?'

'Well yes it did take place' he admitted. 'The file has been opened with the prosecutor but there are no leads yet. You know my former driver when I was at the ministry of justice now works for the police and they are looking into it.'

'You said I would get the children back all along so how come you now change your tune?' Emma demanded. 'I trusted you. Why did you lie to me?'

'Well, things have gone on for a long time and the children are settled in their new school year at their father's.' he tried to explain to Emma. 'I always said this was a danger.'

'Well let me tell you something Jules.' Emma announced looking him straight in the eyes. 'I am not giving up and furthermore I will not accept this report. I am going to write a book and divulge all the dishonest goings on in your judicial system and contact both the local and the international press.'

Jules, suddenly to Emma's surprise, looked quite alarmed. 'Which journalists would you contact?' he asked. She promptly gave him the names of whom she considered the best investigative journalists in the country focused on dodgy dealings.

'Then of course there are all the international ones.' she reminded him. 'Many of these are much more unrestricted in what they can report and also much bolder.'

'Oh I will help you with the book.' he offered eagerly.

'Thanks Jules but that won't be necessary.' Emma replied.

They chatted about other things for a while then Emma paid and left.

Emma was in a sombre mood. It was the middle of October and autumn was setting in. There was a chill in the air and the days were getting noticeably shorter. Again Emma had no official visiting right to see her own children as the appeal court judgment had expired end of August and they had waited for the experts' report to plan the next step.

The school year had begun and Emma was more convinced than ever that she had been set up. She could not live with losing her children in such unfair circumstances. It was against all her principles of justice, decency and honesty which she had grown up with and in which she vehemently believed. It might take her years to get to the bottom of things and meanwhile she would live for the quality moments with her children, give them love and support and one day they would return, even if they had to walk out and come back of their own accord. She knew they were not happy where they were. If they had been, this would have put another spin on things.

The following Saturday afternoon Emma parked her car in the city centre and set off down the main shopping street to the biggest book store in the country. Her fact finding mission had begun. She was apprehensive about what she would discover. However, she had been manoeuvred into this impossible situation and now she had to find a way to manoeuvre herself out of it. The words of Edgar's lawyer friend echoed in her mind. 'If you can prove you were set up then this changes the picture and you will get your children back.'

Her mum's words also rang as clear as a bell in her head. 'Don't worry you will get what you want at the end of the summer'. Well that would have to be next summer now she muttered as she looked up towards the sky. Meanwhile there was a lot of work to be done.

Chapter 40

Emma glided up the escalator in the large shopping centre clutching her handbag close to her side as she passed through the exceptionally wide doors of the book shop. The place was huge. Books, records, CDs, printers, PCs for as far as the eye could see. Just where was she going to start to find the ones which would give her valuable background information and help her make more sense of her absurd predicament? Find the current affairs section she told herself then take it from there.

Funnily enough for a book shop the lighting was quite dim. It gave the place a relaxing and more intimate atmosphere but when one was looking for a needle in a haystack light was a definite advantage. It was Emma's lucky day however. After five minutes, she had located a special shelf which seemed to contain many books about the various wheeling and dealing of the last thirty years and even 'scandals' a word which could be found in many of the titles or prefaces.

Emma bought them all. As she headed to the cash desk she tried to keep the pile straight. She could just peer over the top to see where she was going. The cashier passed each one through the bar code system and Emma packed them hurriedly into plastic carrier bags, conscious of the people behind her watching what she was purchasing. She paid by credit card and hurried out of the shop and back down the escalator.

She stopped at a newsagents and bought several fluorescent pens. Interesting subjects and paragraphs would be highlighted for easier and future reference. She planned to read at weekends when she did not have the children and in the evenings after work. Winter was approaching so this was the right time to curl up on the sofa with a good book and favourite background music. She missed Olivia and Sebastian so much. The daily void of being separated from her precious children only served to fuel her enthusiasm and determination to get to the bottom of things.

Her first objective was to try to identify the terrain, how things worked or in some cases did not work and why. She now knew for certain that some things did not work the same way as they did in England. It soon became clear after reading the first two books that there were some fundamental problems in the system which only served to help the more unscrupulous members of society take advantage of and profit from the situation, often at the expense of others.

For the first time Emma really began to understand the disillusionment of her local friends with their system and their apparent lack of interest and enthusiasm for politics and general suspicion and lack of faith in the judicial system.

The judicial system had been grossly underfunded for years and had not kept pace with modernisation. Successive coalition governments had become lazy and complacent. The number of cases before the courts had soared, both criminal and civil, and resources could not keep up. Judges and magistrates were badly paid so the best lawyers preferred to remain on the other side of the bar. Judges and magistrates who did decide to put themselves forward were nominated for their political affiliations. This is turn led to an artificially high rate of cronyism. A surprising element was that once nominated to become a judge or a magistrate there was no training afforded. Every company Emma knew trained their staff. Emma's discoveries made her feel uneasy.

At the same time as reading the many books, Emma decided to ask colleagues and friends about their experience and knowledge of the judicial system, especially the provincial court which had originally taken away custody of her children. A good colleague provided the first interesting story.

'Oh that provincial court. That is a place I can tell you.' Emma's colleague began.

'Why is that?' Emma asked curiously.

'Well until I came here I used to work for a company based in the same town. One day my boss told me he wanted to move to another area but it would not be wise since by remaining where he was, he was sure to win every single legal wrangle in which he found himself.'

'Now that is interesting.' Emma replied.

'Yes they certainly seem to help out their friends over there.' the colleague concluded.

'Unfortunately I have learned that to my own detriment.' Emma added.

The colleague nodded then shrugged her shoulders. 'I agree with you that it is not right but what can we do?'

A good colleague sent Emma in the direction of Raymond who seemed to have experienced a lot of problems with the owner of his previous house and the affair had ended up in the provincial court. Raymond worked in logistics and was an expat. Emma went to his desk with an inventory question then just before leaving broached the subject.

'Ann tells me you have been having problems with the local judicial system.' Emma piped up. 'If it's any consolation, me too. What happened to you then?'

'You too? he asked in surprise.

'Yes and not just a little bit.' Emma elaborated.

Raymond suddenly seemed quite relieved to meet someone else who was getting a raw deal and he opened up and started to tell Emma his story.

'When we first came here we rented a house then after two years the owner told us he wanted to sell it so we had to move. When we came to do the inspection of the premises to get our deposit back he claimed we had made a lot of damage and demanded a large sum of money. We had not damaged the property and therefore we refused to pay what he was asking. The owner then decided to take us to court. You know I spent over 5000 € just in legal fees and this has been going on for the last three years. Then I made some enquiries and it would appear that the owner did not sell the house as he claimed and he has played the same game with another couple of expats in the past too.'

'It is scandalous.' Emma remarked. 'You must not pay. You have to fight this sort of thing.'

'Wait.' Raymond continued. 'The best is still to come.'

Emma waited wondering what on earth she was going to hear next.

'Well the last time we went to the provincial court' Raymond almost whispered not wishing to be overhead by anyone but Emma. 'things did not go too well for us. When I was looking for the exit, I mistakenly opened the door to the office of the judge and the lawyer working for the owner of the house was sitting there with his feet on the judge's desk smoking and laughing with the judge. They both looked really embarrassed when they saw me so I quickly said sorry, closed the door and made a speedy exit from the court.'

'Incredible.' Emma commented quite shocked by this revelation. 'What gets me is that they simply think they can get away with things like this.'

'Well I might repatriate back home soon.' Raymond continued. 'Then I won't pay the owner anything and they can try to recuperate the money and good luck to them.'

'Good for you.' Emma commented. 'But you won't get back the 5000 € you already had to splash out in legal fees not to mention all the stress and hassle of being dragged through the court.'

'I know.' Raymond retorted sadly. 'Now what happened to you?' he asked Emma.

'Another unbelievable story.' she began. 'My two young children were snatched away from me and my ex-husband was given custody by this court and I don't even have a visiting right to see them over a year later and now he is pushing me to pay him maintenance to subsidise his luxury tastes and those of his former mistress.'

'No you are kidding me.' Raymond uttered in total surprise. 'But small children should be with their mother. They can't do that to you.'

'Well they just did' Emma replied 'but I have decided not to take it lying down.'

'Right you are.' he replied sympathetically. 'Don't give up. Children need their mother. Especially young children.'

They smiled at one another then Emma returned to her office taking a small amount of comfort from the fact that she was not the only one getting a rough deal in this provincial court.

By chance, a week later Emma bumped into Bob in the office. He was a serious sort of person, a thinker who worked in the accounts department. He seemed very cultivated and knowledgeable and was obviously up to date with current affairs, the sort of person who closely followed the news and read the newspapers.

'How are things going?' Emma asked.

'Could be better.' he replied. 'We still have problems with the implementation of the new financial system.'

'So I heard.' Emma answered sympathetically. 'All new systems take time to run smoothly. You guys in accounts are the first to switch to the new software. You have to make the mistakes so that the rest of the company can enjoy a smooth implementation.' she joked.

Bob smiled.

'Tell me Bob.' Emma began. 'I know you are right up to date with current affairs. What can you tell me about the provincial court down the road? I have an issue there and have a distinct impression that things work differently there than the norm.'

'Well.' he replied sweeping his hair back in one swift gesture. 'Let me think for a moment. Well yes, there are few strange issues. The biggest one being that the court has often been accused of covering up the series of killings in the 1980s which cost the lives of dozens of innocent people who were gunned down inside and on the parking of petrol stations in a series of Rambo like operations.'

'Oh yes.' she replied. 'I remember this sad affair quite well. I worked with a girl whose best friend's mother was one of the victims. She was really cut up by the whole thing. I also have a friend who knows an elderly couple who lost their only son in the massacre. They never got over it. Who covered it up and why?' Emma asked thinking to herself sometimes what a small world it could be.

Raymond hesitated for a second deep in thought 'Well the chief prosecutor is often mentioned. Well nobody really knows who is responsible for or should I say behind this affair. They caught the perpetrators but never the commanding officers and this despite a parliamentary enquiry. Some more experienced journalists wrote that it was part of a far right campaign to destabilise the government at the time.'

'Strange.' Emma commented shaking her head. 'Well if the parliamentary enquiry could not even get to the bottom of it, I don't suppose we will ever know. Huge shame for the poor victims and their families.' She added.

'Yes there I fully agree.' Raymond concluded.

Chapter 41

Emma had explained in simple terms to Olivia and Sebastian that the experts' report had taken much longer than expected to complete and as a result they would return to their new school at the start of the new school year and continue to live with daddy. However, everything would work out fine and if they wanted they would eventually come back to live with mummy and go to school again with their good friends. In any event mummy loved them and would always be there for them.

In October Emma asked Paul to have the children for one specific weekend as her company had organised a day and evening at a theme park with a barbecue afterwards. Paul reluctantly agreed but claimed afterwards that she would not be able to see her children for three weeks. She saw them just four days in five weeks. To top things, Paul had nothing special planned so it was yet another tactic to show Emma who was in charge, ignoring the rights of the other parent and the desire of the children to see both parents equally as outlined in the recent experts' report.

Emma was upset but what could she do? It just strengthened her resolve that the time she spent with her children would be real quality time. She cooked them their favourite meals then they watched a good video curled up together on the sofa. They saw their friends and did lots of interesting activities together. She gave them lots of love and attention.

Emma avoided asking questions but the children confided in her. Paul and Lea were arguing quite a lot. This did not surprise Emma. Paul was a dominant person wanting everything his own way. Lea loved money and things were not going too well on the financial front.

Olivia and Sebastian confided in Emma that they had to wear the same clothes for school for practically the whole week as Lea did not have enough space in the washing basket for their clothes, something Lea's own son was not subjected to. They were not allowed to wear the new clothes Emma had bought them. They were not allowed to use Lea's shampoo and for weeks there was nothing else available. On several occasions they arrived at Emma's for the weekend without having washed their hair for two weeks. It literally stuck to their heads. Friends were witnesses. Emma almost cried but dare say nothing for fear of giving the adverse party some much sought after ammunition to use against her.

'Tell your father.' she urged the children. 'Mummy we don't dare.' was the answer. 'He will only be angry with us then Lea will be even meaner when daddy is not there.'

To add insult to injury, Victor Falconer continued to send letters insisting on Emma's contribution to the upkeep of the children. Mrs Sinclair had advised Emma she had better try to gather as much information as possible as the law was going to support their demand. This only added to Emma's frustration. Mrs Sinclair suggested that Emma try to find out as much as she could about Paul's boat.

Emma called a colleague who knew everything there was to know about boats. They went on the internet together. They soon discovered that there was only one distributor in the country selling Paul's boat and Emma wrote to them as a prospective client asking for the purchase price, consumption, running and maintenance costs.

The previous summer she had not even had a holiday and had stayed at home with the children. Paul had rented a villa for three weeks in the south of France and had gadded around the coast and creeks every day on this speed boat. She meticulously kept copies of everything she spent on the children knowing she was going to need them in the future. It all seemed so unfair.

What now hurt and upset Emma the most was the criticism Olivia and Sebastian were subjected to regarding the clothes she bought them. Emma's mum's last visit to the outside had been to go into town and buy her grandchildren nice new anoraks and winter shoes. Lea insisted the anoraks grandma had bought were ugly. The shoes Sebastian had chosen himself were ridiculed. Lea called Paul over and in front of Sebastian said his shoes were really ugly.

Olivia was accused of looking like a tart because she wore a top from Gap bought in Paris. They were only ten and eleven years old. Emma was sad. Take no notice she reassured the children. You look great. It is unfortunate your father is supporting this behaviour. Lea should look in the mirror then she would be less critical of others. The children picked out the most neutral clothes they had and wore these when they returned to their father's place. Emma could only encourage them to do so.

Jules Mercier had continued to call Emma at least once per week. These seemed difficult times for everyone. Jules was having problems not only with his health but also with his wife Dominique. The marriage was floundering and for once Jules was lost. The tables were reversed and ironically Jules started to turn to Emma for moral support.

She agreed to have dinner with Jules and Dominique in a Greek restaurant on the Saturday evening. The evening started off well. Dominique had just returned from a week's holiday in the south of France which she had spent on her own. She described it as a cooling off period and one of reflection. Jules had been concerned but was happy that she was back. Emma and Dominique had always got along well. They laughed and joked and talked about many different things. Then just before coffee was served, Jules started criticising and almost shouting at Dominque. Emma was surprised and initially said nothing.

'Do you hear him Emma?' Dominique retorted looking to Emma for support. 'He is aggressive, domineering and disrespectful.'

'Jules' Emma said. 'Please calm down there is no need to speak like that. That is not solving anything.'

Emma suggested that the two of them speak offline and plan their next holiday together. After all they had not enjoyed any quality time away as a couple for at least five years.

'You are in a rut.' Emma told them both. 'You need to re-evaluate and start to invest in rebuilding your relationship.'

They both nodded but Emma knew it was too late. The distance between where they came from and where they were today being just too great. A castle, 30.000 € a month income, prestige, power, a chauffeur driven car, the good life to a small rented house and two precarious jobs not knowing how much each would be paid at the end of every month and if it would cover all the bills.

The time came to pay. For once Emma had had enough of being the cash cow and she had been offering the advice this time. She sat tight. Jules true to form also. Dominique looked sympathetically at Emma. It was a look which said so much. They understood one another.

'I will pay.' she said taking out her cheque book.

'Thank you so much.' Emma said gratefully.

Jules sat contentedly sipping his cognac and lighting up a fat cigar secure in the knowledge that he was firmly in charge. When they said goodbye, both Dominique and Emma knew that it was the last time that they would meet, at least in Jules' company.

Chapter 42

One week later Jules turned up on Emma's doorstep on the Saturday afternoon looking absolutely wrecked. Luckily she had two English friends over for the weekend.

'Emma I need to speak to you.' he urged. 'Dominique has left me.' he spluttered.

'OK come around Monday evening and we can talk.' Emma replied.

Jules turned up at 7 pm sharp. He was obviously shaken and for once surprisingly vulnerable.

'Do you have 20 € for me?' he asked sheepishly. 'I am waiting for my commission from the estate agent next week and need to put petrol in my car.'

Emma looked at him and almost felt sorry. 'Here is 10 €.' she said. 'It should last until next week if you don't drive too much and then you can reimburse me when you get paid.'

'Thanks.' he replied.

Emma knew she would never see the money again.

'Dominique left me.' Jules told Emma again.

'I guessed it might come to that.' Emma replied.

'We make such a nice couple you and I.' Jules commented. 'Are you sure that you do not want to get together?'

'Absolutely.' Emma replied trying to sound nice but as convincing as she could. 'You need to find your feet then look for someone your own age. What are you going to do now?' Emma enquired.

'I am going to buy a small flat in the south of the city.' Jules replied.

'Oh have you got some money after all?' Emma asked softly.

'Not a lot. My son is paying. I am moving in in a couple of weeks. Will you come and see me from time to time?'

'Sure.' Emma replied not wanting to deflate an already flat balloon.

Meanwhile Emma had been carrying on with her reading material. She was trying to gauge the circles in which Jules moved from the information he had shared with her in the past.

She had prepared a nice salmon dinner and they sat down to eat. Emma poured Jules a glass of red wine and slipped into the conversation 'Jules do you know Paul Jordan?'

'Oh yes I know him really well.' was the nostalgic reply. 'He is a friend of mine.'

According to the book Emma had just completed Paul Jordan was a character with apparent great charm. He had worked in the ministry of justice as head of the cabinet and also held a high position in the public prosecutor's office. He was to everyone's surprise first arrested for having provided parts of a judicial file to drug dealers being investigated internationally. Then it transpired he had granted pardons to dubious characters. Monies he received illicitly were allegedly used to finance a major political party. He was sentenced to several months in prison for violation of professional secret and forgery followed by another five further convictions connected to the underworld.

A little later Emma asked Jules casually if he knew Alan Lambert.

'Oh yes I know Alan well too.' came the enthusiastic reply.

Emma moved the conversation over to Jules' impending move and asked him about his new flat.

Alan Lambert had for many years been the enigmatic head of the police and was arrested for forgery and corruption. Police informants accused him of receiving bribes and being linked to the underworld. The investigations dragged on for several years and most of the accusations were subsequently squashed by the instructing judge. However, according to the author, this was enough for the minister to ask the former police chief to retire quietly.

From Jules' answers, Emma already knew that Jules' former circles left much to be desired.

Emma cleared off their plates and the two of them sipped their second glass of red wine and waited for the coffee to filter through.

'Jules' Emma began. 'I am concerned about the provincial court and the judgment taking away my children. The judgment is too one sided. I think there is some corruption at play here.'

'Corruption? No I don't think so.' Jules replied.

'I am afraid so.' she continued. 'Doesn't it bother you being part of such a system?'

'They are not all corrupt.' Jules replied almost defensively. 'In a case I recently tried to influence, the judge got himself replaced at the last minute.'

Emma stared at Jules trying very hard not to look shocked and trying at the same time to think very fast what the follow up question should be.

'Oh!' she continued. 'So how does one influence a court case then?' She raised her glass and quietly swallowed a mouth full of red wine, waiting for the answer.

'Well' Jules began very thoughtfully. 'We know one another in many cases. We have a language, signs. We very rarely put things in writing. A phone call or a contact face to face. We ask one of the parties, the magistrate, the prosecutor's office or the court clerk to give a favourable outcome and it normally works. In such cases the judgment can be decided upon even before the court hearing.'

'Oh' Emma said. 'So that's how it is done. Now let's get you some coffee. Would you like dessert? I have ice cream or sorbet.'

She served the coffee and they both settled for sorbet. She changed the subject and they talked about a host of different things. This was quite a revelation and Emma was anxious not to raise suspicions or push her luck.

When Jules had left, her mind went back to the emergency court hearing in the provincial court where she had lost temporary custody of her son and daughter. She remembered how Jules had very clearly asked her not to stand next to him in the court room. Could he have passed a sign to the judge or prosecutor's deputy at this time in Paul's favour? She felt uneasy. She almost wished she had not made the discoveries of the last few weeks but she knew she had to continue as there was more to come.

Chapter 43

A few days later Jules Mercier called Emma again.

'Can I come around for a meal end of the week?' Jules asked. 'I am on my own and can't really cook.'

'Sure.' she replied. 'You know what? I will invite Valerie and Cathy too and there will be the four of us. It should be fun.'

Cathy and Valerie had both met Jules before. Valerie in particular questioned his loyalty and the damaging advice he had seemed to give so far in Emma's case but then Valerie had always been very perceptive. Jules had picked up on this and as a result, he did not really like Valerie. Emma on the other hand would not accept any criticism of her good friend from Jules. Let the girls challenge Jules with me Emma thought to herself. She briefed them beforehand on the plan and they both arrived punctually for dinner on the Saturday evening.

Jules arrived half an hour late. He looked absolutely wrecked. He proceeded to tell the three girls excitedly that he had been partying until the early hours of the morning and had met lots of interesting women. Apparently he also had a new girlfriend already, a teacher whom he had met the week before. He went on to proudly claim that he had screwed her on the desk of her classroom. Emma teased him adding ironically that she hoped the incident had happened outside of school hours. The three friends looked at one another with a smile and raised eyebrows. As Emma was serving dinner in the kitchen, Valerie probed Jules about Emma's case.

'Shame about the children.' she said.

'Yes.' Jules agreed 'but she will get them back through the appeal court. They are serious people there.'

As Valerie got up to give Emma a hand in the kitchen, Jules muttered under his breath 'That is what she thinks, she won't get them back.'

Valerie had excellent hearing. Cathy also picked up on it. Jules was clearly exhausted and the wine had gone to his head. The girls had made sure his glass was nicely topped up throughout the evening. His mutterings were louder than he had intended. However, they all believed that he did not even realise that he had been overheard. When he left, the three friends compared notes. It was now crystal clear that Jules was working against Emma. It was still too early to blow the whistle but now they knew for sure.

Jules called Emma at the beginning of the following week.

'Did you get some sleep then?' she teased him.

'Oh yes but what a weekend.' he replied excitedly. 'I feel so young again.'

'Better pace yourself.' Emma suggested. 'You are not thirty anymore and carry on like that and you will burn yourself out or even worse.'

Jules laughed. 'Can I come around for dinner again this week.' he asked. 'I really enjoy your company, not to mention your cooking of course.'

'Fine' Emma replied. 'Come over Wednesday evening.' She still had things to discover.

Jules arrived at 7 pm sharp this time. He proceeded to tell Emma about his new girlfriend. She apparently knew all about his past but had told Jules that it did not bother her. What past Emma asked herself. Better not ask too many questions this time she thought. Just let him speak.

'What can I do on Saturday evening with her?' Jules asked Emma eagerly. 'What do young people do nowadays on a date?'

Emma laughed. 'Lots of things. Just be imaginative. Well you could go to the cinema then out for a nice meal afterwards.' she proposed. Emma knew it was not a very original idea but it was the only thing she could muster.

'Good idea.' Jules retorted. 'What's on at present? What would you recommend?'

'Well apparently there is a good film which just came out called 'Eyes wide shut' and it seems to be getting quite a bit of coverage. It stars Tom Cruise and Nicole Kidman and was made by the acclaimed film director Stanley Kubrick, apparently just before he died.' Emma explained.

'OK then we will go and see that one.' he replied.

Over dinner their conversation turned to the web.

'It is a great tool.' Emma explained to Jules. 'You can search for almost anything and find it. You know there is some funny business going on in the courts and I am sure Victor Falconer has something to do with it. I have been looking up things on the web. You always said that some people are untouchable but now with the free flow of information more readily available than ever before, perhaps this will change in the future.'

Jules looked surprised. 'What search engine are you using?' he asked.

'Just the normal ones' she replied. 'You know AltaVista, Yahoo, Ask Jeeves.'

'And the key word?' he added.

'Oh just general stuff like judiciary and politics.' Emma replied casually.

One day Emma came across an article about a business man called Arthur Falconer. He seemed to be very well connected. Valerie and Emma wondered if he was related to Victor Falconer and because of the political and business influence, strings had been pulled in the provincial courts. It was worth investigating. One of the books Emma had purchased contained a section about his escapades and also a couple of photographs. She had been astonished when she opened the book to see the physical resemblance to Victor Falconer.

Her search on the web had subsequently revealed that according to a well-known newspaper Arthur Falconer had paid a large sum of money to secure his part of the business in the famous Rollo affair. This had come out by accident as a result of investigations ongoing into the assassination of another minister. In the Rollo affair, bribes had apparently been received by various people in public office from two foreign companies to secure a large defence contract. Some of the money was believed to have been used for illicit funding of the political parties. There was a much publicized trial through the Supreme Court where a dozen individuals were found guilty, including several ministers.

'Do you know Arthur Falconer?' Emma asked Jules over coffee.

'Oh yes. I know him personally.' he replied. 'He got a large number of votes in the recent election.'

'Oh' Emma said. 'What does he look like?'

Jules thought for a moment then added 'He is medium height and build with blond curly hair and comes from the south of the country.'

'Is that right?' Emma replied pushing back her chair and walking over to pick up the book. She opened it at the page with the photos.

'Afraid not Jules.' she continued. 'He is short, dark and stocky and comes from the same town as Victor Falconer. There you are take a look.' Emma said thrusting the book under his nose. 'Don't you think he looks very much like Victor Falconer, Paul's so charming and upright lawyer? They could be brothers or at least cousins wouldn't you say?'

Suddenly Jules went very pale as if he had seen a ghost and his voice began to shake. He took the book, flipped it over, read the title and looked again at the photos and asked Emma where she had found the book.

'In the bookshop.' she answered. 'It only came out two months ago. You did not answer my question Jules.' Emma reminded him.

Jules stood up and said he had to be going asking if he could take the book with him to read.

Emma said he could but he should bring it back as she needed to finish reading it.

Jules left in a hurry. The colour did not return to his cheeks. Emma was very surprised by the magnitude of his reaction. She cleared off the table and called Valerie to explain what had happened. Valerie laughed ironically reminding Emma that she had told her that there was something strange and she had felt it all along. She confirmed to Emma her belief that Jules Mercier was at the centre of the set up but not to give him his marching orders yet as Emma might still discover other useful pieces of information.

'That is exactly what I was thinking.' Emma replied. 'Sleep tight and see you tomorrow.'

Chapter 44

Jules Mercier called the following week again as if nothing had happened. He had spent an excellent weekend with his new girlfriend and wanted to come by for dinner and tell Emma all about it. She confirmed to him that it was fine to come over the following evening. She did not mention the recent incident with the book either as she did not want to be confrontational and by playing dumb, perhaps she would learn something else which could turn out to be interesting and actually help her case.

It had dawned on her over the last few weeks that they had played with her like a pawn, with the stability of her children, her emotions, her sanity, her health, her life without the slightest scruple. She was shocked and deeply hurt but determined to keep going and regain custody of her children. She blamed herself for having been so naïve.

Jules arrived promptly at 7 pm.

'What are you cooking for dinner tonight?' he asked as he walked through the door and straight into the living room.

'Steak.' Emma replied. 'I know you like that and it will build up your strength again after the last few troublesome weeks.'

He smiled. 'Yes I love steak. Have you got béarnaise sauce too?'

'No only green pepper sauce but it's just as good.' she reassured him 'So why don't you tell me about this wonderful weekend you spent with the new love of your life. You sounded so excited on the phone.' Emma beckoned.

'Yes well it was great.' he explained excitedly, his eyes sparkling and his voice full of enthusiasm. 'We went to the cinema. That film you recommended it was wonderful. Just like the good old times over here.' he said with an air of nostalgia combined with an unexplainable air of exaltation.

It was a strange combination. Emma had no idea what he was talking about. She planned to go and see 'Eyes wide shut' with her American friend the following week. She was just pleased that Jules seemed to have enjoyed it so much. With hindsight, it was just as well that she had not seen the film when Jules expressed his utter delight and enchantment. She might have given away her feeling of utter and total shock. Luckily when it came the following week, she was in the cover of darkness in the cinema, in the safe company of a trusted friend.

Revelation followed revelation and suddenly Emma started to feel punch drunk. That weekend Jules was moving into his small flat and he insisted that Emma come around and see the place and they go out for dinner afterwards in his new neighbourhood. It was a weekend when she did not have the children or anything else planned so she agreed.

She parked the car on the communal parking and looked up at the apartment block. It was modern and stylish and surrounded by gardens and trees. Emma could not help thinking about the castle Jules had apparently told her he had owned or even the smart villa where she had first met Jules when she had visited him on that sunny fateful Saturday morning for guidance in her mutual consent divorce.

Emma checked the long list of door bells and after locating Jules' name she pressed the bell. Jules familiar voice echoed back from the parlour phone. He opened the main entrance door and Emma navigated her way up to the sixth floor in the lift. The flat was small but comfortable. The balcony was wide and overlooked gardens and towering trees.

'What do you think?' Jules asked Emma almost immediately.

'It is nice.' she replied. 'There is a lot of nature outside and the place is easy to up keep. At the same time, you are in the capital and not far from the cultural events, restaurants, theatre, exhibitions. You never liked gardening anyway.' she reminded him with a smile.

Jules smiled 'It is a bit of a come down from what I had before.' he lamented.

'It is fine.' Emma reassured him. 'You have to look on the bright side. Just think how many people are worse off than you.'

Jules stared at Emma for a second then walked out onto the balcony to take some fresh air. He lit up a fat cigar then after a few minutes came back inside.

'I had a hell of a weekend.' he continued almost proudly. 'I asked a girl to come around to help with the cleaning and we ended up in bed together. She made passionate love. It was wonderful. She is only nineteen you know and I really hope that her husband does not find out because no doubt he is the jealous type.'

Emma looked at Jules in surprise before adding 'Don't you think it would be wiser to pick someone a bit closer to your own age? That girl is young enough to be your granddaughter. Doesn't that bother you?'

'No.' he replied. 'I know her parents and I asked them for the telephone number.'

Emma did not understand anything anymore and she did not want to. There was something decidedly distasteful about this whole story which disturbed her so she did her best to block it out.

'Let's go to dinner.' Jules suggested sensing Emma's silence and apparent withdrawal.

They had decided upon a local restaurant where they could sit outside in the garden and which overlooked the communal swimming baths. They chose a table in the middle of the garden and ordered a drink. Autumn was approaching but it was a balmy and mild evening.

Emma looked out over towards the swimming pool. Memories came flooding back of the good times she had spent just two years before with mum and Aunty Hilda and the children in that very pool. At that time, they were still all together. She had everything even though she was constantly harassed by Paul and Victor Falconer. Now she had nothing. How things could completely change in such a short space of time she sighed to herself.

Suddenly Jules became quite nostalgic. 'You know in the past I had everything. Now just look to which level I have sunk today.' he said with a certain degree of regret and bitterness.

'What do you mean?' Emma enquired.

'I was involved in a large affair in the past.' he confessed for the first time. 'A large amount of money disappeared. My lawyer was one of the brothers. In front of the judge he stood up and performed a series of bows.'

To Emma's surprise, Jules stood up in the garden and promptly performed the bows he was so aptly describing. She looked at him in amazement, quickly turning around to ensure they were not being scrutinized by any curious diners.

'Saved me of course.' he continued. 'My son sorted everything out. Of course they did not get all the money back either.' he concluded with a satisfied smile.

Quite simply Emma did not know what to say so she said nothing. The dinner arrived shortly afterwards and they both tucked in. True to form, afterwards Emma paid the bill while Jules complained about the speed of the service.

'What do you expect for that price, Lobster?' she asked. 'Now really Jules, do stop complaining.'

Emma drove Jules back to his new flat. He urged her to come back with him.

'I have no curtains and I can't sleep with the light coming in. You have to help me to hang the curtains at least in the bedroom.' he explained.

She reluctantly agreed. 'Just the bedroom curtains then. Where are they?' Emma asked.

Jules pointed to a pile of neatly folded curtains on one of the chairs. Emma kicked off her shoes, stood on a chair and started to hang the curtains. Jules observed her attentively.

'You know?' he started. 'You are such a good friend to me. Nobody cares about me, not even my own family. You are one of the kindest people I know. I consider you as a real friend. One of the only ones I have.'

This was a tough moment for Emma. She knew that Jules was double crossing her. She already had some serious reservations about his past. The fact that his children almost disowned him came as no surprise either anymore.

Emma was not a good actress so she simply replied 'Thanks don't worry about it.' before hurriedly attaching the last hook in the curtains, springing down from the chair, hopping back into her shoes and making a beeline out of the flat under the pretext of being tired. She breathed a sigh of relief as she started the car engine and drove out of the complex, direction home. Jules watched her leave and waved at her from the balcony.

Chapter 45

Early the following week, the planned evening out at the cinema with Emma's American friend Mary Jo took place. They had decided to go and see Eyes Wide Shut. Both girls were rushed off their feet at work so they left the office rather late and it was a mad rush to arrive at the cinema on time for the start of the film. The film was just beginning as they slumped with relief into their soft seats. The two friends decided to go out for a bite to eat after the film, sharing in the meantime a large bag of popcorn.

The film started quite slowly then suddenly the point arrived when Tom Cruise's character Dr Harford arrived in a castle to gate crash a very private gathering where the participants were all clad in long black cloaks and ominous looking masks. A password was needed to gain entry. The gathering in the large hall of the castle close to New York city was impressive but frightening. It was obvious that the individuals were all powerful, rich and members of a closed and secret society. It smacked of masonry. One lady died in suspicious circumstances and the musician disappeared in an equally questionable series of events. A sort of venerable father or high priest dressed in red presided over matters in the middle of the hall muttering mumbo jumbo and knocking on the floor with his gavel. Following the ceremony, the proceedings developed into a mass orgy in several rooms of the castle.

As soon as Emma grasped what was transpiring, Jules' enthusiastic and excited words about the film came flooding back to her 'It was just like the good old times over here.'

Suddenly everything seemed clear for Emma including the powerful forces at work against her. She could not contain herself.

'Oh no. Holy Shit.' she muttered glad to be sitting in the dark while making this startling discovery and in the safe company of her good friend Mary Jo.

'What is the matter?' Mary Jo asked in surprise.

'Holy Shit.' Emma repeated in utter shock and despair.

After the film, the two girls went for a bite in one of their favourite eateries. As they walked to the restaurant Emma was uncharacteristically quiet. Mary Jo noticed.

'Hey Emma is everything OK? You are not your chatty self this evening.' she pointed out.

Emma was still digesting this latest revelation. Eventually she decided to share her realisation with Mary Jo. She needed to speak to someone about it. 'You know the retired judge who helped me with my divorce, well he participates or participated in the sort of stuff we saw in the film. These masonic like gatherings and erotic goings on seem to be international.'

'Oh boy oh boy oh boy.' Mary Jo replied her voice deepening with each word.

'You can say that again.' Emma muttered. 'Now it is painfully clear just what I am up against and it is going to make it all the more challenging to regain custody of Olivia and Sebastian.' Emma admitted suddenly overcome with apprehension and weariness.

'Oh boy.' Mary Jo repeated as it began to sink in what Emma had said.

There was a marked silence for what seemed like an eternity then Emma added 'I have to keep on fighting no matter what. They say information is power but in this case, I would rather not know. I prefer the saying that ignorance is bliss.' Emma confessed.

At this point she could not help thinking to herself what a strange set of circumstances had led her to this startling discovery. What an unexpected stroke of fate.

'You will be OK you just need to keep going forward step by step. We are all behind you one hundred and fifty percent.' Mary Jo added encouragingly.

'That is all I can do. I don't have a lot of choice. Now let's go and get some food. I am starting to feel hungry.' Emma replied philosophically taking Mary Jo's arm. She did not want to spoil the evening for her good friend.

'Holy shit what a dilemma.' she murmured once again as they turned the corner and entered the restaurant.

Chapter 46

Later that week Jules called Emma and asked if he could come around to dinner. She was still in a state of shock after seeing the film and making the connection but she could not afford to show it. Emma agreed and two days later they had a quiet dinner at Emma's home. As usual the conversation turned to recuperating the children. For once Jules was apparently more candid.

'You will get them back' he started to explain 'but only when they have had enough of Paul and arrive at the age of puberty, you know when they start to get hair under their arms and on their genitals and then they will decide of their own accord to come back to you.'

Emma looked at Jules in surprise but also with suspicion. Whatever induced him to say things like that she asked herself. She felt very uneasy. The conversation turned again to the court and her suspicions.

'You know I am not going to let this drop Jules.' she said. 'I feel very strongly about the injustice in my case. Where I grew up people don't get away with things like this. No justice system is perfect but what I have seen here defies belief.'

She got up to walk into the kitchen to check the dinner adding 'If things don't get sorted out very soon then I am going to escalate the whole thing and it won't be pleasant for the instigators.'

Jules followed Emma into the kitchen.

'If that is the case' he replied matter-of-factly. 'then we will have to get rid of you either in a car accident or by poisoning you.' He pointed to the bottles in the wine rack.

She stared hard at him. He quickly changed the subject. They talked about generalities as Emma tried hard to digest what she had just heard.

233

'I am going to Marseille for the weekend to see some friends.' Jules announced as he was leaving.

'Have a good time.' Emma replied closing the front door behind him.

The full meaning of Jules' words suddenly hit home. Emma felt very frightened. She thought about the powerful fraternal friends in the film and how easy it was for them to bump people off and make it look like an accident. At the same time, she was furious. They set me up, tear my young children away from me then when I fight to get them back, they threaten to shut me up for good. My children need me. This is outrageous. she thought to herself indignantly.

A few days earlier Emma had just finished reading a book written by three journalists over a two year' period. It was an exhaustive piece of investigative journalism about how a case involving the abduction and murder of several children had been covered up. The book left so many questions unanswered and contained so many anomalies that it left Emma very concerned indeed. Witnesses spoke of orgies involving minors and some of the names mentioned seemed to move in the same circles as Jules Mercier. One of the witnesses explained how people who were invited to the parties and were uneasy about the whole thing suddenly seemed to disappear in suspicious car accidents. That the youth court judge used to collect him and others from a children's home and take him to the parties where he was subsequently abused.

Emma spent a few restless nights tossing and turning as her mind whizzed around and around and she tried to make sense of these troubling elements which had suddenly all seemed to fall into place over such a short period.

The surprises were not over yet. Jules arrived back from Marseille. A couple of days later Emma received a strange phone call just before midnight from a female. The woman explained to Emma that she had found Emma's mobile phone number on the telephone pad of her Nigerian boyfriend. Apparently the Nigerian boyfriend had a very dodgy acquaintance and he had been the one to write down her number. The woman asked Emma what nationality she was. Emma replied that she was Dutch.

'You sound English or American.' the woman continued. 'Where do you live?'

Emma gave a false town.

Finally, the woman explained the reason for her call. She was worried about the company her boyfriend was keeping and wanted to warn Emma that her telephone number was now with this almost mafia like character. Emma tried to keep calm.

'Well I think you should also be quite worried yourself.' Emma replied to the woman. 'That is about the company you are keeping. Take care now and thank you for calling.'

Emma hung up. She had a distinct feeling that Jules was behind this and the voice may have been that of his new girlfriend. The girlfriend had called Jules once on his mobile while he had been having dinner with Emma and the tone sounded very similar.

Emma could not have been more worried. She picked Olivia and Sebastian up for the weekend. As usual they enjoyed every minute of their limited time together. Emma tried hard not to show that anything was wrong. She checked her car brakes every time she set off and drove with extreme caution especially on the motorway. She started buying small bottles of water and wine and would not drink anything at home which did not have a new seal on it. She never left her drink unattended when she went out.

It was while she was driving back that Sunday evening in the rain after dropping off the children back at their father's house that her mobile phone rang. The windscreen wipers swept from side to side making an occasional squeaking noise, the rain swished around the tires of the passing cars and the spray from the lorries engulfed Emma's car as she carefully overtook them. Emma really did not enjoy driving in heavy rain and then to make matters worse also in the dark. Emma was listening to the soothing sound of the Carpenters. She turned down the volume and flipped her mobile phone onto hands free.

'Hi Emma.' a friendly voice called out. 'How are you doing?' It was Emma's friend Tom.

'Fine.' Emma replied. 'I am on my way back after dropping off the children and true to form the heavens have opened and it is throwing it down. You know how much I adore driving in the rain. How are you?'

'Listen my friend.' Tom exclaimed getting straight to the point. 'I have some very interesting news for you.'

'What now?' Emma thought to herself. After the last few weeks nothing could amaze her anymore.

'It is Jules Mercier.' Tom continued excitedly. 'He has been in jail. He was involved in a large scandal involving the disappearance of several millions and rumour has it, in well informed circles, that it was linked to the Rollo affair and illicit financing of the political parties.'

'Oh sugar.' Emma retorted. 'Now that would make sense.'

'I can't tell you anything more than that but do check it out.'

'Thanks a lot.' Emma replied and Tom was gone.

Emma turned up the volume and the Carpenters started to sing 'On top of the world'. It seemed so ironic. She concentrated on the road in front of her. Her head was spinning. She remembered going to visit Jules at his home one year earlier during the Rollo trial. He loved all things English and had asked Emma to buy him a flat tweed cap for winter. She had taken the cap around to find him intently watching the early evening news.

'Look there.' he had said pointing to one of the ministers accused of corruption. 'He is a really good friend of mine.'

At the time Emma had thought nothing of it. Now things were suddenly fitting together like a giant jigsaw puzzle. She also thought back to her recent discovery on the web that Arthur Falconer had allegedly also been involved in the Rollo affair but the Supreme Court judge had decided to limit the number of the accused to keep the trial at a manageable level. So this latest revelation about Jules was probably correct.

Emma wondered what she was going to do. She was scared for her own safety, hurt and angry about being set up, felt helpless because she had no one in authority to turn to for help and above all she was desperately missing her children. How was she going to get out of this fix? She decided to take the bull by the horns and write to the British Prime Minister. She outlined her story and asked if he could possibly help. Also if Jules and company did try to bump her off, her story would be on record and they might not get away with it.

Emma sent a copy of the letter to family and friends in five different countries and requested them to go to the international press if anything happened to her. She stuck the stamp on the letter and popped it into the post box. Hopefully things would improve. Someone somewhere had to help her. Emma also advised Mrs Sinclair of her concerns and the fact that her file and story were abroad in several countries just in case something did happen to her. Emma felt silly about over reacting but she had never been so scared in her life.

Chapter 47

Emma was more convinced than ever that it would be impossible to get a fair hearing in the provincial court. The only viable option seemed to be to push the case through the appeal court based on the first appeal opened by Hubert Belette asking for a social enquiry to determine why the children were being locked up overnight on their own and where the provincial youth court judge had simply closed the case. After all, the appeal court had the right to take all elements into account and make a judgment on the overall case.

Mrs Sinclair advised Victor Falconer that she would be asking the appeal court to handle the proceedings. Victor Falconer had naturally been pushing for a final custody hearing in the provincial court where he had had a very successful track record so far.

Victor Falconer was soon up to his old tricks again. He aggressively accused Emma of having forced Olivia to write a letter to a friend confirming she wanted to go back to her old school and was not happy in her current school. This is what Olivia said she had also confirmed when she was interviewed by the experts. Victor Falconer claimed the letter had been written prior to Emma trying to abscond the previous summer to England with the children. Emma explained to Mrs Sinclair that this would have been difficult since Olivia mentioned her new mobile phone number which had only been activated one week before she wrote the letter. Mrs Sinclair looked at Emma and a smile crossed her face. Emma read her mind.

'I will send you proof of purchase of the phone and also a confirmation from the mobile phone company that the line was only very recently activated.' Emma suggested helpfully.

'Good.' Mrs Sinclair replied.

Emma called the operator and briefly explained the situation. They were very helpful and three days later the fax confirmation arrived.

Emma continued with her background reading in the evenings and at weekends when she did not see Olivia and Sebastian. She had already made her way through half of the large pile of books she had picked up weeks earlier.

Yet another book shed some background on the workings of the system. Apparently the three main political parties, the so called pillars of society, had shared power for several decades on national but also on local level. It had even been known for political coalitions to anticipate the results of the forthcoming elections and sign agreements before the results were known. Financial aid was distributed proportionately between the regional ministerial cabinets. Such a practice was so common that the major political parties had got used to the idea of mutually keeping an eye on one another to ensure there was nothing cooking in secret. It was in this climate that a corruption of an unimaginable size had flourished and that the public markets had been sliced up in a regulated manner by the 'godfathers' of politics.

This had given the political parties considerable power. They were responsible for the nomination of almost everyone in a public function from the caretaker of a school to the CEO of the largest public concerns. However most revealingly it was claimed that the prominent members of political parties not only got involved in the granting of a building permit or actually overturned fines but also did not hesitate to intervene in the course of justice. For a long time, the judicial system remained deaf and blind to this invasion of corruption which rotted the country and warped all the normal mechanisms of decision. The political nomination of judges and magistrates of course played a major role. Emma's mind went back to Jules Mercier's time at the ministry of justice from where a great many of the nominations were made.

The experts who had seen the children were also most probably nominated as the courts used them almost exclusively and of course their livelihood depended on it. She felt uneasy reading this analysis but at least the mechanism which made the system tick became clearer and clearer and her own predicament made more sense than it had done up until then.

Emma continued to see her precious children every second weekend or four days a month. Things seemed to move so slowly but Emma told herself that she had to hang in there. Her friends and family continued to be extremely supportive. Courage and patience Valerie kept reminding her. You will prevail her good American friends kept telling her by email or when she had them on the phone. Be strong and don't let these dishonest individuals get you down her sister Laura repeated in their weekly telephone calls.

Various friends reassured Emma that the truth would come out in the end, that the children were growing up and they would become smarter and braver with time and that Paul could not keep them indefinitely against their will. Emma really did not know what she would have done without the unbending support of family and close friends. Material comfort was good to have but real friendship was invaluable. She vowed that if any of her friends ever needed her help in the future, they could count on here through thick and thin.

Weekends together with the children were very special times. Emma planned lots of interesting activities alone with Olivia and Sebastian but also surrounded by their mutual friends. She wanted them to remember the good life they had enjoyed together before they had been torn away from her and which their father was now trying to blot out. Above all she wanted to keep the children as stable as possible and confident that she loved them and was there for them.

She told the children one Saturday night as she hugged them to look out of the window at the moon. It was big and bright and Emma told them it could be seen from almost anywhere. If you miss mum Emma continued, then just hug Paddington bear and think I am looking at exactly the same moon so really not far away at all. Olivia and Sebastian had both smiled.

A few weeks later Sebastian confided in Emma that Olivia had been sleepwalking at her father's place and had gone down to the ground floor in the middle of the night, unlocked the door and walked around the garden. She had done the same thing a few nights later climbing to the fourth floor and opening the window. Emma was suddenly very worried but dare not show it. She asked Sebastian if their father was aware of the situation. Apparently he was and had thankfully put a bell on her bedroom door so if Olivia started sleep walking again, he would hear it and go and bring her back. Emma was relieved.

Then Sebastian added that Lea had taken the bell away as she did not like being woken in the night. Emma was upset but also worried. She did everything to hide it. She asked Olivia if she remembered anything when she sleep walked. Olivia replied nothing so Emma reassured her not to worry, to sleep peacefully and to forget about the moon. To just remember that mum loved her lots. That was the last Emma heard of Olivia sleep walking but she spent many an anxious moment hoping and praying that everything would be OK.

It was while doing some shopping one lunchtime in the local supermarket that Emma noticed a book which had just been published and was prominently displayed on its own stand. She popped the book in her shopping trolley and started to read it the following weekend. It was a book which was to leave a deep impression on her.

It was written by a young woman named Ella who had been brought up as a child prostitute from a very tender age. By the time she was eight, she was receiving clients almost every day. When she was still a child, her parents introduced her to a pimp who took her destiny in his hands. Ella explained that from time to time she recognized her clients on TV under the guise of senior politician, member of the judiciary, or top industrialist. The rapes were less of a problem she declared. What really bothered her were the torture and sometimes murder of children. The pleasure of the client only intensified with the fear of the child, the ultimate form of sexual pleasure culminating in the fear of death of the victim.

The author testified that she had witnessed dozens of murders during her hellish childhood. She had survived only because she was strong, healed quickly and had developed various characters in her personality which enabled her to block out the most horrendous memories. Some children were tied to boards and cut with razor blades and burnt with candles. Others were let loose naked in large gardens of prestigious estates and hunted like game or chased by dogs.

Most of the children had been knowingly pushed into prostitution by their parents. Others had been lured in later. As Ella approached her sixteenth birthday, she was conscious that her time to die was nearing fast. Children in her situation were apparently called angels as they supposedly disappeared and went to heaven. An adult's testimony could more easily be listened to and eventually investigated. It was much easier to discredit that of a child, especially when the parents were consenting.

However, Ella had developed a superhuman will to survive. She met a young man whom she married and who pulled her away from the network. Destroyed by a lifetime of unbelievable abuse, Ella followed many years of therapy so when she decided to write the book, with the goal of helping other children, she was a much stronger and balanced person.

The book really upset Emma. She had already seen many things in her life and travelled quite widely but this surpassed everything. She kept repeating to herself what a cruel, sick and horrible world they all lived in. For two weeks after finishing the book, she would spend many a restless night tossing and turning in bed and when she did wake up, would feel hot tears rolling down her cheeks. She guessed given the fact that she had been so unjustly separated from her own children, this just made her sensitivity to the plight of other children so much higher.

Chapter 48

Emma was just digesting the book when Jules Mercier called her again. They had not spoken for over two weeks. He had left Emma a couple of messages but she could not bring herself to return his calls, especially after the startling discoveries of the last few weeks.

'How are you doing darling?' he asked Emma cheerfully.

'I am fine.' she replied.

'Can we have dinner one of these days?' he enquired. 'Do you have any news yet about filing with the appeal court? You are bound to get results there.' he continued in a positive voice.

Emma simply did not trust Jules anymore. She now realised only too clearly that her naivety about the honesty of judges had cost her and her children very dearly indeed. What she had recently read about how the judicial system functioned here had only added to her mistrust.

'Sorry Jules.' Emma announced. 'I am extremely busy so I cannot see you this week or next. I will call you when things are less hectic.' With that Emma hung up.

It was another rainy Friday evening when Emma picked up Olivia and Sebastian and they had just arrived back at the local butchers. She left them in the car on the parking in front of the shop window as she hurried in to buy some fresh meat to make one of their favourite dishes, shepherd's pie. Her mobile phone rang. It was Jules.

'Sorry can't talk now.' she answered. 'The children are in the car, I am in the butchers and I have to hurry home to cook dinner.'

'What about the court hearing? Do you have a date yet for the appeal court?' he asked.

'Not yet.' Emma replied. 'We submitted our written defence but Victor Falconer is dragging things out again as one might expect.'

'This is extraordinary.' Jules went on. 'I have never seen such a case in my whole career.'

'I bet.' Emma said ironically biting her lip and adding 'Well I have, my own and it smacks of a set up.' She ended the call, ordered the meat and returned to the car to spend a nice weekend with her children.

Jules did not call Emma back that weekend but she knew he would the following week so she started to prepare herself for the rupture of their friendship. She had never been a great actress and under the circumstances she had no will to carry on pretending. The phone rang Tuesday morning in the office. It was Jules.

'Hello.' he announced. 'Are you OK?'

'Fine' Emma replied curtly.

'I have the impression you are annoyed with me Emma. What is the matter?' he asked in a concerned voice.

'Well why don't you tell me?' Emma asked and waited for the reply

'It is not my fault the children are still with their father.' Jules started after a short silence.

'I think otherwise.' Emma shot back trying not to raise her voice.

'What do you mean?' he asked anxiously his voice slowing down.

'You damn well know exactly what I mean.' Emma hit out. 'You set me up for whatever reason be it financial or otherwise. You have been working against me from the outset.'

'That is ridiculous.' Jules almost shouted obviously unprepared for such a conversation.

'Really.' Emma continued dryly. 'Well how come you have been in jail notably for the Rollo affair and how come you know Arthur Falconer, who is most likely also related to Victor Falconer. Both of you should also have suffered a similar fate were it not for the leniency of the judiciary and Supreme Court who did not want to extend the investigations to too many people to keep it to a manageable size. Yes, and the minister who was found guilty is a good friend of yours too. You told me yourself.'

'I don't know Arthur Falconer.' Jules cried back his voice starting to tremble. 'It is Andrew Falconer whom I know.'

'Don't lie to me anymore Jules.' Emma said calmly. 'I have had more than enough. I trusted you implicitly and you let me down big time. You really are a double crossing low life.'

'It is not true.' Jules protested again.

'Fibber.' Emma shot back. 'Now get out of my life and stay out. You have done more than enough damage already. And should you and your band decide to carry out your threat to have me disappear in a car accident or poison me, then I just want to let you know that I wrote to the British Prime Minister outlining full details of my case including your name and sent copies to friends in five countries. So if anything happens to me, yours will be the first door they will come knocking on. My friends will also contact the international press and post everything on the internet.'

Emma did not give Jules the opportunity to continue the conversation and she simply put down the receiver. By now she was trembling. This had been a very difficult and painful conversation. Her good colleague in the neighbouring office who could not fail to hear the conversation came into her cubicle. She was aware of some of the background and had been a great support.

'You had to do it.' she reassured Emma. 'He deserved it. Well done. Now just concentrate on getting your children back.'

'I know.' Emma sighed. 'But I have made another enemy.'

'Oh he was already firmly working against you even when he was nice so don't worry now. He can't hurt your case more than he has already done.'

'Hope you are right.' Emma replied squeezing her colleague's hand which she had reassuring placed on Emma's shoulder.

Chapter 49

One dark November evening Emma arrived home from work just in time to change and head out to her exercise class. A letter from the Foreign and Commonwealth office in London was in her letterbox. She opened it and started to read. The Prime Minister wished to thank her for letter which had been passed to the FCO for reply.

The desk clerk hoped that Emma would understand that the British government could not interfere in a private legal matter nor the affairs of another country as it would not accept another country interfering in theirs. However, the FCO understood Emma's concern for the children and hoped everything would be solved in the very near future. They understood that she had changed lawyer and recommended Emma proceed through the local legal system with her new counsel.

Emma was relieved and happy to have received an acknowledgement. The fact that the Prime Minister wished to thank her for her letter did wonders for her moral although she did actually wonder if he had actually read it himself. He must get hundreds of letters each day she told herself. The British authorities could not get involved but at least they now had her story officially on record.

Emma wrote back thanking the desk clerk for her acknowledgement. She added that unfortunately there was more to her case than met the eye and she hoped that the British authorities would understand that she was far from being a trouble maker, just a loving mother concerned for the welfare and future of her children.

Christmas was approaching and Emma was so much looking forward to having the children again for more than a mere weekend. They arrived on the Saturday evening. Olivia seemed tired and shivery. Olivia confirmed that she did not feel too well going on to explain that Lea had asked both children to clean the whole staircase with water as she was expecting visitors and one of them was allergic to dust. It had been cold in the stairs and Olivia had caught a chill. Emma gave her a big hug reassuring her that she was home and need not worry about any more cleaning as Cathy had been the day before and everything was picco bello. Olivia smiled and gave Emma a big hug adding 'Mum I love you.'

'Me too.' Emma replied affectionately. 'Now run along and play with your brother.'

Emma was mad. How dare Lea treat her children like modern day Cinderellas? A couple of weeks earlier Olivia and Sebastian had told Emma how they had both cried because on Wednesday afternoons they were forced to tidy and clean their bedrooms and upon inspection, Lea had declared that things were not tidy enough so she had taken every soft toy and other small items she could find and had thrown them into the middle of the room and demanded that the children start again from scratch.

For Emma this was downright mean and spiteful. Paul did not seem interested to redress the situation. Emma had suggested Olivia and Sebastian tell their father that this was unfair. They had simply replied that he did not care. He had promised them that he would talk to Lea when she was mean with them but nothing ever changed and she was then even meaner to them next time their father was not there.

During dinner that evening Olivia unexpectedly announced that she wanted to meet Mrs Sinclair. Me too Sebastian added.

Emma explained that this was not possible while the case was still ongoing. Both children replied that they then wanted to write to Mrs Sinclair directly adding that it was their wish to come home and live with Emma. Emma agreed and told them to give her the letters when ready and she would post them to Mrs Sinclair. During the holidays both children wrote their own letter to Mrs Sinclair. They explained that they did not like their stepmother as she was mean to them and made them cry. She favoured her own son and often criticized them. Olivia mentioned her sadness that Emma always had great difficulty to get through to them on the phone and Lea refused to let them call back the same day. Lea had also insisted that Paul confiscate the mobile phone Emma had just given the children.

Sebastian complained that they were forced to wear the same clothes all week for school in contrast to her own son who could change his clothes every day. Sebastian wrote that their stepmother accused them of drinking one litre of milk every day and eating a whole loaf of bread while, in reality, Sebastian himself was only allowed half a glass of milk and one slice of bread each morning. They washed their hair rarely as Lea would not let them use the shampoo without her permission but she only made these remarks when their father was not around which was quite often. Finally, both children wrote how much they missed Emma their mum and asked Mrs Sinclair to do everything in her power to reunite them as soon as possible.

The content of the letters gave Emma hope that one day they would be together again. She had not influenced or given any help to Olivia and Sebastian to write the letters. The content had to come from them as Emma knew that most probably one day they would confidently and convincingly have to say something similar in front of a judge.

Emma knew deep down that it was still going to be an uphill struggle. Paul liked to control people and there was also the financial aspect which could not be underestimated. The children reminded Emma that their father had said that she still owed him lots of money. Paul had apparently told Olivia and Sebastian that if they stayed with him he would build a nice villa with a swimming pool with the money mummy would have to pay him each month.

Emma did not want to use the children as a go between so she just smiled and added let daddy dream.

The most revealing comment came over dinner one evening.

'Do you know what daddy said?' Olivia confided. 'We heard him say to Lea that Jules Mercier is not as daft as he thought at the beginning. I don't think he knew we were listening.'

'He also asked us recently if you still see Jules Mercier.' Sebastian added.

'Oh not very often.' Emma replied casually.

Well well Emma said to herself this was just another element proving that the whole thing had been a premeditated set up from the very beginning. What a group of charming people she had unfortunately got tangled up with.

Chapter 50

The New Year came and everyone got back into the routine. Emma already looked forward to the half term holidays in February because she had booked a skiing holiday with Olivia and Sebastian in Austria and they were all excited about spending a week together in the snow and the mountains. They had already bought their ski suits in the January sales. Until then she would see them for just four days a month.

Meanwhile Emma needed to find out more details about Jules Mercier's imprisonment and what exactly he was accused of. The more she knew for the appeal court hearing, the better they would be able to defend themselves. Somebody, somewhere had to believe that she had been set up and do something about it. However, she knew that it would not happen on its own and was acutely aware that she had to be proactive.

Against her better nature, she put on her detective hat again. She decided to write to one of the most experienced journalists who often covered cases of corruption in quite a forthright way, unusual for the country. The next day she received a call from the journalist and they arranged to meet in a restaurant the following Friday. She was nervous. She had never met a journalist before and this was her private life they were talking about.

Before the meeting with the journalist on the Friday, Emma visited the PR department of her company to check if they had a standard non-disclosure agreement she could repurpose. She did not want anything published without her prior agreement. Unfortunately, they did not have anything appropriate, so Emma decided that she would have to see how things went with the journalist and clearly agree on what could and could not eventually be published before the start of their conversation.

Emma had arranged to meet the journalist, Mr Godfroid, in a restaurant in a quiet suburb of the capital midway between their two offices. Emma slid nervously into her car and drove the fifteen minutes to the venue. She looked around as she locked the car door. What would this journalist look like? She entered the restaurant. It was empty apart from an old gentleman in a grey checked suit who had just been served his soup. He tucked his serviette into his shirt collar and slowly began to eat, blowing onto his spoon as the steam rose from the piping hot bowl. He seemed to be a regular. The tables were tastefully laid with starched yellow table cloths and cotton serviettes. The wine glasses stood to attention. There was a skylight at the side of the table and the sun shone brightly through, illuminating the flower decorations on the neighbouring tables.

Emma kept glancing nervously towards the door then discreetly at her watch. The tables were well spread out so nobody would be listening to their conversation Emma reassured herself. Suddenly a confident and tall looking gentleman appeared in the doorway. As the restaurant was otherwise empty, they made immediate eye contact, smiled and Emma stood up to introduce herself and shake hands.

'Pleased to meet you.' she said. 'Thanks for agreeing to touch base.'

'Pleasure.' the journalist replied. 'I am curious to hear your story.'

Mr Godfroid sat down opposite Emma and beckoned over the waiter. He had obviously been there before.

He ordered them both a drink then turned to Emma in a business-like manner but with a smile which put her more at ease.

'Well why don't you start from the beginning and tell me your story.' he encouraged Emma.

'What I have to say I would like to be kept at this stage in complete confidence.' Emma began. 'Can I count on you for that? Can I also ask if you are a freemason?'

Mr Godfroid looked at Emma then replied 'You have my word of honour that what you say will be treated in confidence. We only publish with the agreement of the client and no I am not a freemason.'

Emma sighed with relief. Thank goodness for that she told herself.

'It is a long story and it is quite complicated but I will do my best to summarise. Please interrupt me if anything is not clear and I will try to explain further.' Emma urged.

After she had finished outlining the story they had already finished the starter and were half way through the main course. Emma nibbled like a mouse. Her otherwise healthy appetite and appreciation of fine cooking seemed to have deserted her. If Mr Godfroid noticed, he was good enough not to show it. He was evidently enjoying his meal as he tucked enthusiastically into each course. He was an obvious dab hand at this sort of thing. From reading his articles, it was clear that he was a seasoned and tough journalist. This was precisely why Emma had contacted him. She wondered if it was not a double-edged sword.

'Well.' Mr Godfroid suddenly said, taking a serviette and wiping around his mouth following a sip of wine 'you are right when you said you have been naïve to have complete confidence in one of our judges. Judges here are unfortunately not above reproach.' he added with a certain amount of conviction coupled with irony.

Emma smiled. To hear this from an experienced journalist made her feel strangely relieved. Things were slowly beginning to make more sense.

Mr Godfroid guided the conversation onto the orgies which took place among some members of the elite including politicians, industrialists, members of the judiciary, police etc.

'If it is among consenting adults then I have no problem with it.' he stated.

'Me neither.' Emma agreed. 'What worries me is that freemasonry and cronyism are being used to distort the course of justice. Justice is perfect nowhere but what I have seen here so far is frankly unbelievable and unacceptable in a modern western democracy.'

'The thing which concerns me about these orgies attended by the elite is that they may be used by less honest members of society as a form of blackmail against members of the judiciary or the government.' he continued.

There was a moment of silence as Emma reflected on what Mr Godfroid had said.

'You know these child witnesses and that recent book, these people are crazy and cannot be taken seriously,' he continued.

Emma was surprised by the comment. 'Oh why is that?' Emma asked. The book she had just finished reading about the alleged abuse of children was still very clear in her mind.

'They are completely unstable. Can you imagine if only half of what they said is true then you would want to go home and get drunk every single night because it is just too horrible to contemplate.'

'I know it is horrendous.' Emma replied. 'But just imagine that even a small part is true then it is our duty as citizens and parents to fight for the truth to come out and for these things to stop. I recently read the book and found it very disturbing indeed.'

'Oh it is just pornographic.' Mr Godfroid replied emphatically.

'I found it heart-breaking. Maybe there are a couple of anomalies but no one can invent such a moving story. You just can't make this stuff up.' Emma explained.

Mr Godfroid looked at Emma for a couple of seconds then continued. 'This Ella, I visited her parents. A pretty shabby house but they showed me photos of her youth, happy, carefree. She is simply a mythomane inventing these stories. She had a perfectly normal upbringing with normal parents. She is mentally ill.' he continued.

Emma did not want to get into a long discussion on this topic with Mr Godfroid. She had understood from a couple of different sources that Ella, the author who had written the book and had been forced into prostitution as a small child, had been brought up by her grandmother who had been running a series of brothels for years. Not the cosy home environment Mr Godfroid was eluding to.

'Well about your story.' Mr Godfroid continued. 'I have all the files on the Rollo affair at home and nothing about Jules Mercier in them.'

'Well nothing happened to him publicly in this respect and I suppose even if there is substance as rumour has it, then it would have been effectively covered up.' Emma continued. 'After all he was a member of the judiciary and it seems it was the world of politics the courts eventually went after, not one of their own.'

'Yes that is a possibility.' Mr Godfroid replied.

'What can you tell me about the city where my ex-husband and his lawyer live?' Emma asked.

'Well only that over there things really do not happen like they do in the rest of the country.'

'Do you mean it is a second Palermo?' Emma asked with a smile.

'Sort of.' he replied equally amused.

'Even if you agree I would have problems to publish your story.' Mr Godfroid continued. 'We can report on almost everything apart from divorce cases as this contravenes the protection of privacy law.'

Emma smiled. She was beginning to relax. 'This is not about a simple or even contentious divorce case. This is about something more complex and serious that is to say the distortion of justice by some members of a secret society, the freemasons.' Emma protested.

'I will talk to my editor but I don't think I can help any further by publishing the story.'

'Well thanks anyway.' Emma said as they shook hands and said their goodbyes. Mr Godfroid paid the bill. They parted under the proviso that they might meet up again one day. They had had a pleasant and interesting conversation. Emma had discovered a few things but not as much as she had hoped. She had a small suspicion that Mr Godfroid knew more than he was letting on. One thing on which they both agreed was that the judiciary had a tendency, in some cases, to create its own reality.

Chapter 51

The meeting with the journalist Mr Godfroid had taken longer than expected and Emma headed quickly back to the car for the one and a half hour's drive to pick up the children for the weekend. She looked at her watch. It was already 2.45 pm and she would be at least fifteen minutes late. Since the first appeal court ruling a few months earlier, she had been granted the right to pick up the children directly from school every second weekend. She decided to call the school to announce that she would be slightly late so the children would not worry.

It was an effort to dial the number as the headmistress had ignored Emma's requests for a copy of Olivia and Sebastian's school reports after the temporary transfer of custody and Emma had felt completely excluded and discriminated against. She put on a brave and cheerful voice. No problem the secretary replied promising to inform Olivia and Sebastian who, she confirmed, would play in the school yard until Emma arrived.

Olivia and Sebastian were pleased to see their mother. They ran into Emma's arms and she hugged them both. They headed back in the car for another short but enjoyable weekend.

A couple of weeks later, Olivia announced that their father insisted that Emma no longer go to the school to pick them up but to the house instead. On the few occasions Emma had been to the school to collect her children, they had run into her arms. Their friends had followed and Emma had given them all sweets.

'Your mummy is pretty and so nice.' their friends had commented. The teachers had stared at Emma somewhat curiously. This sort of demolished the bad image which Paul had obviously tried to paint of Emma as the alcoholic and devious mother who had abducted her frightened children against their will and tried to abscond to the UK in complete contravention of the law. Emma did not argue. She just wanted the children to be spared the stress and problems which their father could cause when contradicted. There were much more important battles to win.

Mrs Sinclair gave Emma a call. Victor Falconer had still not forwarded to her his papers for the next stage of the custody hearing despite several requests from her side and this, three months' after the final report from the experts. She explained to Emma that Victor Falconer was pushing her very hard to return to the first provincial court although she had indicated to him Emma's firm wish for the case to be handled by the appeal court. She told Emma that she thought that they should meet to discuss together which course of action to take, then to push forward very forcefully.

Emma gave the matter some serious thought. She jotted down all the reasons for not returning to the provincial court. She surprised herself when she read them all. The whole thing was definitely very strange. She felt uneasy. Emma was starting to see things less emotionally and more logically and even to get a complete overview. Yet at the same time she had the nagging feeling that there were still some missing pieces and additional elements which she had to discover. She started to prepare herself psychologically for the next round of surprises.

The following day she met Mrs Sinclair who, after reading Emma's list, accepted that Emma had enough good reasons to feel uncomfortable about returning to the provincial court for the custody hearing. She promptly informed Victor Falconer in writing that she intended to plead their case in front of the youth court section of the appeal court who, in her opinion, were perfectly competent to pass judgment on the present situation owing to the law of evocation. She insisted that Victor Falconer send his court papers in the very near future otherwise she would ask the court to define a date by which he would be obliged to do so. Poor Mrs Sinclair Emma sighed to herself. If she had only known what she was taking on with my case, she may have thought twice before getting involved.

The following week, true to form, Victor Falconer went into attack mode with another official letter. Again Emma had given the children a mobile phone and asked them to keep it activated so that she could call them every day between 4.00 pm and 7.00 pm. In addition, she had asked them to call their friends without informing their father. Of course, on returning home, the children had told their father rather than hide the phone as Emma, their mother, had suggested they do. Olivia and Sebastian were completely free to call whomever they wanted including their friends but were not interested in staying in contact with Valerie, Cathy or her daughter. It was preferable that Emma, who tried to call every day, limit her calls to between 5.30 pm and 7.00 pm so as not to disturb their harmonious family life.

By now Emma was used to such nauseating letters packed full of untruths from Victor Falconer. Mrs Sinclair replied promptly. Unlike Hubert Belette she was not going to allow Victor Falconer to continue inventing things and presenting it as evidence of Emma's bad will in the next court hearing. She also replied officially.

Emma had never tried to call her children more than three times a week and always at reasonable hours. She had given them back their mobile phone as often she encountered an engaged tone when she tried to contact them or an answering machine on which she left a message but never received a call back. Or she had to free the line while in conversation with her son and daughter as other members of the family needed to use the house phone. She had never asked the children to hide the phone and asked herself how she could have even thought of doing so, since by definition, the phone rings.

On the contrary, Emma had asked the children to inform their father that they had recovered their mobile phone. The paper she had given the children contained the SIM number and the telephone number of some friends but she had never insisted that the children make calls to these numbers. Mrs Sinclair asked why the children would not be allowed to call their mother on a mobile phone which she had given them and was concerned enough for their well-being to ensure that the phone was not abused. Finally, she wanted to point out that Emma had never put any obstacle in Paul's way to prevent the children talking to their father when they were with her.

Emma sighed. When would these unprovoked attacks stop? Emma was beginning to bounce back and although she found such incidents frustrating, she was more determined than ever not to let them get her down.

Chapter 52

Emma and the children were looking forward to their skiing holiday together. It was only a few weeks away. Meanwhile, Olivia and Sebastian had taken up horse riding at a farm five minutes away from Emma's home. Their friends had told them how much fun it was. As soon as Paul had discovered that the children had taken up horse riding and were enjoying it, he arranged for them to do the same on alternative weekends which Emma appreciated as they would be able to practice on a weekly basis.

On the Sunday afternoon, Emma stood in the pale winter sun watching Olivia and Sebastian cantor around the enclosure on their horses with their teacher. Suddenly a gust of wind blew a jacket from the fence and Olivia's horse bolted instinctively. Emma watched everything in slow motion as Olivia flew over the horse's head and landed on the ground with a decisive thud. Oh no Emma shouted ducking under the wooden fence and running over to where she was lying. She asked Olivia if she was OK. Olivia confirmed she was fine. With Emma's help, she picked herself up and dusted down her clothes. The teacher arrived and asked Olivia if she was hurt. No she replied bravely explaining that she had landed on her thumb but proceeded to move it up and down confirming again that she was fine. Undeterred, she even asked to continue with the lesson.

The teacher recovered the frightened horse and rode him around the enclosure a few times to reassure him before Olivia climbed back on. During the afternoon Emma kept checking with Olivia that her thumb was fine and she could move it without difficulty or pain. That evening she drove the children back to their father's place and in the dimly lit street hugged them goodbye for another two weeks. To Emma's surprise, she received a phone call from Paul next morning. He seemed almost triumphant.

'You know Olivia's thumb is broken.' he announced. 'I hope you have an insurance.'

'Sure I do.' Emma replied. 'You know it was an accident which can happen anywhere.' she started to explain only too aware that all would be done to use this latest unfortunate incident against her. 'Following the fall the teacher and I checked and Olivia said she was fine. She could move her thumb perfectly normally. There was therefore no reason for me to worry or for me to take Olivia to the hospital.' Emma explained as convincingly as she could.

'Send me details of the insurance because I am going to need them to recuperate the medical bills,' Paul instructed.

'Fine.' Emma replied and Paul hung up and was gone.

Emma sat at her desk dreading what a big deal Victor Falconer and Paul would try to make out of this latest event. She had been in this movie too long and knew she was in for another potential battering. She sighed deeply. She thought it better to give Mrs Sinclair the heads up that more official letters were probably on their way. The following day she sent off details of the insurance to Paul. As Emma had expected, by the end of the week two official letters had already landed on Mrs Sinclair's desk from Victor Falconer. She asked Emma for her input to help her formulate a reply.

Emma sat down and started to read the letters. They were so predictable. She wished she could have punched Victor Falconer in the chops. He was the most dishonest and unethical individual she had ever had the misfortune to encounter. As far as she was concerned, he was an expert at distorting the truth and wreaking havoc on innocent people's lives.

The first letter began that Olivia had complained upon returning to her father's home the previous weekend that she had a severe pain in her hand. She had explained to her father that she had fallen from the horse during her lesson and that Emma had brushed it off and had simply told her that it was not serious. Noticing that her hand was swollen, Paul had gone to the hospital on the Sunday evening where an x-ray had revealed the existence of a fracture of the thumb. Enclosed were two medical certificates.

Paul had contacted the riding school to learn from the manager that there was no insurance policy as Emma Brown had refused to take one out despite the repeated advice from the owners of the stable. As it was a nasty fracture of the thumb, just above a growth area, immediate care was necessary. Left untreated, there could have been a deformity of the hand. As it was impossible to put in a plaster cast, the hospital staff had bandaged the thumb and recommended that Paul see a specialist as soon as possible to decide if a surgical intervention was necessary. The owner of the riding stable had seemed quite put out declaring that for months he had asked Mrs Brown to do the necessary to insure her two children. Mrs Brown had apparently had the forms at home for a long period and had never filled them out. Emma shook her head in disbelief. These people were unbelievably devious and also so dangerous.

She started to read the second letter. Olivia had been examined by a specialist and her hand had been put in plaster. One could only hope that there would be no need for an operation. However, any sport was seriously out of the question for the next two months. Paul was in no doubt that Emma would respect this provision, notably that Olivia would not be able to go skiing in the half term holiday, nor swimming or horse riding. The letter enquired if Emma planned to make any particular arrangements for half term.

Then to Emma's disbelief went on to allege that Emma had sent Paul a copy of the insurance and in reality it had been backdated by the owner of the riding school. Emma had then gone on to explain to Paul that by this means he could recuperate the medical expenses from the insurance. Victor Falconer concluded sarcastically that he presumed that Emma would take full responsibility for all these manipulations.

Emma was livid at the audacity of it all. Obviously Victor Falconer was planning to use this distorted version of events in the appeal court hearing to show what an irresponsible and dishonest mother Emma was. She took the two letters along and went to see the owners of the stable. It was embarrassing as Paul and company had also put into question their integrity. Luckily, Olivia's best friend's mother kept a horse in the stable and had known the owners for many years. She gave the owners a call and confirmed the authenticity of Emma's story, adding that she had been a witness to the manipulative excesses of Paul and his lawyer over the last three years.

The stable owner willingly confirmed that Emma had in fact never refused to take out an insurance and on the contrary had taken home the forms immediately, returned them signed and paid the premium when the children had booked their first lesson. As soon as Paul had notified them of the accident, they had sent off the accident declaration forms the same day. All the forms bore the date at the beginning of the year when they were presented to the riders. Everything had therefore been done normally and nothing backdated, the proof being that the insurance company would handle the claim favourably.

Emma passed everything onto Mrs Sinclair to formulate the official reply. She asked Mrs Sinclair to remind Victor Falconer that there was a certain code of ethics in the legal profession and he was obviously falling short of upholding what would be considered acceptable behaviour in a civilized Western society.

Mrs Sinclair's official letter explained that Olivia's thumb had moved normally following the accident and had been examined by the owner of the stable as well. If there would have been any sign of a problem, Emma would have gone immediately to the hospital.

As often happens, fractures do not manifest themselves immediately which was the case here since Olivia's thumb had only swollen after taking a hot bath upon her return. There was no reason for Emma not to take out an insurance as it only cost 20 € for the full year. As soon as Emma had discovered the accident she had immediately done the necessary for Paul to be reimbursed.

Furthermore, as soon as she had found out about the fracture and in order not to disappoint her children who had looked forward to the skiing holiday, she had booked a holiday in the sun in a club full of fun activities for children. During the holidays the children could be reached easily on Emma's mobile phone. Mrs Sinclair concluded that she regretted the constant trial on which her client found herself and did not understand the reasons for it in view of the affectionate presence which Emma gave her children each time she was fortunate to spend time with them.

Emma, Olivia and Sebastian had a wonderful holiday. They had never taken a holiday in the sun out of season before. It was twenty-five degrees in early March and the sun did wonders for their moral after what seemed like a long winter. Their bungalow was a two-minute walk from the golden beach. The entertainment and the food in the club were extremely good. They also went sightseeing, the highlight being a trip to the desert and a camel ride with the nomads as well as a horse drawn carriage ride through an oasis.

The children had been asked by the school to prepare a project of their half term holiday with photos and a narrative. Emma and the children chose post cards of the country and the culture and wrote together the text based on their own experience and impressions. Olivia and Sebastian were pleased with the result. Emma was really happy for once to be able to help them with something to do with school. They received top marks and a special word of praise from the teacher. Emma was proud of them.

Victor Falconer eventually deposited his written defence with the appeal court and sent a copy to Mrs Sinclair. She immediately made an appointment to see Emma.

'I am so sorry about the content.' Mrs Sinclair started to explain to Emma sympathetically. 'I felt sick reading it so I can't begin to think how you must feel. However, you have to go through things very carefully and give me your feedback for our additional input. Especially the most recent events, noticeably during your holiday. I have to reply you see. Our first set of court papers were very conciliatory in the interests of the children but we can't leave unanswered and uncontested the tirade of accusations which Victor Falconer is now presenting to the appeal court judges.'

Emma had not yet read them but already felt full of trepidation followed by consternation. She felt her indignation beginning to rise again.

'Tell me something.' she asked Mrs Sinclair. 'How dare he send such a pack of lies to the appeal court? Is he not worried that they will see through things and reprimand him for being so dishonest, confrontational and making a mockery of the judicial system?'

Mrs Sinclair shrugged her shoulders. 'I don't know.' she replied. 'I would not do it but some lawyers act differently.'

'Tell me about it.' Emma replied ironically. 'The courts should do their job thoroughly and put some order in their house when they encounter people like Victor Falconer.'

Emma could not help thinking that around every corner there was a new surprise waiting and not many of them were pleasant ones.

Emma took the submissions and supporting documents home. With a heavy heart, she took out her highlighter pen and a pad and pen to jot down the pieces of additional evidence she was going to need to counteract the latest list of lies. Every time she had to do this she could not help feeling angry. Why did she have to do this? Why could the judges not scratch below the surface, see where the real problem originated and put things right?

Victor Falconer wrote that it was stinging to note that yet again Emma did not appear to apply the same principles to herself as she did to Paul. She claimed not to put any obstacle in Paul's way preventing him from enjoying regular contact with his children. However, recently during her holiday in the sun, the opposite could be claimed. Emma called the IT department of her company and they gave her a detailed print out of the calls made on her mobile phone clearly showing that during the week away, the children had called Paul five times and had spoken to him on at least three occasions.

Paul had insisted that Olivia and Sebastian send him a postcard. Emma had encouraged them to do so. Again, she was the object of a vicious attack. Concerned about systematically vexing Paul in a very petty minded way, a good example of Emma's negative approach was the postcard the children wanted to send in the half term holiday. In fact, it was sent by Emma herself without even mentioning a name, just the address and she had dictated what the children should put on the card. In her defence, Emma pointed out that first the card was in their handwriting and she had nothing to do with the content. The children had simply written that they were having a good time, the weather was great and the food delicious.

Lea had tried to play down the holiday telling Olivia and Sebastian before they left how bad the food and hygiene were at their destination. When their father asked about the food during a phone call, the children had confirmed it was really good pointing out that it was only to be expected because they were in a four-star club after all.

Olivia had asked to have her hair trimmed and styled in the club's hair salon during the holiday. Victor Falconer's court papers explained that Olivia had been to the hair dressers with her father just before the holidays and came back from the holiday with her mother with her hair styled in such a bad way that upon her own insistence, she had to visit the hairdressers again with her father before resuming school. Emma sent Mrs Sinclair a photo taken of Olivia just after leaving the hair dressing salon which proved beyond doubt that her hair was perfectly cut and styled.

Emma was angry but worried. There were thirty-seven pages of such lies and dozens of official letters and confirmations from Paul's acquaintances about how well the children were faring in their father's home from people they had seen a couple of years ago or only once. Luckily the children's current teacher refused to cooperate. He told Sebastian to tell his father that he did not want any problems later. It was nothing short of character assassination on a huge scale.

Emma had no choice but to go point by point and give Mrs Sinclair the necessary evidence to refute as many of the accusations as possible. Emma really hoped the appeal court judges would dig a bit deeper than the provincial courts had done so far. Friends tried to reassure her that in the appeal court there would be three skilled judges and it would make a difference. I really hope so Emma kept replying.

Chapter 53

Easter came and went. Emma took Olivia and Sebastian to England for the week to visit her sister Laura and her family. Laura always organised lots of interesting activities. They went to Woburn safari park, Windsor and LEGOLAND, tenpin bowling, the cinema and otherwise just pottered around. Emma's treat was to saunter over to the village shop and buy a daily newspaper and eat her favourites such as Cornish pasties and sausage rolls. It was so nice to have her children with her for the whole week.

Before she knew it, it was time to drop the children off at Paul's mother's house in the country for the second half of the school holidays. Paul's mother had told the children to invite Emma to come in for a chat and a cup of tea when she arrived.

Paul's mother had fallen out with Lea. Emma had known it was inevitable and just a question of time before these two possessive and narrow minded women decided they did not see eye to eye. Paul was caught in the middle as unfortunately were the children. Paul's mother was not allowed to visit Paul's home nor call her grandchildren on the landline. She had been told that she had to use the mobile phone Emma had purchased them when she wanted to speak to her grandchildren. This seemed rather ironic after the unrelenting support she had given her one and only son before, during and after the divorce.

As Emma hugged and kissed Olivia and Sebastian goodbye she asked them to tell Paul's mum that she would not be coming in. Olivia blew Emma a kiss as Paul's mother opened the door and came tottering down the drive to meet them. Emma looked straight ahead and drove off direction home.

It was becoming obvious that as the experts' report had specified that the children were fine in both parental homes and had failed to recommend with which parent Olivia and Sebastian should reside principally, that the children were going to be auditioned eventually by the youth court judge. True to form, Paul was trying to keep the time they spent with Emma to a minimum. During the Easter holiday he had instructed his mother, as so often the case, to do some ground work for him. Tell me about life with mummy she kept probing. She confided in Olivia that she thought that both children were better off with their mum. Olivia fell into the trap.

'Me too.' she replied. 'I am not happy in daddy's home and I don't like Lea. I wrote to mummy's lawyer telling her all the things I don't like and asked her to do everything to reunite me with mummy as soon as possible.'

'Me too.' Sebastian joined in.

All of a sudden, panic crossed Paul's mother's face as she exclaimed 'Oh my goodness, oh my goodness. I am going to have to tell your father about this.'

She went immediately to the phone. The two children sat despondently as she made the call to Paul. He was very angry and forced Olivia and Sebastian to sit down upon his arrival and write a letter which he dictated confirming that Emma had forced them to write the letters to Mrs Sinclair a few months earlier. To top it all, he asked them to write that Emma had threatened that if they refused to do so, she would hit them. Emma had never hit her son and daughter. She was saddened. It was clearer than ever that this was going to be a long hard fight up to the bitter end. Poor children she told herself.

The following weekend Olivia and Sebastian were together and enjoying dinner when they explained to Emma what Paul and his mother, their grannie had done. They asked Emma not to give up. They reiterated that they wanted to come back and live with her insisting that she had to carry on fighting. Emma hugged them both.

She would carry on fighting until her children told her that they were fine where they were. So far this was far from being the case.

Emma was sure that Paul loved his son and daughter but he controlled them by fear and she could never accept his attempts to shut her out of their lives nor the way this whole affair had been premeditated and handled from the beginning. Emma told Olivia and Sebastian that they were going to have to start to stand up to their father and tell him what they really wanted.

'If you want to come back you will have to have the courage to tell him one day.' Emma told them.

'But mum you don't understand. He gets so angry when we talk about things like that. We are frightened when he shouts.' Sebastian explained.

'I know.' Emma continued. 'But you have to help me too. I can't do everything on my own.'

'OK I will.' Olivia confided.

'Me too.' Sebastian added meekly.

'Good,' Emma exclaimed. 'Now who wants dessert?'

Emma spoke to a good friend about how she could go about proving that she had been set up.

'I know it but I need proof, preferably before we go to the appeal court.' Emma explained.

'Well you need to prove first of all that Paul and Jules Mercier knew one another before you went to him for advice about your mutual consent divorce. That it was a plot and premediated.' the friend explained.

'How?' Emma asked.

'Check your old phone records. Call the provider and ask them for details of the incoming and outgoing calls for the six-month period preceding your separation when you first spoke of divorce seriously for the first time.' she suggested.

'Good idea.' Emma replied. 'He may have used his mobile but then you never know. We might just get lucky if he called from the house phone.'

She wrote to and called the provider. Unfortunately, she drew a blank. They apologized for not being able to help but said they did not keep records from four years ago. Emma was disappointed. She found it difficult to believe but could not really argue. She would have to find another way.

Again Paul started to be contentious about the split of weekends. Emma had no official visiting right and Paul seemed to be making the most of his dominant position. Mrs Sinclair became impatient especially when she caught Paul lying to Emma about not being able to see her children one weekend which should have been hers. Paul claimed that the school fete ran the whole weekend so Olivia and Sebastian would not be available to see their mother. Mrs Sinclair picked up the phone herself and called the school to learn that the school fete was only on the Friday evening.

In addition, it was Mother's Day on the Sunday and the children had made Emma a present at school which they looked forward to giving her. Paul called Emma on Friday evening after Mrs Sinclair's exasperated fax had gone through informing Victor Falconer and Paul that Emma would pick the children up on the Saturday morning.

'Don't even bother coming because we won't be there and you will have wasted your time.' he told her emphatically.

'But it is my weekend.' Emma protested. 'On top it's Mother's Day and I am not going to wait three weeks again to see my children.'

'Too bad.' he bellowed. 'That is how it is and that is how it will stay.' and with that Paul hung up.

Emma sat in the car in front of the house. She had just done the shopping and bought the children their favourite desserts. Tears came to her eyes. Tears of sheer and utter frustration. She now faced the weekend on her own. How she loathed this system, these people. It was nothing short of diabolical.

Emma picked up the phone and called Laura her sister and Valerie. They were sympathetic. He is a real bum they told her but he won't change so you just have to let it pass over your head. When the children are a little older they will see clear.

Emma was determined to put on a brave face. She had received a voucher for her birthday for a day out at a local spa complete with treatments and a massage. She called the spa and luckily, as it was Mother's Day, they still had a couple of spare slots. She went along and was pampered from head to foot. As she ran afterwards on the treadmill in the gym she thought of her children. She ran faster and faster and gritted her teeth in determination. She was more resolved than ever that the truth would come out. How dare these unethical people and this system continue to treat her so unfairly?

She called Olivia and Sebastian on the Monday evening and asked them if they had enjoyed the weekend. They explained that they had accompanied Paul to his mother's home to celebrate Mother's Day. 'Very nice.' Emma replied promptly changing the subject.

Chapter 54

It was the time that the internet and online sales were becoming increasingly popular. Emma discovered Amazon. It was so easy to find what one was looking for and with a couple of clicks the books dropped into the letter box a few days later. Emma soon had four Amazon accounts in four different countries and continued to keep track of existing and new books which came out and might help her further her research. Two books caught her attention. She read the descriptions and evaluations. They sounded rather heavy but they might reveal something interesting. She ordered them online and started to read them the following weekend.

Apparently, the former defence minister had allegedly been seen by several witnesses participating in sex parties with children from a high-class prostitution network. He had been accompanied by the chief prosecutor of the provincial court as well as a well-known arms manufacturer. The arms manufacturer had apparently made his fortune during the period his good friend had run the ministry of national defence. According to the author of one of the books, these luxury prostitution networks targeted the political, economic and judicial world. A means by which organised crime could spread its influence by blackmail and corruption up to the summit of the state apparatus. The arms manufacturer's company had apparently delivered a large order of armoured vehicles and witnesses had claimed a bribe of several millions had been paid to the defence minister for awarding the contract.

During a subsequent enquiry, the defence minister had confirmed that his arms dealer friend was someone for whom he had a great deal of esteem and who was certainly an example to follow for many industrialists. This opinion was apparently not shared by the public prosecutor's office who pursued the arms manufacturer through the courts regretting that the defence minister could not be found on the same bench. The arms manufacturer was sentenced to two years in prison and received a large fine for forgery and tax evasion. As it turned out, the arms manufacturer also owned a factory in Malta. According to the second book, this company served to overturn the arms embargo against Iran during the war with Iraq.

Emma started to feel decidedly uncomfortable. She thought back to the proud admission by Hubert Belette that arms contracts had been his specialty and that he had negotiated several in Malta. Emma had also recently learned via a friend that Hubert Belette had been imprisoned and had been banned from practicing as a lawyer for several years. The natural question she now asked herself was if this was all connected.

To add fuel to her suspicions, one of the close friends of the arms manufacturer was the police chief whom Jules Mercier had admitted to Emma was a good friend of his and who was already suspended as investigations into his alleged links with the underworld were ongoing. She thought back to the stash of arms discovered in Jules Mercier's former villa after he has moved houses. Oh no, Emma lamented. What a fine old mess she had probably been unwittingly drawn into.

As for the defence minister, the head of the local secret services had been contacted by other Western secret services to confirm that they had a problem with the minister of the national defence. He had apparently put his many private business interests above state security and made regular trips to Eastern Europe to source products more cheaply at a time when the cold war was still ongoing. He had enjoyed a very close relationship with a lady from Eastern Europe who was also suspected to be a spy.

The defence minister was subsequently found guilty of fraud and tax evasion. He was accused of over one hundred offences and found guilty of over thirty, receiving a suspended sentence and a heavy fine. For once the judge seemed to be on the ball. Wrapping up the case he told the defence minister that he was a large and irreclaimable fraudster who had imposed laws on others and who should have been the first to respect them. According to the book, this was the end of his career. Not the defence minister's but the brave judge's who had spoken out and done what should have been done years earlier.

Emma could not believe what she was discovering. What a quandary, what a situation she muttered to herself shaking her head in disbelief. Just when she thought she had seen it all. However, her instincts told her that there was even more to come and she braced herself with a certain amount of trepidation for the next round of revelations.

Chapter 55

Emma visited her doctor.

'Well we can do the operation end of July.' the doctor announced looking in his diary. 'I will send you the papers to hand over to the hospital on your day of admission. You need to arrive the day before to do all the pre op tests.'

'Fine.' Emma confirmed shaking the doctor's hand and leaving the surgery.

It was not a serious operation but it was under general anaesthetic and the first time Emma was going to undergo an operation. She was a little apprehensive. Better keep it very quiet she told herself. This might just be a prime opportunity to bump her off and make it look like an accident. She already had a suspicion that her phone had been tapped. She told only Valerie and Mary Jo of the impending intervention and then face to face. They would come and visit her during her five-day stay. She did not want to worry family and friends abroad so she would tell them once she was out and on the mend. She could call work the day after the operation, tell them where she was, when she would be back and send them the necessary medical certificate.

Emma arrived at the hospital. Valerie had accompanied her then had driven her car home and parked it in front of Emma's house. Emma would not be able to drive for at least one week following the operation so Valerie planned to come and pick her up afterwards. Valerie was Emma's rock. Emma did not know what she would have done without her.

It was a beautiful summer's day and Emma introduced herself to the lady, Pauline, who was sharing her room in the hospital. She seemed very nice. Smart, sophisticated, cultured with a good sense of humour. The two were to be operated the same morning so they would go through this experience together. Pauline and Emma hit it off right away and they were already joking together as they went through the pre op tests. The operation took place early the next morning. Before Emma knew it she was back in her sun filled room drowsy but relieved to have successfully survived the anaesthetic.

Next day was Sebastian's birthday and she just had to call her children. They were in the south of France on holiday with their father. Emma still felt a little disoriented but was greatly cheered up by the sound of Olivia and Sebastian's little voices on the end of the phone. They had celebrated Sebastian's birthday earlier with their friends from the former school and would then have another celebration in two weeks' time during their planned summer holiday together in Tenerife.

During the post op days and between visits, Pauline and Emma chatted about a huge variety of things. Conversation seemed to come very naturally. Emma discovered that Pauline worked for one of the local councils where Jules Mercier had admitted to Emma that he had been involved with in the past.

Emma casually slipped into the conversation 'Oh by the way have you heard of Jules Mercier?'

'Oh yes,' Pauline replied thoughtfully adding 'but my husband will probably know more. There was a big scandal. It was covered at the time in most of the papers.'

'Oh.' Emma replied. 'Yes I had heard that a large sum of money disappeared and there was talk of corruption.'

'You know what?' Pauline suggested. 'Go to the head office of the Daily Herald a large national newspaper and ask them to do a search for you. My son did it recently for a project he was preparing for school. Apparently they have now put every article on computer and you can run a search then you will find the date of the event and the article. With this you can then go to the national library and ask to see all the other newspapers from the same period and see what they had to say as well.'

This seemed like an excellent idea and Emma was suddenly excited to find out more about this dishonest individual whose catastrophic advice had inflicted such suffering on her and the children over the previous couple of years. Soon it was time to leave the hospital. Pauline and Emma said goodbye and swopped telephone numbers. Valerie came to pick Emma up.

As the operation had been in the region of the abdomen, Emma was still a little sore when walking and it would be a couple of days before she could drive again. She was happy to be in the comfort of her own home. She planned to rest for the weekend then on Monday visit the newspaper and start her research on Jules Mercier's incarceration.

On Monday morning, Emma parked her car on a busy wide road in the capital. She carefully checked the traffic before crossing, aware that she could not move as quickly as normal. Living dangerously had unfortunately become a way of life for Emma of late but she told herself that it was preferable to take only calculated risks. Emma entered the premises of the newspaper. The reception area was spacious, bright and tastefully decorated. The receptionist was very friendly. Emma briefly explained what she was looking for. The receptionist pointed Emma in the direction of another young lady sitting at a computer screen on the other side of the reception area.

'Can I help you?' she asked Emma with a smile.

'Yes please.' Emma replied easing herself slowly down onto a chair. She could feel the muscles in her abdomen pull after the recent operation. 'I would like you to check for me what you have as articles on a former judge called Jules Mercier.'

'For what period?' the young lady asked.

'Everything you have. As far back as your records go.' Emma requested.

'Fine.' the young lady said tapping in the name. 'Now let's see what we come up with.'

Emma waited in expectation. Hopefully they would find something. A lot of people seemed to know something about the scandal Jules Mercier had been involved in but getting something more concrete on the affair was proving more difficult. Emma had bumped into Edgar a few weeks earlier at work and he had asked Emma how things were going. She had explained that they were plodding along and that she had discovered meanwhile that Jules Mercier had been in prison involved in a big scandal, adding some even maintained that it was connected to the Rollo affair. Edgar had looked at Emma initially in surprise before nodding in acknowledgement.

Emma could not help thinking that he should have mentioned it when he helped her change counsel and she could have confronted Jules Mercier there and then. However, on the other hand, she guessed that she would not have uncovered so many other things had she had not stayed on good terms with Jules Mercier for a little longer.

It seemed like an eternity as the computer ran its search. Suddenly there was a ping and the young lady's face lit up as an article appeared on her screen.

'Got something here.' she announced with satisfaction. 'From the beginning of the decade. Embezzlement of several millions. A judge held under suspicion.'

'Can I have a copy?' Emma requested in anticipation.

'No problem. It will cost 5 cents.' the young lady replied.

'Can you find anything else?' Emma continued as the document began to churn out of the printer at the side of her desk. Emma waited eagerly to read it.

The young lady typed in a few more key words and they both waited.

'No, unfortunately not.' came the reply. 'That seems to be everything.'

'No follow up article?' Emma asked in surprise. 'It seems strange that the outcome of the arrest, the details of the charges or the eventual outcome of the trial have not been covered.'

'Sorry.' the young lady repeated. 'That really is everything the computer is giving me.'

Emma thought to herself that it smacked of another cover up as, might be expected under the circumstances.

'Do you have a department with photos open to the public too?' Emma enquired. While she was here she might as well check this out too.

'Yes of course.' the young lady answered most helpfully. 'I will call them now and ask them to come down and meet you then you can go upstairs and see if you can find what you are looking for.'

Emma thanked the young lady gratefully for all her help. She occasionally bought the weekly magazine from this particular newspaper because she found the articles on current affairs interesting. She decided to continue to do so as the receptionists had been so helpful. She stood up slowly as the young man from the photographic department came down to meet her. He walked quite briskly and Emma tried to keep up with him. She could feel the stitches pulling if she walked too fast.

'What are you looking for in particular?' he asked cheerfully steering Emma over towards the stairs.

'Anything you have on Jules Mercier.' she replied as he took the article from her and read it through quickly. 'Maybe you have some photos of him with friends, politicians, businessmen and the like.'

'I know the appeal court counsellor in whose hands the instruction of the file was given.' he admitted to Emma's surprise. 'He was the father of a good friend. He was a really good man. Unfortunately, he died recently.'

'That is a shame.' Emma remarked.

Apparently because Jules Mercier was himself a judge and therefore part of the judiciary he could only be tried by the appeal court and not a normal court of first instance. In the case of the ministers in the Rollo affair, this was one level higher, with the Supreme Court being the official body to handle the proceedings.

Emma asked herself if this was the gentleman and judge in the appeal court who had let Jules Mercier off following the freemason bows. Suddenly the image of Jules standing that Saturday evening in the garden of the restaurant on that balmy summer evening imitating the bows of his lawyer during the closed trial and his words 'it saved me' came flooding back to Emma. It seemed almost surreal.

They entered a very large room full of hundreds of hanging files. A few busy employees looked up as they walked in. Emma said hello and smiled. The young man checked his records and confirmed that a photo of Jules Mercier was on file. Emma followed him expectantly to the wall of hanging files. He took one down. Inside was a black and white portrait taken a few years before.

'Is that all you have?' Emma asked trying to hide her disappointment.

'Afraid so.' the young man replied.

Emma thanked him and headed towards the lift. Who other should come through the door at that moment than the journalist Mr Godfroid with whom Emma had had lunch a few months earlier. They spotted one another at exactly the same time.

'Hello.' Emma said. 'Remember me?'

'Yes.' he replied 'Mrs Brown. So how are you?'

'Just fine.' Emma replied. 'Just checking out a few things in your offices. Nice place you have.'

'Yes we like it too. Just got back from the east. Big investigation.' he continued.

'I keep reading your articles.' Emma added. 'Keep digging and keep us all up to date.'

The lift arrived and Emma said goodbye. After her meeting with Mr Godfroid she had written to him to thank him for lunch and to ask him to kindly send her any copies of articles he or the paper might have on Jules Mercier or Hubert Belette which she could eventually submit to the appeal court. The letter had remained unanswered.

When Emma got back to the car, she sat in the driver's seat and read the article through slowly and carefully. Jules Mercier had been in prison for six weeks when the news of his arrest broke in the papers. He was accused of forgery and embezzlement. The amounts involved amounted to tens of millions. The appeal court refused to confirm the figure pointing out that they had asked for an expert assessment to put a figure on the size of the sum which had disappeared and also the exact nature of the malpractice. It was clear however, that these sums must be considerable. The police were helping the instructing judge with his enquiries.

'Phew.' Emma said to herself. There it is black on white. God she had been so naive. On her way home she drove over to see Valerie.

'Look.' she said handing over the article. 'There it is. Our good judge Jules Mercier. Wonderful isn't it?'

Valerie quickly read the article then laughed. 'I knew he was up to no good. Now you know. You should use this to get your children back. Send a copy to Mrs Sinclair.' she suggested.

Next day Emma had an appointment at the hospital to follow her progress. She felt quite tired after the adventure and discovery of Monday. She was on convalescence leave until the end of the week so on Wednesday she planned to go to the national library. Once she got back to work things would be manic again and it would be difficult to find the time. It was important to find out as much as possible and to collect written evidence. She missed Olivia and Sebastian so much.

The national library was enormous. Emma parked the car as near as she could and slowly made her way up the wide and imposing steps to the entrance on the first floor. Emma was curious about what she would discover. She had arrived early to allow herself as much time as possible. A call the day before had briefed her on the system. She was sure the library had not changed for decades. Every two hours copies of all the daily papers which had been requested were brought out and could be studied. Records dated back to the late 1800s. A form had to be submitted one hour in advance. Maximum three papers could be requested at any one time. The papers were huge. They were in heavy binders, each one covering the issues from the whole month.

As Emma now had the date from Monday's article, she knew where to focus. She managed to fit in three sessions. There was an air of constant silence followed by a sudden spate of activity. The first set of newspapers had arrived. There were three people sitting waiting patiently and above all quietly. The attendant asked almost in a whisper who had ordered this one. 'Me.' Emma whispered back half raising her hand.

The library attendant edged his way over and put the large binder on the wooden stand in front of Emma. It was heavy and it landed with a decisive thud. Every noise in the library seemed to be amplified. The paper was starting to yellow and it had a distinct fusty smell to it. Emma opened the first page and started to slowly leaf her way through, carefully reading each article before stretching her arm as far as she could to turn the large pages. She had lots of time and there was no need to rush. She broke off during the first session for a cup of tea in the library cafeteria. For lunch, she preferred to go outside and found a pavement cafe where she ate a sandwich and enjoyed the fresh air and, above all, the noisy activity around her.

For her day's efforts, she had discovered two more articles. She ordered copies. It would be one month before they would arrive. Nobody here was going to die from stress she reassured herself. She left the library in the middle of the afternoon and was glad to beat the rush hour traffic as she made her way home. It had been an interesting day and a couple of additional elements had transpired from the other two articles. Emma had jotted down details on a notepad.

The judicial authorities were keeping an absolute silence about the details of the case. The public prosecutor's office had been equally silent about the details handled by its hierarchy stating that it could give no comment in the matter.

Emma was pleased to have discovered a little more but further details of the case were not to be found anyway. The silence from all corners was deafening. As soon as Emma had copies of all three articles, she made an appointment to see Mrs Sinclair to discuss the approach they would take for the appeal court hearing. She wanted to spill the beans. This was an obvious set up and the truth had to come out.

They had just received a date for the custody hearing from the appeal court and Emma was disappointed that it was two weeks after the start of the new school year. She had pushed so hard for it to take place before the summer recess. The children's schooling was going to play a major role in any decision. Mrs Sinclair had reassured Emma that children could still change school up to the end of November and they already had a written confirmation from the headmaster of Olivia and Sebastian's former school that they had a place waiting from them for the new school year.

A week later Emma set off to Tenerife for a two week' holiday with Olivia and Sebastian. A good friend from London had given them her apartment to enjoy a holiday together. Emma had not had a summer holiday the year before as she waited for a date for the planned audition of the children by the experts. Emma, Olivia and Sebastian explored the island. They went on a jeep safari in the hills, visited the volcano, went to an aqua park, and took a local bus to the other side of the island then a boat to see the dolphins. Sebastian loved dolphins and his bedroom was like a dolphinarium. He often spoke of becoming a marine biologist one day. They met two students on the boat who were studying marine biology in Scotland and they eagerly explained all about dolphin behavioural patterns to Sebastian which he found fascinating.

Emma and her children were close. After being separated for most of the year they found themselves together day and night for three whole weeks. The bond strengthened further. Emma was more determined than ever that the autumn appeal court hearing just had to sort things out and her children would be able to return home. The thought of being separated from them for yet another year with all the difficulties and obstacles which Paul and Lea continued to put in her way was more than she could bear to contemplate.

Chapter 56

Emma had often gone over old ground to analyse again how she had met Jules Mercier which had subsequently led to all the problems she was still facing today. Janine, a middle-aged lady had been introduced to Emma and Paul by a neighbour when they still lived together in the farmhouse and the children were only three and four. Occasionally Janine picked up the children from school and would look after them until Emma went to collect them after work. It had been Paul's suggestion.

Janine's five children were already grown up but two still lived at home. Janine had been a high flyer and successful stock broker before she met her husband and had given up work to look after her family. Janine's husband had become one of the top bankers in the country taking Concorde and often flying to the US, Singapore, Hong Kong and all over Europe. Janine's husband had gone on to have an affair with his secretary and sired a child out of wedlock. It had broken Janine although she never admitted it. She had even gone with her husband to officially give her consent to recognise the child so that it could bear his name as they were still officially married. Janine refused to divorce.

Her inward suffering and outward generosity were apparent and Emma suspected also a potent combination which subsequently pushed her to hit the bottle. Janine seemed to get on well with Paul's mother who called her from time to time to discuss the well-being and progress of her precious grandchildren. Jules Mercier had confided in Emma that Janine had joined Alcoholics Anonymous.

It had been Janine who had called Emma and pushed her to consult Jules Mercier to help her with the mutual consent divorce. Janine and Jules had been going to the same golf club for years and seemed to move in the same circles. After her separation from Paul, Emma had seen Janine on a couple of occasions but met her only once following the fateful provincial court judgment transferring temporary custody to Paul and not even granting her a visiting right.

Janine had told Emma thoughtfully that it was a pity that she had tried to go to the UK as this is what had been her downfall. Emma had defended herself pointing out that the divorce settlement ratified by the court allowed for this and that she had double checked with Hubert Belette and Jules Mercier who had confirmed it was OK. Emma added that they had gone on to reassure her that she did not need to check further with the courts. Janine had remained silent and had changed the subject.

With the newspaper articles now in front of her highlighting the questionable past and integrity of Jules Mercier, Emma wanted Janine to at least have the courage to answer a couple of questions which had been nagging at her for nearly two years. Emma sat down and wrote Janine a letter.

Emma started off by hoping that Janine was fine as well as the family. She then attached the three newspaper articles and stated that the content would probably not surprise her as she had always been an intelligent lady who had kept well up to date with current affairs. Emma highlighted the next sentence in bold type. By enthusiastically recommending Jules Mercier as an honourable retired judge and therefore an excellent counsel for her divorce, did she not doubt his sincerity and/or his motives and eventual loyalty? Today it would appear that Jules Mercier worked with the lawyer he had recommended Hubert Belette (himself struck off from practicing for several years) in favour of the Archer family. An honest judge would never have given such compromising advice.

She wrote that Hubert Belette had even admitted to Emma that Paul and his mother had tried to buy his services prior to the first provincial court hearing. Every day one reads crazy stories in the papers about what some people are prepared to do when they need money. Emma confirmed the set up risked to become public one day and like every loving mother she would fight to the end to be reunited with her children. She thanked Janine in advance for being good and honest enough to give her a reply to her questions. As a p.s. she wrote that Paul's mother seemed highly interested to know if they had seen one another recently.

Emma posted the letter and waited. She did not really expect a reply. She was making more of a statement. A letter did arrive back at the end of the year. It was a Christmas card addressed to Emma, Olivia and Sebastian. A different writing was on the card and the envelope. It wished Emma and the children all the best and above all good health. It arrived three weeks after the sudden death of Janine in her early fifties from a brain haemorrhage. It was very strange and Emma could not begin to make head or tail of it.

Chapter 57

In the midst of all this activity, Emma continued to read whenever she had a moment. She had just finished an interesting and enlightening book about the goings on in the city where Paul and Victor Falconer lived. The authors wrote about the unyielding power of the masonic lodges on every aspect of life in the political and business domains and also the judicial arena as the latter was, in most cases, simply a nomination of the first. They went on to explain that it is normal that as a result of their membership of freemasonry, that eminent members of the political parties are in possession of information which they might otherwise not have. Relationships, it was common knowledge, were made in freemason lodges and no longer inside the party as a result.

Freemasonry was an important pivot as it became an organ of surveillance and control. This explained the large feeling of unease Emma had felt when she had had to appear in front of the court in Paul's home city and Victor Falconer had appeared so absolutely sure of himself. The minute he had encountered opposition when Emma had challenged him in, he had turned to his masonic brother representing the prosecution who had immediately sprung to his aid and had recommended an open ended extension of the first judgment in all its forms, including exclusion of any official visiting right for Emma to see her children.

It was also clearer to Emma what Mr Godfroid the journalist had meant when he had cryptically pointed out that in this city things were done very differently.

The authors went on to explain that a competent judge who had investigated two files concerning the shady dealings of several politicians much too well had suddenly found himself discharged of all financial files. In fact, the financial cabinet was simply being dissolved. In this city, the only one in the country, the prosecutor's office no longer had any investigative magistrates specialised in financial affairs. In their opinion, there was no doubt that this decision was imposed by the political class and a certain fringe of freemasonry directly concerned by the previous two files. Emma was flabbergasted and could not believe to which point the rot seemed to have set in. She shuddered. This city was where her dear children were being held hostage. How could she possibly expect a fair hearing in any court with such forces at play?

Emma's next surprise came one Sunday afternoon when she was surfing the web. She came upon an article which dealt with one of the most sensitive files in recent history. What struck her however, were the number of striking similarities with her own. The file was referred to as the Perry file and it had been opened nearly twenty years earlier.

It involved the provincial youth court where Emma had lost temporary custody of her children and the custody battle arising out of a divorce case between a dentist and his wife. The wife had admitted to participating in orgies with her new lover and the fine flower of the establishment. Minors had been present. One women had died in a car accident as it was deemed she knew too much. She had been given too much to drink and her car had been tampered with. Another was seen giggling and being taken up to her room by two men then her lifeless body was discovered two days later with an empty bottle of sleeping pills by her side. The death was classed as a suicide. The minors were brought to the party by a youth court judge who selected them from children's homes. Two of them later committed suicide.

Hoping to gain custody of his children, Mr Perry hired a private detective to record his wife's admissions. He thought that would be enough to gain custody of the children. However, a few days later his home was burgled and the only thing which had disappeared was the cassette. He obtained another recording from the detective and went to the police to lodge a complaint. The new deputy public prosecutor in the provincial court refused to add the cassette to the divorce file and Mr Perry's wife was awarded custody of the couple's children. Later the deputy public prosecutor closed the police file.

Another article on the web revealed to Emma's surprise and dismay that Mr Perry's former wife had enjoyed a successful career working for the justice minister, the same minister Jules Mercier had worked for. Coupled with everything Jules had already told Emma, she was pretty sure that he also moved in these circles. The provincial court seemed pretty hazardous, both the youth court section and also the prosecutor's office. Mr Perry had lost custody of his children, his house had been burgled like Emma's to recover a cassette containing compromising evidence. They had both received death threats.

Emma hoped so much that the appeal court would see clear, make a fair judgment returning the children to their mother's home and help Emma out of her current nightmare. Like Mr Perry twenty years before, she knew she would never be able to accept the injustice and would have to continue to fight for the truth to come out.

Chapter 58

The summer seemed to pass by so quickly. Emma spent quality time with Olivia and Sebastian. Parting afterwards was always difficult. With time it failed to become any easier. With a date now set with the appeal court for middle of September, Victor Falconer did not hesitate to exchange official letters for every small anomaly or misunderstanding attempting to pin the blame on Emma and accuse her of being uncooperative, aggressive, and acting against the real interest of the children. It was so ironic and also nauseating. He was completely unscrupulous which made him all the more dangerous.

Mrs Sinclair was vigilant and together with Emma, they tried hard to minimise any occasion which he might be able to seize upon. Emma had a decidedly stubborn streak especially when it came to injustice and refused to let it get to her. She was spurred on by the fact that Olivia and Sebastian kept telling her to keep fighting, that they loved her and wanted to come home.

The day before Emma was due to drive the children back to their father's Paul called. He wanted them to come back a day earlier than agreed as it suited his plans for shopping for any last minute items and to go to the hairdressers. True to style Paul did not ask Emma but instructed the children to tell her. Paul now wanted to add insult to injury by asserting his authority in contravention of a clear and written agreement. Emma told Olivia and Sebastian that she would drive them back to their father's home the following day as officially agreed months earlier.

Paul was not happy. He shouted and bellowed at the children so loudly on the phone that Cathy and Valerie could hear every single word. Olivia cried following the call and Cathy hugged and comforted her. Sebastian was frightened and tearful. Paul had also taken the opportunity to insult Valerie over the phone. Emma arrived home from work to be updated about this latest episode.

She was angry and disappointed. She knew that she could do absolutely nothing apart from take a deep breath, reassure the children herself and hope that the appeal court would see clear in the coming weeks. She had never put so much hope in anybody or anything in her whole life.

Mrs Sinclair could not leave unanswered the constant tirade of libellous and completely unfounded accusations directed against Emma by Victor Falconer. Emma was very conscious that time was on Paul's side and they were certainly playing for it. The longer the children lived with Paul, the more he could argue that they were settled and it was in their best interest to remain there.

Mrs Sinclair had assured Emma that the appeal court was competent to handle the case. She had done her homework and had asked other experienced colleagues for their opinion. They had all agreed that as per the judicial code the superior jurisdiction was entitled to take care of judging all elements in a case going back to the very beginning with the mutual consent divorce, the bad advice, the acts of destabilisation, the first appeal against the provincial court temporary ruling etc.

Victor Falconer's friends were in the provincial courts and that is where he wanted to fight this out, confident of a positive outcome. He put forward a rambling argument that the appeal court was not competent to handle the case referring to a previous Supreme Court ruling. Emma could not judge. She had to rely on the experience, support and good judgment of Mrs Sinclair.

Mrs Sinclair's written defence was clear, well structured, and backed up by real evidence. She briefly outlined the history, the fact that Emma had received full custody when the divorce was granted, that the terms of the divorce stipulated that Emma could go and work abroad with the children, that she had been very poorly advised indeed by Jules Mercier, a retired judge, who had subsequently recommended the services of a lawyer, Hubert

Belette, who had let her down very badly and been extremely negligent. Emma was happy that Mrs Sinclair had actually written their names. She hoped that the appeal court judges would know about their dubious pasts.

Mrs Sinclair also continued that Victor Falconer had no proof of his many allegations against Emma if it were not for a series of official letters full of the untruths of his client which could not seriously be considered as evidence by the court. She asked that the appeal court reconstitute full custody of the children to the mother for the next two school years so they could finish their junior schooling in their previous school with their friends. The headmaster had been very supportive providing yet another letter that he welcomed Olivia and Sebastian back to their previous school with open arms. He was a smart and kind man deeply respected by all staff and pupils at the school. He had quickly grasped what had happened. In his limited capacity, he was doing what he could to help.

As a subsidiary request, Mrs Sinclair requested that should the court rule that the children had to stay with their father until the end of the next school year, that Emma should receive an official visiting right to see them every weekend as proposed by the experts in their report. It was recommended by both parties that the children in any event be heard by the youth judge in the appeal court.

Paul was not happy that Emma had refused to bring the children back early and instinctively she knew that she was probably going to have to pay for it. A couple of days later, Emma's problems to talk to her children on the phone started again. The fax had been connected to the phone line and set off whistling every time she called. When she eventually reached Olivia and Sebastian after sending a fax, they explained that Lea's daughter had run up a 500 € phone bill spending hours on the phone with friends and as of now, Emma had to call them on the mobile phone she had purchased them. However, the mobile had to stay in Paul's study in the basement and if they could not hear it ringing, which was inevitably the case, then Emma had to leave a message. The children could then check their messages from time to time and call Emma back.

Emma called Paul and politely suggested that he put the mobile in the living room or the children's bedroom where they could hear it ring as it was much easier and pleasant for everyone. Paul replied dryly to Emma that the children were not waiting all day long for her calls then just hung up. He then instructed Olivia and Sebastian to tell their mother during their next call that if Emma called at 6.55 pm then she could only talk to them for five minutes because at 7 pm it was deemed too late and she would have to call back next day. Paul also changed the mobile PIN code so that if the children took the mobile phone out of the office and forgot to recharge it, they could not reactive it.

Emma shook her head. She had never put these sorts of obstacles in Paul's way. However, she was sure it was done to upset her in the run up to the appeal court hearing. She asked for a print out of her mobile phone bill. In one week, she had had to leave fifteen messages to reach the children just three times. She sent a copy to Mrs Sinclair. Emma noticed that the children' resolve to have the phone in an accessible place was beginning to strengthen. It was just a question of time and the children would start to rebel.

Chapter 59

The day of the hearing approached. Emma's apprehension but also hopes of a positive outcome and end to the ongoing nightmare mounted. The night before the hearing she took a long and relaxing bath and went to bed early. She double checked her alarm clock to see it was set correctly and also set the alarm on her mobile phone as a back-up. She tossed and turned for most of the night afraid of falling asleep too deeply and waking up too late.

Emma arrived in town forty-five minutes early. She decided to go for a cup of tea and a pastry in the nearby gallery. She made her way up the escalator looking at herself in the smoked glass mirror. She had put on her best navy blue suit and looked smart but serious. As she sipped her lemon tea, she thought about Olivia and Sebastian going to school some hundred kilometres away as she was fighting for their future in the appeal court.

She tried to imagine how the hearing would go. Mrs Sinclair had prepared well. Victor Falconer too but he lacked evidence. Would this matter she asked herself for the umpteenth time. So far it had not, but this time they were in the appeal court. So far nobody had really examined her case in detail or in any depth.

She headed over to the court building. There was a distinct autumn chill in the air. She stood for a second looking up at this huge imposing building. She walked slowly up the steps to the entrance. At the top she stopped and stared at the shrine of several missing and murdered children which had been covered very actively in the press. She looked at their photographs and the flowers. Tears came to her eyes and she shuddered.

She passed through the huge wide doors and into the dimly lit corridor. There were already quite a few lawyers walking around in their familiar black gowns. Emma was ten minutes early. She reached in her bag, took out her phone and called Mrs Sinclair to see where she was. Mrs Sinclair had just arrived and was heading off to the lawyers' chambers to put on her robes. Suddenly she came around the corner much to Emma's relief.

So far there was no sign of Paul and Victor Falconer. Mrs Sinclair and Emma made their way along the long corridor to the court room. They sat on the polished wooden benches waiting for the arrival of the three judges, prosecutor's deputy and court clerk. They chatted to relieve the tension. Suddenly Victor Falconer and Paul arrived and headed over to shake hands and say hello. This was the part Emma least appreciated. She found that it was so hypocritical. After reading so many lies and vicious attacks on her character, she was supposed to behave as if this was a business meeting, shaking hands and smiling. She played the game but it required a great deal of self-restraint. 'Be nice.' Mrs Sinclair whispered to Emma. 'Don't show them that you are mad or upset.'

The court officials arrived and they filed after them into the court room. Everything was in wood, highly polished with a distinct shine. The tall windows overlooked the roof tops of the capital. This time the officials sat high up on the bench. Paul and Emma sat on the much lower front bench with their respective counsel behind them. The judge in the middle was a middle-aged man with a friendly almost fatherly looking face. The court clerk was a distinguished looking lady. The prosecutor general's deputy exuded a certain haughtiness coupled with a touch of arrogant authority. His nose seemed to point upwards and he had a certain air as if he was displeased about something.

Mrs Sinclair began to present her case first. She spoke for forty-five minutes putting her heart and soul into it. She was objective. She reiterated Emma's proven capacity as a good mother, described her suffering which stemmed from being separated from her children. She mentioned Jules Mercier by name reminding the bench that he had had quite a reputation and had been instrumental in Emma's predicament providing poor advice and direction. Judging by the age of the court officials, it was highly likely that they were aware of his past. However, they did not show it.

Mrs Sinclair highlighted the lack of evidence to substantiate the case of the adverse party and their unwillingness to act in a responsible and fair manner sharing the time and contact which should be enjoyed by both parents. The judges and the court clerk listened attentively as did Paul. The prosecutor general's deputy and Victor Falconer had an almost casual air about them. Emma discretely watched the expression of both parties. She had been in this movie before, and now much wiser, did not wish to miss anything. There was too much at stake.

It was now Victor Falconer's turn to present his case. He started off in his distinct regional accent going over past history when he had successfully concocted the file against Emma together with Hubert Belette with the stream of official letters. He played on the previous judgments from the provincial courts which had been in his favour. However, he was not a match for Mrs Sinclair. Emma thought that half way through he realised it and decided it was time for a little help.

Emma still did not know whether it was a word, phrase or specific gesture but she did know that a masonic sign was passed and it was immediately picked up by the prosecutor general's deputy. His face changed instantly from the cold, distant and aloof to the friendly, receptive, completely attentive and helpful during the second half of Victor Falconer's counsel's speech.

Again Emma did not want to believe what she was seeing. This was the second time Victor Falconer had played this card in open court. Emma looked carefully again at the prosecutor general deputy's expression and she knew for certain that something was definitely amiss. It was confirmed in his wrapping up of the hearing. The judges seemed in favour of auditioning the children and even spoke of fixing a date. The court clerk nodded in agreement. The prosecutor general's deputy replied decisively and with a great deal of authority that the children were settled with their father and this is where they were going to stay. Mrs Sinclair tried to reason with him. He abruptly cut her off. It was obvious he had firmly taken Paul's side.

They left the court room. Emma said very little. Mrs Sinclair asked Emma to drop her off at her office. They stopped at a corner shop to buy two diet cokes. As they sipped the drinks, Mrs Sinclair asked Emma what she had thought.

'I don't know.' Emma replied. 'We will have to see the judgment.' She was not yet ready to tell Mrs Sinclair what she had seen or suspected. She needed to digest it first herself.

Mrs Sinclair seemed to think it had gone quite well and, as the judge had indicated, there was a good chance that the children would be auditioned on their preference of main residence before the final judgment. Deep down Emma knew instinctively that she had been snookered once again by unethical forces at play and just waited for the proof to show up in the judgment. She could not begin to describe her disappointment and utter disillusionment with the system.

Emma went back to the office and tried to work for the rest of the day. She did not have the energy to do any shopping that evening and flopped lifelessly onto the sofa and watched a film to take her mind off things. She slept for fourteen hours waking up only at 2 pm the following afternoon.

Never before had she felt so utterly drained and wanted to seek complete solace in sleep. She woke up feeling rather groggy and slowly set about trying to persuade herself not to give up the fight. It was just another setback. They had lost another battle but not the war she tried to convince herself. The mountain in front of her seemed almost unconquerable. She had put all her hopes and faith in the appeal court and now it seemed to be just like the provincial courts in the grips of a few elite belonging to a secret society. Emma found it very difficult to shake off the cynicism which had suddenly engulfed her. This was a serious and unexpected set back and she was going to need some time to assimilate and come to terms with it.

The written judgment was due in three weeks but it took over five weeks to arrive. Just before it was pronounced, Emma wrote to Mrs Sinclair to tell her that as far as she was concerned the hearing was just a continuation of the setup which had begun four years previously and that Victor Falconer had again used his freemasonry connections to further his cause. Mrs Sinclair called Emma. She admitted that she had also found it very strange and that perhaps Emma did have a point after all but that it was difficult, if not impossible, to prove.

Emma's sister Laura was equally disappointed. She told Emma that she believed her when she said she thought she had been set up by secret society members who influenced the court system but added that unless Emma could prove it, she was no further forward. Emma knew she was right. Laura added that she felt like taking the world's biggest bulldozer and flattening both the provincial and the appeal court.

'Don't ever bring continental justice to Britain.' Laura said. 'No system is perfect but what is going on over there defies all belief.'

Emma had to laugh at the thought of Laura sitting behind the giant bulldozer. Emma's other international friends took a similar approach. It strengthened her resolve. Emma's good friends and family knew that she was not a nutcase and actually believed her but they all admitted that it would be very difficult for her to prove. However, Emma decided she had no alternative but to plod on and hope for a break through. She could not give up for the children's sake. Her determination slowly returned.

The judgment eventually arrived. Mrs Sinclair faxed it through to Emma with a cover note. The appeal court agreed with Victor Falconer that the current case concerning custody of the children should not be handled by the appeal court and that the first provincial court was the competent authority.

Mrs Sinclair confirmed to Emma that they had two alternatives. They could return to the provincial court and as both the children would both be over twelve the following summer, by law they could demand that they be auditioned and their wishes taken into account in the final custody decision. At least then Emma would have an official visiting right to see her own children whatever the outcome which was more than she had had for the last three years. The second alternative was to go to the Supreme Court and appeal against the appeal court decision but this would take a very long time.

Emma was caught between the devil and the deep blue sea. She knew that by returning to the provincial court she would be at an enormous disadvantage. The Supreme Court was not a solution either. She could not take her case to the European Court of Human Rights either until she had exhausted all possible routes in the country including the Supreme Court and by then the children would be adults, she would be bankrupt and most probably a complete wreck.

Mrs Sinclair concluded her fax by saying that she was sorry for the lengthy procedure but she remained convinced that the strategy they had adopted would bear fruit. Emma really hoped so. Anyway, what choice did she have?

Olivia and Sebastian were disappointed when Emma told them that they would not be heard after all by the judge in the appeal court and that their parents would have to go back to the provincial court for the final decision the following autumn. Meanwhile they would be staying with their father for the current school year.

Paul of course seemed triumphant. Victor Falconer stepped up his claims for money to cover child maintenance. Paul had apparently left his previous company and had become an independent consultant as he enjoyed a certain notoriety in his sector. Olivia and Sebastian had told Emma that Paul and Lea often argued about their finances and they had heard Lea complain to a friend that it was a pity that they did not have lots of money.

On the other hand, Paul had consistently refused to produce any details of his income over the last two years despite several requests from Mrs Sinclair. Emma remained determined. She would not be paying him a penny until she was legally forced to and then not retroactively. Not after being set up and treated in the manner which she and the children had been treated not to mention the blackmail on her dying mum.

Relations between Lea and Paul's mother continued to deteriorate. Paul's mother was also restricted to calling her grandchildren on the mobile phone and between limited hours in the evening. She seemed to be reaping what she had sown and was slowly becoming aware of the fact.

During the summer she had tried to question Olivia and Sebastian again on Paul's behalf about where they preferred to live. However, wiser following the betrayal the previous Easter, Olivia and Sebastian had refused to be drawn into the conversation. Saddened by their lack of trust in their grandmother, Paul's mother had started to cry and complain that it was such a pity that things had turned out the way they had. She called Emma to ask for her permission to call her grandchildren on the mobile phone Emma had purchased.

'You don't have to ask for permission. You are their grandmother. You can call them when you want,' Emma replied matter-of-factly. 'I am not difficult like your son and daughter in law but I think you know that.'

'Emma I am sorry that things have turned out as they have. Children should be with their mother.' Paul's mother announced trying to sound sympathetic.

'Don't be hypocritical.' Emma answered calmly. 'It is a little late for such sentiment. You did everything you could to help your son snatch my children away from me, you and that rich nephew living in the USA with his wealthy and powerful contacts. I was set up and you know it so please stop your amateur dramatics.'

For a moment there was a deafening silence then a gasp at the end of the phone followed by another silence. Emma waited for the reply. It eventually came.

'Emma you do not give me a chance to defend myself.' Paul's mother lamented.

'Well go on defend yourself but at least have the courage to admit it.' Emma prompted.

Again there was a long silence.

'As I said,' Emma continued. 'you can call your grandchildren on their mobile and when they are with me whenever you want. As for the rest, you have made your bed so you can now lie on it. I have enough problems of my own to sort out. Enjoy the rest of the evening. Goodbye.'

Emma hung up. She had suspected for a long time that it was highly likely that favours were being done among the rich and powerful and that this was at the origin of the set up and all her problems. It was less likely that Paul would have had the contacts to pull the strings as they had been pulled.

Emma thought back to the words of Hubert Belette three years earlier. When Emma had complained that everything had started with Paul's mother, he had almost panicked and replied rashly,

'Whatever you do don't touch Paul's mother.' How strange this comment had seemed at the time and completely out of context. However, again it was nigh on impossible to prove.

Chapter 60

Chris a British colleague walked into Emma's office.

'How did it go in court?' he asked in a concerned manner. 'Did you get the judgment?'

'Afraid so.' Emma replied. 'But we are no further forward. I am more convinced than ever that this whole affair is being manipulated and that freemasonry connections are instrumental.'

'Oh.' he replied in surprise. 'That is really unfair. You know I read a book several years ago about the power which freemasons have in Britain and how this power is being abused in some cases in the courts and in the police force. It was a fascinating book. I will see if I can dig it out at home and I will bring it for you to read.'

'Yes please.' Emma replied. 'I would be very interested to read more about these people.'

The next day Chris walked into Emma's office with a big smile waving the book in his hand. (The Brotherhood by Stephen Knight, published by HarperCollins). He handed it over and said he hoped she would enjoy reading it and to let him know what she thought. Emma thanked him and took the little book in her hand. The pages were beginning to yellow. It had been published fifteen years before. The cover was already intriguing. It showed two men in white gloves shaking hands, a special handshake by which freemasons make themselves known to one another for the purpose of mutual aid and assistance.

Emma left work on time that day and headed home to start reading. She was so engrossed in the book that she forgot to eat. Before she knew it, it was already 11.00 pm and her stomach started to rumble. She made a quick sandwich and continued until 5.00 am the following morning. She simply could not put the book down. Her own predicament began to make much more sense as she turned each page. She was not alone in being set up, nor was she imaging things. This in itself was a significant relief.

When writing the book, the author collected input from hundreds of masons who were becoming disillusioned as a result of infiltration of the movement by less scrupulous members of society who were allegedly using freemasonry for their own and in many cases less than honest means. Many who had helped did so anonymously as they feared recrimination from other members of the brotherhood. Among them were government officials, politicians, judges, policemen, lawyers, churchmen, and past and present officers of both MI5 and MI6. As one can imagine, the book sent shock waves upon its publication. It was the first of its kind and many people from all walks of life started to ask serious questions about the effects of this secret society on life in Britain.

Emma was grateful to the author for highlighting a really important issue which had had such a profound and painful influence on her life for the last five years. Whoever wrote 'information is power' knew what he was talking about she thought to herself.

It was at this point that Emma made a major decision to take her courage in both hands and start to write an account of her own story. First if needed, to provoke an enquiry into her own case if she did not regain custody of her children pretty soon and secondly to highlight the problems faced by hundreds if not thousands of other innocent victims so that the necessary measures might be taken to curb the numerous miscarriages of justice.

Emma learnt from the book that Freemasonry is a secret society with several hundred thousand members in the UK. *'All are male and have sworn on pain of death and ghastly mutilation not to reveal masonic secrets to outsiders, who are known to the brethren as the 'profane.'* Freemasonry is a secret society originating in Britain with independent offshoots in most of the non-communist world. The brotherhood's stated aims are morality, fraternity and charity. However, many people have suffered when freemasonry has entered into areas of life it should ideally not be i.e. the judiciary and the police. In short, according to the author, *'the abuse of freemasonry causes alarming miscarriages of justice'*. Emma could only identify with this statement which in one way gave her a certain degree of comfort that she was not the only one in such a compromising situation.

A part which Emma found particularly interesting was that there is an elite group of freemasons over whom the United Grand Lodge has no jurisdiction. These are the brethren of the so called higher degrees. One enters at the first degree to become an apprentice mason and can rise to the third degree or Master Mason. The other thirty degrees beginning with the fourth (that of Secret Master) and culminating in the thirty third degree (Grand Inspector General) are controlled by a supreme council and are headquartered in London. Entry to the higher degrees is by invitation only. The Ancient and Accepted Right of the thirty third degree is the only unified masonic group run on truly international lines.

The Supreme Council in London is one of many Supreme Councils in various parts of the world of which the head is the Supreme Council of Charleston USA which operates a worldwide network of masons in the most powerful positions in the executive, legislature, judiciary and armed forces as well as industry, commerce and professions of many countries.

According to the author, some of the masons providing input for the book believed that interest in the craft had been steadily decreasing and because the lodges wanted to reverse the trend and give recruitment a boost, they gradually began to lower their standards. Some members sponsored people they hardly knew and it became easier to join for people of dubious morals who were looking to get more out of the craft for personal gain than what they could give back.

Something which really surprised and almost shocked Emma was that in the book, one mason estimated that if only five percent of masons abused the craft for selfish or corrupt ends, it would mean some 25.000 of them doing so in Britain at that time and he put the figure at much closer to twelve or thirteen percent. Examples of how masons might damage a non-mason or help a fellow mason were quite revealing for Emma too and hit home hard. It all seemed so familiar when she thought about her own case.

This feeling was only accentuated when one person interviewed in the book explained that solicitors and lawyers were apparently very good at damaging others. *'By getting someone involved in a legal matter you had him. Masonic solicitors were allegedly past masters at causing delays, generating useless paperwork, ignoring instructions, running up immense bills, and misleading clients into taking decisions damaging to themselves'.*

One highly placed mason told the author that *'Only the fighters have any hope of beating the system once it is at work against them. Most people, fighters or not, are beaten in the end though since victims do not know who they can trust and they can get no help because their story sounds so paranoid.'* He pointed out that there was *'no defence against an evil which only the victims and the perpetrators know exists.'* Again this all seemed so familiar to Emma who was still fighting hard and, up until now, had obstinately refused to be beaten.

Many people who contacted the author were concerned that *'freemasons in the judiciary and legal profession exercised a pernicious influence over the administration of justice. Allegations of collusion between judges and lawyers on behalf of brethren in the dock were rife. There were claims of huge masonic conspiracies between rival firms of solicitors and suggestions that freemasonry was such a Grey Eminence that proceedings in open court were merely an outward show, while everything was decided in advance long before cases involving Masons reached court.'* The author also heard of a number of cases of *'civil battles lost and won on the basis of masonic signs in court. Even the odd murderer was said to have got himself off by pulling the trick at an opportune moment.'*

Emma went to work next day feeling pretty drained following her 5 am ordeal. However, she felt relieved that at least in the UK, the illicit use of freemasonry to distort the course of justice had become an issue fifteen years ago. Here on the continent it was obviously still a well-kept secret. However, in moments of inattention, Jules Mercier had already let slip quite a few of the secrets about signs being made in court, judgments agreed up front. Reading the book confirmed to Emma that these things really happened and on a much larger scale than she had initially thought possible.

She still did not know what she was going to do or how she was going to get out of this impossible dilemma. Going public internationally seemed her only hope if things did not work out for her before the next school year. She set slowly to work on her book continuing in parallel her research. It also helped to heal some of the pain when she wrote down her story. She was under no illusions that it would be an uphill struggle still requiring a great deal of courage and patience.

The web was a great asset and books continued to arrive via the post. Emma checked on Amazon and there was a sequel book about freemasonry published a few years later by a renowned British journalist. (Inside the Brotherhood, Explosive Secrets of the Freemasons by Martin Short. Published by HarperCollins).

She ordered it. A few days later Emma opened the letterbox to find a fat brown box sitting there. The box appeared to have been opened. As she lifted the lid it was obvious that someone had taken a look inside. The plastic bag had been torn open and there was an ugly jagged tear along most of the cover. Emma was shocked. Who could have done this? A disgruntled customs official, someone who packed the book in the warehouse, a masonic postal worker or even Jules Mercier himself checking her letter box? Emma went to look for the sticky tape. She painstakingly repaired the cover and sat down to read. The book was extremely well written and quite frankly fascinating, all seven hundred pages of it. With each chapter Emma felt even more confident that she was not imagining things and nor was she alone in her plight.

The author made some very well founded observations. The one which Emma thought summed things up so well was *'Since freemasonry claims above all to be a 'system of morality' it lays itself open to justifiable attack when well publicized events show members acting corruptly. These reinforce suspicions held among non-masons about incidents they have observed but never fathomed. Crimes condoned or unpunished, favours granted or withheld, the inept promoted, the able destroyed, the offending parent awarded custody, the corrupt deal which costs the company or the taxpayer a fortune.'*

In examples given, even masons had ruined fellow masons so Emma could not help thinking what chance did she have as an insignificant foreign member of the 'profane' in a judicial system loaded with masons who had taken a solemn bloodcurdling oath to protect and assist one another, even in circumstances they might otherwise deem dishonest, even immoral.

The author also noted that anyone's chances of appearing before a mason-free slate of three magistrates was almost nil, unless all of them were women. Emma could not help reasoning however, that unlike the UK, women on the continent could also become freemasons and then there were female and also mixed lodges so even this did not apply in Emma's case.

In the court hearings Emma had been through so far, on at least two occasions the prosecutor's deputy had been a women and she had found both individuals to be cold and even aggressive. She wondered if the masonic mole in these cases had been female.

Jules Mercier's words came flooding back to her at dinner two years earlier. That anyone of the three so the judge, the prosecutor's deputy or the court clerk could be asked 'to give a favourable outcome' even the court clerk and that decisions were often made up front about who would win the case, the hearing itself being just a formality, a facade.

Another element which left a distinct impression on Emma was the claim by many 20th century writers that the big secret and ultimate aim of freemasonry is world domination. So it really is an international issue Emma told herself. She had always been interested in modern history and current affairs and was absolutely amazed to read on the web details of the Italian story of lodge P2. At the same time, she could not fail to be concerned about anything similar the general public still did not know and people's ability, or lack of it, to control their own destiny.

P2 was an Italian masonic lodge, fascist in nature, and referred to by some as a 'state within a state' or a 'shadow government'. At its height, it comprised four cabinet ministers, all three heads of Italy's intelligence organisations, forty-four members of parliament, hundreds of military officers and the cream of the country's industrialists, bankers and diplomats. The lodge and its impressive membership list were unmasked in 1981 following the discovery of a series of financial irregularities by investigating magistrates. Some claim the lodge was preparing a right wing coup along the lines of the one in Chile in the 1970s. One prosecutor's report described P2 as a secret sect combining business and politics with the intention of destroying the country's constitutional order. As a result, and following a parliamentary enquiry, secret organisations were outlawed in Italy.

Again much of the content for the book had been provided by masons becoming increasing concerned that freemasonry was being brought into disrepute by a growing number of dishonest members. They hoped to at last put pressure on its leaders to put the craft's house in order and discipline and expel brethren acting corruptly or inappropriately.

Again the book sent shock waves through the UK and was taken seriously. It led to a parliamentary enquiry in which the author was a key witness. His recommendation was that masons in certain positions in society, notably the judiciary and the police, be required to declare their membership which in turn be made available publicly. In the first report of the Home Affairs Select Committee published in March 1997 on Freemasonry in the Police and the Judiciary the concluding paragraph stated *"We recommend that police officers, magistrates, judges and crown prosecutors should be required to register membership of any secret society and that the record should be publicly available."* Alas, the recommendations were never implemented as they proved to be too complex to administer.

Now Emma had even more information than before but how could she best use it to reveal the truth and be reunited with her children? She still had no golden bullet but she kept on searching. Strangely Emma's instincts seemed to be sharpening. She had often joked that Valerie was somewhat psychic. Valerie could not watch any police film because after ten minutes she had already figured out who had done it and everyone complained that she had spoilt the ending for them. Valerie, like Emma, had been through some pretty harrowing times. She told Emma to wait and see as she too would start to anticipate what people who wanted to harm her would do next.

Chapter 61

Of course Paul and Lea were not going to make things any easier as far as having a normal telephone contact with Olivia and Sebastian was concerned. Emma found it so unnecessary and downright spiteful. However, she knew they would not change. The mobile was still in Paul's office and each time she had to leave several messages before receiving a call back. She only tried to call maximum three times a week. When unsuccessful for two days, she would try to reach her son and daughter on the land line. Lea's children passed Emma to her children without further ado.

One Friday evening Emma fell face to face with Lea herself. Lea reminded Emma in a very condescending and unpleasant manner that she had already been told on several occasions that she was only to call on the mobile and leave a message.

'I have tried and already left three messages.' Emma replied. 'So please pass me my children.'

'No.' Lea replied stubbornly.

'Please pass me my children.' Emma asked again forcing herself to stay calm.

'No.' Lea repeated.

Emma could not contain herself any longer. 'You bitch now pass me my children at once.' She shouted.

Lea hung up and Emma redialled the number. Lea answered.

'Pass me my children.' Emma asked for the third time.

'No.' Lea replied and started to laugh. 'Over here we are the ones who command not you.'

'Not for much longer.' Emma shouted back and hung up.

She had never felt so angry, trapped, frustrated and humiliated in her life. How dare these people, this system continue to treat her in this inhuman way? Olivia and Sebastian were also perturbed by the story. She was their mother. Surely she had the right to speak to her children normally on the phone. In addition, the children had confided in Emma again that Lea had been really mean to them recently during one of Paul's regular absences and they had been reduced to tears.

Emma took a deep breath and wrote to Mrs Sinclair. She outlined the incident. She told her to expect another official letter from Victor Falconer especially as Christmas was approaching and he could probably do with the extra income. She reiterated that she was not going to crack and this only strengthened her resolve to target those responsible with the precision and force of a ballistic missile. She was going to go public and their days were numbered.

To her surprise, no official letter arrived this time and telephone contact slowly improved. Had she hit a sensitive note? She did not know. She just knew that she was hopping mad and kept asking herself how many other innocent lives these characters were going to try to ruin with their unscrupulous behaviour?

Chapter 62

One Saturday morning in December Emma was leafing through the TV magazine to see which programmes were scheduled for the following week. A documentary caught her attention. It had been made by a group of foreign journalists and covered the anomalies of an ongoing investigation into the abduction of several children whose bodies were later discovered.

Unfortunately, the documentary was due to be aired by a TV channel which Emma could not capture. Undeterred, on the Monday she sent an email to a good colleague and friend Michael and asked him if he did not mind recording the programme and sending her the cassette. No problem he had assured her adding that it was a pleasure to be able to do her a favour.

The end of year arrived and Emma enjoyed a whole week with Olivia and Sebastian. Laura and the family came over from the UK and the whole family spent a fun week together.

Middle of January Emma had to fly to Canada for an international sales meeting. She had almost forgotten about the recording Michael had made for her. When they met he reminded her adding with a smile that he had brought the cassette along with him. They agreed to have breakfast in the hotel next morning before the meetings. When Emma arrived, a brown envelope containing the recording was already on the table. She asked Michael if he had already watched the documentary and if so what did he think. She was surprised and intrigued by his response.

'Yes.' he replied. 'I watched it together with my wife while we were recording it for you. We were absolutely amazed. Unbelievable story. Really smacks of mafia like tactics and a massive cover up.'

'Oh really?' Emma added with surprise. 'I will watch it when I get back to Europe and let you know what I think. Thanks again so much for taking the time to record it for me.'

When Emma arrived back home a few days later she unpacked her case. She opened the brown envelope and took out the black cassette inside. She made herself a sandwich and a cup of tea and sat down on the sofa to watch what she knew instinctively was going to be another revelation.

Several children had been abducted and their bodies had been found several months later. There was a debate and much speculation ongoing as to if the children had been abducted by a lone predator or if they had been abducted to order to be used at VIP sex parties attended by members of the government, the judiciary, top businessmen, the police, the army etc. The investigations appeared to have been sabotaged. Investigating police officers and magistrates who seemed to be making good progress were suddenly dropped from the investigations on a technicality. Files were split up and given to different regions and courts to investigate so no one had the full picture any more.

The most alarming phenomena according to the journalists were the disappearance of key witnesses in an unexplainable manner and in what could only be described as suspicious circumstances. Car accidents, a fire, a drowning, a suicide. One victim appeared to have been poisoned. This was discovered only after his body was exhumed and samples sent to the USA by the family to be analysed.

The former child prostitute Ella who had written the book Emma had found so moving, appeared in a lonely fight to have her witness statements believed and acknowledged. She had ironically concluded that in this case as a witness you were either declared mad like herself or found dead.

The Perry file was also mentioned. Mr Perry had meanwhile moved to live in Southern Europe but had taken a full copy of the file and the recording with him. One of the journalists explained that the youth court judge in the Perry file was today the president of the provincial court. 'Shit.' Emma remarked. She wound back the cassette and listened to this part again. She felt uneasy and had a very bad feeling about the whole affair. There were too many similarities with her own case which indicated that the same people might be involved.

Emma remembered that Victor Falconer had written a letter directly to the president of the provincial court over three years ago asking that the case requesting a social enquiry to look into why Olivia and Sebastian were being locked up alone overnight be presented in front of the judge before any exchange of written defence papers or counsel's speech. His request had been acknowledged and the case had simply been closed by the judge despite the request of the prosecutor's deputy and verbal agreement of both parties i.e. Paul's and Emma's counsel to present their case at a future date to be specified by the court. Emma thought back to Jules Mercier's thinly veiled threats that if she became a risk she would be eliminated in a car accident or poisoned. She went to bed and fell into an uneasy sleep.

The more Emma discovered, the more alarming things looked. Now she knew where the expression ignorance is bliss came from. Aunty Lilly, Emma's dad's only remaining sister gave Emma some much needed encouragement. You are strong she reminded Emma. Don't let these dishonest characters get you down. You mum and dad were both fighters and so are you. Olivia and Sebastian need you. We love you and are behind you all of the way. Emma had given her a hug. She was a wise old lady. She had been a sister on a nursing ward and had seen a lot but also helped an awful lot of people in her life. Aunty Lilly's husband had been decorated in the war for rescuing twenty people from a burning building during the Coventry blitz. Aunty Lilly reflected sadly that there were a lot of evil and dishonest people in the world driven only by greed and power. However, there were also thankfully a great many decent and honest people and for this reason one had to fight for what was good and right. Emma could only agree with her.

Emma continued to see Valerie on a regular basis. Valerie too was a constant source of encouragement. She suggested that the two of them return to see the renowned medium. Valerie was missing her own father who had died unexpectedly and much too early. She felt she needed to receive another message from him. Valerie encouraged Emma to take along a picture of Aunty Hilda. When they had visited Nice with the children on their last holiday together, Emma had taken a lovely picture of Aunty Hilda on the flower market. She took it out of the picture frame in the living room, put it in her bag and the two of them drove off towards the capital.

Emma placed the photo face down on the large table among the many other photos people had carefully deposited, regained her seat next to Valerie and waited for the medium to arrive. The séance soon got off to a start and Emma waited in anticipation. Would Aunty Hilda be chosen and would she want to leave Emma a message?

Suddenly the medium held up Aunty Hilda's photo and Emma raised her hand and announced that the photo was hers. To Emma's relief, the medium went on to explain that Aunty Hilda was fine and was in the happy company of Emma's mum and their parents. Then to Emma's surprise, she went on to explain that Aunty Hilda was laughing and wanted to remind Emma that she had had to take one of her exams three times before she succeeded. This had always been a private joke between the two of them. Emma had been a good pupil and had normally had very good results. This one exam had eluded and plagued her and Aunty Hilda had found it amusing. Oh gosh Emma thought, she really is there. How else could the medium have possibly known this?

The medium went onto explain that Aunty Hilda just wanted to remind Emma that everything would be fine. Emma felt comforted. Valerie smiled at her. They both knew what this meant. The message had not been as clear or as strong as the one Emma had received from her own mum a year ago but it was along the same lines and for Emma this could only mean one thing. That one day her fight to be reunited with her children would be successful.

Chapter 63

Emma reminded herself that it had already been three winters that she had been separated from Olivia and Sebastian. Victor Falconer with the help of the courts had succeeded in dragging out this affair for so long. Had someone told Emma just after the temporary judgment that three years later she would be no further forward and have no official visiting right to see her own children she told herself that she would have cracked and gone completely crazy. When friends praised her courage and perseverance Emma just shrugged and replied that she believed all loving mothers would have acted in exactly the same way. Her friends and family were not so convinced. They replied that they thought most people would have cracked or given up by now.

Laura in her down to earth analytical manner had commented that long term Emma had to come out of this nightmare victorious for two reasons. The first being that despite all efforts from the adverse party, Emma had not and now would not crack, go mad or do something stupid. Secondly that despite the limited contact Emma had with her children, Paul had failed to win their hearts as he had planned and steer them away from her. This was comforting and it also gave Emma the necessary courage and determination to continue her lonely crusade.

'You rock the boat.' Laura had pointed out. 'They don't like it. They are not used to it. You are a trouble maker and to make things even worse, a foreign one at that.'

'But they took my children away from me.' Emma protested. 'Everything was fabricated. It is obvious what happened if anyone reads the file carefully.'

'It doesn't matter.' Laura replied. 'They don't care. They have their way of doing things. However, you have no choice, you have to carry on through the system warts and all. Just think that they cannot give you any less than you already have today so all the chances are that your situation can only improve. With time the children will be coming back of their own accord anyway. But unfortunately, this will take time.'

It was over dinner a few weeks later that Emma saw the first sign of a rebellion from Olivia. One of their friends had come over and they were talking about their passports and the fact that they both had dual nationality. Then suddenly Olivia announced that she was not very proud of her other passport, the non-British one. Emma asked her why. Olivia's reply surprised Emma.

'Because they are dishonest and they tore us away from our mum. They did not ask me what I wanted, they just took us away and now we see you so little. Instead we have to put up with that pest Lea every day. On top of that dad is not there very often.'

'Well you know I am doing everything I can for you to come back home.' Emma replied. 'You will be heard by the judge this year and you will have to say very clearly what you want. When you are twelve years old they are obliged to listen to you by law.'

'I want to come back too.' Sebastian added almost as if he was afraid of being left out. 'I love my mum and I am coming back.'

Emma smiled. This was something which neither Paul, Victor Falconer nor the courts could control long term.

Mrs Sinclair had sent her written defence to the provincial court. They now awaited the additional submissions from Victor Falconer's side. Emma had the distinct impression of having been in this movie before. When they arrived, Victor Falconer's papers were the same as they had always been, a libellous assassination of Emma's character and capabilities as a mother.

Emma continued to be amazed that there was no ethical code of conduct. She was convinced that Victor Falconer was so confident that his freemason friends in the courts would continue to help him. In addition, there was such a remote possibility of him ever being caught pulling the strings.

On Emma's recent trip to Canada for the international sales meeting, the welcome pack Emma had received had contained a post card and stamp to write home. She had sent the postcard with the photo of a seal to the children and this was now being used as evidence that Emma was a business woman and would never be there for her children. The meeting had taken place during a weekend in which the children were with their father and Emma had arrived home the following Tuesday.

To counteract the claim, Emma requested and received a confirmation from her employer that she travelled rarely, the four day annual sales meeting being the exception. Paul on the other hand, according to Victor Falconer's court papers, was now an independent consultant, a decision he had consciously made to spend more time with his children. He could certainly no longer be classed as a businessman. Ironically Emma knew that Paul had more responsibility and had to travel and was absent more than ever before.

Emma asked herself how two parents could get on in the interests of the children when one was constantly attacking and trying to completely destroy the image of the other parent. Mrs Sinclair's tactic had been to slowly rebuild and restore the devastating image built up of Emma by Victor Falconer aptly aided by Hubert Belette, which she had done quite successfully, at least on paper.

Victor Falconer was still trying to use this so called evidence combined with the fact that the children were now three years in their father's home and were settled and any further move would be detrimental for them. It was all part of a very elaborate and clever plot which Emma had unwittingly fallen into lock stock and barrel. It had taken her two years and a lot of pain to figure it out. Now she still had to prove it.

At the beginning of his final set of submissions, Victor Falconer began with a series of general observations. Apparently, Emma seemed to have lost sight of the fact that the present procedure had been ongoing for three years. Only now was she insisting that it was urgent. Without going back to the blocking of the procedure which had been instigated by her previous counsel (the procedure being as per Victor Falconer's main case papers from three summers' ago) the debate Emma was now asking the court to address should have taken place long ago had Emma not been so obstinate in wanting the appeal court to take the matter under its jurisdiction.

This despite Paul and Victor Falconer's warnings that the appeal court was overtly not competent to handle the case. Perfectly conscious of these errors and the context which presided at the introduction of the present procedure by Paul, Emma now wanted to completely erase the past. Victor Falconer went on that one could not forget the past, and as Paul had shown three years ago when he had been awarded temporary custody, there were some serious threats for the future well-being of the children caused by Emma's approach and behaviour in the past whatever she declared as her good intentions today to further her own cause. It was nauseating.

Emma was now painfully aware that the case three years ago had been concocted against her by two consenting lawyers who undoubtedly had had inside help from the court too. The appeal court was to all intent and purposes competent to handle the case. Victor Falconer had asked for and received help from the prosecutor general's deputy to swing it back to the provincial court on a technicality. The brotherhood had identified themselves to one another, the request for help had been dispatched by Victor

Falconer and sympathetically acknowledged. Emma had seen it with her own eyes – and this for the second time.

She now knew after reading several books that this sort of thing actually went on. She thought back to the recording she had made of Paul three years ago where he had mockingly announced that Hubert Belette was not telling her everything, by appealing against the provincial court she had put her hand in a mangle, that she was going to have some serious serious problems. Now it all seemed to make more sense. Jules Mercier had remarked to Emma on a few occasions that some people were untouchable and they knew it.

Chapter 64

Mrs Sinclair wrote to Emma with her final court papers adding that if the children did not express very clearly their desire to come back and live with their mother, the judge would probably leave them for another year with their father until they had finished junior school. She wrote that they would then have a stronger chance to regain custody before the start of their new secondary school. She appreciated it was easier for her to say then for Emma to do. Emma decided to tell Olivia and Sebastian very clearly that their future was now to a large degree in their own hands. Much depended on their wish and how strongly they expressed it.

Every second weekend with Olivia and Sebastian was a treat for Emma. They saw friends, did interesting activities together, often hugged one another. Emma still had no official visiting right and Paul was generously granting her, completely voluntarily of course, every second weekend and half the school holidays. By this means he could say to the court that this was the ideal arrangement despite the expert's report from eighteen months previously recommending a shared custody with the non- guardian parent seeing the children every weekend. Emma had to collect and also drive the children back each weekend which entailed a round trip of three hours by motorway. Paul had told the children that he did not want to spend any money on petrol.

Victor Falconer kept sending letters demanding that Emma pay Paul for the upkeep of the children. Paul refused to produce any detail about his financial situation. According to Victor Falconer, he was now an independent consultant so details about his income were of no value.

Emma continued to buy Olivia and Sebastian nice clothes, spoilt them with treats and interesting activities. The children had few treats at their father's home, participated in no additional activities such as sport, dance classes, brownies, beavers, private language

327

classes, things Emma had willingly paid for while they were at home with her. It seemed so unfair. She dug in her heals and became more determined than ever that the truth would come out one day.

She stepped up her activities in the evenings after work to take her mind off things. She started aerobics on Tuesday's with a friend. On Wednesday's she went to the gym. She took up squash on Thursday's with colleagues. She continued to read books and surf the web during her spare weekend. She was hungry for knowledge and above all proof which she could use to show the courts that she had been set up.

One evening while she was surfing the web Emma discovered a book which had just been published. The short description outlined the lonely and courageous fight by a police officer from the special research brigade to highlight corruption within the prosecutor's office. The magistrate and member of the justice ministry involved in the shady dealings was none other than Paul Jordan.

As Emma had already discovered, Paul Jordan had worked in the ministry of justice as head of the cabinet and also held a high position in the public prosecutor's office. He was to everyone's surprise first arrested for having provided parts of a judicial file to drug dealers being investigated internationally. Then it transpired he had granted pardons to dubious characters. Monies he received illicitly were allegedly used to finance a major political party. He was sentenced to several months in prison for violation of professional secret and forgery followed by another five further convictions connected to the underworld. Above all, Jules Mercier had admitted that he knew him well and he was a big friend of his.

Emma wrote to the author, Terry Talbot, to order a copy. She admitted that she was very interested to read the content since she herself was in a difficult situation fighting for her rights in a system which seemed to prefer to cover up misdoings rather than fix them. A few days later the book arrived through the post. Emma pulled down the blinds, settled on the sofa, put on her favourite soul music, made herself a cup of lemon tea and started to read.

The detective in question was described by his superiors as an example to follow. He became known in the force as 'the Incorruptible'. All attempts from the underworld to coax him into taking bribes to turn a blind eye to their illicit activities had failed. He was also hard working and available day and night for his colleagues if necessary. He had followed a tough training doing his military service in the crack para commando unit. Above all he believed in justice and could not take no for an answer. Emma could firmly empathise with this last point. She already knew they had something strong in common.

Several years after his retirement Terry Talbot set to work to write his book with the goal of showcasing the existence of protections against which investigators and honest and conscientious police offers came up against, which in no way facilitated the already difficult task they faced in the field. He claimed to have been the victim of mafia like procedures but this not prevent him from sleeping because he had a clear conscience. Significant was his understanding of why certain enquiries came to nothing. A dishonest magistrate or police officer could easily sabotage an enquiry.

Terry Talbot claimed that his relationship with Paul Jordan only began to deteriorate when he understood that the former had figured out various irregularities in certain investigations and represented a potential danger to him. He was prevented from investigating certain cases and unjustly disciplined. Only when Paul Jordan was arrested and found guilty of various misdemeanours, did people realise that Terry Talbot had not been wrong after all. His boss admitted that Terry had been right but too early.

During Paul Jordan's trial the general counsel had spoken about the bitterness and humiliation felt by police officers who had been deceived from within by a magistrate whose job it had been to direct them and he recommended a long prison sentence and a lengthy ban from public office. The corruption charges were dropped and the eventual verdict included a light prison sentence and a small fine. In Terry Talbot's opinion, there had been political pressure. Terry Talbot was later involved in two more enquiries which he maintained were equally sabotaged. One was related to arms trafficking and the other to the counterfeit printing of tens of millions.

Terry Talbot concluded his book with some sobering thoughts. In reality, he believed that politicians wanted to neutralise the enquiries which concerned them and that they had not given to the police the necessary means to work more effectively. He maintained that it was in the field and not sitting comfortably behind a desk that one learned what happened in the criminal world and that colleagues today confronted with similar issues should not lose faith and continue to fight against crooks, many of whom invariably finished falling sooner or later.

It was a thought provoking book which Emma enjoyed reading. It basically confirmed what she had already figured out about the system. She had not learned anything new about Jules Mercier or Hubert Belette but they certainly seemed to fit the mould of the shady characters who seemed to turn up in many a scandal.

A couple of weeks later the phone rang one evening. It was Terry Talbot.

'Good evening.' he announced introducing himself. 'Sorry to disturb you but I was curious to find out what you thought about my book.'

Emma gulped in surprise quickly trying to regain her composure. After all she had never spoken to a detective before.

'Oh fine, very good.' Emma replied. 'It was well written and very well documented with evidence but then, if I read between the lines, you were a very good detective so I would not have expected anything less.'

Terry laughed. 'So you also have problems with our system?' he asked as any good detective would.

'Yes I was also set up by some unscrupulous characters one of whom told me he knows Mr Jordan very well.' Emma explained.

'Who is that?' Terry asked. 'Perhaps I know him.'

'I really think it is better not to discuss this over the phone.' Emma continued. 'You never know who might be listening.'

'I understand.' Terry Talbot replied.

Emma thought for a moment. This gentleman had a lot of experience. He had written a book. He knew so many people in the system. Perhaps he could give Emma some information about Jules Mercier which she had not yet discovered and which might help her. He might even give her some tips about how to write a book. The plan to actually now move ahead with this project following the bitter disappointment of the appeal court outcome was more apparent than ever. Like herself, Terry Talbot seemed to be an honest person fighting for truth and justice.

'Let's meet for lunch.' Emma suggested. 'Then we can discuss things at our ease and in private.'

'Fine.' he replied promptly asking 'Where and when?'

Emma appreciated his efficiency.

'Next Monday if you are free.' she replied. She suggested one of her favourite Italian restaurants close to the office and only twenty minutes from where Terry Talbot lived. 'I will book a table for two for 12.30 pm.'

'Fine.' Terry said. 'Look forward to meeting you there.'

Emma booked the table. She knew the waiter well. He was fun and always very helpful. She entered the restaurant and looked around for an elderly gentleman sitting alone at a table. Emma was sure Terry would have spotted her first. Actually he had, as he was sitting down behind the bar out of sight. Emma's waiter friend came over and indicated with a smile that Terry was at the table obscured by the bar.

Typical Emma smiled to herself as she hung up her coat and headed over. Terry Talbot stood up to greet Emma and they smiled and shook hands. His handshake was firm and strong. They sat down and started to chat. Conversation flowed easily and they hit it off immediately. Terry asked a lot of questions but so did Emma. Emma thought that she would be nervous but funnily enough she was not.

They discovered that they had quite a few things in common. They were both stubborn and, by nature, fighters so that they agreed that this was probably a deciding factor in not cracking under immense pressure when one was up against the system all alone. They joked that they were both from areas of their respective countries renowned for their gritty, determined sort of folk.

Emma asked Terry Talbot lots of questions about his book. How long it had taken him to write it, his motivation, why he had not gone through a publisher. He admitted that he would have liked to but no publisher would have touched it as they were nervous as the content was not very complementary of the system. He admitted that everything was documented and proven but the couple of publishers he had approached were not prepared to take any risks. Therefore, he had arranged to print the book at his own expense and keep selling a few copies every month.

A website promoted the book. In fact, this was where Emma had discovered it. In addition, whenever Terry Talbot went to police gatherings or other events he mentioned it and quite a few people ordered a copy afterwards.

Emma asked Terry what the reaction had been so far. He confirmed that it had been good. Like herself, people had found it convincing, interesting and backed up with proof. He added wistfully that of course some entities did not like to be reminded of the truth.

Terry Talbot did not know Jules Mercier nor Hubert Belette. He promised to keep their meeting and the content of their discussions confidential. Emma confided that she had received thinly veiled death threats from Jules Mercier. Terry was sympathetic. He reassured her that if she had everything documented and also abroad, then they would probably not dare to do anything. He added with a smile that he thought they had eventually backed off in his case because he knew too much and had also documented it just in case.

They parted company thanking one another for an enjoyable lunch and chat. Terry told Emma that if she needed any help or advice she knew where to find him. He also wished her the best of luck with the next court hearing. Emma thanked him and promised to get in touch with a foreign manufacturer to obtain an instruction manual in local language for a recent purchase Terry had made, something he had been struggling with for a while. She received the instruction manual two weeks later. She knew he would be pleased and she posted it to him. Terry called Emma the day it arrived to thank her.

They were to remain in touch for several years and spend many enjoyable lunches together exchanging ideas and theories about many of the unsolved cases of the previous two decades.

Chapter 65

The weeks flew by and before Emma knew it, it was already Easter. The days became longer and the weather milder. Emma was looking forward to spending a full week with Olivia and Sebastian during the Easter break. Laura had decided to spoil them. She was sympathetic about all the expense Emma had incurred over the last couple of years. She was even more sympathetic about all the stress the set-up had caused Emma and the children and continued to encourage and praise her sister's resolve. She found the situation completely inadmissible like many of Emma's international friends.

Laura had booked the family into a manor house on the English coast complete with spa, gym, pool and a very good restaurant. Emma found it comforting to be in a typical English environment again. For a few days at least, all her problems seemed removed and far away. They visited Hastings, Eastbourne, Beachy Head, the smuggler's caves, the mediaeval town of Rye and Dover Castle. An action packed week, full of tradition, history and educational activities for the children.

As Emma rolled onto the car ferry for the trip back across the channel, she had a heavy heart although she tried hard not to show it to Olivia and Sebastian. In a couple of months, she would be back again in the provincial court to fight for the future of her children. Instinctively she knew it would lead to nothing. She was defiant but also fed up. Somehow, somewhere there had to be a break through.

It was a Tuesday evening and Emma had just arrived home from her aerobics class feeling sweaty and tired. She was busy preparing a quick bite to eat when the phone rang. It was a good colleague.

'Emma I just wanted to tell you that this evening there is an interesting programme and debate about freemasonry on TV. It starts in half an hour. I saw it in the TV magazine and thought you might learn something to help your case.'

'Thanks very much.' Emma replied gratefully. 'Yes I will watch it. You never know. See you tomorrow. Have a great evening. Bye.'

Emma ate her dinner on a tray in front of the TV. It was indeed a very interesting documentary followed by a debate. The adverse effects and misuse of freemasonry to distort the course of justice was clearly beginning to manifest itself on the continent too. As far as Emma was concerned, this was a positive development. A chief prosecutor, a smart and articulate man, had actually put his foot down and called on the press to reveal the major irregularities, cover ups, conspiracies in the courts all traceable back to freemasonry. He openly admitted there was a real problem of freemasonry in the judicial system.

A lawyer went onto explain the many resulting miscarriages of justice. How dozens, if not hundreds of innocent people, were pushed to ruin, even suicide every year by the illicit practices of the brotherhood. How a judge had locked away a file in a custody case for three years and the poor mother had been deprived of all her rights. Emma sat mesmerised.

Two journalists had spent two years investigating the many anomalies and had just published a book. It was definitely a book which Emma would order. It could even reveal something interesting which might help her case. One thing was for sure, she was far from alone.

The problems seemed to be the same as those encountered and revealed a few years earlier in the UK. The heads of the different masonic lodges were also present during the debate. Naturally they defended their movement which they presented as honourable, inoffensive, and full of good intentioned members. Of course the majority are, Emma reminded herself. However, the heads of the masonic lodges were all unconvincing when it came to presenting their plan about how to deal with undesirables or members of their society found to be using the brotherhood for dishonest means. Emma reasoned that having sworn an oath to mutually assist fellow masons, it was probably a dilemma for masons to actually sanction a brother, even if he was behaving inappropriately.

That evening Emma went to bed relieved that things on this side of the channel were also beginning to hot up. She thought to herself that it really was about time that this became public knowledge and that someone made a stand. Thank goodness we still had a handful of brave and well informed journalists to reveal the truth, even if it does mean opening up a Pandora's box she told herself.

Emma ordered the book online the following day and it arrived one week later. (Les Frères Invisibles (The Invisible Brothers) by Ghislaine Oppenheimer and Renaud Lecadre published by Albin Michel).

By just scanning the book cover, she knew she was in for another interesting read. This is starting to sound all too familiar Emma lamented to herself as she turned the pages. For more than fifteen years one scandal had followed another. The authors claimed that all the political parties were implicated, sections of the police and even the justice system. After a close examination of a large number of files dealing with business matters, even corruption, each time the common thread turned out to be the implication of freemasons. *'That the masonic networks and their cult of absolute secrecy under threat of having one's throat cut offered an ideal shell to protect the intrigues of a growing number of dishonest members.'*

The book, like those in the UK, pointed out that a great many members are sincere and they are the first to worry about the most serious and growing number of derivations. Again, similar to the UK a few years before, thanks to the revelations of highly placed masons revolted by the trend, the authors were able to *'unravel the codes and customs and lift the veil on the existence of invisible powers, often above the law.'*

The first chapter already revealed some additional signs of recognition among the brotherhood. The promotion to a superior grade or degree was referred to as a salary raise. There was even a coded alphabet dating from the XVIII century from where the custom originated among masons to use capitals followed by three dots. Three dots in the form of a triangle, two parallel lines with a dot or the line framed by two dots which certain masons made appear in their signature as a sign of recognition.

The book actually went onto explain that one way to swing a court decision in one's favour consists of filing the court papers in advance of the hearing in which the signature of the lawyer carries the three dots. It is a way to draw the attention of the judges, hey look I am a mason and it would be good to get a favourable outcome.

All of a sudden, this seemed really interesting to Emma. She took out her own file containing the court papers on the off chance that she would discover something. She suddenly stared in disbelief. The first letter sent to her by Victor Falconer and setting off the official hostilities the month the mutual consent divorce had been pronounced had a very clear three dot triangle in the signature as did dozens of subsequent official letters to Hubert Belette in which he painted a very grim picture of Emma's character. Letters where Hubert Belette had been completely negligent and he had not answered most or even shown some of them to Emma. These letters had been subsequently attached as evidence to all Victor Falconer's defence papers filed up front with the courts.

In concocting the file against Emma, the sign of recognition which also constituted a request for help had come from Victor Falconer. Emma was now sure that Jules Mercier and Victor Falconer had been in this together from the beginning. Any masonic magistrate, prosecutor's deputy or court clerk looking at these letters signed in this way would also immediately recognise the request for help and probably oblige as Emma's diabolical track record had proven so far.

Emma carried on leafing through the court papers in her file. It got even better. The day before Hubert Belette had met Paul in the appeal court to fix a new date for the hearing under the pretext that the appeal court had itself postponed the hearing to handle an urgent paedophile case, Victor Falconer had written a letter to the General Counsel of the appeal court enclosing a copy of a letter addressed the same day to the president of the appeal court. In the letter, he was at pains to point out that he had still not received any news from Hubert Belette or any reason for his silence. Victor Falconer requested that the case be postponed pointing out specifically that this could not be held against his client. On the second page, clear to see and completely out of context, were the three dots of the triangle. There was no apparent reason this should have been in the letter if it was not a sign of recognition again between the masonic brethren.

Hubert Belette had told Emma that he has seen the General Counsel on two occasions to raise some issues with him about their case. Was this one of the issues? Did the General Counsel brush him off? Did Victor Falconer get worried and already plead his own defence? Whichever it was bizarre and also very suspicious.

Six weeks later, Emma had dumped Hubert Belette to the surprise of the adverse party and Mrs Sinclair had taken on the case. The same section of the appeal court assigned an expert to interview the children. It turned out that the expert was not free and others had to be found leading to a very convenient delay which only played in favour of Victor Falconer and Paul. Coincidence perhaps but it smelt very bad. For Emma, there were too many bad coincidences for one to believe that it was merely coincidence. She was dumbfounded but pleased by the discovery. It stacked up and it was what she had expected but to see it black on white was quite a shock. What she would eventually do with her discovery now was something else.

Another section of the book which seemed all too familiar to Emma and which she could not help drawing a parallel with her own case was that a member of the Grand Lodge admitted that in several courts dealing with commercial matters a brother would always arrange with his lawyer for his affair to be judged the day where the hearing was presided over by a comprehensive brother. For Emma, this all seemed to compare nicely to what Jules Mercier had previously admitted. So it did happen and it was true. Emma asked herself how many people would continue to deny it. Probably still a great deal if the happened to be working in the courts she told herself.

Emma could not help asking herself what recourse one had if one discovered that one had been set up by secret society members with help from within the judiciary. It was delicate but it seemed to be widespread. How long would it take before it was recognised as a European or even a worldwide problem and would this disclosure and subsequent solution ever be allowed to happen? Emma had no answers but the questions kept nagging away at her.

The authors of the book maintained that eighty percent of complaints brought against the judicial system were closed without further action. However, the European Convention on Human Rights stipulated that everyone has the right for his case to be heard by an impartial court. The European court had gradually refined the definition of impartiality. According to its jurisprudence, it has to be objective and 'visible' in the eyes of the justiciable so that the latter is not tempted to put in question the integrity of the court. The judges must not only be impartial in their conscience but inspire an absolute confidence in people who appear in front of them.

The book's authors seriously asked themselves how this could be possible for a judge, magistrate or prosecutor belonging to the brotherhood who had sworn a blood oath to protect the secrets of freemasonry. In 'appearance' according to the terminology of the European court, a magistrate swearing such an oath could not be altogether impartial when he swapped his robes for an apron.

Emma could not agree more as she had experienced this first hand. She regularly asked herself if the issue would ever be publicly acknowledged one day and, even more importantly, addressed.

Chapter 66

Papers had been filed by both parties with the provincial court since the beginning of the year. Emma knew from experience that there would be additional submissions from both parties before they were given a date for the hearing. Mrs Sinclair wanted the children to be interviewed by the youth court judge prior to any custody hearing. The measures were still temporary but in the next hearing there would be a definitive decision concerning custody. Instinctively Emma knew that they would start messing her around.

She told Valerie two months before it happened that she expected that they would try to assign their case to a judge sympathetic to Paul's cause and that is exactly what did happen. Emma had to attend yet another public hearing to hear what the judge had decided was the next step. The youth court judge, a sympathetic looking lady, agreed that the children should be auditioned prior to the final hearing. However, they both had to be twelve years old which fell into the summer period.

Olivia was already twelve but Sebastian would only be in the summer. Once again, it was going to be conveniently very tight for the start of the new school year. Emma had hoped together with Mrs Sinclair that this judge herself would be the one to preside in their case. She had a reputation for being quite astute but also fair.

When the confirmation from the court dropped through the post a few weeks later in the familiar brown envelope with the black stamp, Emma opened it quickly, anxious to read the content. She stared at the name of the youth court judge assigned and swore under her breath. It was dear judge Granger, the charming judge whose reputation for favouring the case of the father had extended to many a lawyer's offices. The same judge who had so abruptly dismissed Emma's case three years ago asking for a social enquiry when Paul was locking up the children alone overnight. The same judge who had mockingly chided Emma for being concerned that her young children were being sent out alone on the streets of the city, the same city where two children of the same age had recently been abducted and found dead several months later. The same judge against whom Hubert Belette had appealed.

Emma's sentiments were in complete disarray jumping between disbelief, predictability, unfairness, bad luck and premeditation of the opposing party. She called Mrs Sinclair. She was equally disappointed with this development. Mrs Sinclair agreed with Emma that this appointment would definitely not help their case.

She called Emma back next day confirming that they might be in luck after all. Victor Falconer was on holiday on the date assigned and he insisted on the hearing taking place after his return. Emma asked when he would be back. They calculated that it was one week before the return of the normal youth court judge and therefore judge Granger would probably still preside. However, Mrs Sinclair had another important case the following week which she had already committed to so the two lawyers wrote to the court and a new date was confirmed for both the interview of the children and the custody hearing, both in the first few days of the new school year.

The name of the presiding youth court judge was not one Emma had seen before and Mrs Sinclair was not familiar with the judge in question either. Emma asked her to try to find out who it was. Given the history of her case, Emma was anxious to know up front what they were going into.

Victor Falconer had already filed his second set of submissions with the court. The judge and court clerk could read them up front to familiarise themselves with the case. Emma was pretty sure however, that behind the scenes some court officials were already quite familiar with her case.

Again Emma felt sick reading Victor Falconer's latest defence papers. They were so full of wicked untruths presented in such an aggressive and unfair way. An outright assassination of her character. One sentence, in particular, caught her eye. In paragraph five entitled attitude of the parents in face of the problems, Victor Falconer was at pains to point out that the court was in possession of all the official letters exchanged between the parties and their counsel containing each of the points developed. The court could therefore judge for itself about the well-founded arguments and precisions made by Paul.

Emma smiled and shook her head. There were over sixty official letters attached to Victor Falconer's papers as evidence, each one full of untruths from his side or negligence from Hubert Belette's side supporting their case which they had painstakingly built up against Emma. The first letter the court officials would probably see to set the scene would be the one to Emma just after the divorce with the distinctive three dot triangle in the signature. The message being loud and clear. Hey I am a mason help me out. Many of the subsequent letters to Hubert Belette also had the same distinctive signature.

Mrs Sinclair had put together an excellent defence showing with firm evidence that not only had Emma been extremely badly advised but that she was also not the uncompromising troublemaker, bad mother and career woman which she had been painted out to be. In addition, all the official letters could not be taken seriously by the court as evidence as they were full of simple invention from Paul's side. Finally, since temporary transfer of custody to Paul, all efforts had been made to make the limited contact Emma had with her children as difficult as possible and Paul still insisted on controlling and being the judge of each of Emma's movements which certainly was not in the best interests of the children.

Emma thought to herself if any court really wanted to scratch beneath the surface of this case and think rationally about the origins, they would soon see that it was a set-up, a clear manipulation resulting in a gross injustice. She was also painfully aware that nobody in authority wanted to see the origins or handle it properly. For Emma, it was a mixture of incompetence, discrimination and corruption with the brotherhood helping one another out to secure the desired result. She shared her concerns with Mrs Sinclair aware that there was only so much she could do.

Emma decided to have a wonderful summer holiday with Olivia and Sebastian then she would discover what the provincial court turned up in the autumn.

Emma had not booked any summer holiday as she first wanted to see what the court would decide about interviewing the children. With the revised court dates now clear, she could make plans. She was careful not to spend too much money, acutely aware that she still had legal fees to pay and eventual maintenance payments to Paul.

She asked the children what they thought about a camping holiday and they replied enthusiastically that they thought this was a great idea. Emma bought a tent which slept five, a small gas stove and some camping furniture as well as inflatable matrasses. They already had sleeping bags. She loaded up the car. Luckily she had a large estate car so everything fitted in, just. This was going to be an adventure and Emma knew that they were going to have lots of fun together.

Their first stop was a four-star camp site in the Dordogne with three pools, waterslides and the most modern of amenities. They met up with a good English friend of Emma's and her family. They canoed together down the Dordogne river, visited the grottos and caves, swam in the pools, went horse riding and barbecued every evening. In the morning Olivia and Sebastian got up, went to the small shop to fetch the fresh baguette then cooked bacon and eggs on the small gas stove in the open air. They were very resourceful and Emma was proud of them.

Their next stop was the coastal area south of Bordeaux. They had arranged to meet Cathy and her family. There were summer festivals and they visited the nearby Atlantic coast and rolled together down the Dune de Pila. Cathy's family invited them several times to dinner. Olivia and Sebastian decided not to tell their father that they had spent time with Cathy as they knew that he would not have approved. They then headed for the Pyrenees. They climbed mountains to reach desolate lakes, visited breath-taking sights including the snow-capped Cirque de Gavarnie. It was a completely different free way of life, where everyone contributed to the daily tasks. They worked together well as a team.

One evening as they headed down the mountain, Emma noticed that the skies were overcast and darkening. She instinctively turned on the radio and heard that a storm was forecast. They drove to the local supermarket and bought pork chops, sautéed potatoes and a big fresh salad. Before preparing dinner, Emma took out the waterproofing spray and gave the tent another coat of protection from the outside and carefully checked that the pegs were firmly anchored in the ground. She was not sure how big this storm would turn out to be.

The thunder started to rumble in the distance, suddenly everything became very dark, and a wind started to blow. At the same time the first drops of rain started to fall and echoed loudly as they landed on the roof of their tent. Emma took out an umbrella and held it over the small gas stove as she continued to cook dinner. The chops sizzled in the pan and smelt invitingly good. The three of them had done a lot of walking that day and were all feeling pretty hungry. Olivia headed off the fifty metres to the toilet. By now it was almost pitch black. Suddenly Emma heard Olivia calling out in the dark.

'Mum, mum come and help me. I have fallen over and cut my foot. I can't walk. It's bleeding.'

Emma knew Olivia hated the sight of blood. Suddenly a large streak of lightening lit up the surroundings and Emma saw Olivia in the distance holding her foot. She cried out to Sebastian to hold the umbrella above the small stove so the dinner could finish cooking then sped off into the night to rescue Olivia.

'Jump on my back.' she urged as she arrived at her side. 'I will carry you back to the tent then we can patch up your foot.'

Olivia obediently jumped on Emma's back and they headed back through the sweeping rain and wind to their tent. Emma had already lit a small gas lamp and she helped Olivia onto her inflatable mattress then rummaged through her toilet bag to find the disinfectant spray and plasters. Emma cleaned the wound and stuck a big plaster on Olivia's foot.

'It will be fine tomorrow. Just don't put any weight on it this evening.' Emma reassured her.

The three of them sat in the tent and tucked into their evening meal. Meanwhile the thunder and lightning continued outside. They all felt safe and comfortable in the warm confines of their small shelter. It was another unique team building experience. Next day the storm was gone and when they opened the tent, they were greeted with blue sky and sunshine.

The children had so much energy. For the first time as they climbed to two thousand metres, Emma was following Olivia and Sebastian and not the other way around. Sebastian was already as tall as Emma. It hit Emma hard how fast her son and daughter were growing up. In a few weeks' time they would be in court being interviewed by the judge about their preference of residence and their future. How Emma hoped they would be brave and express themselves clearly.

Olivia and Sebastian had told Emma on several occasions and also during the holidays how much they were looking forward to coming home. Emma knew that Paul would put them under pressure. She knew him well. He would lose financially if they came back and he also needed to be in control.

To Emma's dismay, the children confided in her before the holidays, just after the date of the audition had been confirmed, that their father had called them into his office. He had told them to stand in front of his desk and they were going to have a rehearsal. He was the judge and he was going to ask them some questions and they had to reply exactly as they planned to do in the forthcoming audition in the provincial court.

At first Olivia and Sebastian stood there and said nothing. Paul slowly became angry and started to shout at them. He bellowed that they would not leave the room until they had told him what they were going to say. Both children started to cry. Paul insisted to continue with the questioning. The children were told to stand up straight. Finally, Olivia told her father that she loved him but did not like Lea. She missed and preferred life back at her mum's place, in her old school with her friends and therefore wanted to go back.

Suddenly Paul broke down. He told them that he thought that he was giving them a good upbringing and he would ask Lea to be nicer to them in the future. Emma was sure Paul did love his children in his own way. However, despite Victor Falconer's rhetoric to the court that Paul was a hands-on father, he was rarely at home and the children were left with Lea or her daughter, people they did not feel entirely comfortable with and deprived of regular contact with their own mother. It all seemed so unfair but this is what they were up against.

Chapter 67

Emma drove the children back to their father's place following the holiday. The following weekend they were off to England for a wedding. The niece of Paul's rich American cousin was marrying an English chap. Paul had decided rather late that he was not going to the wedding so Olivia and Sebastian were scheduled to travel with their grandmother. Paul's mother had asked Olivia to bring along a pretty dress for the wedding and Sebastian a suit which Emma and her American friends had bought them for their birthdays. Lea had prepared them a small case but it contained nothing more than a pair of old shorts and a couple of t shirts.

Emma wished the children an enjoyable and safe trip and settled back into the routine of work. It was early on Thursday morning when Emma's mobile rang. She had just got out of bed and wondered who would call at such an early hour. It was Olivia.

'Mum you have to help us.' her little voice implored. 'We are at the station ready to get on the train to London and we don't have our passports. Can you fax our British passports through to London?'

'Don't get on the train without any valid paperwork.' Emma advised immediately. 'In fact I don't even think they will let you on. Stay put and I will come immediately to the station with your passports and you can take the next train. They are quite frequent. You just need to call your uncle Bob and tell him you will be arriving a little later for him to pick you up. Wait in front of the station and I will be there as soon as I can.'

Emma hurriedly got dressed and rummaged in her desk for the two passports. She grabbed an apple and headed for the car. What on earth are they doing without travel docs she could not help asking herself. Surely Paul and his mother should have checked this out in advance.

She parked the car somewhat illegally with the warning lights flashing and dodged around the building works as she headed towards the station entrance. Olivia and Sebastian ran towards her followed by Paul's mother. Emma hugged the children and handed them their passports. Paul's mother approached very apologetic and grateful. She looked frail and quite pale. It had been well over a year since Emma had last seen her and she was a bit shocked at how she looked.

'Emma thank you so much.' Paul's mum said for the third time.

'It is OK.' Emma replied. 'It is the least I can do in the circumstances. You know your son should be responsible for seeing that the children have the necessary paperwork to travel. He can't expect an old lady like yourself who travels so little to take care of everything.'

'Dad is furious at grannie and at us for calling you.' Olivia added. 'He said we should have called him instead. He shouted at us all on the phone. We called you because you can come faster from home than he can.'

'I know and it is OK.' Emma reassured them. 'Don't worry anymore. Have a good trip and call me when you arrive back. Do you have a way to contact Uncle Bob and tell him when to pick you up now at the other end?'

'Yes.' Olivia explained. 'Other friends are waiting for us and they have a mobile and will call Uncle Bob as soon as we know exactly when the next train will arrive in London.'

Emma was relieved. She watched the three of them walk away together towards the departures. She only hoped that Paul would not try to confiscate their British passports when they returned or cause any other problems.

Emma planned to visit her sister Laura with the children first week of September. She had booked them on a low-cost flight. It was

Emma's weekend as confirmed in previous correspondence. She had not realised it but also the weekend before Olivia and Sebastian were due to be auditioned by the judge.

An official letter arrived from Victor Falconer three days before their planned departure. Paul did not agree that Emma saw the children that weekend. Emma was livid. She had already paid for the flight tickets and her sister had arranged a weekend full of activities including a night out at a musical in London for which she had already paid for the tickets. Mrs Sinclair replied with a copy of the reservations insisting that Emma see the children that weekend and pointing out that she had been more than helpful in the recent passport incident.

Victor Falconer shot back with another official letter accusing Emma of not behaving appropriately, of putting her own wishes in front of everyone else's including those of the children, of not adhering to past agreements. He accused Emma of having made the reservations in a unilateral manner, typical of her bad attitude. He confirmed that Paul was not aware the children had left their ID cards at home before their trip to the wedding in England, which he had given to them and asked them to carry with them at all times.

Victor Falconer insisted that Paul knew nothing of the existence of Olivia and Sebastian's British passports which was in total contravention of local law which did not allow dual nationality and this even more so, since custody of the children had been granted to the father. This whole incident was another clear example of Emma's poor state of mind, not to mention her general mentality.

Emma should have been used to it after five long years. She was nevertheless shocked by the tone and content of the letter but also indignant. She wrote back to Mrs Sinclair enclosing four letters signed by Paul just after he was awarded temporary custody confiscating hers and mentioning the children's British passports when she first saw her children at the weekend. She added that it was therefore astonishing to note in Victor Falconer's last letter that Paul was not aware of the children's British passports which they had acquired shortly after their birth with the full agreement of Paul, their father, who had even asked that she do the necessary for him to obtain dual nationality. Emma also told Mrs Sinclair that she believed Victor Falconer had now completely overstepped the mark and she was going to write to the new justice minister and demand an official enquiry into her case which was an absolute disgrace.

A letter came back confirming that Emma could see the children that weekend and go to England as planned.

Shortly afterwards Olivia and Sebastian confided in Emma that Victor Falconer had been angry with their father since he claimed he risked facing serious problems. Emma could not figure out if this was because of the recent passport incident and her threat to escalate the whole case to the new justice minister or the fact that Uncle Bob had called Emma to thank her for her help with the passports. Bob was the brother of Paul's very rich influential cousin living in the USA who doted on Paul's mother and who Emma and her family had long suspected of being at the origin of the set-up. Bob had confirmed that the American side of the family had been very disappointed by Paul's attitude and the no show at the wedding as well as the chiding of Paul's mother over the passports and it was now clear which parent was in the right and the wrong.

Emma had briefly explained to Bob without going into any detail that she had lost custody of her children as a result of corruption in the system which one day she would do her utmost to expose. Bob had told Emma that he thought it was an unbelievable story and a film could be made of it. Emma had replied in a jovial manner that he was spot on.

Chapter 68

A good and worldly friend with a degree in child psychology who knew Olivia and Sebastian well advised Emma to go along to the court to see the children before they were heard by the judge. She told Emma that their father would put them under a lot of pressure just before the hearing and if they saw Emma they would know that she supported them all the way and it would probably encourage them to be even more courageous. In addition, Emma could gauge if there were any further irregularities at play. Emma agreed with her. She told Olivia and Sebastian in advance that she would be there and they seemed pleased.

Emma arrived at the provincial court and quietly entered the reception area. She waited for the court clerk to finish her telephone conversation then smiled and introduced herself.

'Hello. I am Emma Brown, the mother of Olivia and Sebastian Archer. They are due to be heard by the judge at 3 pm. Can you please tell me which waiting room I should go to?'

The court clerk looked surprised. 'Oh. The audition has been postponed by half an hour. We called your ex-husband to inform him. After all he is the one with custody of the children. We did not think it necessary to call you.'

'Well here I am anyway.' Emma smiled back. 'Not to worry I will go and have a cup of tea on the town square and come back in half an hour. Where is the waiting room please?'

As she headed back to the court she wondered what she would see. From the cafe window, she had looked out for Paul's car but had not seen him arrive. As she turned the corner there he was sitting with Olivia and Sebastian. He looked startled to see her.

'Hello.' she announced with a smile kissing both children. 'Look I have brought you some sweets and your favourite magazine.' Emma added trying to sound as cheerful as possible.

Paul looked at both children sternly. They froze and looked down at their shoes. They obviously felt intimidated.

'I decided to come at the last minute.' Emma announced looking at Paul. 'After all I think it is only normal that we are both here and it is not very far from my office.'

Paul nodded but said nothing. Meanwhile a lawyer sat at an adjoining table speaking into a small handheld recorder, recording the notes from a recent hearing. For a moment, this was the only noise to break a very deafening silence.

Suddenly the court clerk, a demure looking man, walked out of the office where the children were to be heard. He nodded as he quickly passed by. He avoided eye contact. He looked uncomfortable. Emma tried to make light hearted conversation. Olivia had been ill with a temperature and had been off school for two days so Emma asked her how she was feeling. Better had been her reply but not yet one hundred percent.

At last the youth court judge arrived. She was a middle-aged lady. She shot a glance at both Paul and Emma and then smiled at the children asking which one wanted to go in first. Sebastian volunteered. Both children were gone for about half an hour. When Sebastian came out Paul stood up and asked him to follow him out into the courtyard. Olivia meanwhile had been ushered in to see the judge so Emma sat alone in the waiting room.

She looked around at the posters on the wall. There was one showing a couple and the message advocating mediation to limit conflict between separating parents. Emma smiled ironically. She had gone along with the mutual consent divorce in the interest of the children and had been manipulated and set up big time. She doubted that Paul would have chosen mediation. He had been far better served by Victor Falconer, Jules Mercier and Hubert Belette bending all the rules in his favour.

Suddenly Sebastian returned to the waiting room and Paul beckoned for Emma to join him in the courtyard. Emma stood up. Whatever could he want?

Paul began. 'The children are going to express themselves today and we do not know which way it is going to go. We have to think and act in their best interest. I have told them that if they want to come back to you I will fully support that.'

Emma listened calmly. 'Go on.' she prompted.

'It is a pity that things have deteriorated to such a degree.' Paul added. 'If we had to go through it again, I would definitely favour the mediation route.'

Emma felt like laughing but she had to play the game.

'Yes, it is a pity.' she admitted. 'If you are concerned about the best interests of the children then why have you done everything to separate them from me during the last three years? After all I am their mother and I love them. Believe it or not they love me too and also need me.'

'I did not.' Paul blurted out defending himself.

'Well maybe not personally as you were not always there but what about your wife?' Emma asked.

'Well, Emma let's be fair. She was very mad with you. It is your fault she lost her job.' Emma said nothing. She did not even want to get into this futile discussion again. It was simply untrue but moreover, nothing justified a deliberate attempt to separate a loving parent from his or her children. 'Well at least we are talking together as mature parents.' Paul concluded.

'Yes that is at least a step in the right direction.' Emma replied.

They both went back inside and waited for Olivia to emerge from the judge's chambers. She came out shortly afterwards with the judge. The judge asked Paul and Emma if they would like to see a copy of the report adding that for her it was very clear. They both agreed. Emma wanted to see the content in preparation for next week's hearing. The judge asked them to wait for a few minutes until the court clerk finished typing it up.

A few minutes later the court clerk came out and handed the report to Emma. It was short and simple. The children were happy in their father's home. They loved both parents and wished that they would get along. Sebastian did not always appreciate his stepmother but this was not seen as a major problem. If Olivia had a magic wand, her wish would be that her two parents would get back together again as this would solve all the problems. Neither child wanted to make the other parent unhappy by expressing a wish to live in one household or in the other.

Emma handed the report to Paul to read and they walked together with the children out of the court room and to the exit.

'You know.' Emma explained to Paul. 'Olivia and Sebastian have very clearly said that they want to do their secondary schooling at the very good school next to my office, where several of their friends from their former school will also go.'

Emma looked at Olivia and Sebastian and they both nodded and told their father that this was true.

'We will cross that bridge next year when we come to it.' Paul replied.

'Why don't you move to the centre of the country again?' Emma suggested. 'Then we can have the only fair solution in any custody hearing, an equal shared custody?'

'It is not that simple. We will see next year.' he concluded.

Suddenly the court clerk came hurrying towards them.

'Do you have the report?' he asked. 'You can't take it with you. There are no copies allowed. It can only be consulted in the court.' he announced almost reproachfully.

He took back the report and scurried across the yard and into the court building.

Emma said goodbye to the children and went back to the office. She was concerned. Deep down she had not expected anything else. The courts were never going to give her back her children. It was a scandal. Unacceptable.

That afternoon Olivia called Emma in the office. Her father had gone out to a business meeting.

'Mum' she began. 'This whole thing is just not serious. It is a joke.'

Taken back by her comments, Emma asked her to explain why.

'We are supposed to be allowed to say where we want to live.' she explained. 'We are over twelve years old now. Well this judge began the interview by saying to us both that we should not tell her all our secrets because she would have to write things down. I told her I wanted to come back to you and then do my secondary schooling at the good school at the side of your office. Mummy guess what she said? She told me it was not my decision and it was the parents and the court who would decide. The main thing was that I was working well at school so that I could get a job later. She did not write anything down about my wishes or comments at all.'

Emma was astounded. She asked Sebastian if there was anything else which seemed unusual in the audition.

'Well I told the judge that Lea had told dad that we were retarded and we did not appreciate this.' Sebastian explained.

'What did the judge reply?' Emma enquired.

'Oh just that we should speak to Lea about it, that's all. I also told the judge that I wanted to come back and go to the secondary school next to your office and the judge did not write this down.' Sebastian announced.

Emma remained calm. Even this audition seemed to have been manipulated. Emma asked the children what their father had said after their chat together.

'Oh just that the school we want to go to next to your office is full of snobs and that we are much better off staying with him. And that the only thing which interests him is that you start to pay him money and fast.' Olivia confided.

'Charming.' Emma replied. 'Don't worry we will get there eventually. They can't continue to separate us forever against our will.' she reassured both children.

'They are dishonest.' Sebastian suddenly announced confidently for his age.

'I know.' Emma replied. 'but you had better not say that too loudly for the time being.'

Emma called Mrs Sinclair. She explained calmly what the children had just told her and expressed her disappointment yet again about the partiality of the courts. Mrs Sinclair listened carefully. She promised to go to the provincial court herself the following morning and look at the content of the audition before filing her final papers for the hearing the following week.

Mrs Sinclair had been completely reasonable in all her requests backed up by experience and common sense. For the coming school year, she asked the court for shared parental rights and a visiting right for Emma as recommended by the experts every weekend, once the entire weekend and then the Saturday of the following weekend, half the school holidays and six of the eight weeks in the summer so that they could finish their primary schooling at their father's place where they had been for the last three years. A much fairer deal than had existed up until today could only serve to re-establish a serenity which in the best interests of the children as well as both parents.

For their secondary schooling, Mrs Sinclair requested that the children should come back and live with Emma in accordance with their wish and go to the good school close to their mother's office with their friends from their former school. A decision needed to be made since it was necessary to enrol the children in advance. On the financial front, despite specific requests for over two years, Paul had refused to present the slightest element justifying his financial status so the court was requested to issue a ruling that he do so before any decision on payment of maintenance by Emma could be made.

Emma felt Mrs Sinclair had done all she could and she would just have to see how the custody hearing would go. She was not hopeful but tried to keep an open mind. Albeit unsuccessfully.

Chapter 69

The day of the custody hearing arrived. Emma woke early. She had agreed to meet Mrs Sinclair on the parking of a large supermarket, a stone's throw away from her office. Together they planned to take Emma's car and head for the all too familiar setting of the provincial court. The custody hearing was scheduled shortly before lunch. Emma preferred to travel together with Mrs Sinclair so she could update her on the latest developments and reassure her. More importantly she was not alone when she entered the court.

However, Emma could now not help feeling a foreboding every time she had to set foot inside the provincial court. This had only been accentuated by her recent discoveries via books, the web and television documentaries about the strange goings on and cover ups involving this court. She tried hard to suppress these feelings and remain confident and optimistic. She was painfully aware that in any event she had no choice but to go through the official channels as uncomfortable and as one sided as it all seemed.

Emma dropped off Mrs Sinclair in front of the court entrance and eventually found a parking spot in a secluded side street. She made her way over to the court building. She had put on a chic black pinstriped suit. The waistband pinched her as she dreamed of being a few kilos lighter but she felt smart which boosted her confidence. Emma joined Mrs Sinclair in the waiting room. Mrs Sinclair had already given a copy of her latest written defence following the audition of the children to Victor Falconer who was in the throes of examining the content.

As Emma walked in, the two opponents stood up to greet her and shake her hand. Emma decided to give both Paul and Victor Falconer the handshake of the apprentice mason pressing her thumb between their index and middle finger. She wanted to see how they would react. She looked them both straight in the eyes as she shook their hands. Paul looked startled then blushed slightly.

Victor Falconer was not quite as flappable but there was a slight element of surprise in his otherwise expressionless face. A few seconds later he left the room.

Emma had not been aware during their marriage that Paul was a freemason but he knew that Emma was not a fan of anything occult so perhaps he had kept it hidden. Then again he could have joined after their separation. It was in Paul's nature to try to gain a competitive edge if he could in both the private and professional context. For Emma, Victor Falconer was the bigger culprit for misusing the philosophy and society for dishonest means, abusing his power as a member of the legal profession and deliberately distorting the course of justice.

A few minutes later Victor Falconer returned with the written defence he had prepared following the audition of the children and Mrs Sinclair and Emma started to read them together. The content was as aggressive and warmongering as ever. Victor Falconer continued to attack and put in question Emma's capacity as a suitable mother who should see her own son and daughter with any regularity. He had written in his submissions that Emma had double standards and had already refused to let Paul see his children every weekend if they came back and did their secondary schooling in their mother's home and this even more surprisingly so as Emma was now claiming this visiting right for the coming school year. Mrs Sinclair and Emma picked up on this point at the same time and Mrs Sinclair called Victor Falconer over.

'What is this? she asked. 'It is simply not true.'

'Oh I thought .....' he replied trying to look surprised.

'You think lots of negative things all the time but you should check them out properly first.' Emma interrupted.

Mrs Sinclair was kicking Emma's leg under the table urging her to be quiet. Emma was no longer intimidated by Victor Falconer. His dishonest tactics just made her angry.

'I made a mistake.' he admitted. 'I will tell the court when I hand over the court papers this morning.'

They filed upstairs into the small wooden waiting room. Victor Falconer and Paul stood over by the window chatting and joking. Victor Falconer was informing Paul what good contacts he had in the judicial system in his own city and that the president of the bar was a very good and longstanding personal friend. This was so indicative of how things seemed to work over here. Have a friend or a brother in the system and all your worries are over Emma thought to herself. She often wondered what happened if both parties had a friend in the system. She supposed it was down to which was the better friend and which insider had the most authority, i.e. the higher degree in the masonic hierarchy.

Emma's thoughts were interrupted by the court clerk who read out their names. Suddenly a lady appeared, obviously a parent from the previous hearing. She punched the air in triumph, a huge smile on her face. She was obviously very happy with the outcome. If she was so happy Emma could not help thinking, then it was highly likely that her ex-husband had got a raw deal. Emma was still to see a good decision come out of this court.

They filed into the small court room. Sitting at the table in front of them on the left was the prosecutor's deputy, a young stern looking woman with short hair and glasses. The lady judge who had interviewed Olivia and Sebastian the previous week was positioned in the middle and on the right the dour looking court clerk who had come running after them to retrieve the original report covering the audition of the children. He continued to look down, this time into his court papers. Emma had checked his name. It was the same court clerk who had served Judge Granger nearly five years earlier, the judge who had simply closed the file despite the request by the prosecutor's deputy at the time to proceed with a social enquiry as the children were being locked up alone overnight.

The judge opened the proceedings. She looked directly at Emma and said that she regretted having given Paul and herself a copy of the report to review following the audition as the parents had pounced on the children afterwards and she felt sorry for them. Emma looked her directly in the eyes, her expression attentive and neutral. She was not guilty and had no intention of looking down as if she was. She had not pounced on the children. Paul had called them out individually to hear what they had said to the judge during the time Emma had remained in the waiting room. This was a good start she thought to herself.

Emma had informed Mrs Sinclair of what she considered irregularities and omissions from the report based on what the children had told her when they called. Why the judge directed this comment directly at Emma remained a mystery. The judge continued by admitting that she was the wife of the prosecutor's deputy who had presided over their case five years ago. As an appeal had been made against the judgment by Emma's previous counsel, she felt she had to tell Emma. She added that she would understand if they asked her to stand down because they had some concerns about partiality. Mrs Sinclair and Emma looked at one another. Her husband had apparently supported their case five years earlier. It had been judge Granger who had shown such a distinct lack of partiality. Emma nodded. Mrs Sinclair confirmed it was OK and they could proceed accordingly.

There was one hour scheduled for the hearing. Victor Falconer set off with his counsel's speech. It was more of the same. Emma had not accepted the divorce and had tried to abduct the children in secret to England against their will. They did not speak a word of English and were very frightened. Anyway, they had said on so many occasions that they wanted to live with their father and his new family with whom they got on admirably well. They were now very settled and doing well at school and the current situation should be upheld. Emma had refused to pay maintenance despite many requests and the court should oblige her to do so, retroactively and with interest of course. Emma's request to see the children every weekend as recommended by the experts was excessive and Paul, of his own accord, had already allowed Emma very generous visiting rights to see her children which were working perfectly well today.

Having to listen yet again to this series of lies made Emma feel sick. Victor Falconer spoke for a full hour. As he finished the judge looked at her watch. Emma was sure that he had done it on purpose. She was also peeved that the judge had not stopped him after half an hour.

'I think you should put forward your case now.' Emma said aloud to Mrs Sinclair. 'It is only fair that both sides of the story are heard.'

'I would like to put forward my defence.' Mrs Sinclair said standing up and addressing the judge. 'I am surprised by the length of Mr Falconer's counsel since it was clear to all parties that one hour has been allotted for the whole hearing.' she pointed out calmly.

The judge nodded. 'How long do you need?' she asked.

'Up to half an hour.' Mrs Sinclair replied.

She began. She was good. Clear, well structured, confident, precise, and fair. She began by correcting Victor Falconer's picture of the past. She mentioned the terms of the mutual consent divorce allowing Emma to go to England with the children for professional reasons, that she had been very badly advised by Jules Mercier and Hubert Belette.

Suddenly after ten minutes the judge interrupted Mrs Sinclair abruptly.

'Why are you talking about the past and not finding a solution for the situation today?' she demanded.

Emma was as surprised as Mrs Sinclair.

'I am just addressing the issues raised by Mr Falconer during a whole hour.' Mrs Sinclair defended herself. 'I wanted to put the past into context then come with the proposed solution for the present and the future.'

'Carry on but talk about solutions from now on.' the judge almost growled.

Mrs Sinclair continued. She formally requested that the children go to the school the following year for their secondary education situated close to Emma's office and return to the maternal home. This was an excellent school and the children had expressed a clear wish to go there together with their friends from their former school. Emma knew that both children had clearly told this to the judge the previous week but she had failed to include it in her report. Emma watched the judge's expression closely. Mrs Sinclair continued that as adolescents it was important that the children could have a daily contact with their own mother and this would compensate for the years she had lost out on as her children were growing up and she had had no rights at all. Mrs Sinclair also legitimately pointed out that Emma had been completely excluded from the current schooling of the children. She therefore asked that a decision be made regarding transfer of the children at secondary school level back to their mother one year down the road.

'I can't make that decision today.' the judge retorted. 'The children will have to be heard again next year.'

'But we have to put their names down now,' Emma said as confidently and constructively as she could. 'Places at good schools are taken up quickly.'

The judge fixed Emma for a moment with a piercing stare.

'She is right.' Mrs Sinclair added supportingly.

'Then you can go ahead and put their names down and Mr Archer should do the same thing at his end and we will see next year. Often parents enrol their children in more than one school.' the judge decided.

As was customary, the prosecutor's deputy gave her opinion in the wrapping up session. The young woman had said very little during the hearing but had fixed Emma throughout with a penetrating stare. Emma held her head high, her expression attentive and neutral. She was not going to be intimidated. She also did not want to come across as being too sure of herself either. She already had such bad press from Victor Falconer, she really did not need to add to it.

The young woman set off, her voice loud, very confident and oozing with authority. She looked directly at Emma as she spoke.

'I would like to begin by saying that I do not care at all about how the parents feel in this case. The only thing which concerns me is the well-being of the children. If one of the parents has a problem with this, they should consult a psychiatrist.'

Emma was dumbfounded. She thought she had seen everything but this really was unbelievable. Emma continued to look directly at the prosecutor's deputy. She fought hard for tears not to come to her eyes. She did not want to give her this additional pleasure. It was already very obvious that the prosecutor's deputy did not like Emma and she was making no bones about hiding it. Emma was sure that this woman had presided over at least one if not two of their previous cases. The arrogance and the piercing voice came back to haunt her. The court clerk continued to look down into his papers. He looked uncomfortable. The judge watched the reactions of both Paul and Emma.

The prosecutor's deputy continued. 'I think Mr Falconer is also correct. The mother's request to see her children is excessive. I would recommend upholding the current arrangement. Regarding maintenance, by law, the non-guardian parent has to pay.' she barked looking at Emma again with a penetrating stare.

'I suggest you start doing so immediately. In any event this is something I recommend be clearly covered in the judgment. These are my recommendations.' she concluded looking at her watch. She was obviously half an hour late for her lunch break.

The judge announced that the judgment would be issued within the next two weeks. All parties stood up and filed out. Victor Falconer and Paul smiled and warmly thanked the judge and prosecutor's deputy. Emma politely said goodbye and left. She was the first down the stairs. She felt livid but helpless.

'It is unbelievable.' Mrs Sinclair muttered to Emma shaking her head. 'That young woman, the prosecutor's deputy, her approach, her reaction is inadmissible. There is a complete lack of any psychology so important in a family case.'

'To be honest I expected nothing more from these people.' Emma replied flatly. 'In her case she is so full of her own importance, she cannot see further than the end of her own nose. In addition, who knows what she got as a brief from the freemasonry set pulling the strings behind the scenes.'

Emma went to pick up the car leaving Mrs Sinclair at the entrance of the court. She had no intention of seeing Victor Falconer and Paul any more that day gloating over their latest victory. She drove Mrs Sinclair back to her car. They decided to get a quick bite to eat together. Emma was not really hungry but she forced herself to eat something.

'Do you want to change lawyer?' Mrs Sinclair suddenly asked her. 'Take say a freemason to level the playing field a little?'

Emma was surprised by the question. Mrs Sinclair had obviously noticed the continuing injustice at work and felt, Emma assumed, that she could not effectively fight the forces at play against her.

'No.' Emma replied resolutely. 'You were recommended to me as one of the best in the country in the field of family law. As far as I am concerned, the system should function correctly and not in the inadmissible fashion it does today. It needs one huge shake up. If nobody ever stands up to them, it will just go from bad to worse. No wonder four out of five people in this country have no confidence in their own judicial system. I bet they don't know even half the real reasons why it is so bad though.' Emma said with a weak smile.

She was feeling tired as the impact of the morning's proceedings began to hit her.

'I will send you the judgment as soon as it arrives.' Mrs Sinclair assured her as they said goodbye to one another.

Emma went back to the office. Her colleagues asked her eagerly how things had gone. 'Bad' was her reply adding that the system was dysfunctional and discriminatory at best and corrupt at worst.

Despite assurances that the judgment would be issued within two weeks, Mrs Sinclair received nothing. Emma knew that Paul must have received it because after three years he actually proposed to come and collect the children on the Sunday evening. Sharing the journey was a standard term covered in official custody arrangements. For three years as Emma had had no official visiting rights, she had had to assume the journey both ways if she wanted to see her children. Emma informed Mrs Sinclair and she contacted the court.

'It is not our problem.' was the curt reply she received. 'It was sent out so it you have any complaints contact the post office.'

Mrs Sinclair requested a duplicate copy. When this failed to arrive, she got in touch with Victor Falconer to fax a copy through to her.

Even to Mrs Sinclair, such procedures seemed highly irregular. For Emma this was the last insult. She had had time to digest the court hearing and had made up her mind to take things further. She wrote a fax to Mrs Sinclair expressing her concerns. Her family and friends also found the whole situation scandalous, bizarre and unacceptable. The children had clearly told the judge of their desire to come back and live with Emma but for some reason this had not been noted. The prosecutor's deputy was completely out of line. One could only note that in the best case it was due to incompetence and discrimination and in the worst to cronyism and corruption favouring fellow members of the brethren. Emma asked what measures she could take to open an official complaint and ask for an enquiry to be undertaken.

Mrs Sinclair came back and confirmed that Emma probably had a case against Jules Mercier and Hubert Belette, however, she doubted that they had anything on Victor Falconer and they should meet to discuss things in more detail. Emma disagreed about her assessment of Victor Falconer. She believed he had played a key role in distorting the course of justice, in constantly and unrelentingly morally harassing Emma for five years, in assassinating her character, in consistently lying to the courts, in concocting a file with Hubert Belette later produced as so called evidence, in putting freemasonry signs in his correspondence both to the courts and in letters attached to his court papers, in passing freemasonry signs during his counsel's speech successfully soliciting help from sympathetic freemason magistrates and members of the prosecution, not once but twice.

Eventually Mrs Sinclair faxed Emma a copy of the judgment. Emma took a cup of tea and sat down to read it. It started that it was obvious from the experts' report and the interview with the youth court judge that Olivia and Sebastian were saddened by the conflict between their parents and apparent rivalry between their mother and their step mother. They loved both parents as much as one another and were sad that if they said they wanted to live with their mother, their father would be sad and vice versa. The children wished that their parents would take the responsibility to decide on where they lived understanding that the children could not be cut in two. The parents should put the priority of the children before their own.

Emma's requests to see her children as per the experts' report were excessive. She could see them for five weeks in the summer and not six so as not to separate them from their father for too long and then every second weekend in term time. The court could not make a decision as requested by the parties on the children's wish for their secondary schooling but at that time the situation would need to be re-evaluated after hearing the children. The children were to be registered as officially living with their father.

The judgment went onto recommend that as parents if they could not conduct themselves like responsible adults, the court highly recommended that they follow a mediation in the interests of the children, all the more so, as they now exercised joint parental authority. Meanwhile Emma was ordered to pay temporarily 200 € a month maintenance even if she were to appeal. Paul to produce his financials and then a decision about retroactive maintenance would be made by the court, the more diligent of the parties to then fix a date for the hearing.

Chapter 70

Emma hoped that now things had been made official by the court for the next year at least, things would eventually run more smoothly.

The following weekend Emma set off to pick up Olivia and Sebastian for the weekend. She rang the doorbell only to be told that they were with their father picking up his new BMW. They arrived forty-five minutes later. Emma had sat waiting for them making a few calls to friends to pass the time. The children were very apologetic saying that they had told their father that they did not want to go with him as they knew their mum would be there at 5.30 pm and they did not want her to have to wait.

The following weekend, Emma called Olivia and Sebastian on Sunday morning. They were forced by Lea to interrupt the call. When Emma called back she discovered the mobile had been switched off. She later discovered that it had been confiscated until the evening.

The following weekend Emma was told to arrive one hour later as Paul wanted to go for a walk with the children and the dog in the woods. Olivia almost cried on the phone. 'Call him because he is insisting we go with him. I want to come with you for the weekend.'

Emma could not understand why Paul and company were continuing with their inacceptable behaviour if it was not to provoke or upset her. She tried to reach Mrs Sinclair and left her a message.

Emma had a copy of the judgment in her bag and was tempted to go to the local police station and make a complaint that she was being hindered from collecting her children for the weekend. Instead she called Paul and left him a message.

She calmly told him that she found his behaviour completely unacceptable and completely against the spirit of and the advice laid out in the judgment. If the children were not ready when she arrived, then she would personally write to the youth court judge, even if she appeared to be on his side, because of his and Victor Falconer's freemasonry connections, and tell her that he was making a complete mockery of her and the judicial system in general. In addition, Emma found the idea of mediation an excellent one which could only help sort out this sort of misunderstanding and she would be contacting the mediation group to make a first appointment in the interests of the children.

The phone rang five minutes later. It was Olivia to confirm that they would be back in time for when Emma arrived to pick them up. Mrs Sinclair returned Emma's call just when things had been sorted out. She was relieved.

'Your ex-husband is in reality a demon she sighed. An angel in the courts but a demon in real life.'

Mrs Sinclair called Emma in the office a few days later. 'Go to the fax and look at the latest letter from Victor Falconer.' she urged. 'Apparently you have not yet made the first maintenance payment and they will make an official complaint if you do not confirm that it is on the way.'

Emma protested that she had only received a copy of the judgment a couple of days earlier and she was arranging the payment that week. They had never received the judgment from the court and Victor Falconer knew this because he had had to fax them through a copy.

'I know.' Mrs Sinclair sighed before adding 'They also complained that you made the payment for the children's skiing holiday directly to the school and Mr Archer wanted you to transfer the money to him so he could centralise everything.'

The following weekend the children were late as Paul had made an appointment for Olivia to see the doctor for a check-up. She was not ill so Emma requested Paul to make such appointments next time when she was not scheduled to pick up the children. True to form, he just hung up on her.

Then he asked the children to call Emma and tell her to come to pick them up on Saturday morning instead of Friday evening as outlined in the judgment as he had been working abroad for several weeks and wanted to spend time with them. Olivia and Sebastian had obstinately refused. Emma was relieved that the children were beginning to stick up for themselves and did not want to have their weekends with Emma shortened.

Laura and Valerie were sympathetic but honest enough to remind Emma yet again that Paul would never change and that she just had to let it go over her head. Emma knew that he would continue to dog her existence for as long as he could, unfortunately with the unequivocal backing of the court system which only saw what it wanted to see.

Emma contacted the secondary school next to her office and made an appointment to visit the headmistress and enrol Olivia and Sebastian in the school for the coming school year. She asked Mrs Sinclair to prepare a letter to Victor Falconer asking Paul to let her take the children along to visit the school. Of course Paul refused under the pretext that the timing was very bad. Emma went along alone and explained to the school principal that the children were familiar with the school and as they had friends already there and had visited the premises with the brownies and beavers.

Olivia and Sebastian confided in Emma that their father had seemed very agitated when he received the letter. They had tried to reason with their father asking him to let them visit the school with Emma but he had just shouted 'out of the question' and abruptly interrupted any further protests. Emma knew it was going to be tough right up until the very end. She collected the new school prospectus and Olivia and Sebastian studied it eagerly and started making plans for their extra curriculum activities.

Emma explained clearly to Olivia and Sebastian 'You know you will also have to tell and convince your father that this is what you really want and are determined to do. You cannot rely on the courts. You have seen how they can manipulate and turn things around. You will have to tell both your father and the judge very convincingly next year that you want to and are coming back to live with your mum.'

'Yes mum we know.' both children had reassured Emma.

'I really hope so. It is your choice. Your destiny and your future are firmly in your own hands. I cannot do much more now to help you apart from offer you a good stable and loving future if it is back here where you wish to be. Meanwhile we have to make the very most of the valuable moments we have together.'

Emma was painfully aware of the long and difficult road which still lay ahead of them and hoped that by being honest with her children, they would find the courage to express their wishes so firmly that the impossible would happen and they would not be prevented from returning to the maternal home. Emma had never felt closer to Olivia and Sebastian. She knew that it was not easy for them either.

Things were helped a little by the fact that life in their father's home was taking a turn for the worse. Emma wrote to Mrs Sinclair with a short update. Paul was constantly away from home most days of the week. Lea also seemed very preoccupied with her professional activities. The couple argued a lot. Olivia and Sebastian complained there was no one to help them with their homework. Lea's daughter cooked in the evenings then not wanting to leave them alone took them along to a student bash. They returned home at midnight and admitted to Emma that this was a bit late when they had school next day. Lea continued to criticize Olivia who went out of her way to avoid her. Olivia was beginning to rebel as she entered her teenage years. Things came to a head and a shouting match followed.

'You are a horrible child.' Lea shouted at Olivia. 'It is a good job that you are not my daughter otherwise I would hit you.'

'I will never be your daughter thank goodness and you had better not touch me.' Olivia retorted back.

Paul supported Lea's stance and Olivia was subsequently punished for two weeks. Lea simply added that when Olivia would be older she would turn into a delinquent. Olivia was shocked and hurt by the comment. Emma reassured her that it was nonsense and would not happen. A further punishment ensued as Lea accused Olivia of not joining in the conversation at the dinner table and living in a world of her own. Olivia complained to her friends at school and they agreed that her stepmother was a strange and unpleasant woman.

'What do you want me to say?' Olivia protested to Emma. 'The subjects they talk about are not interesting. They are always mocking or criticising others or disagreeing, even arguing about tastes and personal things, things which really are not important'.

As a result, the children's school reports were not good, much to the consternation of their father. Emma told Olivia and Sebastian to do their best and not to worry. She told them that if they needed any help at secondary school, she would personally help or pay for private lessons.

Olivia and Sebastian commented that they had not seen Paul's mother since the wedding in England some four months previously. Apparently, there was tension between Lea and Paul's mother. Paul went to visit his mother in secret on Monday evenings. Paul's mother told her grandchildren on the phone how much she missed them. The children wanted to see their grandmother at New Year but so far Lea had refused. Emma encouraged Olivia and Sebastian to insist on going to visit their grandmother the first week of January. Emma had taught them to make pancakes and spaghetti bolognese so, if push came to shove, they could even cook for the old lady.

Emma did not appreciate how her ex mother in law was being treated even if she believed she was partly to blame for Emma's own situation and her separation from her children. She felt the poor treatment of this lonely old lady to be cruel and unnecessary. Paul's mother had fallen ill and was confined to bed for three weeks then hospitalised. She told Olivia and Sebastian on the phone that she hoped she would see them again before she died. Emma could not help thinking how ironic the whole situation had turned out to be and what a big mess had been created which she was still fighting to sort out alone and with a great deal of forces at play against her.

Emma requested Mrs Sinclair to inform her about the possibilities and channels to lodge an official complaint and ask for a formal enquiry into her case. Laura had advised her sister to check carefully all the routes open and weigh up the pros and cons and chances of success. She reminded Emma that she had already spent so much money in legal fees and the authorities would do their best in any event to keep things covered up. She also told Emma to ensure that any possible enquiry would not harm her chances of recuperating the children the following year for their secondary schooling.

Emma's close friends liked the idea of the book and encouraged Emma to start writing, even if one day she would decide not to publish or would postpone the eventual publishing until a later date. Valerie advised Emma to write to the new justice minister. Most locals believed he was doing his very best, albeit in the wake of many obstacles, to improve the administration of justice in the country.

Emma set up an appointment with Mrs Sinclair one evening and decided to show her part of the written proof she had about Victor Falconer's involvement in the set up with Jules Mercier and Hubert Belette. Emma was tied up in a meeting most of the afternoon so when she listened to Mrs Sinclair's message postponing the meeting, she was already in front of her office. Mrs Sinclair seemed in a hurry, almost flustered so Emma offered to come back at a later date.

'No you are here now, so do come in but let's make it short.' she suggested to Emma.

'Thanks.' Emma replied. 'Here is a copy of the appropriate pages of a book published this year by two very good journalists about the misuse of freemasonry in the courts. Here highlighted in yellow is a description of some of the signs freemasons put in their signatures to identify themselves to one another and ask for assistance either from the lawyer of the opposing party or from presiding magistrates and other court officials.' Emma explained as if making a business presentation to a captive audience.

Suddenly Mrs Sinclair looked very interested, almost intrigued.

Emma continued. 'Here are some letters from Victor Falconer to Hubert Belette. Look at the signature. Do you see what I see?'

Mrs Sinclair picked up the letter and examined it. 'Quite. Can I keep this?' she asked.

'Of course. There are lots more like that. Not to you, just to Hubert Belette and a couple directly to the courts, the president of the provincial court and also to the appeal court. All the originals are in a safe deposit box abroad as is a very detailed account of my story.'

'I have some close friends who are freemasons. Can I show them this and ask for confirmation of the authenticity?' Mrs Sinclair asked.

'Yes you may.' Emma replied. 'These copies are for you. You know most freemasons are good people. I am sure that the majority of members are not proud or happy that their society is being misused by some less scrupulous members.' Emma added.

She remembered the book published in England and the admission by a top mason that approximately twelve percent of masons would use the society to further their own cause and do so in a dishonest manner. With what Emma had learned about the way things were structured and worked over here, she guessed it was probably closer to twenty percent but nevertheless still a minority. However, probably much more heavily weighted in the judicial system she reminded herself woefully.

'You know if you lodge a complaint against the characters you believe set you up, I can't handle it.' Mrs Sinclair suddenly explained looking a little concerned.

'I know.' Emma replied. 'That is why you need to explain very clearly what options I have then I will need to eventually look for an expert in suing other lawyers. I understand, like most other things, it must be a specialized field. Maybe I need to take a tenor from abroad on a no win no fee basis.' Emma reflected.

Emma stood up to leave very much aware that Mrs Sinclair was under time pressure but also seemingly surprised by what Emma had handed over to her.

'Call me as soon as you have more news.' Emma asked shaking Mrs Sinclair's hand as she left.

Emma hoped that Mrs Sinclair's freemason friends were highly enough placed to be able to do something behind the scenes to neutralise their situation. Perhaps even sanction the behaviour of Jules Mercier and Victor Falconer in this neverending saga and help Emma get at least a fair hearing and outcome in the summer of the following year.

Christmas was approaching. The first flakes of snow began to fall as Emma wrapped up the Christmas presents. She planned to spend Christmas in England with Olivia and Sebastian, Laura and her family. The whole family would be together for a traditional Christmas. For a week at least, she would be able to relax and enjoy the company of her children. The New Year was not far away with the new set of challenges which it would no doubt bring with it.

Chapter 71

The day before Emma's departure to England for Christmas with the children, Mrs Sinclair forwarded to her a long letter from Victor Falconer outlining Paul's financial situation and claiming from Emma a substantial sum of money in retroactive maintenance going back over the last three years. Paul was planning to start building his luxury villa in the spring and every Euro he could extract from Emma would be a bonus. Emma could not help thinking that the timing was as usual spot on. Two days before Christmas. Oh well, she sighed as she quickly scanned the content. She would deal with it when she was back on New Year's Day and draft an appropriate reply.

'Find out exactly what the jurisprudence is for retroactive maintenance.' Laura advised. 'Show everything you have paid for the children over the last three years. When you are dealing with figures it is more clear cut and there is less scope to manipulate the situation.'

Other friends told Emma that they had suspected that it was all about money from the start and that Paul just did not have any scruples. As for the support he had so far received from the judicial system, well it was nothing short of a disgrace.

It was Emma's indignation and refusal to accept such injustice which gave her the energy and determination to surge on when friends told her that many people would already have given up. Over Christmas, she recharged her batteries in the familiar and comforting surroundings of the little village where Laura lived, conscious that once she arrived back she would need all her resolve, focus and strength to see this through to a successful conclusion, still with the odds very much stacked against her.

The more Emma discovered, the more she realised just what an uncompromising situation she had been drawn into. Over the last three years, she had found many pieces of the jigsaw and slowly the pieces were fitting together. There were still a few gaps, things which did not yet fully make sense. In her spare time, she continued to read extensively and surf the web for more detail. Instinct and a strengthened intuition told her things were connected. She began to feel like Miss Marple.

It had all seemed to start with a few financial scandals in the 1970s and the discovery of an interconnected luxury prostitution network. The former defence minister, later found guilty of many cases of fraud, had nominated a young magistrate who in turn had quickly been promoted to chief prosecutor of the provincial court. In the years to follow, the prosecutor had seemed to cover up a series of misdemeanours.

At first he had admitted that the Perry file just did not exist. Then he admitted to a parliamentary commission that he had not hidden the Perry file in his safe but kept it in his office to protect the private life of the people mentioned. According to other sources, the defence minister and the chief prosecutor had taken part in orgies themselves. The conclusion of the parliamentary enquiry set up to investigate the petrol station killings was clear in its findings. The orgies mentioned in the Perry file had existed although there was no proof that children were involved. They also concluded that several files had not been treated normally, notably several which had passed over the desk of the chief prosecutor in the provincial court.

Emma had gathered from what Jules Mercier had let slip that he had also taken part in these orgies and she could not help making the link. If this was the case, he really did have string pulling friends in high places, notably in the provincial court which she had long suspected and which he had also hinted at.

Reading other articles on the web written by experienced journalists and former police officers who had been removed from various investigations concerning the attempts in the 1980s to destabilise the country, Emma could not help drawing a parallel with what had happened in Italy during the same period. The local petrol station killings were believed to have been perpetrated by the far right to force the state to take a less liberal stance in the midst of the cold war.

In Italy in a similar case, one of the driving forces was apparently the masonic lodge P2. There was speculation that a right wing coup had been planned although this had been averted following the almost chance discovery of the lodge and its impressive membership from the highest echelons of the Italian establishments by the financial police investigating numerous irregularities of its Grand Master.

Two parliamentary enquiries had failed to determine who exactly had been behind the local petrol station killings which had taken place when Emma was married to Paul and within a few kilometres of where they lived at the time. However, there were rumours that a coup d'état from the far right had been planned involving the former defence minister, commander in chief of the army, one of the highest judicial figures in the land, the commander of the police and the former justice minister. The one Jules Mercier had worked for, much to Emma's surprise and dismay. Thankfully, unlike Greece, the military takeover never came to fruition and at the end of the 1980s the Berlin wall fell and the cold war was effectively over.

After a little more surfing and reading Emma stumbled upon the existence of Gladio, the codename for a clandestine (NATO) "stay-behind" operation in many Western European countries during the Cold war. It was set up to prepare for, and implement, armed resistance in the event of a Warsaw pact invasion and occupation. The existence of Gladio became public in 1990 and was the subject of a European Parliament resolution, outlined in part below (1):

'In certain Member States military secret services (or uncontrolled branches thereof) were involved in serious cases of terrorism and crime as evidenced by various judicial inquiries.

Whereas these organizations operated and continue to operate completely outside the law since they are not subject to any parliamentary control and frequently those holding the highest government and constitutional posts are kept in the dark as to these matters.

Whereas the various 'Gladio' organizations have at their disposal independent arsenals and military resources which give them an unknown strike potential, thereby jeopardizing the democratic structures of the countries in which they are operating or have been operating,

Greatly concerned at the existence of decision-making and operational bodies which are not subject to any form of democratic control and are of a completely clandestine nature at a time when greater Community cooperation in the field of security is a constant subject of discussion.'

With the resolution, the European Parliament called on the governments of the member States to take the necessary measures, 'if necessary by establishing parliamentary committees of inquiry', and the judiciaries to 'clarify any action they may have taken to destabilize the democratic structure of the Member States.'

Emma could understand the need for such an operation given the political landscape at the time and the determination of the West to protect its system of democracy and freedom but clearly for use in the worse- case scenario of an invasion and occupation. However, reading between the lines and various articles on the topic, it became clear that the Gladio cells may also have gone a step too far and been behind some terrorist attacks on home territory in several countries across Western Europe in the 1970s and 1980s. This to destabilize governments deemed to be too far left. Elected governments with coalitions too heavily dominated by communists and socialists, to bring them back into the fold. This also involved manipulating the population through fear. A so called 'false flag' strategy of tension.

Emma sat up as she read that apparently the masonic lodge P2 was involved in the Gladio operation in Italy. A determined judge was able to uncover direct evidence. Emma's head started to spin. She could not help thinking that the world was going completely mad. How could fellow countrymen turn on their own people in a modern democracy she asked herself several times? It was completely unacceptable. Some might even call it treason.

As a result, Emma could not help wondering if the local petrol station killings were also the brainchild of a secret lodge, even involving Jules Mercier and his friends and associates, many of whom were strategically placed and keen masons. People whom Emma had read had been accused of various wrong doings, even criminal acts and who were obviously all perfectly capable of behaving in an unethical manner.

Emma remembered the time she had arrived at Jules' home to find him watching the evening news and seemingly amused that the police had found a stash of arms in his former house which now stood empty. The fact that two parliamentary enquires and the strange handling of the investigations by the chief prospector of the provincial court had turned up very little and the chief prosecutor himself was on the ultra- conservative far right of the political spectrum together with the minister who had nominated him, only added credence to this theory. Stop it Emma had told herself when she started to add up two and two. It was all too much to contemplate.

Emma found this new look at history fascinating but at the same time it hit home just how utterly powerful the freemasons were, also internationally, and how difficult it was going to be for her to regain custody of her dear son and daughter. Emma could not help thinking that her unfortunate predicament had had a profound effect on her personnel evolution and view of the world. She felt that as a result she had become a much richer, spiritual and compassionate person. This had no doubt been facilitated by more than a fair share of pain and suffering.

However, on the positive side Emma had developed an incredibly resilient and positive stance. Despite her separation from her children which she would never accept or get used to, she remained cheerful and determined to enjoy life to the full. Everyday counted. Quality of and approach to life seemed to have greatly improved compared to the days when she had been married to Paul. She liked herself and more importantly those around her which in turn attracted positive interactions with nearly everyone she met. She told herself that she did not deserve to be depressed or miserable. Her mind had become surprisingly alert awakened by the array of emotions, challenges and a survival instinct following the death threats and obvious manipulations in the courts.

Before her unfortunate adventure, like most people, Emma had accepted unequivocally almost everything heard from official channels and read in the media or seen on TV. Now without being paranoid, she tended to question most things running them past a logic test. She knew that only if she was strong and very switched on would she ever realistically be able to beat the freemasonry manipulations and deceit and be reunited with her children.

Emma had experienced some of the negative sides of freemasonry and had felt its darker power. She loved her children, her family and her good friends and, as funny as it sounded, she felt that this was more powerful than everything else that was being put in her way and would ultimately be what would see her through in the end.

The triumph of good over evil or right over wrong. Whichever, in any event, she truly believed in it.

Chapter 72

On the 1st of January with Olivia and Sebastian back with their father, Emma poured over the papers Victor Falconer had sent concerning Paul's financial situation and exaggerated claim for retroactive alimony. Mrs Sinclair was awaiting Emma's feedback before presenting their case. This is what it had all been about from the beginning Emma muttered to herself. Control and money. Unfortunately, like so many other things in life.

Paul had adamantly refused to declare his earnings for nearly four years despite numerous requests, content with simply claiming excessive maintenance from Emma's side. When the court, on Mrs Sinclair's insistence, eventually obliged him to do so, it was obvious why he had held out.

Paul was earning thirty percent more than Emma plus he was receiving 250 € child allowance per month plus the 200 € per month Emma was now paying him. Victor Falconer was claiming 15.000 € in retroactive maintenance arguing that this was based on the monthly sum Paul had offered to pay in the mutual consent divorce. Of course, now as a self-employed individual, he could declare very little and his income was obviously low as he needed to invest in his new business.

Victor Falconer was at great pains to point out that in the absence of any financial contribution from Emma, Paul had had to limit costly leisure time with his children, restricting himself to weekends walking in the country, swimming, cinema, excursions once a month for an average of 80 € which was considered as totally reasonable. Again for Emma, the irony was astounding but it no longer surprised her. She expected nothing more.

What she could not accept was the insistence on bleeding her dry and literally driving her into the ground. Emma knew Paul did so little with the children even at weekends. He occasionally took them to visit his mother in the country, went swimming twice a year, to the cinema extremely rarely. For the rest of the time they were left very much on their own playing together in their bedroom.

Emma was certain the courts would give Paul the benefit of the doubt unless she came up with some pretty firm evidence to the contrary. She was determined to stay calm and approach this as another business transaction with a cool and logical mind. For the whole of New Year's Day and three evenings that week she worked diligently putting the defence case together. She tried to be as structured as possible listing each point which she hoped Mrs Sinclair could then build into a convincing case, addressing the many arguments put forward by Victor Falconer. Mrs Sinclair summed things up objectively.

Paul had been in complete agreement to voluntarily pay the 400 € a month maintenance in the mutual consent divorce because he could afford to do so and he had earned three times more than Emma in the year in which they separated.

In the last three years Paul had earned thirty percent more than Emma, shared the household bills with Lea and had also benefitted from 250 € child allowance. Emma's colleagues in finance were helpful and had run a financial report on Lea's new company showing a 1 million Euro annual turnover and an estimated income for the owner of 80.000 € before tax.

Every summer Paul had rented a villa for a month in the South of France and enjoyed daily trips on his speed boat which was also moored there. Emma could only afford to go camping with the children and had not even taken a summer holiday at all the year before.

Emma had paid for four extra curriculum activities during the time she had had custody of her children. That year, as well as paying

200 € a month maintenance, she had paid 500 € towards a skiing trip with the school. Paul had paid for no extra curriculum activities and had even asked Emma to contribute an extra 50 € a term towards a gym class. When Emma refused and asked him to take it out of the monthly maintenance she was paying, he simply cancelled the class much to the disappointment of Olivia and Sebastian.

Paul claimed money for medical expenses but failed to produce any receipts. Emma had paid for new glasses for Sebastian as Paul refused to renew his old ones and for Olivia to have specialist treatment for a protruding tooth which Paul refused to split equally.

Paul claimed expenses for the fall Olivia had had from the horse which Emma contested as everything was reimbursed by the insurance she had taken out.

Finally, Emma attached a list of fixed costs she had every month, amounting to nearly half of her net salary and a list of items she had bought for the children over the last three years from clothes, shoes, leisure totalling over 6000 €.

Middle of January Emma wrote a short email to Paul asking if she could have an extra weekend with the children at the end of January as Paul had confirmed she needed to recuperate one weekend. Emma hoped that he would be able to reply to such a simple request directly without involving Victor Falconer.

Instead a few days later Mrs Sinclair forwarded yet another official letter from Victor Falconer accusing Emma of not paying the maintenance specified by the court. Emma was perplexed but also furious. She knew this was a ploy to build another case against her demonstrating her poor will for the next court hearing. She dug out her bank statements proving she had paid the maintenance and sent them to Mrs Sinclair.

Emma then sat down and wrote an email to Paul. She was angry. Just where was this all going to end she asked herself. She had no intention of spending the next five years of her life as she had spent the previous five constantly attacked, harassed, falsely accused by these two deceitful individuals and separated as much as possible from her own children. She was going to show them that she was determined to stand up to them and, given half a chance, expose their dishonest tactics.

She confirmed to Paul that Olivia and Sebastian had told her that the extra weekend end of January was fine but asked Paul to confirm it to her directly himself as per her email request.

Emma continued that she was very surprised to learn from Mrs Sinclair that another official letter had just arrived from Victor Falconer as she could categorically prove that she was punctually paying each month the maintenance imposed by the court. It was unfortunate that Paul could not contact her directly if he had a problem of this kind and that he obviously was having difficulty communicating like a responsible parent with joint custody as clearly set out in the latest judgment in the interest of the children.

On the contrary, true to form, Paul and his lawyer were trying to set her up again, falsely blackening her name in an attempt to mislead the court. She added that she would no longer accept this sort of behaviour from their side and if it continued she was going to officially complain to the highest judicial authorities in the land and ask for an explanation for the number of striking anomalies in the handling of her file. There was, in her opinion, a code of ethics for lawyers as well as others which had been greatly overstepped by Paul and Victor Falconer in the last five years.

A few days later, another letter arrived from Victor Falconer. Emma went along to meet Mrs Sinclair. To Emma's surprise Victor Falconer's letter rambled on about various issues then briefly mentioned Emma's email to Paul. For the first time the tone was much calmer. The sarcasm and personal attacks were noticeably absent. The tone almost submissive. Mrs Sinclair scolded Emma for having been so direct. Emma just hoped that this had set the record straight and she would be treated with more respect going forward.

Half term holidays arrived and Emma took Olivia and Sebastian to Amsterdam for three days. It had been fifteen years since Emma had last visited the city and she was eager to rediscover the delights with her children. They spent three very busy days visiting and sightseeing and eating out in a variety of restaurants. Emma could not help thinking how fast they were growing up. Olivia used her perfume, tried on her clothes. Her feet were only one size smaller than Emma's. Sebastian was now even taller than Emma and his shoe size two sizes bigger. Emma did not mind. She loved sharing her things with Olivia. Emma also noticed that Olivia and Sebastian seemed to know more and more what they wanted.

The children continued to complain that Paul their father, was rarely at home. He had been to Florida for ten days leaving them with Lea's mother. Paul's mother was very unhappy that she could not look after her own grandchildren and called every day to check how things were going. Paul arrived back, stayed one night, then disappeared again for another five days. Emma felt frustrated and helpless. She was at home almost every day and they were forced to be separated even though they really all wanted to be together. The whole thing was absurd. She only hoped the custody hearing would take place as planned in June. Emma had prepared her children psychologically as much as she could and knew how.

'Dad will shout a lot when we tell the judge we are coming back.' Olivia admitted calmly. 'But I don't care though because he can't shout forever and once we are back, we are home and safe and happy again.'

Emma nodded and gave her a hug of encouragement. She was only too conscious however, that one could never underestimate Paul or the system.

Emma followed up closely with Mrs Sinclair that the written defence was filed well ahead of time from both parties anxious to avoid that the other party play the system yet again and drag things out for a fourth year into the start of the new school year.

They agreed that Mrs Sinclair would be ready with her written defence middle of March and send it to the court. Emma had given Mrs Sinclair as much ammunition as she could. She now hoped and prayed that they would eventually make some progress. She had no choice but to hang in there and go step by step, as long and as drawn out as it all seemed.

Chapter 73

Shortly after Mrs Sinclair filed her court papers, Victor Falconer reverted cancelling his previous submissions from February as Mrs Sinclair and Emma had highlighted too many untruths in the content. When will they stop being so economical with the truth Emma asked herself wearily. Probably never she told herself realistically.

Mrs Sinclair asked Emma to study Victor Falconer's new defence papers and give her comments so she could formulate a reply at the earliest. Emma sat down that evening with a cup of tea and, as on so many previous occasions, went line by line noting any obvious anomalies and adding appropriate comments which she believed might help their case, at least on paper.

Of course, the main objective of the next hearing was to secure retroactive maintenance as far as Paul and Victor Falconer were concerned. However, they were at great pains to point out in their papers that money certainly was not a prime consideration for Paul, unlike for Emma of course.

From her side, Mrs Sinclair emphasised the importance of the judge re-auditioning the children as set out in the last judgment on their preference of main residence going into their secondary schooling before any decision be made on the final custody arrangement and resulting maintenance payments.

Emma trudged her way laboriously through another fourteen pages of lies and wicked attacks on her person. Luckily her feelings of sheer indignation had long outweighed her feelings of hurt. She had produced receipts over the last three years showing that she had spent a monthly average of 175 € on clothes and activities for her children excluding holidays and that Olivia and Sebastian wore these clothes to go to school too on occasions. According to Victor Falconer's written defence, this should not diminish what Emma should pay in retroactive maintenance since she had bought the clothes of her own initiative without the opinion of her son and daughter who did not like to wear them for school. According to Victor Falconer, Olivia and Sebastian even insisted that Emma come and collect them from home and not school so they did not have to wear these terrible clothes in front of their friends. Also, the new glasses which Emma had bought for Sebastian without Sebastian's opinion had caused a similar problem.

Emma shook her head. It was so spiteful and downright untrue. Mrs Sinclair put the record straight in her reply. Sebastian had chosen the glasses himself so where was the apparent problem? It was Paul himself who insisted that Emma collect the children from home and not directly from the school as he wanted to exclude her completely from their schooling, something which Emma had accepted to avoid additional conflict which was not in the children's best interest. It had nothing to do with their clothes which at the age of thirteen and twelve they chose and wore of their own accord.

Victor Falconer also claimed in his court papers that Olivia and Sebastian had clearly expressed their firm desire to remain with their father and had told this clearly to their mother who was perfectly aware of their wishes. Emma's mind flew back to the conversation nine months previously when Olivia and Sebastian had told Paul in front of her that they wished to do their secondary schooling next to Emma's office and go back to live with their mother. Paul had remained calm and added that they would discuss it further nearer the time.

Mrs Sinclair shot back reiterating that the audition of the children was the only measure susceptible to demonstrate objectively the wish of the children and Emma formally contested the allegations from Paul and asked how he would know that Olivia and Sebastian had told Emma directly that they wished to reside in their father's home.

Victor Falconer attacked Emma for taking foreign holidays on several occasions with her children asking how it was possible with the salary she was declaring. Mrs Sinclair confirmed that when they went to England and the USA they stayed with friends. One summer they had stayed at home and another stayed free of charge at a friend's place in Tenerife who was sympathetic to all the problems and expense Emma had occurred. the previous year they had been camping. She went on to point out this was in stark contrast to Paul who in the first half of that year alone had spent ten days in Florida, one week in Greece, rented an apartment at the seaside over Easter and a villa in the south of France for a month that summer where he enjoyed using his power boat which he insisted cost him nothing. However, he failed to produce the mooring costs over the winter, his insurance, transporting the boat into the water and the costs of putting and keeping the boat in the water in the summer in some of the costliest locations on the Cote d'Azur.

To crown things, Victor Falconer had specifically requested in his court papers that the audition take place in term time before the summer holidays when the children were with Paul and that Emma should be banned from attending and seeing the children in the waiting room, in order to avoid perturbing and destabilising them. He had added that apparently their mother had turned up on the previous occasion of her own initiative with magazines, sweets and other treats for the children generating a real atmosphere of stress which was intolerable.

Emma asked Olivia and Sebastian if they wanted her to be there ahead of this year's planned audition.

'Of course mum you must be there.' they both retorted. 'Dad is already threatening us and putting pressure on us to say we want to stay with him. We don't. We want to come back. If you are there he will not dare threaten or frighten us.'

To Emma's surprise Sebastian admitted 'He was the one who was perturbed last time you arrived not us. Did you see the expression on his face?'

Actually, Emma had not. It had been a great effort for her to walk into the waiting room looking relaxed and smiling and putting the children at ease. She had not paid attention to Paul's reaction. One thing she was certain of however, was that he would do everything possible to manipulate matters up to the last minute. Emma was determined to be there for Olivia and Sebastian. However, she played devil's advocate and also prepared them for the eventuality that she might not be authorised to be there and that, come what may, they would need to remain strong and not be negatively influenced.

The children had confided in Emma that their father had told them that they were going to be in very serious trouble if they told the judge that they wanted to come back and live with their mother and if so, they would never see their father again as he would not want anything more to do with them. Sebastian had added resolutely that if this was the case then it was his loss and not theirs. Emma admired their resolve but knew, more than most, just how menacing Paul could be when he risked not getting his own way. Emma knew they were far from out of the woods yet but kept encouraging her children to be brave and tell the truth as they saw it to the judge. They had to be honest about where they wanted to spend the next six years of their life.

To strengthen his case as he saw it, Paul continued to blacken Emma's image whenever he could. Olivia and Sebastian shared their disappointment with their mother. Paul often repeated to them that Emma was a bad mother and would ruin the rest of their lives if they went back to live with her. Lea could not resist joining in whenever she got the chance. Emma was pleased that Lea had taken Paul off her hands and was probably realising that she had got more than she had bargained for. The children's dislike of Lea grew with every incident. Emma updated Mrs Sinclair. With many years of wisdom behind her Mrs Sinclair replied philosophically that Paul had been an unpleasant bully with Emma during their marriage so there was no reason to believe that he would be any different with his current wife or any other women he might meet in the future. That she was really better off without him. Of that Emma was certain.

'Eat properly Olivia.' Lea had snapped. 'Hold your cutlery properly and stop making noises when you chew. Now we all know where you get your bad manners from. From your mother of course. English people have no manners.'

Olivia stood up and left the table and went up to her room leaving her meal practically untouched. Paul followed her up the stairs and grabbed her arm firmly.

'Don't you take that attitude with me young lady. We are the boss here not you.' Paul chided.

'I am not going to listen to you criticising my mother.' Olivia replied defiantly.

Paul said nothing but left the room banging the door firmly shut behind him.

Emma lamented to friends and family that the courts could not see more clearly. It never ceased to amaze her how things could have gone on for so long and how unfair the whole thing had turned out to be. Her sister Laura found it unbelievable that Emma had not been given the opportunity to express herself in court, that people seemed to be able to put what they wanted in the court papers and it was difficult to see who was telling the truth and not. That there were so many grey areas in family cases.

Victor Falconer had never stopped attacking Emma for several years inventing one untruth after another. Mrs Sinclair had explained to

Emma that it was part of an overall strategy to exasperate the court so that they would leave the situation as it was since the parents were simply not making an effort to get on. She reiterated that this is why it was so important that they be seen to be looking for peaceful solutions and not taking a belligerent stand.

Mrs Sinclair reminded Emma that her reputation had been incorrectly decimated through the earlier joint work of Victor Falconer and Hubert Belette and Mrs Sinclair and Emma had spent the last four years methodically building it up again. Emma felt exasperated that if this was a strategy used by the more unscrupulous lawyer why were the judiciary not aware of it and coming down hard on people making a mockery of the judicial system.

Emma knew that the real answer however, lay in the freemasonry connections who had worked diligently against her on several different fronts. She was also now almost certain where the roots of her problem lay, and it was far more complicated than anyone could even begin to imagine.

Emma could not prove it but she had gained peace of mind knowing how this scam had most likely been accomplished. She had long been aware that to have done what they had done there needed to be some powerful forces at work against her behind the scenes. Laura and several close friends agreed. Laura had said that to wield that sort of influence you needed really high status or a great deal of money or both.

It could only have originated from Paul's very rich, well connected and influential cousin living in America who had set the wheels in motion, maybe even unwittingly, to help his adored aunt, Paul's mother, have more contact and influence over her grandchildren's upbringing following the divorce. This had been confirmed by the reactions of Hubert Belette and Paul's own mother when Emma had challenged them.

However, Emma was beginning to think that the adverse party had not expected that things would drag on for so long, that Emma would return to the country the minute she lost temporary custody of her children, that she would not crack, that she would continue to fight and that the longer things went on, the more she would discover and put two and two together, although she deliberately kept her discoveries low profile in the interests of her own safety. In short, they had underestimated the lengths to which a loving mother is prepared to go to be reunited with her children and offer them a good and safe future.

Emma learnt from a reliable source that Arthur Falconer's fortunes were changing. From being one of the country's top business men, it was becoming apparent that some of the deals his company had initiated under his close guidance had not all been very kosher. One investigation involving black money paid to the local mafia to win a huge international contract resulting in substantial losses might not be the last to transpire.

Rumours predicted that probably more was to come. This was apparently why the judiciary had warned the new government to be careful about giving Arthur Falconer a ministerial post, something he had craved at the last election. In brief, his reputation had gone downhill in what one could call good circles. Emma hoped this might also be the start of a general downhill trend in the fortunes of the adverse party.

A further development she hoped might play in her favour was the ostracism of Paul's doting mother almost completely from the lives of her grandchildren by Paul and Lea. She was now even forbidden to visit or call her son's home. She kept in contact with Olivia and Sebastian via the mobile phone Emma had purchased. Lea forbade Paul to even visit his mother although he did so in secret and Paul's mother confided to Olivia and Sebastian that she was frankly ashamed of her own son and the way he behaved under Lea's influence. Paul's mother told Olivia and Sebastian that she hoped that they would go back and live with Emma as she was available at home to look after them and much nicer to them and even her than her own son and daughter in law.

Even the American side of the family admitted that Paul seemed to have lost it. Paul's mother had been deliberately excluded from the recent family celebrations for the second communion of Olivia and Sebastian. A practicing catholic she had gone to church in the small village where she lived and stood there crying pitifully, a lonely, abandoned old woman. Emma found the whole thing sad, unnecessary and strangely very ironic. Paul's mother wanted to send Emma an official photo of the communion as Emma had done when the children had celebrated their first communion five years earlier. Paul had found out and had gone bananas threatening to confiscate any further letters she tried to send to her grandchildren if she did so.

Emma asked herself if the powers behind this set up would have the foresight or the will to undo the mess they had instigated and which had seemingly backfired. Probably not was her conclusion. They had moved on since then and the mess was Emma's and Emma's alone to sort out.

With all these disturbing and thought provoking issues whizzing around in her head, Emma anxiously awaited the date of the audition and the next custody hearing.

Chapter 74

When the postman rang the doorbell, Emma instinctively knew what it was. The envelope from the provincial court arrived in the form of a registered letter. The introductory hearing was in two weeks' time. Meanwhile Olivia and Sebastian were with Emma for the weekend and they needed to try on and order their uniforms for the new secondary school close to Emma's office. The specialised shop was only open that weekend. Both children excitedly tried on the different pieces of clothing. The choice was much bigger and the garments much more stylish than Emma's own school uniform had been. Olivia and Sebastian each chose shirts, a tank top and a jumper. They agreed to go back at the end of August for the trousers and socks which were not yet in stock.

Emma asked both Olivia and Sebastian 'Now are you sure you want to go to this school? I understand if you want to stay with your dad. In that case I don't need to spend money unnecessarily on a uniform. You need to be honest with me.'

'No no mum we definitely want to come back we really do.' they both chanted.

'The school at dad's place is dreadful.' Olivia continued to Emma's surprise. 'It is dirty and we went for an open day and it was awful. They sell drugs outside and the older pupils racketeer the young ones. If they don't hand over their spending money, they beat them up.'

'No that can't be true.' Emma protested in disbelief. 'Whoever told you that?'

'It is true mum honestly.' Sebastian added.

The children went onto explain that Lea's son had started at the school the year before and had been the victim of a racketeer attempt. He had fended off the attackers only because he was exceptionally tall for his age but it had left him rather shaken.

'This is unacceptable. You can't go there. Tell your dad.' Emma urged.

'No.' Olivia replied. 'He will not listen. It is all the same to him. He wants us to go to this school and that is all. He never asked our opinion. We don't want to. We are coming home.'

Suddenly Emma felt quite scared that her son and daughter would end up in such a school. They had expressed very clearly, at least to her, their wish to come home but just imagine the court manipulated things again and they had to stay with their father. Her anxiety soured to new levels.

Local friends encouraged Emma to write to the new justice minister if the system continued to distort the truth. They assured Emma he was trying to improve things although it was not an easy task. Emma had to agree with them. If Olivia and Sebastian were held against their will for the next school year at their father's place and forced to go to this school, then she would have no choice. She had to carry on fighting. She would not bleed alone nor let these dishonest characters ruin hers and her children's lives in all impunity.

The date of the introductory public hearing arrived. They were awarded a date for a private hearing one month later and in any event before the end of the school year. However, the presiding judge refused to give them a date for the re-audition of the children. She could not locate such a provision in the last judgment. As they went outside the court room Mrs Sinclair said to Victor Falconer that she wanted to receive a date for the children to be heard by the judge at the earliest since it was clearly marked in the previous judgment. Victor Falconer replied, as one would expect, that he could not recall such a provision but added that had no objection to the re-audition.

Emma reiterated that it was definitely in the judgment as she remembered it distinctly. Then to her surprise, Mrs Sinclair commented ironically turning directly to Victor Falconer that they would not have been in this predicament today had it not been for the extreme negligence of Hubert Belette. It was the first time that she had spoken in public of any malpractice. Victor Falconer looked surprised, nodded and started to defend his position.

'Don't start.' Emma interrupted. 'You know only too well that Hubert Belette is a crook who has been in jail not to mention Jules Mercier who suffered a similar fate.'

Paul looked down at his feet as Emma spoke. Before she could say anything else, Mrs Sinclair pulled her by the arm and they headed out of the court.

'You are nervous today.' she commented to Emma. 'I will have to give you some tranquilizers for the court hearing.'

Emma laughed then continued. 'No you won't. I promise I will stay calm because you told me it is the only way to succeed but seriously when will they stop their nonsense? You know I have to share a secret with you. I have this almost uncontrollable urge to give Victor Falconer a gigantic kick straight in the balls. If only I could, and then get away with it after all the heartache he has caused the children and I over the last five years.' Emma confessed with a wry smile.

'You can't possibly do that.' Mrs Sinclair replied and then her face broke into a broad smile. Maybe she had a lively imagination.

'I know.' Emma replied with a grin. 'But it is not for lack of wanting.'

One week later a letter dropped through the post again from the youth section of the provincial court. The children were to be heard by the youth court judge in nine days' time and then the final custody hearing was scheduled to take place one week later. Emma was advised at the same time as Paul and there was no provision banning her from being present in the waiting room just before the children met the judge as requested by Victor Falconer.

Emma called Olivia and Sebastian that evening and advised them. They sounded surprised and a little nervous. 'Brace yourselves she told them this is your only and last chance to change things.'

Four days later Paul had still failed to give Olivia and Sebastian the letter from the court addressed directly to them advising them of the interview they would have with the judge. Emma became suspicious especially as Olivia and Sebastian advised her that Paul was constantly asking them if Emma had mentioned anything about the forthcoming audition with the judge.

'Tell your dad I told you.' Emma urged the children. 'It is your legal right to go and speak to the judge. In any event, do not sign anything which could be a letter your dad prepares for you advising the court that you do not want this interview as you are perfectly OK where you are in your dad's home.' Emma advised.

'No mum we want to see the judge.' both children reassured Emma.

Emma called Mrs Sinclair for support and advice.

'Both children will be older than twelve this summer.' she replied. 'If they don't turn up for the interview all is lost. There is nothing more I can do then.' she concluded in a matter of fact manner.

Three days before the hearing Paul gave the letter to the children. Emma had advised Olivia and Sebastian that it was the same youth court judge as the previous year.

'Oh no.' they replied. 'We told her things last time which she did not even write down including that we wanted to come back and do our secondary schooling with you.'

'Well maybe she wanted to protect you from the pressure which your father might exert on you.' Emma explained before adding 'This time you are both one year older and wiser. You must insist on what you want and insist she writes it down. Refuse to take no for an answer. Tell her you were surprised she did not write everything down last time and you would like her to do so this time. Give good reasons for your decisions. She can only manipulate the proceedings to a certain degree.' Emma concluded as reassuringly as she could.

'If she does not let me come home I am going to the police and I am going to make a statement.' Sebastian announced to Emma's amazement.

Emma sincerely hoped it would not get that far. In three days' time she would find out. She lit a candle and prayed every evening that things would work out this time. Goodness they needed a lucky break for once.

Chapter 75

Emma was normally a sound sleeper. The night before the audition was an exception. She tossed and turned and waited for the distant sound of the birds to start chirping as dawn broke around 4.30 am and the first rays of light seeped through the bedroom shutters. It was a big day for the children. It was all down to them now. Emma had spent some time with them the evening before on the telephone urging them not to worry, to be themselves and to tell the truth as they saw it. Emma could only hope that things would turn out fine. Over the last four years she had experienced so many setbacks she almost dared not hope for the best.

The morning in the office seemed to drag by. Emma tried to busy herself with as many things as possible while keeping a close eye on her watch. Early afternoon she bought magazines and some of the children's favourite chocolate bars and set off on the all too familiar route to the provincial court.

She only managed to eat half her sandwich. Her stomach was nervous. She had no appetite at all. She arrived half an hour early and parked the car on the large historical square. Mrs Sinclair had advised Emma on several occasions that whatever she did she was to remain calm. Emma felt weak. She dashed into a newsagents and bought an energizing drink which she consumed quickly. She needed additional strength and a boost to ironically remain perfectly calm and composed. After ten minutes, she started to feel the positive effect.

She walked slowly along the cobbles towards the youth court. Paul had told the children to let Emma know that it was no use her coming along because they were going to arrive at the last minute anyway. Emma knew she would be very unwelcome as far as Paul was concerned and Victor Falconer's court papers had been very explicit in this respect. However, she was only there on the specific request of Olivia and Sebastian and she was going to put on a very positive and serene face however uncomfortable she happened to feel inside.

She sat in the waiting room, in the corner, out of view of the entrance and buried herself in a current affairs magazine. One minute before 2 pm the door opened and in walked Olivia and Sebastian with Paul. They walked over to Emma and gave her a kiss before taking a seat on her righthand side. Paul nodded at Emma avoiding eye contact. He was obviously not pleased but there was little he could do now to stop her being there.

'Hello.' Emma announced chirpily.

The dour looking court clerk flitted by, looking downwards and barely acknowledging the waiting group. He was preparing the judge's office for the audition. Emma looked around at the posters on the wall. The same ones as the previous year promoting mediation for couples going through a divorce. How ironic it all seemed, almost surreal. Emma turned to the children and asked them how their exams had gone that morning. She smiled at them reassuringly, updated them on recent news from friends, told them she had received the confirmation for the holidays. They smiled back nervously.

Emma asked Paul if she could collect Olivia and Sebastian earlier on their last day at school so they could all arrive at a reasonable time in the evening in England. Paul agreed and asked the same favour for his forthcoming holiday to the south of France. Emma replied that there was no problem. It was strange to be communicating in a very calm and constructive manner knowing all too well the dangerous undercurrents just below the surface.

'I would like the exact address of the place you are going on holiday.' Paul continued. 'If you have a heart attack or something else happens to you, then I need to know where I can collect the children.'

For a second Emma was taken by surprise. Then she replied 'Don't worry. In any event we can always be reached on my mobile. Of course, you can have the address if you wish. However, you really don't need to worry because I am in excellent health with a very strong survival instinct and have absolutely no intention of dying at a premature age and certainly not during my long-awaited holidays.'

Paul smiled at the jovial irony of Emma's response. Emma felt uncomfortable. Maybe she was too sensitive but after the thinly veiled death threats from Jules Mercier, one could not be too complacent she told herself.

Suddenly the door opened and the youth court judge appeared. She nodded to Paul and Emma then smiled at Olivia and Sebastian.

'So last time Sebastian came first. Shall we do the same this year?' she asked the children.

'No I will come first this time.' Olivia replied standing up and walking towards the judge's office.

Olivia had told Emma the evening before on the phone that she knew what she wanted and what she was going to say to the judge. She had added that she had prepared it carefully in advance. For Emma, it appeared that Olivia was keen to put it behind her.

The audition should normally have lasted half an hour per child. Nearly one hour later the youth court judge appeared with Olivia. Emma had good hearing and heard her ask Olivia before opening the door if she was alright and not frightened. Olivia had replied that it was OK.

The youth court judge looked sternly towards Paul and Emma.

'Can you please come into my office for a second?' she asked them both.

They followed her in and she closed the door.

'Oh no.' Emma thought to herself. 'I am going to be the bad one again and get shouted at for being here to morally support my children.' she shuddered to herself bracing herself for another onslaught.

'I don't call in the parents very often' the judge began. 'but I have to say that this audition was very difficult for Olivia who actually cried. She is in the middle of her exams at school and I find it very unfair and inconsiderate of you, her parents, to have asked for this audition at this delicate time.'

She looked at both parents waiting for an explanation.

Emma drew a deep breath before explaining calmly 'If I am here today it was at the specific request of my son and daughter. The last thing I want to do is make things difficult for them. Mrs Sinclair wrote in her court papers that the audition could have taken place early July at the beginning of the school holidays. Mr Falconer insisted that it take place before the end of the school year.'

The judge looked at Emma and nodded in acknowledgement.

Emma continued. 'I understand the point you are making your honour, I really do. Believe me I only want peace in the best interest of the children. Unfortunately, it is made rather difficult by all the constant attacks I still endure from the adverse party as you can clearly see from the papers they have filed with the court.'

Emma did not know what Olivia had said but this time to her surprise the judge looked at her sympathetically. Perhaps at long last the truth was coming out and the judge was actually beginning or wanting to see things more clearly.

The judge then turned to Paul who muttered some excuse for Victor Falconer.

'I wanted to let you know my feelings and I will be mentioning it to the prosecutor's deputy in the actual hearing too.' the judge concluded.

They filed out of the office back into the waiting room. Sebastian stood up and followed the judge into her office. Olivia sat reading a magazine her head downwards. She looked up briefly at Emma and gave her a tense smile. Emma wanted to take her in her arms and hug her but she knew it was the wrong time and the wrong place.

'Follow me outside.' Paul suddenly said to Emma. 'I want to have a word with you.'

Emma stood up again and followed Paul out into the court yard.

The window of the judge's office where Sebastian was being auditioned was open so she suggested to Paul that they go to the other side of the court yard so as not to disturb the proceedings. The last thing they needed was yet another reprimand from the youth court judge.

'Whatever the outcome of the hearing this time,' Paul began 'I am a very flexible person and you can see the children whenever you want. Any extra weekend here or there. We can talk and arrange things.'

Emma looked at him in disbelief. 'Well that is new and very welcome.' she replied. 'But why have you done everything you possibly can for the last four years to cut me off from my children, completely exclude me from their schooling, even made telephone contact extremely difficult?'

'I have not.' Paul protested.

'Well let's say more Lea as far as the telephone is concerned.' Emma continued. 'Because you are rarely there but then of course with your backing Paul. As you may recall, when I had custody you never had any problem in either area.'

'It is not true.' Paul shot back already getting agitated. His short temper had not subsided over the years.

'It is impossible to dialogue with you Emma. It has always been the case. You will never change.' Paul announced his voice rising.

Emma looked over towards the open window at the other side of the court yard and hoped the judge could not hear them. She shrugged and turned to go back inside when Paul added condescendingly 'I think it is an absolute disgrace that you have still not paid any child maintenance for the last four years.'

Emma turned around to face Paul. 'Really.' she retorted very calmly but resolutely. 'Now let me tell you what I find absolutely disgraceful. That you and your mother with help from your rich American cousin with his influential friends have set me up, torn my children away from me, blackmailed my dying mum, burgled my house, burgled the premises of the experts, and all this with help from corrupt officials inside and outside the judicial system. Not to mention your extremely unpleasant and dishonest lawyer who is far from white either. To be quite frank Paul, I am sick and tired of you all, especially the system which allows this to happen, and if I do not get my children back this summer I will take my chance by reporting this whole unsavoury affair to the new justice minister and contact at the same time the international press.

Should you have forgotten one piece of interesting evidence is the recording I made of you blackmailing me about my dying mum and her wish to see her grandchildren for the last time, admitting that strings are being pulled in the courts in your favour, pre-empting all the problems I will have in the future in this respect. The original is in a safe deposit box in London should you be wondering and full details of my case are with several sets of friends in several different countries just in case.'

Paul looked at Emma in total surprise and shook his head in denial.

'I don't know what you are talking about.' he added with a mocking smile as if she was completely mad.

'Well you would say that wouldn't you.' Emma replied. 'Let's go back inside.'

They sat in the waiting room in relative silence until Sebastian came out from his audition shortly afterwards. He seemed unperturbed although Emma could not underestimate how difficult it had been for him too. Normally the judge would have shown the parents a copy of the reports. She did not offer and Emma certainly did not want to ask as she wanted to spare the children a scolding or even worse from their father which she knew was the part they were dreading most. They stood up and after thanking the judge left together. Emma gave the children a huge hug and a kiss and promised to call them later. She waved them goodbye and went back to her car.

Back in the office Emma called Mrs Sinclair as she had promised.

'How did it go?' Mrs Sinclair enquired eagerly.

'I don't know exactly until I have a chance to speak to the children this evening on the phone.' Emma confessed. 'But you are going to get reprimanded next week in the hearing for requesting the audition during exam time. Victor Falconer should as he insisted on this but my guess is that we will all get it in the neck as usual.'

Emma went on to explain to Mrs Sinclair in detail what had happened and her exchange with the judge.

'Let's meet end of tomorrow morning.' Mrs Sinclair suggested. 'We really need to know the content of the judge's reports to know where to go from here. Come and pick me up and we will drive to the provincial court together.'

'No problem.' Emma replied really hoping and praying the content would be positive for her this time.

Emma received an sms from Olivia that afternoon. She was obviously back at her father's place. Emma's mobile was on her desk and the familiar peep peep alerted her to the incoming message. Emma opened the message.

'Love you to bits mum. I am coming home. Call me this evening. Xxxx.'

Emma's heart lit up. Gosh, she really might have pulled it off Emma muttered to herself. She sounds confident. Maybe, just maybe this time it will work. For the first time, Emma dared to believe that they might have a chance. She left work on time and hurried back home. It had been a harrowing day for all of them. She just wanted to flop on the sofa and listen to what Olivia and Sebastian wanted to tell her. They had been so brave. She was so proud of them.

Emma poured a glass of red wine and called Olivia and Sebastian on their mobile. They were alone and felt free to talk.

'Mum I told the judge I wanted to come back. I insisted I wanted to come back. I asked her to write it down and sat there while she did it. It is in the report mum. I am coming home.' Olivia announced.

Emma's eyes filled with tears.

'Are you OK? The judge said you cried.' Emma asked.

'No I didn't.' Olivia replied. 'Well only a little bit but it is over now and we can look forward to a really good future together.'

Olivia did not give any further details and Emma certainly did not want to ask. It had been tough enough for all of them. If Olivia wanted to discuss it more over time, there was no problem. Emma felt it had been a very painful experience for Olivia and for the time being she preferred to block out the details. Suddenly she seemed so mature for her age.

'I am so proud of you darling, so proud.' Emma whispered. 'We will have a great weekend. What do you want to do this weekend?'

Sebastian came to the phone.

'Hi mum I am coming back too.' he chirped. 'I said I wanted to go to the new school next to your office. I said I missed you. I said I did not get on with Lea, that she is really mean to us.'

Unbelievable Emma thought to herself. What brave kids. The truth is coming out after all. It was just as Emma's mum had said on her death bed. It was what Valerie had predicted from the beginning. The children will see clearer as they get older. You will need a great deal of courage and patience but you will get there in the end she had repeated to Emma endless times. In Emma's darkest moments her kind and wise words had kept Emma going. Emma's sister Laura and her good friend Rachel had continued to repeat the same thing. It was now actually about to happen. Ironically Emma felt numb, shocked, empty but she knew that once these feelings wore off she would feel incredibly happy and relieved.

When Emma picked up Mrs Sinclair next morning to drive her to the provincial court she was feeling cautiously optimistic. She told Mrs Sinclair that she would wait for her in a side street. They had agreed it would be best if Emma were not seen the following day by any of the court officials. Emma popped into a little grocery store and bought them both a fresh drink for the return journey. She hoped and prayed that what Mrs Sinclair was reading at that very moment was enough to have the children come home and for them to start a new life together. It was make or break after four years of fighting.

Mrs Sinclair arrived back at the car. She opened the door and sat down in the passenger seat. She turned to Emma and smiled.

'It is positive.' she announced. 'You will get the children back.'

Emma smiled and for the second time in two days she felt tears welling up in her eyes.

'That is wonderful, absolutely wonderful. Thank you so much for all you have done.' Emma said gratefully to Mrs Sinclair. 'Are you sure they can't do anything to overturn the report or anything else for that matter to keep the children with their father?' Emma asked suspiciously trying to pre-empt another manipulation which might have been in the works.

'Normally nothing.' Mrs Sinclair replied. 'The report is very clear. The children have expressed a very explicit wish to return home to you. Your ex-husband will have little choice but to respect this.'

Emma headed back to the office to tell her colleagues who had been so supportive over the years. They were thrilled and hugged and congratulated her. Emma emailed Laura her sister and a few close friends. She decided to call them personally that evening when she got home. Laura emailed her back. This was indeed great news but she would leave the champagne in the wine rack and only pop it in the fridge following the hearing and subsequent judgment. Like Emma she was all too wary that things could or may still, by whatever means, be turned in Paul's favour. They had seen so much over the last six years that they were extremely cautious. As the saying goes once bitten twice shy.

Paul was still unaware of the content of the reports but would find out over the next couple of days. The only question Emma now asked herself was what would be his reaction. Hopefully he would not be too hard on the children. On the Friday, Emma had planned a business trip abroad for the day with two colleagues. They were travelling by car and had planned to pick up Olivia and Sebastian for the weekend on the way back. She called the children late afternoon to see how they were doing.

'Dad questioned us this morning about the audition.' Sebastian confessed. 'We told him we want to come back and live with you. We let him know that we told this to the judge. He was very angry and shouted at us on the phone accusing us of not telling him the truth. He told us that he is very disappointed. We both cried. He is coming home before 9 pm so you just have to collect us before then otherwise he will shout at us again.' they both pleaded.

Emma felt sorry for the children. It was inevitable that Paul would blow his top but hopefully things would calm down afterwards. Emma's colleague put his foot on the gas pedal and they arrived just after 8 pm and more importantly before Paul. Olivia and Sebastian jumped into the car and they roared off direction home. They hugged each other. Arriving home, they headed off to McDonalds to get a bite to eat and celebrate their new found togetherness.

Emma and the children spent a wonderful weekend. Friends and family from all over Europe and the USA were thrilled that things seemed to be working out at last.

'During the audition I was so stressed I nearly fainted.' Olivia confessed to Emma that weekend. 'But you know mum my love for you was stronger than my fear of all the rest.' she announced proudly.

Emma thought to herself what lovely brave kids she had. What a pity they had had to go through such an ordeal in the first place.

Sebastian had an even more amazing story to tell. On the Thursday evening he made a rushed phone call to Emma talking almost in whispers.

'Mum it's me. Listen if dad calls you, you must tell him I have never heard of Jules Mercier OK? Can't stop now but I will tell you more at the weekend. Love you. Bye.'

Emma really could not imagine what he was talking about.

The following Friday evening Sebastian told his story.

'Mum you are not going to believe this.' he began.

Olivia joined in. 'Listen to what Sebastian has to say mum. It is really strange.'

Emma braced herself for what was going to come next. Could they still surprise her? She had already seen and discovered so much over the last four years. What could she now expect on top?

'Mum do you remember four years ago when we were only small just after they had taken us away from you? Well I kept a diary in the country at grannie's place.' Grannie was their name used by the children for Paul's mother. 'I noted down that I heard grannie on the phone talking with Janine who had recommended Jules Mercier to you and they were talking about Jules Mercier and the influence he had on our case. It was such a long time ago. I don't even remember all the details. Well I locked my diary in my desk and did not think about it anymore. Well, dad called me into his office the other evening after the audition and asked me if I knew Jules Mercier. Of course, I said no. Then he handed me the diary which grannie had taken from my desk. She had actually gone into my drawer, taken out the key and snooped around my personal belongings and given my diary to dad. When I said no he held up the diary and said he knew everything about us and we could not hide anything from him. Well I just did not know what to say. I was so upset with grannie for going into my personal things and taking my diary to give to dad. Grannie also said to us on the phone today that she hopes we do not regret coming back to live with you. This after all the times she has said we are better off with you. It was

416

just a trick as Olivia said last time to get us to confess to something so that she can then tell dad who is angry with us afterwards. I can't believe she did this to me. I am so upset with her. I will never trust her again.'

'I believe that Jules Mercier set us up.' Olivia added. 'You recently showed us the newspaper articles when he was imprisoned. We believe you and that is one of the reasons we want to come back. It is not the only reason or the main reason but it is all so dishonest.'

Emma was amazed. The children were much more perceptive and smart than she had ever imagined. She was sure they had grown up more quickly as a result of everything they had experienced over the last few years.

'Don't worry that is all past now.' Emma replied trying to play things down. 'The main thing is that you are coming back. We will make up for the lost time and have a good future together.'

'Yes.' they both agreed in unison.

Chapter 76

The following Monday Mrs Sinclair called Emma in the office.

'I have just received a new set of court papers from Victor Falconer in which your ex-husband is relinquishing custody of the children and transferring it to you as of the new school year.'

'What?' Emma gasped in amazement. 'Have they really conceded custody?'

'Yes they don't have a great deal of options after the recent reports.' she continued.

Emma sat in astonishment trying to take in what she was hearing.

'Then it is cut and dry.' she replied. 'If they concede there is no need for a battle in court.'

'That is correct.' Mrs Sinclair replied. 'However they are still pressing for retroactive maintenance for the last four years and your ex-husband has offered to pay 250 € a month in maintenance for both children which is the legal minimum in accordance with his new earnings which he has declared as an independent.'

'I am not worried about the maintenance he will pay.' Emma confirmed. 'I can survive on my salary and the child allowance even if he does not pay me anything. What really bugs me is why I have to pay retroactive maintenance for being set up by a suspect court paying for the pleasure of having my children literally torn away from me by corrupt individuals not to mention all the heartbreak and additional expense involved in getting them back.'

'Well maybe we can come to some sort of out of court settlement.' Mrs Sinclair suggested constructively. 'I think the main thing is that the children are coming back.'

'You are right.' Emma replied not forgetting how fortunate they had been. 'But I can't afford the thousands of pounds he is claiming. Just how am I expected to pay?'

Things were moving so quickly and after four years of non-stop fighting Emma still had not completely taken in that her children were coming home.

The custody hearing was taking place early next day and even though she now knew that the outcome was going to be positive, Emma felt a certain amount of trepidation about having to return yet again for another hearing in the provincial court. She felt like a dog which had been beaten too often. She was still subconsciously dreading another unexpected and decisive blow against her.

Emma got up early next day and put on a smart cream trouser suit. She was the first of their group to arrive at the court. A court clerk approached her asking her if she had come for a minor offence hearing. She almost laughed. She thought to herself no but I can give you an impressive list of candidates suitable for a not so minor offence hearing if you really want.

She was joined by Paul and the infamous Victor Falconer who had so plagued her existence for the last six years. They both shook her hand. Victor Falconer was uncharacteristically chatty and pleasant. It was so hypocritical but Emma had learned from Mrs Sinclair that sometimes it paid in such circumstances to be super hypocritical in return. It did not come naturally and she had to make a concerted effort to remain calm, charming and constructive.

Mrs Sinclair arrived in a flap. She had had a bump with a lorry on the motorway and he had demolished her left wing mirror. The lorry driver had been rather irate and had ranted and raved at her although she claimed the lorry driver was at fault. She was a little shaken and as a result had forgotten her glasses in the car. Emma offered to go and get them for her as she finalised with Victor

Falconer Paul's visiting rights which would then just need to be ratified by the court. Just as Emma arrived back, they were ushered into the court room. How Emma hoped this would be the final time. She thought she could never face going into another court room in her life.

They all sat down. The judge and the prosecutor's deputy looked down at the assembled group. Emma felt calm but still numb. Was this really happening she asked herself waiting for the proceedings to start. The youth court judge updated the prosecutor's deputy about the difficult audition she had had with Olivia and the latter looked at Paul and Emma sternly. It was the same prosecutor's deputy who had presided the previous year and had given Emma such a hard time. Emma took a deep breath.

Mrs Sinclair spoke briefly. She expressed her regret but added that the positive thing to come out of the audition was an agreement, at long last, between both parents concerning the main residence of the children which could only be beneficial in their long term interest. The youth court judge looked pleasantly surprised.

'That is indeed a very positive development.' she replied.

The prosecutor's deputy nodded in agreement adding 'I am glad you have reached an agreement on who is best placed to look after the children on a daily basis.'

Good old Mrs Sinclair Emma could not help thinking. She had got things back quickly onto a positive footing. It was Victor Falconer's turn to present his case first. For the first time ever, he did not launch into a virulent attack on Emma which she had to sit and listen to. Somehow, thankfully this time, it was no longer appropriate. He referred to the court reports following the audition and reiterated the fact that had his client known how much the children wanted to come back to their mother then he would have prompted this move of his own initiative even earlier.

Emma cringed in disbelief. What else could she do? It was completely unreal. It was a classic.

Victor Falconer then went on to stress the deterioration in his client's financial situation and his offer to pay the minimum in maintenance in accordance with the legal requirement of all non-custodial parents to contribute to the upkeep of their children. He insisted on pushing hard for retroactive maintenance from Emma with interest.

Mrs Sinclair stressed that Paul had earned his living extraordinarily well over the last few years, with his base salary, incremental child allowance and generous severance packages received from previous employers following restructuring. His standard of living and income explicitly laid out in the court papers were indicative of this. With her salary, Emma could not possibly pay the exorbitant sums claimed by Paul over the last four years.

The prosecutor's deputy wrapped up the hearing in customary fashion. She pointed out that all parents had to face up to their financial responsibilities and there was absolutely no excuse for not doing so. She would therefore expect Emma to pay retroactive maintenance to Paul. As she did not know the details of the file, the exact amounts would need to be determined by the judge based on the financial circumstances of the parties concerned.

Emma smiled to herself. This relatively young lady was very apt at making bold statements about text book law without unfortunately seeing beyond the end of her own nose let alone scratching the surface which in their case led to a real hornet's nest. Emma really hoped it was unintentional.

The youth court judge looked at Emma directly and asked her if she wished to add anything. Emma hesitated for a moment. A thousand and one things rushed through her mind such as yes I want to say that I was set up by unscrupulous characters who have made a complete mockery of the judicial system, that it is an utter disgrace how the children and I have been treated, that it is an absolute insult that I pay the slightest amount to my ex-husband as his family was part of instigating the setup, that it is I who should receive generous compensation from the authorities for the heartache, trouble and expense I have been put through over the last six years. I hope you read our court papers carefully and found the press article where Jules Mercier the honourable judge and freemason supreme was arrested for embezzlement and fraud and put two and two together.

Emma inhaled deeply. Instinct told her to quit while she was for once ahead. With a lot of hard work and a little luck she could make up the financial ground. Olivia and Sebastian were back home and she would ensure that they had a very good future. At the end of the day, that was what really counted.

'I would just like to thank you, that's all.' Emma finally said looking at the judge and forcing a smile.

The judge nodded and smiled back. The court clerk for once looked up and nodded approvingly too.

The judge concluded that the judgment would be issued within ten days. The group stood up and filed out of the court room in silence. It had been so quick, so easy. Actually, after four years of battle for Emma almost too quick and too easy. She had to see the judgment written in black and white then she would start to believe it she told herself.

Mrs Sinclair walked with Emma back to her car.

'I really can't thank you enough.' Emma told her again. 'You were wonderful. We beat them against all the odds. I was beginning to think that it would never be possible but we did it.'

'I knew we would eventually get there.' Mrs Sinclair replied. 'I always told you that remaining calm and constructive pays dividends in the end. It just takes time. When I take on a case, I often have two adversaries. My own client and the real adversary. Often at the beginning, one's own adversary is the most difficult to address. When you first came into my office you were angry, hurt and totally confused. Now you are calm, collected and victorious.'

Emma had to agree with Mrs Sinclair but what a learning curve and at what price she asked herself.

'My sister always referred to you as a wise old bird who knew where you were going and who would get there in the end.' Emma added.

Mrs Sinclair liked the reference to the wise old bird and they both started to laugh.

'Mr Falconer told me you threatened your ex-husband last week to go to the press and minister of justice.' she suddenly quipped.

'Well not really threatened.' Emma explained. 'I just put the record straight that I had no intention of putting up with anymore of their, excuse the word, shit.'

'You also said something against Victor Falconer?' she enquired.

'Yes I said he was far from being whiter than white but I think that is pretty obvious the way he functions, his ethics or rather lack of them and so on. Anyhow do you agree?' Emma asked.

Mrs Sinclair smiled and elaborated. 'I just told Mr Falconer that you had been very unfortunate to find a former judge who had been arrested for fraud and embezzlement who in turn recommended to you a lawyer who was obviously so grossly negligent, and has a reputation in the whole country among the legal profession for being so, and who was not only struck off from the bar once but

423

twice. Now that is above the law of averages for any person however unfortunate they happen to be.'

They laughed again. It was indeed absurd but for the first time Emma could actually see the funny side. God how naive she had been she reminded herself.

'Well I suppose that it comes as no surprise if I tell you that Victor Falconer was part of the plot and set up as well.' Emma added.

Mrs Sinclair smiled but did not reply. She had done her bit and obviously defended to some degree the system she had worked in all her life and would continue to work in for the next few years until she retired. They shook hands warmly, parted company and Mrs Sinclair promised to contact Emma as soon as the judgment arrived.

That evening Emma called Laura to put the champagne in the fridge. Laura was in Italy and her flight had been delayed. Emma's brother in law Frank answered the phone. He was thrilled that things had been officially sorted. His father and grandfather had been members of the English judiciary and his father had been deeply worried at the beginning about the developments in Emma's case so Frank appreciated more than most the magnitude of the victory.

'We are proud of you Emma.' Frank said. 'Christ talk about grit you sure have it. Quite honestly I think that is what got you through combined with your inbred stubbornness that dishonesty was not going to win the day.'

Frank was often spot on in his observations and Emma had to give him credit for his assessment of the situation. Emma had refused to give up despite immense and continued pressure as, like most loving mothers, she could not contemplate living without her dear children and would have carried on battling until the very end, especially as she knew that they really wanted to come home.

Less than two weeks later the judgment was issued. The only unknown was the amount of money which Emma would be required to pay to Paul in retroactive maintenance. As it turned out, it was less than half the amount he was claiming. Nevertheless, it was still over 6000 €. Mrs Sinclair had initially suggested that if it was excessive they could go to appeal. This suggestion had sent shudders down Emma's spine.

Emma called Laura who immediately suggested she just pay up and move on adding that she could still afford it. Emma knew her sister was right. The most important had been achieved. Money was important as a means to an end but love, family, friendship and good health came much higher up the list.

Emma called Mrs Sinclair to ask her for her final bill for the excellent result she had achieved. She planned to sell shares bought with the inheritance her mum and dad had left her to cover all the outstanding expenses including the retroactive maintenance she now needed to pay to Paul. Emma's parents had worked hard all their lives. A significant part of the money they had left her had already been consumed in legal expenses to fight the battle of her life. Over half of this sum had been paid to the two crooks Jules Mercier and Hubert Belette.

Emma considered herself fortunate to have had the means without which her battle would have ground to a halt even before she met Mrs Sinclair. Emma's parents had been very principled and therefore she knew that they would have approved of her investment to regain custody of her children and have justice prevail at the end of the day. All their lives they had encouraged Emma and her sister Laura to be financially independent with good jobs to support themselves. Today Emma knew for certain that her parents were watching over herself, Olivia and Sebastian and would have been proud of the result they had achieved together, against all the odds.

Chapter 77

Emma hoped that the nightmare was now firmly behind her. Her experience had taught her that one should not dwell on past misgivings. Life was too short and now she and the children had to make up for lost time and live every day to the full.

Since the judgment Olivia and Sebastian often repeated how happy they were to be coming home and how much they loved Emma. It was therefore with great pride that Emma helped them get ready for their first day at secondary school. They both looked so smart in their new school uniforms and Emma took photos in front of the house in the autumn sun before the three set off together. Emma dropped Olivia and Sebastian in front of the school gates, gave them both a hug, sat watching them greet their friends and enter the school building then drove the two minutes to her office.

The children were excited to be starting a new school and to be united with their friends again. It had been fun choosing the uniforms, files, school bags, books, shoes. Emma was an integral part of their lives again. She still could not believe it at times. After school, the children did their homework then walked the short distance to Emma's office and the three of them drove home together. They were soon into a pleasant routine. It was almost as if they had never been separated.

Emma had already sent Paul the prospectus from Olivia and Sebastian's new school encouraging him to discuss with them which extra curriculum activities they should choose. She assured Paul she would request the school to send him directly all correspondence about parents' evenings, plays, and open-days so he felt fully involved. She planned to photocopy their school reports and sent them to him as soon as they were issued. She also assured him that she was flexible about any extra weekends he might want to spend with his children.

Emma was very much aware that children need both parents and, despite the exclusion from her children's lives and the spitefulness show to her by Paul in the past, she did not intend to emulate any part of this behaviour. She knew first-hand just how utterly painful and unnecessary it could be both for the parent on the receiving end and the children.

Emma now felt mature, confident and able to take everything in her stride. She told herself that no one could frighten her or make her panic into taking poor advice as she had done six years previously. Olivia and Sebastian also saw things much more clearly and refused to be manipulated as they had been in the past.

Emma knew that Paul had to take a constructive step in his own way. Since the judgment, he had accused her of manipulating the children in their decision. He criticised the choice of their new school although it had an excellent reputation and both children were keen to go there. On several occasions, he told Olivia and Sebastian that he hoped that they did not live to regret it. Most surprisingly of all he blamed Lea for driving the children away from him. Lea begged Olivia and Sebastian to confirm to their father that it was not her fault that they had expressed their wish to return to live with their mother. Olivia and Sebastian admitted to their father that it was not the main reason.

Emma also reassured Paul's mother that she could call her grandchildren on the land line or their mobile whenever she wanted. Emma encouraged and paid for Olivia and Sebastian to accompany the old lady to the USA for two weeks to visit the family, something she had wanted to do for three years already. In the summer holidays, Emma drove Olivia and Sebastian to the country to spend one or two weeks with their grannie.

One year after the children returned to the maternal home, Emma went house hunting and purchased an old house with lots of character and a beautiful garden a short distance from where they had been living. She put the rest of her savings into the property conscious that it was a good investment for the future. Hers was the only name on the deeds and the mortgage so she knew that she would probably never be faced with having to sell up and start again from scratch.

There was quite a lot to renovate but Emma had help from Valerie and her cousin as well as the neighbours who were charming and she soon became quite a dab hand at DIY herself, something she had never thought possible. One of her bigger personal achievements was that she learnt to walk into a DIY store and navigate her way directly to what she was looking for. This in sharp contrast to the beginning when she spent hours trying to locate what she needed and walking endlessly and aimlessly up and down the aisles.

A close friend jovially pointed out that Emma was recuperating her children at a challenging time as they were about to enter puberty and their teenage years. Emma had smiled. She was sure they would have their ups and downs like all families with teenagers in the house but she felt confident that the bond between them was very strong and that the problems would be minimised as a result. She used to show Olivia and Sebastian the Harry Enfield sketch with the unruly teenager Kevin and they used to all laugh together with Emma adding wistfully that she sincerely hoped that they would never become like Kevin. Mum they had protested almost indignantly, how can you say something like that?

Several years later, there were clear signs that Paul's mother was ageing and becoming forgetful. When she set fire to the kitchen while making jam, Paul decided that it was time for the old lady to move into a home for her own safety. He selected a comfortable place not far from where he lived. Relations with Lea had not thawed so he went to visit his mum once or twice a week on his own. Even at Christmas the old lady often spent the festivities in the home with the other residents and not with Paul and the family.

Emma invited Paul's mother over one weekend. She was curious to see the new home where her grandchildren now lived. She met the neighbours and some of their friends. She seemed content that Olivia and Sebastian were in good surroundings, happy and were doing well at school. Emma took them to a nice restaurant and Paul's mother seemed to enjoy being out and about again. She wrote Emma a very big thank you letter and for the next two years whenever they spoke, she reminded Emma about what a good time she had had.

Olivia and Sebastian were growing up fast and would soon be celebrating their nineteenth and eighteenth birthdays. The children were beginning to spend more and more of their free time with their friends as is normal at that age and Sebastian had met his first girlfriend. Adapting to the situation, Emma had built up a busy social life too with lots of friends and activities.

Emma had made a conscious decision not to enter into a relationship with anyone while her children were growing up, all too aware of what they had been through with Lea and wanting to enjoy worry free and quality time with them. Emma now felt the time was right to have someone special in her life to share enjoyable times, holidays and intimate moments again.

One day she met David. David was very different to Paul. He was fairer, a little less tall with laughing blue eyes, a kind carefree character and a keen interest in travel, good food and current affairs. He had a small business, had divorced nearly twenty years earlier and lived with his youngest son in a house on the outskirts of the capital. He met Olivia and Sebastian and they seemed to get along well. The relationship developed and soon the couple was spending half the week living together either at David's or Emma's home.

Emma had had little contact with Paul since the children came to live back at home. He worked very hard and had managed to successfully build up his own business. He was still with Lea and they returned every year with the boat to the south of France. As Olivia and Sebastian were getting older, they were able to decide what they wanted to do and arranged their spare time directly with their father. Emma was happy to go along with their plans and do everything necessary to keep the status quo and above all the peace.

She was happy things were going well for Paul. He could also spoil his son and daughter as a result and always bought them nice presents at Christmas and for their birthdays including the most recent iPhones and Mac computers which they needed for school.

One day Paul suggested that the two parents meet to discuss the children's university education. Emma agreed and they met up in one of her favourite Italian restaurants not far from Emma's office. Ironically it was a restaurant she had been to so often before with Jules Mercier. The staff were still the same and the menu and food just as good as always. It was strange to see Paul again after such a long time. He looked a little older, a bit greyer around the temples, with a few more wrinkles from the sun.

They did not discuss the past. It already seemed so far away. Instead, they had a very civil and constructive conversation. Twelve years after their separation and divorce, they were able to talk objectively and calmly about their children and how they could jointly support them in the final leg of their education. Emma also felt happy and confident that she had recently met David and things were going well between them. Paul mentioned it briefly but Emma did not elaborate. They led two very different and separate lives and that is how Emma wished to keep it.

She offered to pay for her part of the meal but Paul insisted on picking up the tab. Emma did not argue and thanked him for the pleasant lunch. She tried to remember how many lunches she had paid for Jules Mercier. She could not remember exactly but she knew it was a lot.

Chapter 78

Paul's mother's health started to deteriorate. She had become frail and weak and had told Olivia and Sebastian that she did not think that she would live for very much longer. She had given up the will to carry on. This pained them both.

Emma told Olivia and Sebastian that if they wanted she would drive them after work on the Friday afternoon to visit their grannie, all too aware that things could deteriorate fast and then they might regret not having gone to visit earlier. It was a three hour round trip but Emma was now used to driving longer distances and her car was comfortable and powerful which made the journey easy and pleasant. Olivia had written her grannie a letter which she gave to her when they arrived. Paul's mother opened it and read it as tears welled up in her eyes. It was a moving moment.

Paul's mother was delighted to see her grandchildren again. She could not believe that Sebastian had a girlfriend already and seemed quite shocked much to their amusement. Emma thought that she must still consider Olivia and Sebastian as the little children who needed looking after and caring for, remembering the best moments when she came regularly to the farm house to look after them when they were just two and three years old. Gosh what a lot of water had passed under the bridge since then Emma thought to herself.

Paul's mother thanked Emma gratefully for having driven her beloved grandchildren to see her again. Emma encouraged her to get well and build up her strength so they could come back more often and visit her. She left Olivia and Sebastian alone with their grannie for twenty minutes and went outside to take some fresh air. When Paul's father passed away, Emma had been the one in the hospice to notice and had alerted the nurse who checked and informed the family. It was as though he had waited for Paul and Emma to arrive so Paul's mum would not be alone when it happened. It all seemed such a long time ago. Nearly twenty years. Olivia and Sebastian had been toddlers at the time.

Emma was sad. She felt the old lady would soon be joining her husband. She did not want to tell her children what she feared. She did not know if they guessed or not. They stayed for another hour until the evening meal was served then they said their goodbyes and left.

Paul's mum grabbed Emma's arm as she stood up and told her to take good care of her grandchildren and give them a good future. Emma nodded. She looked for a last time at the old lady who waved and smiled at her as she closed the door. One week later Olivia and Sebastian received a call from their father. Grannie had died peacefully in her sleep.

'I am really glad we went to see her last week.' Sebastian remarked.

'Me too.' Olivia added.

Emma was not invited to the funeral and she did not ask to go. She decided to visit the grave to pay her last respects a couple of weeks later on 1st November, all Saint's Day. It was a Sunday and Emma had a leisurely breakfast with David. She then went to the local market and bought two huge plants and set off alone for the drive to the little village in the country where Paul's mother had lived for many years and was now laid to rest.

It was a wonderful crisp autumn day and the sun was shining brightly. The sky was exceptionally blue for the time of year. Ninety minutes later she pulled up outside the old cemetery. It had been around twenty years ago since Paul's father's funeral and Emma tried to remember where the family grave was located. She thought she would find it first then come back for the two plants. They were not easy to carry.

After about ten minutes Emma found the grave of her former parents in law. The cemetery was abundant with colour as most graves had already been decorated in the last couple of days with flowers from relatives of the deceased in preparation for All Saint's Day. Emma negotiated her way past the graves back to the car to pick up the two plants. The gravel path crunched under foot with each step she took. She had chosen a yellow and a purple chrysanthemum. They were robust plants and Emma reassured herself that if it did not freeze too early, the plants would still look good in several weeks' time, perhaps even up to Christmas.

Emma placed the two plants on the grave and stood back to look at the headstone. She turned around and glanced out into the surrounding forest. The nature exuded a distinct calm and beauty. The air was pure and fresh. She inhaled deeply. Paul's mother was now at rest with her husband.

Emma's mind drifted back in time picturing Paul's parents as they had been nearly thirty years ago when she had first met them. Paul's father had been a calm and pleasant man. He had spent six years as a prisoner of war in what today is Poland. He had been liberated by the Cossacks and Emma remembered his stories around the dinner table that he and his fellow prisoners had been more afraid of their liberators than their captors.

He had been fishing in a lake for food when a Cossack approached, his arm completely decorated with watches. The Cossack tutted then pulled out a hand grenade and lobbed it into the lake. There was a resounding explosion then dozens of dead fish floated to the surface. The Cossack had been able to convey in a wry sort of way that his was by far the most efficient way to fish.

At the end of the war, it had taken Paul's father over six months to make his way back home. Mainland Europe was in total disarray and there was no way to update his parents that he was on his way. One day he arrived at the bottom of the road where they lived. His

Alsatian dog sensed his presence and came bounding down the road towards him. He had always claimed that these loyal dogs only ever had one master and never forgot him.

Emma tried to imagine the scene and how Paul's dad must have felt coming home unexpected after nearly six years in captivity, with a long world war, which he had been fortunate to survive, behind him. Paul's mum had not had an easy time either. Her father, a successful local business man, had died of pneumonia when she was very small just two weeks before the release of penicillin which would have saved him. Paul's mother's mother had had to bring up her four young children on her own and shortly afterwards, war was declared and the country was invaded and occupied.

Emma asked herself to what degree people's characters had been shaped by what they had gone through in childhood and early adulthood and what role fate played in their overall destiny. What had guided Paul's mother to spoil her son so much and to want to take over the role of mother from her own daughter in law? Emma had no answers. She just knew that things had not turned out as the other party had planned.

Emma looked at the grave again and hoped that the pair would rest together in peace. She pictured them reunited above, just as she had learned from the medium that her own parents had re-found their family and were happy to be together again.

Emma stayed another ten minutes deep in thought, said a final goodbye then headed slowly back to the car. It was as if a page had turned. So much water had passed under the bridge in those last thirty years. Emma drove through the thick forest to the motorway heading back home to Olivia, Sebastian and David who were waiting for her. This was the future. She had said her goodbyes and made her peace. A door had closed on the past.

Emma never heard anything again from the honourable retired judge Jules Mercier nor from Hubert Belette, the lawyer he had so highly recommended. She was not even curious to know what had become of the unfortunate and dishonest pair. She just knew she had paid a very high price for being so naïve and trusting as had her children.

Twelve years later three friends contacted Emma in the same week. A group of journalists had posted on the internet the names of the influential people whom various witnesses had identified as taking part in orgies with the cream of society, in some cases in the presence of minors. Jules Mercier's name figured in the list as did several of the people he had worked with or had confirmed to Emma were his acquaintances or friends. Some of the orgies had apparently taken place in a large castle in the country about forty minutes from the capital. Emma was curious and looked up a picture of the castle on the web. She had driven past the motorway exit hundreds of times. What a small world it was she could not help thinking to herself.

It did not come as a surprise. Emma had already figured it out herself many years earlier. She remembered the scene in the film 'Eyes Wide Shut' and some of Jules' inadvertent comments and shuddered. However, to see it confirmed in writing and posted in such a public location did surprise her. She remembered her conversation with Jules in the late nineties just after the use of internet was gaining momentum. Emma had pointed out that maybe one day the truth would come out and that going forward not everything could be covered up as effectively as it had been in the past.

She hoped that the people who had participated in these unsavoury pass times and others who were planning to would be much more restrained in the future, that indeed society would no longer tolerate such divergences from its leading figures who should frankly be setting an example. Many of the people named had since passed away. Others were old and long retired. It was time for the winds of change to blow stronger than ever. A new outlook and generation of more honest and responsible players. A better society and a more secure and just future.

Emma had a long discussion with the mother of one of Olivia's friends, Stephanie, over dinner one evening. The conversation turned to freemasonry and Emma did not hide her reservations that certain members were using the brotherhood to further their own interests to the detriment of non- masons, adding quite simply, that this should not be allowed to happen. She explained with conviction that it was proven that major miscarriages of justice had been perpetrated as a result.

At first Stephanie was surprised. Emma could see Stephanie asking herself how Emma seemed so well informed. After a short period of reflection, Stephanie admitted, with a certain amount of pride, that she was herself a mason. She then went on to explain just how difficult it had become to enter the craft nowadays as the leadership, aware of the anomalies of the past, had tightened up their membership vetting process to catch and refuse entry to anyone wanting to join for the wrong reasons. This was music to Emma's ears.

However, Stephanie was referring to a woman's only lodge strongly focused on helping the less fortunate. Stephanie did admit that it was conceivable that there might still be some lodges focused on business and politics, where some members might still unfortunately be tempted to join primarily to further their own cause. It was an interesting discussion. Emma guessed that the situation was fortunately not as out of control as it had been fifteen or twenty years ago. However, she was convinced that some less scrupulous individuals were still taking advantage of the system, and always would, unless measures were put in place to prevent them from doing so.

Emma surfed the web one rainy afternoon to discover what Victor Falconer had been getting up to. He was the final piece of the puzzle and she was curious to find out after so many years. He seemed to be still going strong as a lawyer and she found a recent picture of him. He still wore that penetrating stare and had that unflappable air about him. Onwards and upwards Emma thought to herself as she noticed that he had also been nominated as a justice of the peace. Emma smiled ironically and shook her head. She could not help thinking how happy his masonic friends and acquaintances must be, secure in the knowledge that should any case they be involved in find its way into his court, their chances of securing a positive outcome would be greatly elevated.

The last time Emma saw Paul was at Sebastian's graduation. They drank champagne together and proudly applauded shoulder to shoulder as Sebastian was presented with his degree. Other families and friends stood chatting together in the garden behind the university. Paul, Emma, Olivia and Sebastian looked like any normal family. They chatted together easily as if the past had never happened. Paul explained to Emma that he was going to the south of France and was looking forward to spend some quality time on his speed boat. Emma wished him a pleasant holiday. They talked about what their individual preferences and plans were when they eventually retired.

At the end of the evening Paul gave Emma a kiss on both cheeks, said goodbye and sped off in his sports car. Sebastian was pleased that the evening had gone so well. Olivia commented just how different their parents were and that she could never have imagined them ever being married together. Emma smiled. Yes, they were indeed very different she thought to herself. They had certainly had more than their fair share of differences along the way. However, the one really good thing which Emma and Paul had achieved together was to have two wonderful and intelligent children who had grown into adults they were truly proud of. This was their lasting legacy. The rest was history.

After her experiences, Emma hoped that she would never have to seek help again from a lawyer or even worse find herself in a courtroom. As the saying goes, never say never. She was to be unwittingly drawn into another unbelievable adventure spanning several years, this time in a different country and for different reasons. Learnings from the past, with a firm belief that justice has to win the day would again prove instrumental in helping to eventually secure a positive outcome. The only thought which often sprang to mind was 'Oh no, here we go again.'

Epilogue

As Emma discovered, real events can turn out to be so incredible that they are often the subject of the written thrillers or action films popping onto the market on a regular basis. After all, why do these authors and film directors have such a fertile imagination if there is not some well-founded factual basis for their story lines? In today's fast moving society, it may well be that fact encourages fiction and vice versa.

Emma's thirst for answers to fully understand her predicament led her down several interesting paths in areas where she would otherwise never have ventured. Her discoveries have been eye openers to say the least. They affect us all, the world we live in and which we should take responsibility for shaping and, most important of all, the future of our children and grandchildren. Today, as a result, Emma looks at the world in a rather different light.

Information is power and often injustice prevails because some important things are concealed or difficult to prove. Emma believes everything happens for a reason. She hopes that measures will be introduced to bring more clarity into the courts everywhere and to avert subsequent miscarriages of justice by highlighting certain situations which should not be allowed to continue or happen to any other unsuspecting individuals.

The world is getting smaller by the day. Emma is fortunate enough to have travelled widely and thanks to her job, has been in daily contact with many different nationalities. It is reassuring to see that there are still a great many good people in all countries and despite language, cultural and sometimes religious differences, these people share the same basic needs and honourable and respectful values.

Several very interesting books and web articles have appeared over the last three decades outlining the key role that secret societies have played and indeed still play in steering our lives and world events. As one might imagine, they tell a different story to that taught in school and outlined in history books.

From the ancient mysteries of Egypt, to the Knights Templars of the 13th century, the first bankers on whose theories the modern banking and monetary system is apparently founded, through to the Illuminati, the 20th century Council on Foreign Relations, the Bilderbergers and the Trilateral Commission, the upper echelons of Freemasonry, the world's largest secret society, play an important role in all of these societies.

Certain authors go on to claim that the secret societies have been responsible for the American, French and Russian revolutions, the First and Second World Wars, the Korean and Vietnam wars, the assassination of President Kennedy, the fall of communism in Eastern Europe and the more recent Gulf war. Many events which cost the lives of tens of millions of people and untold suffering. Also for the creation of the European Union and the introduction of the single currency, the Euro. One interesting hypothesis is that when nation states are weakened along with a feeling of national identity, world events and the economy become much easier to influence and control.

Man's never ending quest for unlimited power and wealth is said to be the driving force, the ultimate goal of which is global domination, otherwise known as the One World Government. A government which many scholars believe will be totalitarian in nature. One apparent theory is that this is all part of an elaborate, well-structured and long term strategy planned to come to fruition in the next one to two decades, by which time the earth's population will be reduced (by war, epidemic and man-made 'natural' disasters – possibly using 'HAARP'). The middle classes will be slowly decimated by unemployment, financial crisis and drugs as the family unit and religion, particularly Christianity, continue to be eroded. If new 'bail-in' rules are applied with the next financial crisis, a large part of one's life savings could be wiped out practically overnight.

On face value, it all sounds absolutely ludicrous, not to say utterly far-fetched. However, reading these books and online articles with a logical and open mind and following Emma's own brief insight into the inner-workings and manipulations of some well-placed secret society members, she has come to the conclusion that it cannot be dismissed out of hand. With so much at stake, to do so would be unwise.

In fact, some of these trends can already be seen to be happening today. Many question the legitimacy and foresight around the invasion of Iraq. Then there is the subsequent turmoil in Syria, Iraq and Afghanistan and the resulting refugee crisis. On the financial side, the Euro crisis and spiralling EU debt.

Divide and rule, problem creation, reaction, solution (Ordo ab Chao) seem to be common tactics used. With each major crisis come additional measures to gain control and reign in further our individual freedoms. As one alleged leading figure in the Illuminati put it, 'This present window of opportunity, during which a truly peaceful and interdependent world order might be built will not be open for too long. We are on the verge of a global transformation. All we need is the right major crisis and the nations will accept the New World Order.'

Emma clearly remembered what her wise old English teacher cautioned in the early 1970s.

'We have the freedom to end all freedoms. It will be up to you all to make sure this never happens.'

At the time, these words had seemed so profound and such a prospect, so remote. Like most parents, Emma dearly loves her children and wants only the best for their future and the planet we all live on. We need to remain vigilant, united and take an active interest in things happening around us. Our joint actions over the next few years, at the ballot box and with the collective power of the purse, will determine to a large degree what sort of society and even world we leave behind for our children and grandchildren.

Above all, we should not lose sight of the fact that we are ultimately, but maybe only just still, the masters of our own destiny.

Aletia Joiner

Interesting reference material:

Rule by Secrecy by Jim Marrs. Published by HarperCollins.
Non dare call it conspiracy by Gary Allen.
The Brotherhood by Stephen Knight published by HarperCollins.
Inside the Brotherhood by Martin Short published by HarperCollins.
Les Frères Invisibles by Ghislaine Ottenheimer and Renaud Lecadre published by Albin Michel.
Bilderberger. The Secret Centre of Power by Andreas von Rétyi. Published by Kopp.

(1) European Parliament resolution on Gladio. © European Union, http://eur-lex.europa.eu/, 1998-2016.
According to the European Union Commission Decision of 12 December 2011 as provided here, it is permitted to reuse this legislation so long as it is accompanied by the preceding notice.

Printed in Great Britain
by Amazon